Amber

ALSO BY ELLE CASEY

ROMANCE

Red Hot Love (3-book series)

By Degrees

Rebel Wheels (3-book series)

Just One Night (romantic serial)

Just One Week

Love in New York (3-book series)

Shine Not Burn (2-book series)

Bourbon Street Boys (4-book series)

Desperate Measures

Mismatched

ROMANTIC SUSPENSE

All the Glory

Don't Make Me Beautiful

Wrecked (2-book series)

PARANORMAL

Duality (2-book series)

Pocket Full of Sunshine (short story & screenplay)

CONTEMPORARY URBAN FANTASY

War of the Fae (10-book series)
Ten Things You Should Know About Dragons (short story in The Dragon Chronicles)
My Vampire Summer
Aces High

DYSTOPIAN

Apocalypsis (4-book series)

SCIENCE FICTION

Drifters' Alliance (3-book series)
Winner Takes All (short story prequel to Drifters' Alliance in Dark Beyond the Stars Anthology)

To keep up-to-date with Elle's latest releases, please visit www.ElleCasey.com
To get an email when Elle's next book is released, sign up here: http://www.ElleCasey.com/news

Amber

ELLE CASEY

This is a work of fiction. Names, characters, organizations, places, events, and incidents are either products of the author's imagination or are used fictitiously. Any resemblance to actual persons, living or dead, or actual events is purely coincidental.

Published by Montlake Romance Publishing, Seattle

www.apub.com

ISBN-13: 9781542047050
ISBN-10: 1542047056

Cover design by @blacksheep-uk.com

Cover photography by Matthew Hegarty

Printed in the United States of America

For Mary Walker, fellow author and fellow fan of (almost) all things French.

CHAPTER ONE

I'm washing dishes at the communal kitchen sink when a low-slung black sports car pulls up to the house. I don't recognize it as belonging to anyone I know, but I'm familiar with the make and model from a magazine a visitor to the farm left behind last week. It's a Mercedes-AMG GT S Coupe . . . otherwise known as a sorry-about-your-penis car. My mouth turns down at the corners as I toss my sponge onto the counter.

"Barbara!" I shout out into the air. "Someone's here."

"Who is it, Amber?" my mother answers faintly from upstairs. She's busy making everyone's beds, one of the many in-house chores she performs for our large, unconventional family.

My other mother, Carol, joins in, her voice muffled as it comes from inside the pantry where she's running an inventory of the jams and jellies we sell at the local farmers' market. "Is it that woman from the town council again? Because if it is, I'm fully committed to giving her another piece of my mind. She's already had two, but I can dole out a third if necessary."

I smile at my mother's sass. Nobody ever comes back for a third helping of that. "No, it's not a woman. It's a guy." I walk over and push aside the linen curtain that hangs in the window to the side of the front door, assessing our visitor from head to toe. "He's getting out of the car now. And he's wearing a suit."

The stranger stares up at our old white farmhouse as he buttons his coat. His black leather shoes shine like they're made of obsidian. The dark suit seems tailored to fit his broad shoulders and narrow hips. His blue shirt with its bright-white collar looks like it's been starched enough to stand on its own. Diamond cuff links sparkle in the sunlight as he adjusts his briefcase to the other hand.

"And he's got money," I mumble under my breath. Instant distrust rises up and seizes my heart. He looks like trouble, and not the fun kind.

A door opens and closes behind me, bringing with it the smell of potatoes, onions, dried herbs, and something slightly musty. I glance over my shoulder to see that my sister Emerald—Em to everyone who knows her—has come up from the basement.

"What's going on?" she asks, lifting an apron over her head and hanging it on a nearby hook in the entrance to the kitchen before joining me at the front door.

I let the curtain fall back into place. "A suit. Here to buy some organic honey for his girlfriend so he can impress her with his new-age sensibilities." I roll my eyes as Em takes a turn gazing through the curtain.

"Do you know that or are you just guessing?" she asks absently, as she takes in the sight of our visitor.

I sigh. *So gullible.* "Why else would a guy like him drive out here . . . to a hippie commune in the middle of nowhere?"

Em stops gawking to turn and frown at me for a few seconds. "Would you stop calling our home a hippie commune? Come on." She goes back to staring at the stranger. "It's a communal farm. Intentional living. There's a difference."

I wave my hand between us, brushing off her supposed distinction. "Potato, tomato, pa-tah-to, ta-mah-to."

We glare at each other for two seconds before we both break down and smile. I've never found it even remotely possible to stay mad at her for longer than three seconds.

"You are such a dork," she says.

I press my finger to the tip of her nose. "Boop. Takes one to know one."

She slaps my hand away gently, talking under her breath as she shifts her focus back to our visitor. "Boop? Who says boop? Where do you get that stuff, anyway?"

She's wondered on more than one occasion how I stay updated on the coolest trends when we have limited television reception, no newspaper subscriptions, turtle-slow dial-up Internet working on a fifteen-year-old dinosaur of a computer, and very little contact with the outside world. The difference between her and me is that I'm not pathologically shy, and when I do get out to the farmers' market or the local bar, I interact with people and make connections. Em doesn't understand, because she prefers to stay out here in the middle of nowheresville and not socialize.

I ignore the next question she's about to ask in favor of pulling the door open and grinning at the stranger, who is now walking up our front porch steps. I adopt a flirty, mocking tone. "Could I interest you in some organic honey, honey?" I wiggle my eyebrows, trying to make him smile at least. He looks so damn serious in that black suit, like he's coming to attend a funeral.

Out of the corner of my eye, I see Em throw her hand up to her mouth to hide the snicker that threatens to fly out. Entertaining my sisters at the expense of completely clueless men is one of my favorite hobbies. Life on the communal farm can get *really* boring sometimes. I grin harder.

The man stares at us standing in the doorway, no expression on his face as he responds. "No. I'm here to see Sally Lancaster, Barbara Fields, and/or Carol Collins."

More distrust filters in. I sense my temperature rising and my face flushing with anger. He's not playing along at all, which tells me this isn't a friendly stopover to buy some organic honey. We've already been sued by the town several times for zoning issues, and I'm not looking forward to going through that again. I fold my arms over my chest, bunching up the oversize denim shirt I'm wearing over my one and only white camisole. He looks way too much like a lawyer for my comfort. "Sounds serious."

He's not here as a customer, and his suit and car together are worth a couple hundred grand, give or take five figures. My family and I live a very simple, harmless life, and there's no room in it for greed or the kind of bullshit this guy is obviously peddling. My first and only instinct is to get rid of him.

"It is serious," he says, taking a step closer.

I reverse back over the threshold, pulling my sister along with me. "Sorry. Wrong house." I slam the door in his face and stare at the lock, wondering if I should engage it. *Is he the kind of man who'd force his way in?* Our mothers have spent the last twenty-odd years telling us how dangerous the real world can be, and up until now I wasn't sure I bought into their paranoia, because, honestly, we don't get much action out here on the commune, good or bad. But this guy . . . ? He makes me nervous.

"Amber, what in the heck are you doing?" Em whispers, glaring at me.

The doorbell rings.

"Shhh," I whisper back, "he'll hear you." My hand is itching to lock the door, but I don't want to seem like a naïve weirdo who can't handle a conversation with a harmless stranger.

"I can hear both of you," the man says wryly. "I just need to talk to you for five minutes . . . ten max. Please open the door. I know who you are, you know."

Em and I stare at each other. "Who are we?" Em whispers, her eyes as wide as saucers.

My emotions go from angry to good-humored, as if my sister just flicked on a light switch with her silly words. "Did you just ask me who we are?" I giggle.

Em slaps me softly. "Shut up. I'm panicking. You know I panic when people push me. Besides, how can he possibly know us? I've never seen him in my life."

I put my hands on my sister's shoulders and lean in close, staring into her eyes. "Okay, scaredy-cat, here's the deal: I'm Amber and you're Emerald. We're sisters and we live on a hippie commune together . . ."

"Shush." Em twists out of my grip, brushing off my goofiness. Squaring her shoulders, she lifts her chin. "What do you want and who are you?" she demands of the man on the other side of the door. I nod, proud that my normally shy sister is busting out her lady balls.

"I'm someone you want to talk to. Trust me. I come bearing good news."

"Oh, I doubt that," I say, raising my voice to be heard through the door. All the women in this house know how the lawyers for the various levels of government work. They'll lie and cheat to get what they want, but we're not falling for it.

He sighs, managing to sound both bored and annoyed. "I'm here to talk to Amber Fields, daughter of Barbara Fields, born May 18th, 1993; Emerald Collins, daughter of Carol Collins, born May 25th, 1993; and Rose Lancaster, daughter of Sally Lancaster, born June 15th, 1993."

"Wow. He does know who we are," Em says, nodding like she's impressed. "Our own mothers never get the dates right."

My mind races as I consider various possibilities. *One:* he's a hit man, come to collect his due. Our mothers' story that they chose to live in this godforsaken hippie commune in the middle of Maine twenty-six years ago to escape the rat race was merely a lie covering up the fact that they took out a mob boss and were forced to go on the lam. *Two*: he's an insurance salesman, ready to quote us some killer life insurance rates. *Three*: he's a Mormon who's upped his game, no longer riding a bicycle and wearing a short-sleeved white business shirt with a skinny black tie. *Four*: he's a lawyer here to inform us that we've got a big fat inheritance coming to us from a long-lost dead relative.

It's number four that has me opening the door. Not that we need money to support our simple lifestyle, but it might be nice to learn about a family member we've never met. As far as we've been told, we're all we have left in the world. According to our mothers, there are no fathers, no grandparents, no cousins, no *nobodies*—just me, Em, Rose, and our three moms . . . one big happy family sharing space on this two-hundred-acre farm with a few other people who have a tendency to wear hemp and meditate while contemplating their navels.

"What exactly do you want to talk to us about?" I ask the well-dressed stranger on our porch, resting one hand on my hip and the other on the open door, ready to close it immediately if necessary . . . because we're not looking for any life insurance, we're already as saved as we're ever going to be, and no hit man is coming into *my* house.

"May I come in?" He looks past me into the nearby living room.

"I'd rather you didn't," I say, sliding out onto the porch, leaving my sister behind. I shut the door in Em's face, ignoring her exclamation of surprise.

He stares me up and down quietly, nothing in his expression giving me any clue as to what he's thinking. I shrug, completely unconcerned with his assessment. I know what I'm all about and I'm cool with it. "Like what you see?" I ask, lifting an eyebrow in challenge.

"Not particularly."

I hadn't expected such a blunt response. I guess he's not into my natural-fiber clothing and Birkenstock sandals that label me an earth child who lives off the land and does my best to leave no footprint behind. It kind of bursts my bubble if you want to know the truth. My mood goes testy.

He balances his briefcase on one of his arms so he can open it. The top of it is suddenly in my face, blocking my view of him.

"Excuse me," I say, frowning at his complete lack of manners.

A squeaking and crunching sound comes from the driveway, distracting me from delivering my next statement, which was going to be a biting comment directed at his need to drive an overly flashy car. I glance to my right, knowing what I'll see.

The briefcase closes, and the stranger turns to watch my other sister, Rose, approach on her ancient bicycle that needs about a can of WD-40 to get it running well again. We don't use those kinds of chemicals out here, though, so it will continue to squeak until it eventually falls apart—hemp oil can only go so far. There's a scrappy-looking, three-legged border collie—otherwise known as Banana—running beside her. As she parks her bike against the porch, the animal goes over to the stranger's car and starts barking.

"Hey," the man says loudly, the briefcase and the file he removed from it forgotten and dropping to his sides as he descends the stairs. "Be careful. I don't want him scratching my car."

Rose completely ignores Briefcase Guy, walking over to the Mercedes and putting her finger on the window. "Hello there, little fella." She tucks her blond hair behind her ear as she peers into the car.

A small brown head pops up in the window, surprising me. This guy does not strike me as a dog person. He probably kidnapped the poor thing. The tiny dog inside puts his nose on the glass, and Banana jumps up to put his paws on the driver's door, trying desperately to sniff his new friend through the window. When that fails, he begins licking the glass, leaving behind wide swaths of dog drool. The smaller canine inside the car looks confused by this show of affection. I smile because revenge is so very sweet, especially when it comes in the form of a dog-drool car wash.

"Hey!" the guy says, approaching Rose and the dog as he waves the papers at them. "Off! Down! Get *down*!"

I almost think he's yelling at my sister, but then the dog responds by dropping to his three legs, staring at the man with his head tilted.

Rose straightens and loses her smile instantly. "There's no need to shout. He's not deaf and neither am I." She gives the guy a hard look and then walks up to the porch, her pet at her heels. She always has something following her home from her animal clinic down the lane from the main house, but Banana has been a regular for a couple of years now. "You shouldn't leave your dog in a car, even for a single minute. The heat from the greenhouse effect could kill her."

"I know that," he says loudly from behind her.

"Coulda fooled me," she says, brushing past me with a little smile and a wink.

I shake my head at him. "Some people." I turn to join my sisters inside. Em is waiting by the door, watching through the window. As soon as we're all over the threshold, I shut the door behind us and lean against it. My heart is thumping wildly in my chest. I haven't had this much fun in ages.

"What just happened?" Em asks. "Who is that?"

Rose and I look at each other and say the same thing at exactly the same time: "Yuppy guppy with a puppy." We've had several yuppy guppies visit our farm over the years. We have nicknames for almost every group we see out here.

We all burst out in laughter as our mothers appear from various parts of the house. The doorbell ringing and a fist banging on the door instantly sobers us up, though. *Spoilsport.*

"Well?" Barbara asks me. "Are you going to answer that?"

I give her my best innocent look. "Answer what?"

"The door." She glowers at me.

I stick my thumb over my shoulder. "This door?"

She nods.

"Do I have to?" I whine, begging with my eyes. If we ignore him, he'll go away, I know he will. This guy is freaking me out a little too much. I have a bad feeling about what he has in that briefcase of his. It could very well be a subpoena.

All she does is sigh.

"Amber, who's out there?" Sally asks. One of her gray-streaked braids is falling down, so I step over to fix it. I take a hairpin that's loose and slide it into place, securing the plait once more.

"Nobody important." Sally is the most fragile one among us, and we all take pains to make sure she's not stressed.

"He sure looks important," Em says, peeking through the curtain again.

"I *am* important," the guy says loudly. "I mean, the things I have with me are important."

Carol walks through the gaggle of women to the door. "Step aside, girls. Let's see what the man wants."

"Should I get the shotgun?" I ask, smiling at the idea. That'd put the fear of hippies in him, all right.

"Not just yet," she says, pulling the door open and fixing our visitor with a stare. She gets right to the point, as usual. "I don't know who you are, but if you're here to cause trouble, you can just turn yourself right around and get the heck out of here." She sees his car. "And go on back to whatever city you obviously came from."

He holds out a stack of papers. "I'm here to deliver these."

My heart freezes in my chest. It looks like legal stuff. A summons. *Are we being sued? For what?* We have money to live on, but being sued is a different deal altogether. The town council has been giving us crap for so long about our land-use activities, it's almost become a normal part of our lives. None of us ever thought we'd go to court over anything, though. We've always won our cases before they came to a trial.

Carol looks down, refusing to take the documents. "And what would these be?"

He jiggles the papers a few times, but when he finally figures out that Carol isn't going to take them, he places them against his chest. "Please, Mrs. Lancaster, may I come in?"

She looks over her shoulder at Sally. "May he come in, Mrs. Lancaster?"

Sally rubs the loose hairs back away from her face and sighs. "I suppose." She gestures to the dining-room table, visible across the foyer.

He steps through the entrance and walks right into the other room without a single glance or a word for any of us.

We watch as he places his briefcase down on the table and takes out two more stacks of papers to join the others already there. "I don't have all day, and I bill by the hour, so if you wouldn't mind?" He gestures at the other seats before finally looking at us.

We file into the room, exchanging silent glances. This is a first for us, and if nothing else, this man has aroused our curiosity. Clearly, we don't get much excitement around here at Glenhollow Farms.

CHAPTER TWO

My sisters and I each have a stack of legal papers in front of us. Em and Rose are too stunned to speak, but unlike them, I've never suffered that effect when under stress.

"So, what you're saying is, we all have fathers who are alive and well, and after twenty-five years of ignoring us, they've decided they want to give us a pile of money?" I still can't believe the number I saw on that paper. Eight figures? Ten *million* dollars each? Utter and complete *bullshit* is what it is. I can feel my ears burning with the anger that's building up inside me. I honestly don't know who exactly I should be angry at right now, but that doesn't stop me from seeing red. Em reaches over and takes my hand. Her fingers are clammy.

"Not exactly," the lawyer says—*Greg Lister, Esq.*, his business card reads. "They want to meet you. They want to see the women you've become. And in exchange for this *privilege* . . ."—he says that last word with a heavy note of sarcasm—". . . you will be given an inheritance that activates on your twenty-fifth birthdays."

I shove my stack of papers back at him. "Not interested." I stand with the intention of leaving, but Em's grip holds me in place.

"All they want to do is meet us?" Rose asks. She glances up at me before continuing. "Where? Here?"

He shakes his head. "No. In New York, where they live."

"Is it in the city?" Em asks.

"Yes, of course. I said in *New York*." He frowns at her like she's stupid.

"You are aware that there's an entire *state* named New York, right?" Rose asks.

I'm happy to see that she's on the same page as I am—the one that reads: this guy is a total assweed who needs to take his sorry butt out of our house.

"They live in Manhattan. They have a recording studio there, and they like to be near it in the event inspiration strikes."

His explanation does not compute. "A recording studio?" I ask. "Why would they have a recording studio?"

Lister stares at me. After a few seconds, he blinks twice. "Are you being deliberately obtuse?"

Carol clears her throat. "Mr. Lester . . ."

"It's *Lister*," he says, glaring at her. He probably thinks she said his name incorrectly on purpose, but Carol has never been good with details.

"Sure, whatever you say. The thing is . . . we've kept the identities of the girls' fathers and the circumstances surrounding their conceptions to ourselves, so they're not aware of the . . . er . . . situation." She has the grace to look uncomfortable. That, more than anything else, has me worried, because Carol is usually too tough to suffer that emotion.

I exchange glances with my sisters. Seeing that they're both as shocked as I am at this revelation emboldens me enough to speak up for all three of us. "What exactly is going on here, Moms?" I look at the three older women who raised us as one big, happy family.

"Oh, Lordy," Sally says, her gaze going to the ceiling. "I knew this was going to be tough."

"Mr. Lister, could you please excuse us for a moment?" Barbara asks. "We'd like to talk to our girls alone, if you don't mind."

He stands. "Like I said, I bill by the hour. I'll be out on the veranda."

"I hope you don't think you're billing *us* by the hour," I say. I don't like his haughty attitude one single bit. No wonder he drives that car.

"No, of course not. But every minute you take to consider this offer costs my clients more money. Clearly, they're already prepared to pay out quite a bit, but I don't see the need to add to that financial burden unnecessarily, do you?"

I shrug, not sure what my answer is. Maybe they *should* pay more than necessary. They did, after all, either completely abandon all of us or otherwise made it perfectly clear they weren't interested in being a family, for almost twenty-five years. Maybe he considers that a 'burden,' but I'm more inclined to consider it a travesty of biblical proportions. *Yeah . . . Lister can wait until we're good and ready.* I raise an eyebrow at him, silently daring him to say one more thing about it.

He leaves without another word, and I wait until the door shuts behind him before I turn to my mother. "Barbara . . . what the hell?"

"Watch the tone," she says, frowning. She looks first at Sally and then at Carol. "So, sisters of my heart . . . who's going to tell them the Big Secret?"

"I'll do it," Barbara says, sighing. "It was my idea in the first place." It's the saddest I've ever seen her look.

"No, you're not going to take the hit for something we all agreed to a hundred percent," Carol says, her face lined and shadowed; it's as if she's aged ten years in the last ten minutes. She checks with Sally, who's nodding in agreement.

"Tell them, Barb," Sally says. "But no fair playing the martyr. We're all in this together, equal partners. That's what we agreed on before, and nothing's changed."

I sit back down, waiting in stunned silence to hear my mother explain how it is that three women who never let us get away with a single falsehood, who warned us from day one about how we cannot trust people outside our walls, and who lived faithfully by the credos of honesty and loyalty . . . have been lying to us about who we are and where we're from for over twenty years.

"Sally, Carol, and I met in Las Vegas," Barbara says, dabbing at her eyes with the sleeve of her peasant blouse.

"Wait . . . ," Rose says. "I thought you said before that you met in Alabama."

Rose's mother, Sally, holds up her hand. "Can we just let Barb tell the story first?"

"You mean, save all our questions 'til the end?" Rose asks. The bitterness in her voice makes me feel better. I'm glad I'm not the only one angry about what's going on here. I can't tell if Em is mad. She looks more lost than anything.

Sally nods at my mother, silently telling her to continue.

"We met in Las Vegas, backstage at a Red Hot show," Barbara says.

I frown. "Red Hot?"

"The band Red Hot." A smile appears on my mother's lips. "It was *totally* hot."

"*Red* hot," Carol says and giggles. She actually giggles! Carol *never* does that. And then her face crumples and tears well up in her eyes.

Em frowns at me while she gestures at her mother's crazy, out-of-character reactions to the story being told by my mother. We're all riding an emotional roller coaster today, apparently.

I slump down in my chair. Red Hot is a band whose members still to this day tease their long, mulleted hair and wear makeup to complement their tight leather pants and torn T-shirts. They're old enough to have saggy pancake butts and moobs now, but does that stop them? *No.* I obviously have no idea who these women are. Aliens must have come in the night and kidnapped my mothers and replaced them with these fangirls.

"We dropped everything and started following them all over the country," Barbara says. "Jobs, school, everything went by the wayside . . . We didn't care about anything but the music and the men who played it."

"We traveled the *world.* Don't forget London and Paris," Carol adds.

"Ah, Paris . . ." Sally sighs, looking off in the distance.

"Excuse me, but *what*?" I look in frustration at these middle-aged women who appear to be lost in the memories.

"What, *what*?" Barbara asks, coming back to earth. She sounds cranky.

"Are you telling us you were actual *groupies*?"

"Yep," Carol says. "That's about right."

I look at my sisters. "Are you guys buying this?"

Em shrugs, looking deflated. "Maybe. They are pretty open-minded about a lot of things. Spontaneous. I can see them dropping everything to follow their dreams."

"And they know every single lyric to every one of their songs," Rose reminds us.

She has a point. It's true; Red Hot music has been playing in the background of our lives for as long as I can remember. I hate right now that I know all of their lyrics too.

"We stayed with them for two intense years," Barbara explains, twisting one of her long dark locks around her finger.

"It was glorious," Sally says, smiling, her cornflower-blue eyes bright with tears. "I'll never forget it for as long as I live."

I want to comment on the fact that she's so scatterbrained, she probably can't remember what she had for breakfast this morning, so the significance of her pronouncement is pretty damn suspect, but I don't. Sally isn't a bad person, even if she did hide from us who we are and where we came from.

"But then things got messy," Carol says, sighing. She looks deliberately at each of us. Comprehension sinks in.

"In other words, you got pregnant," I say. I'm so disappointed. Our mothers have never called our births *messy* before. I'd be lying if I said it didn't sting.

"Not messy, that's not the right word," Sally says, her blissful expression slipping a bit. "Things got *complicated.*"

"Very complicated," Barbara says. Her tone tells me she's remembering something that's pissing her off. "We were told in no uncertain terms that pregnant women and kids were not welcome on the tour."

"By whom?" Rose asks. "Our fathers?" She looks at Em and me and then at our mothers.

"Not exactly," Sally says. Gone is the faraway look, and in its place is sadness.

"It was the band's manager, Ted," Carol explains.

"And Darrell," Barbara adds. "Don't forget Darrell."

"How could we forget him?" Sally asks. She wipes her tears away and looks off in the distance again.

"Yes," Carol says. "Darrell was one of the original members of the band, the bassist who was replaced later, but he was very convincing at the time when he explained how much it would hurt the band if we stayed."

"He was. And we agreed. It's not that anyone twisted our arms," Sally says, looking to the other women for confirmation.

"No, not at all. We took a long, hard look at what we'd been doing and what we wanted for our children going forward, and the life we were leading didn't mesh," Barbara says.

"A clean break was what we needed. From the environment, from the band . . . from everything." Carol nods once, still very convinced, apparently, that they did the right thing. Her chin only trembles slightly.

I can't believe that all it took was two people to convince our moms to take off from this great life they were having and disappear forever. I feel sick over it and have to pause for a few seconds before I can regroup.

I look toward the front door, jerking my thumb in the direction of Lister. "Was he involved?"

Sally waves her hand around. "No, no, no, he would have been ten years old at the time. We dealt with Ted and Darrell . . . that's it."

"What about the rest of the band?" Rose asks.

Our three moms look at each other, all of them shrugging simultaneously. Carol speaks for the group. "We decided it was best for everyone involved if we made a clean break."

"So you just left?" Em asks. She looks like she's going to cry.

"Yes . . . with a little nest egg that their manager gave us from the band, and we set up our lives here." Barbara shrugs as if that's the end of the story.

My blood pressure rises to new highs. I feel like the vein in my neck is going to explode. "And they've known where you are . . . where *we* are . . . this entire time, but they never bothered to come see you? Or us?" I'm clarifying because I need to know how hard I'm going to have to hate these men for the rest of my life . . . men I've dreamed about finding since I was old enough to understand what a father is.

"No." Carol shakes her head emphatically. "We agreed it would be a complete break not just from them but from the life. We didn't tell them or anyone else where we were going, and we left without any notice and without saying goodbye. They didn't know we were pregnant, and I doubt Darrell told them."

Clearly, my moms are not the people I thought they were. How could women who've been nothing but warm and generous my entire life ever have been so coldhearted? I don't get it. There has to be more to the story. It has something to do with these men, I know it does.

"Why wouldn't he tell them?" Em asks. "Didn't he care about you? Us? Or them, at least?"

"He was only concerned about the music. He felt that women and children would interfere in the life, and we didn't disagree." Carol shrugs as if she isn't talking like a callous monster I've never met before.

"But . . . without even saying goodbye?" Em asks, sounding as disillusioned as I feel. No one answers her. All of our mothers are just looking at one another, unspoken thoughts floating in the air between them.

"The life?" Rose asks. "You act as if that's a thing . . . *The Life*."

"Oh, you know . . . ," Sally says, sounding embarrassed. "The Life—sex, drugs, and rock 'n' roll. It was no place for pregnant girls or babies, and we knew that. Darrell and Ted did us a favor by being honest about it and giving us the means to leave. We thought about telling the whole band what was going on and trying to do the long-distance thing, but we all agreed it was a bad idea." Sally looks to her two partners in crime and they nod.

Barbara jumps in, scowling as she explains. "The press was terrible, always hounding the band, making them miserable. The guys were under tremendous pressure, and it was affecting their ability to write more music. We couldn't imagine getting in the way of that or subjecting our children to the pressures of a public life. We knew if we stayed with them in any capacity—even long-distance—it would happen; our children would be hounded and harassed and forced to live in the public eye, held under a terribly critical microscope."

"Which was unacceptable," Carol says. "Ted and Darrell agreed wholeheartedly; a clean break was the best way to handle the situation, and the only way to make that happen was to leave without saying anything to anyone."

"They offered us enough money to start a new life and we took it." Sally looks away as she brushes another tear off her cheek.

I have never seen her cry like this. Hell, I've never seen any of my three mothers this emotional about anything. And now, I think I know why; they left a part of their hearts behind when they left the band. So many emotions rise up inside me and battle to take over; I'm angry, sad, and disappointed, but most of all, I'm frustrated. I'm too stunned to say anything. All I can do is stare at these women I thought I knew.

"There are five men in the band," Rose says, ever the practical one. "Which one is my father?"

The three older women look at each other with sheepish grins and shrug in unison.

"You mean you don't know?" I ask, shocked that they'd be this irresponsible. These are not the women I've known my whole life. "I can't believe this. Which one is mine?"

They shrug again.

"Holy shit." I shake my head at them. How careless can a woman be? Who *are* these people?

"And me?" Em asks, so quietly I almost don't hear it.

"No," Barbara says. "We don't know. What can we say? We dealt in a lot of free love at the time. We partied, we did drugs, we had sex. With *all* of them." She glares at us, daring us to cast judgment.

Judging another person or her actions is a big no-no in our house. Our mothers have always taught us to be accepting of people and their life decisions. I guess now I know *why* they've groomed us to be this way. Talk about self-serving. Still, I can't fault them for trying to help us be better people. Regardless of my mothers' shared past, the fact remains: judging isn't cool.

I let out a long, heavy sigh, feeling exhausted over how thoroughly my world has been turned upside down. My chest is aching and my head hurts too, but I'm pretty sure I'm only experiencing the very beginning of the pain and confusion. All these years, my sisters and I have speculated about our fathers, assuming our mothers were telling the truth when they said they didn't know who these men were. But we were duped. Our mothers could have answered all of our questions, but they just let us wonder . . . they forced us to believe the lie that they didn't know who our fathers were. I'm trying really hard not to be angry at them for this, but it's not working.

Rose, Em, and I fantasized, imagined, and dreamed about what our lives would have been like with fathers in them . . . only to find out now that it was a conscious choice our mothers made to ensure we'd never know. I'm disappointed not only in them but also in the men involved. How could our fathers have been so clueless? Why didn't they try to track our mothers down after they left? They did it just recently, as evidenced by their lawyer waiting on our porch, but why did they wait until we were almost twenty-five? I'm guessing they wanted nothing to do with raising little girls, too enamored of *The Life*, as my mothers call it, to be bothered.

Rose stands, her face a mask of disgust. "I can't deal with this right now. And I'm not interested in anything that lawyer came here for. I have a very sick cat down at the clinic, and I need to grab a quick lunch before I go back." She leaves the dining room for the kitchen.

"Me neither," Em says, practically running out of the room. She looks like she's about to start bawling at any second.

I stand and walk over to the front door, yanking it open to find Lister standing out there staring off into the distance. "You can come back in. We know the Big Secret now." I know I sound bitter, but I don't care. Anyone would in my shoes.

He searches my face, looking for clues about how our conversation went, maybe. I don't feel the need to help him understand my reaction to this disturbing news, though. I wait for him to respond.

"Are you ready to come back to New York with me?" he asks.

I bark out a laugh. "You can't be serious."

He looks bewildered. "It's ten million dollars. *Each.*"

I shrug. "I don't need ten million dollars and neither do my sisters."

"But . . ." All he can do is sputter at that point.

I gesture in the direction of the dining room, where my mothers are grouped together having a private meeting. "The papers are on the table. Feel free to pack 'em up and take 'em out of here."

I start to walk away, but he grabs my arm to stop me. I look down, praying he'll keep his fingers there for another five seconds so I'll have an excuse to slap him silly, but he lets go.

"You should come and meet them." He looks decidedly uncomfortable, unable to meet my eyes.

"Why?" I ask.

"So you can tell them. Yourself."

"Tell them what? That I'm not for sale?"

He shrugs and then looks me in the eye. "If that's how you see their gesture, as some sort of purchase of affection."

"Isn't that what you'd call it?"

"It doesn't matter what I'd call it."

I fold my arms over my chest, hating that I feel so vulnerable. "What *do* you call it? I want to know."

He sighs and looks at the ground. "I call it . . . regret."

Regret, my ass. It's guilt, and I'm not in a forgiving mood. I shake my head. "I'm not going, and neither are my sisters."

"If you change your mind, just give me a call. I'll leave my card."

"Yeah. Right. You'll be the first to know if and when hell freezes over and I decide to visit those men in Manhattan."

I walk away and leave him standing there. I don't even glance at my mothers as I go into the kitchen and shut the heavy swinging door behind me. I find my sisters standing at the sink hugging, and I join them. Together the three of us cry for a life we never had a chance to live and the men we never knew as our fathers—men who live just seven hours away from where we grew up and who never once dropped by to meet us.

CHAPTER THREE

Three days later, after the anger and disillusionment have abated a fraction, my sisters and I are sitting on my bed in a circle, considering our options.

"I think we should just ignore the whole thing," Em says, twisting the comforter around her finger. "Now that we've talked it over with the moms and we've come to this place of forgiveness with them . . . aren't we just asking for trouble by going to New York, especially when we don't even want their money?"

"We can't ignore it," I say. "We at least need to tell them what we think about them trying to buy our forgiveness." I'm still angry when I think about it. Time has not diminished my emotional reaction to finding out that my sisters and I have fathers out there who've ignored us for twenty-five years. Forgiving our mothers for being young, afraid, and way too dedicated to the success of these music men is one thing, but seriously . . . Who do these guys think they are, showing up out of nowhere and dangling a fortune in front of our noses like that? And ordering us to go to New York? For what? To parade ourselves in front of them for their approval? *Ha!* They've got a lot of nerve, and I, for one, feel the very strong urge to tell them where to get off.

"Are you sure that's what they're doing?" Rose asks, tucking her hair up into a clip behind her head. "Our moms said the band didn't know we existed, so how can they be buying our forgiveness?"

"If they didn't know about us, how did that lawyer know where to find us or to even start looking?" I stare at Rose, waiting for her answer to be different from the one she's already given me five times before. We've been over and over this since we found out about it, but today I'm determined to actually *do* something about it.

She shrugs. "I don't know."

"Exactly." I smack the bed for emphasis. "That's why I need to go there—to ask them how they magically know about us now when they supposedly didn't for twenty-five years. I mean, that's a little hard to believe, don't you think?"

Em nods. "It is. I agree, with that part at least."

"Do you still think I shouldn't go?" I ask her, gentling my voice. This is harder for Em than it is for me; she's shy and non-confrontational, and she doesn't like to make a fuss. Me, on the other hand? I don't mind ruffling a few feathers now and then, especially when there's so much riding on the outcome.

"I don't know." She looks at Rose. "What do you think?"

Rose shrugs. "I think if Amber wants to go, she should. I'm too busy to do it, and you're not interested, but if Amber has the desire, I don't see anything wrong with her going down there for the day to have a face-to-face with the band."

I'm really warming to the idea, picturing myself sitting there and letting them know what's what. "I'll tell them we're not interested, and if they try to play innocent, I'll push for details . . . make them confess."

"Confess to what?" Em asks. She looks worried again.

"Confess to the fact that they've known about us all along and just didn't care enough to bother with us." I snort, imagining their mullet-head selves sitting around and looking over their pasts, wishing they'd done things differently. *Too late; what's done is done.*

"Maybe one of our mothers contacted them," Em suggests. "Maybe that's how they found out."

"No way. Our moms have already confessed all their sins, and they're still sticking to their story that they did the right thing by leaving when the band was away and staying completely gone from their crazy lives." I look to Rose for her agreement and she doesn't disappoint; she nods at Em.

"Maybe there's another reason for them staying away that we don't know about," Em says.

"Exactly." I smile, happy that my sister is now arguing against herself. "And that's what I'm going to find out. What is their damn excuse for being gone for all these years?"

"Orrr, you could just go and tell them we're not interested in the money and leave it at that," Rose says. "Leaving sleeping dogs to lie and all that."

My sisters are such chickens. "Yeah, sure. I *could* do that *or* I could do the other thing. How about I wait and see what happens when I get there and just go with the flow?" I look to my sisters for their approval. I will be their official emissary, and in exchange for them staying behind and not participating, they'll have to agree to trust that I will do the right thing by us. My family has always been the most important thing in my life, and they know that; it's why I'm here working on this farm and not off in some big city somewhere making a name for myself in the business world. They know I'll keep our collective welfare at the forefront of my mind as I go kick some butt in New York City. I'd do anything for my sisters and my moms.

"I'm okay with you doing what you feel you need to do," Em says, sighing.

"As am I. But what can we do to help?" Rose asks.

"You can help me keep this from our moms and figure out how I'm getting there."

"You think we should keep this a secret? Why?" Em asks.

"Because. You heard them. They think they made the right decision walking away, and they'll never agree to me going. They'll say I'm stirring up trouble. But it's not going to stop me, and it'll just cause a big fuss when we argue about it. What they don't know won't hurt them."

"I agree," Rose says. "We've already had enough drama over this."

"What if you go and love it so much you end up staying?" Em asks.

I look at her like she's crazy. "You've got to be kidding me."

"It's not totally nuts; don't look at me like that. You know you're always talking about how boring it is out here and how you wish there was more going on in your life. You could have had a job there if you'd wanted one after college. You had offers."

"She has a point," Rose says.

I frown at both of them. "I'm not going to abandon my family. I'm not like *them*." *Those men.*

"Choosing to live the life you were meant to live doesn't make you an abandoner." Em sounds like she's scolding me.

"Whatever." I'm not going to have this conversation with her or Rose. A long time ago, when I had the chance to leave after finishing college, I made a choice; I came home and dedicated myself to helping my family out with the farm instead of launching a life and career apart from them, and I'm not going to change my mind about that now. Yes, life out here can be incredibly boring, but what kind of person would I have been if I'd just taken off and left them to take care of everything without me? This farm takes a tremendous amount of labor to run, and without me they would have struggled. I was not going to be the one to make their burdens greater. My moms and my sisters *are* my life; I would never deliberately let them down. And now that I know how much our mothers sacrificed to come out here, how they changed their lives so completely so that we could grow up in a safe, loving environment, free of bad influences, I'm even more convinced that the hard choice I made was the right one. I am not selfish like our fathers obviously are.

"Tell us what we need to do," Rose says, taking me by the hand.

I already have this part of the plan figured out. I noodled it through as I lay in bed suffering another night of insomnia. "Help me find an airline ticket and an excuse for being gone that our mothers will buy. I'll take care of the rest."

Em reaches over and puts her hand on ours. "Consider it done."

I lean in and hug both my sisters and they return the gesture. "All for one and one for all," I say.

"You said it," Rose says.

"You're my hero," Em adds.

"Let's wait and see how it goes before either of you starts calling me a hero, okay?" I still don't know what exactly I'm going to do once I get there, but I do know where I'm going to start: with Lister. I know I'm not supposed to shoot the messenger, but I think this time I might make an exception.

CHAPTER FOUR

I step off the plane and flip open my new budget cell phone—one of two my sisters and I bought to communicate with one another while I'm off the farm. They kept one and they're supposed to keep its existence a secret from our moms. I don't want the old ladies to try to contact Lister and cause trouble for my big plan.

As I make my way to the exit of JFK Airport, I send Rose and Em a quick text, telling them I arrived safely and am headed out into the Big City. I didn't check a bag because I don't plan on being here longer than a day, so all I have is my big multicolored-patchwork purse slung over my shoulder.

I'm trying to blend in with the crowd and act like a native New Yorker as I make my way through the airport, which shouldn't be too difficult since there's every size and shape of person in here with me, but damn . . . all I can do is gawk. I've never seen so many people in one place in my life.

I was worried I'd stick out in my homespun hippie wear, but I just passed a woman who's dressed like an African queen, complete with a giant, sparkling, colorful headdress, so I think I'm pretty much invisible to the people who live here. That's fine with me. It'll make it easier for me to get from point A to point B and then back again without any hassles.

I thought about the plan on my way over and I've decided: all I'm going to do on this trip is meet up with those old fogies who call themselves Red Hot so I can give them a piece of my mind and tell them to shove their money where the sun doesn't shine. Then I'll go back to my real life—my wonderful, fulfilling, fresh-air-filled life—and forget they even exist . . . just like they did with my mothers, my sisters, and me. Out of sight, out of mind.

I mean, how dare they demand we come to New York to collect on that guilt money? They actually believe that because we share their DNA my sisters and I are hollow-souled assholes like they are? That we'll take their money and smile and say thank you for ignoring us for twenty-five years? Well, they can think again because I'm about to bring them a little education from down on the farm, and show them exactly what we girls think about their big-city, coldhearted, family-abandoning nonsense. *Huzzah!*

I do a little fist pump to give myself a boost. Neither of my sisters had the lady balls to come with me, but that's okay because I have righteous indignation riding shotgun on this trip, and we are going to kick some butt together . . . set some people straight about what's what.

I walk outside into a stiff breeze that's heavy with the odors of jet fuel and car exhaust. The noise is incredible. I expected this place to be busy, but this is beyond belief. There are cars all over the place, men and women running, shouting, hugging, laughing, arguing, and eating. And God, does it stink here. Not only is there the fuel and exhaust but now something else too. Sulfur? Garbage? "Yuck."

I wave my hand in front of my face to keep the toxins from entering my respiratory system. I knew it was going to smell bad here, but this is something else. A man walks by who I'm pretty sure hasn't showered in a few weeks, so I wave my hand faster. It's not helping. My efforts only serve to push the stench up into my sinuses.

After living on a commune with hippies and free thinkers, heavy body odor is nothing new to me; however, where I come from, odors dissipate quickly. Not here, though. Something about the atmosphere is keeping the odors down at nose-level.

Clearly, New York is trying to smother me with its wicked stench cocktail. Double yuck. This city is already assaulting me, and I haven't even been here for ten minutes yet. *Maybe I made a mistake. Maybe I should go home.* A sliver of panic seeps in.

Three seconds after those thoughts pass through my mind, I reject them. *No. Go away, panic.* I'm not going anywhere. I'm on a one-woman mission, and I'm going to complete it before I run back home to where I want to be . . . or where I belong, anyway.

An answering text beeps on my phone. My sisters wish me good luck and tell me to be careful and not talk to strangers. I smile at their concern as I shut my flip phone and slide it into my bag.

So . . . how exactly does one call a taxi if one cannot talk to strangers? I try waving at one, but he just drives right by. I try again, this time sticking my thumb out, but the same thing happens. There must be some kind of trick to this thing, but I can't figure out what it is by watching the people around me. Everyone else seems to have a ride—a loved one or a business associate picking them up. I walk closer to the edge of the curb and stick one of my legs out, lifting my skirt a little. I know it's old-school, but I'm thinking perhaps a flash of my dainty, lily-white ankle will do the trick.

"Watch out, lady, before ya get run ovah!" an angry taxi driver shouts at me and swerves out of my way, forcing me to jump back. My heart is beating twice as fast as it should now and everyone is staring. I want to disappear into a hole in the ground and tunnel my way back to Glenhollow. *Country girl alert! She's right here, folks! Feast your eyes on this strange and unusual animal who is way out of her element!*

Someone taps me on the shoulder.

I spin around, expecting whoever it is to lecture me about getting too close to the curb. I'm ready to defend myself and say I wasn't anywhere near it, really, but the words freeze in my mouth when I see what's there in front of me.

Heaven.

If heaven were a person, he would be this man holding a pair of sunglasses in his hand. Oh my good*ness*, he is so devilishly handsome, even wearing that dirty baseball hat. How can a man be heaven and hell at the same time? I don't know. *Ask him.* He looks like the devil himself, totally prepared and qualified to lure someone into making bad decisions.

"Hey," he says.

"What?" I ask briskly. I step sideways to put some distance between us, my face burning with embarrassment. He probably saw me lifting my skirt to get some taxi pickup action. I've turned into my mother already and I'm only twenty-four.

He reaches out with his free hand and grabs my forearm as he puts his glasses on. They're the aviator kind that cover up half his face.

I jerk myself out of his grip. "Hands off the merchandise, buddy." Maybe he's not so cute after all. My sisters warned me about New York and what it does to people—it makes them pushy and callous, or so their online research has led them to believe. I should have appreciated that bit of advice more than I did.

"Watch out, you're too close to the street." He grabs me again, successfully pulling me toward him this time.

"Hey!" I look around, wondering if anyone is going to step in and save me from this person who thinks it's okay to put his hands on a stranger. No one seems to even notice, though.

I'm dragged two steps before I dig my heels in and stop my forward movement. "Get *off* me!"

Now some people are looking. *Finally.*

He holds his hands up like I've pulled a gun on him. "Hey . . . I was just helping you not get hit by a car." He looks around at the people still watching and then draws a few small circles in the air with his finger near his ear.

It suddenly hits me what he's saying to them. "Are you suggesting that *I'm* the crazy person in this scenario?" *The nerve of this guy!* And now that I have a better look at him, I decide he's not cute at all. He's scruffy and annoying, and he sure could use some clean clothes.

He points at his head. "Who, me? Suggesting you're crazy? No. Never." He drops his hands and rubs them on his jeans a few times before holding one of them out at me. "Uh . . . nice to meet you." Tattoos wrap around his forearm from his elbow to the back of his hand.

Stranger danger! This is the type of man my sisters warned me about. I'm to avoid him at all costs.

I shake my head. "No, it's actually *not* nice to meet you. Go away." I turn my back on him. Two seconds later it dawns on me that it probably isn't smart to expose my vulnerable parts like that, because crazy people sometimes carry knives, but we have lots of witnesses and several of them are still watching us, so I feel safe. I mean, what's the worst that could happen?

Suddenly, I'm blinded by a flash of light. I throw my hands up to my eyes involuntarily. All I can see are white blobs now. "Ow, what the heck?"

"Ty! Ty! Look over here!" a man yells. More flashes go off.

Then someone's grabbing me by the arm. As my vision returns, I see it's the scruffy guy trying to drag me away.

I panic. Having a thousand witnesses within spitting distance doesn't seem to matter in this place. "Help! Assault! Help me!"

More flashes go off.

"Stop yelling that, Amber," he growls. "Come *on*."

I pause, making him stop with me. *Do my ears deceive me or did he just call me . . .* "Hey! How do you know my name?"

He points to a black car down the curb from where we're standing. "I was sent to pick you up. Come on."

"Who sent you?"

"Please. The paparazzi's here. Do you want your face splashed all over the tabloids, or what?"

My eyes bug out. "Tabloids?" *Why on earth would someone want to put me in a tabloid?* Another flash hits him in the face, glinting off the lenses of his glasses and catching me in the eye again. I spin around to find the culprit and find a short, fat man poised to take another shot with a giant camera that probably has a lens so powerful it'll get a crystal-clear shot of the pimple that erupted on my forehead this morning as I woke up to take this fateful trip.

"Get that out of my face!" I yell, swinging my giant purse around in a wide arc. It hits the end of his super-long camera lens and busts it right off. His equipment skitters along the sidewalk, making people dance out of the way.

The guy who accosted me drags me toward his car.

"You're gonna pay for that!" the cameraman yells.

"Pay for this!" I yell, shooting him a bird.

Some people cheer. Others laugh. Several members of the crowd are pointing their phones at me. The man who accosted me is swearing.

I turn around as we're arriving at his car. "What's your problem?" I ask, slightly out of breath.

"No one warned me I was picking up a hellion. I thought you were supposed to be some kind of peace-loving hippie chick."

I pull myself from his grip as I realize where we are. There's a taxi stand in front of this guy's car, and there's a space for me right at the front of the line. A driver is waving me over. *No wonder they weren't picking me up before . . . I was in the wrong spot!*

I straighten my purse strap across my shoulder, doing my best to brush the wrinkles out of my clothing. "Yeah, well, no one warned me I was being picked up by Mister Grabby Hands either. Now . . . why don't you just bug off and leave me to my business?"

He looks at me like he's confused. Then he smiles. "Bug off? Really?" I get the distinct impression that he's laughing at me.

I make a face at him and storm away, my bag tucked under my arm and my head held high as he laughs behind me. If he thinks he's going to get me into that car, he's nuts. I don't know him from Joseph, and I wasn't born yesterday; New York City is filled with crazy people, and just because he's easy on the eyes and says someone sent him to pick me up, it doesn't mean I'm going to let myself get chained up in his basement.

So he knows my name? *Big deal.* He could have seen it on my boarding pass. Maybe he works for the airline. He's probably a baggage handler, with muscles and tattoos like that. My sisters and I didn't tell our so-called fathers or our mothers that I was coming, so they don't even know I'm here; therefore, Mister Grabby Hands is *not* their emissary and he is *not* here to pick me up, either. I have no idea what he thought he was going to accomplish by getting me into his car, but the important thing is that his nefarious plan was thwarted by my quick thinking and big-city savvy. *Huzzah again!* I will not be a victim. I refuse to be taken advantage of by him or anyone else.

I come to a stop in front of the open door of the taxi. The man smiles as I point to his car. "I can get in here and you'll take me where I want to go?"

He has two gold teeth, right in front. *Snazzy.* I like his style. "Anywhere your heart desires." His voice is like smoooooth jazz. I'm instantly charmed, which is a nice change from what I was just dealing with.

"I'd like to see this man." I hand him Greg Lister, Esq.'s business card.

He glances at it and nods, giving me the card back. "Midtown. You got it."

I slide into the cab and don't look back as it pulls away from the curb and merges into traffic.

CHAPTER FIVE

I look up at the building that is so high I can't even see the top of it from inside the cab. *So that's why they're called skyscrapers.* The trip from JFK to this building has officially blown my mind. I always knew Manhattan was a big place. Even living the sheltered life I have, I read about it and saw pictures of the skyline. But intellectually understanding it's huge and actually experiencing it firsthand are completely different things. There were several points along the way that I lost my breath, but it wasn't from fear; it was from excitement. This place is so very, very different from the farm, but in a good way. I could probably drive over this bridge every day of my life and never get tired of that view.

"Here we are," the cabbie says. "You want to pay using a credit card or cash? Just touch the screen in front of you and make your choice."

"Are you sure this is the right place?" I check the business card in my hand and the number on the outside of the building. It looks correct, but maybe my driver has the wrong street. This address seems a bit much, even for Greg Lister and his fancy car and custom-made suit. It looks like a home base for aliens, all black and shiny. *Are those windows? Can people see out of those big dark panels?* I can't see anything from my side other than the reflection of the surrounding buildings and the clouds in the sky.

Butterflies are going crazy in my stomach. Coming here sounded all well and good when my sisters and I stayed up late into the night weighing the pros and cons over the past week, but now . . . not so much. I can't remember why I argued so heatedly against just letting sleeping dogs lie. Sleeping dogs are great. I *love* sleeping dogs. Who doesn't love a sleeping dog?

"I'm sure," he says. "You can ask security if you're worried about it."

"Security?"

The cabbie points to a person wearing a dark uniform and a badge. "That guy right there."

I have to believe that this cab driver knows his stuff, which means this is Greg Lister's office, and this is the place I need to be. I said I was going to do this, so I just need to go in and get it done, butterflies be damned. My sisters say I'm the brave one and that I never back down from a challenge, and even though I don't necessarily believe that about myself, I'm going to do this anyway. I comfort myself with a personal promise: after I've had the necessary conversation with the band, I can go right back to the airport as soon as it's over and cry about what a disillusioned hippie chick I am where no one can see me—probably in the public bathroom.

I check the flat computer screen in his backseat as instructed. "I don't have a credit card, so I guess I'll pay cash." I press the button and silently hand over two of the six fifty-dollar bills I withdrew from the bank yesterday, even though I'm more than a little shocked at the price of the trip from JFK to downtown Manhattan. *Seventy bucks one way?* I'm going to have to eat fast food to survive on my meager budget.

"How much change you need?" the golden-toothed man asks me, looking at me in his rearview mirror.

"Uhh . . . is that a trick question?"

He shrugs. "May-be." He opens up a zippered pouch and holds out a ten-dollar bill. "That gonna be okay?"

I frown, wondering how I'm going to say this without offending him. "I was never super awesome at math, but I'm pretty sure one hundred dollars minus seventy equals thirty. And that looks like a ten-dollar bill to me."

Suddenly, my door opens and a head is poking itself into the backseat with me.

My jaw drops as I get ready to yell at this impatient New Yorker who can't wait two seconds for me to figure out my change, when I realize it's that *guy* again, from the airport—Mister Grabby Hands. *What the hell!*

I do what comes naturally, which is to start slapping at him like he's an entire nest of wasps that's about to sting my lady parts. "Get out! Get out! Get *out*!"

"Hey! Hey! Hey!" he yells, trying to cover his head.

"Man, what the hell are you doin', comin' in my cab like that?" The driver throws his door open and exits the vehicle. *My hero!*

The guy's baseball cap falls off and I snag it, using it to slap him about the head and shoulders instead of my hands because they're stinging from all the contact I already made with his person. "Assault! Assault! Mugger! Thief!" I shriek, furious that this lunatic is messing up my plans and scaring me into wanting to leave the city before I accomplish my mission.

Suddenly, his head and shoulders disappear from the backseat and he's facing off against the cabbie on the sidewalk. I grab my bag and the ten-dollar bill that fell to the floor and hug them both to my chest. I guess this cabbie is going to get a hell of a tip today. *Dammit. Hot dogs and subway rides for me for the rest of the day.* Sliding over to the far side of the seat, I attempt to exit through the other door, but I'm forced to stop when a chorus of horns blares into my ear, telling me I'll be flattened if I even think about putting a leg outside.

I slide over and try to calculate my chances of escape. The two men are shoving each other just feet away from me, but then the driver suddenly stops. "Hey, man. You're . . . that guy . . . I saw you . . ." He's cocking his head to the side, pointing at him, obviously trying to place Mister Grabby Hands' face.

Mister Grabby Hands looks down at the ground, distracted all of a sudden. "Yeah. Times Square. I know." He searches behind him. "Where's my fucking hat?"

Several people have gathered to watch the show, including a guard from the building. I hear whispers and then people yelling. "Hey! That's Ty Stanz. Tyler! Over here!"

Okaaay . . . So apparently, this guy is a celebrity. He seems less sinister, now that I know he can be identified by any number of people walking down the street, but still . . . Why he'd want to engage in these shenanigans with *me* of all people doesn't make much sense, but I let the incongruity slide on by in my mind. I need to stay focused on finding Greg Lister and then the band. I will deliver my message and then get the hell out of this crazy city and go back home where I belong. My grand ideas about feeling at home in Manhattan are long gone.

I grab his baseball cap from the floor of the backseat and throw it at him. "Here's your stupid hat, you big jerk!"

The stiff bill of the hat hits him right in the 'nads.

He bends over, his legs pressed together with his hands cupping his man parts. "Damn, girl, watch it; that was close." He snatches his hat off the ground, scowling at me.

I quickly get out of the cab and run around both him and the crowd that's growing bigger by the second. The last thing I hear over the sound of people calling out to my attacker is the cab driver. "Hey, give the man some space, would you? Back off! Back off!" My former hero is now canoodling with the enemy, and the crowd standing around him is not berating him for harassing me; they're begging for autographs. *Figures. This is New York, after all. Crazy people everywhere.*

I head for the building, fly around inside the glass turnstile doors, run on tiptoes across the marble floor of the entrance because I'm worried I'll slip otherwise, and arrive at the security desk out of breath and sweaty. *Perfect*. I sure do know how to make an entrance. My sisters are going to laugh and laugh when I tell them what I did. I won't tell them the part where I was scared shitless because some weirdo tried to accost me outside the airport *and* Greg Lister's office.

The guard who stayed in his chair rather than joining his friend outside to handle the fray stares at me. "Can I help you?" He looks as though he's about to die of boredom.

I let out a long sigh to try and control my runaway emotions—a potent mélange of fear, frustration, confusion, and determination. Whoever that guy is outside, he sure is persistent. You'd think he'd be gone by now, trying to escape the mob that's gathered, but he's still there, signing autographs of all things. Thankfully, I feel safe standing here in front of a man in uniform with an actual badge on. That crazy guy wouldn't dare come after me in here. I hope.

"Are you a police officer?"

He slowly shakes his head. "No, I am not."

"But you have a badge." I point to it, in case he forgot he put it on this morning.

"You're wearing a hippie skirt, but I bet you're not a hippie."

I grin, feeling more comfortable by the second. He's big, and now I know he has a sense of humor and that we're connecting. "I'll bet you I am, though. I just arrived here from Glenhollow Farms in central Maine, and I grow all my own veggies and fruits and sell honey from my hives at the local farmers' market."

A slow grin spreads across his face. "No shit."

"Yes, shit. I do. I promise." I hold my hand over my heart.

He chuckles, just a little at first, but then the sound gets longer and louder, until he's throwing out a full-on guffaw. I can't help but smile along with him. I'm pretty sure he's laughing *with* me and not *at* me.

"Girl, you a trip. Where're you headed today?" When he smiles his cheeks turn into big apples on either side of his face. It's totally charming and puts me right at ease.

I hand him Mr. Lister's card. "I'm going here. *If* you allow me past your barriers." I glance over at the turnstiles that people are using electronic badges to get through.

He nods as he reads the address. "Thirty-third floor. Your name?" He leans forward with effort, his belly straining the buttons of his shirt.

"My name is . . . Jessica Albatross." I have no idea why I just said that. Maybe because I saw an article about Jessica Alba in the airplane magazine, and I thought she was really pretty. *Huh.* I'm learning a lot about myself today. Maybe I do panic like Em a little when I'm stressed. I knew I wasn't as brave as my sisters say I am.

I glance over my shoulder. The crowd is still there, and I'm worried that guy is going to try to come after me. If he does, it's better if he doesn't know who I really am; it's better if he's on the lookout for someone named Jessica rather than Amber. I'm happy my big-city savvy came to the rescue once more.

"Jessica Albatross. Really." He loses his smile.

I grin as hard as I can. "I know, right? Crazy name. Blame my father." I twirl my finger in the air next to my ear, just like Mister Grabby Hands did to me earlier.

He slides a clipboard over to me, back to being seriously bored. "Sign in here. And take this badge over there . . . Jessica Albatross." He points at the turnstiles with the plastic card in his hand as I fill in the name and phone number section on the paper. I make up a fake number too: *(555) 867-5309.*

"And bring the badge back to me when you're done."

"Yes, sir. I will do that." I take the stiff plastic card and check it out, bummed it doesn't have my photo on it like his does. I feel pretty official, though, as I clip it onto my shirt. I also feel very safe because now I know Mister Grabby Hands will have to pass the sniff test with this guy before he's allowed in.

"Anything else?" he asks.

"Yes." I look behind me for a second before turning back to him. "Could you please not let that man in here?" I point to the guy slowly making his way toward the door.

"Why not?" He glances at the door but then focuses on me.

"Because. He tried to accost me at the airport and then followed me here."

He frowns. "I'll take care of it." He picks up his walkie-talkie.

I grin at him, feeling like I have sunshine bursting out of me, I'm so relieved and happy.

"Anything else I can do for you?" He looks like he's about to laugh again.

"This is my first badge." I'm smiling like a loon as I look down at it hanging from my white peasant blouse. I know I'm being a total rube, but I can't help it. My mind is spinning with the notion that I'm in New York City . . . the *Big* City . . . I'm about to go hang out in a building that is literally scraping the sky, and my mission to tell these big-city buttheads that they can forget trying to bribe my sisters and me is almost over. I'm totally doing this. Nothing can stop me.

The front door spins around and loud noises spill in. I turn in a panic, and my mouth drops open as I see the huge crowd that's pressing against the glass, trying to enter all at once. "What in the hell . . ."

"Don't worry about it. Just go on upstairs. I'll handle this." The security guard stands up and adjusts his thick leather belt, tucking a bit of his belly under it and smoothing his shirt over his chest.

"Okay . . . Lamar," I say, reading his name tag. "You go get 'em." I point at his chest. "Show 'em your badge."

He shakes his head as he comes around the desk, headed for the front doors. "I will do that."

I take my official visitor's card and go to the turnstiles. I have to lean over really far so the machine can read it, because in my hurry, I'm not able to figure out how to unclip it from my shirt. The crowds behind me are making me nervous. When I'm finally through, I seek out my next goal: elevators. There are two banks of silver ones to my left and right, set deep into shiny black walls that remind me of Mr. Lister's shoes. Everything is so cold and hard here—very impersonal, just like him.

I walk over to the right and press the call button. The elevator just to my left opens up immediately. I go inside all alone and press the number thirty-three. I realize as the doors slide closed and the elevator starts its ascent that this day has been full of firsts: my first plane ride, my first taxi ride, my first assault, my first visitor badge, and my first building over four floors high. The tallest building where I went to college, an hour away, was two stories.

I smile for a moment until I realize what's next. The easy part is over; now comes the hard part. My good humor disappears as I begin to worry. I nibble my thumbnail and wonder what's going to happen when I say what I've come to say. Will they yell at me? Laugh and call me a naïve fool? Toss me out on my butt? The idea that they might feel bad and apologize seems really silly to me right now, even though that's what my sisters and I were hoping for. We talked about getting justice, about saying our piece, about getting these men to feel even just an inkling of the pain we felt when we realized we had living, breathing fathers out there in the world. Now I'm not so sure I can make that happen.

I guess we'll soon find out. I resist the urge to call Em and Rose. I said I was going to do this alone and I am. I've been taking care of my sisters, sacrificing my happiness for theirs, and making the hard calls since day one, and I'm not going to stop doing that today.

CHAPTER SIX

The elevator doors open into a large lobby. I expected to be dropped off into a hallway, so I stand inside the elevator a little too long as I take in the immense open space furnished with leather chairs and couches, glass tables, and metal sculptures. I feel as though I've been riding in a spaceship and I'm being delivered to command central. The doors begin to shut. Thankfully, a man sticks his hand between them, keeping them from closing completely. As they slide open I get a good look at his face.

"It's you," I say, surprised to see Mr. Lister standing right in front of me. He does not look happy.

"Yes, it is. And here *you* are." He looks me up and down.

I lift my chin. He is not going to intimidate me by judging me again. "Yes, I am. I have some things to say to you and your clients."

He glances briefly to his left, in the direction of the reception desk. There are three women and one man sitting there. They look very busy, but I get the distinct impression that they're hearing everything we say anyway.

"Why don't you follow me to my office and we can discuss your plans there?"

I step off the elevator, making sure to leave as much distance between us as possible. "That's fine. But I don't plan on staying here for very long. I have things to do. Places to be." He doesn't need to know that those things consist only of eating a hot dog and seeing Central Park before I leave. If I'm going to make my flight back, I need to keep this short and sweet.

He walks through the lobby, expecting me to just follow him. I'm tempted to stand where I am to prove a point, but when I can't really figure out what that point is, I hurry to catch up. My bracelets jangle together and make pretty tinkling noises as I rush by the reception desk.

Two of the people sitting there look up at the sounds, and I smile and nod at them. "Hi, how are you? Good, I hope." I may be in New York City, but that doesn't mean I'm going to lose all my manners. None of them respond to me, though, as I follow Mr. Lister out of the lobby and down several long hallways. I'd normally be upset by people being so rude, but I'm too distracted with trying to remember which way I just turned to bother with it. I'm definitely going to need a guide out of this place. It's a damn maze!

He finally stops trying to lose me. "After you," he says, gesturing while he stands in a doorway.

I walk past him and enter the biggest office I've ever seen. I'm used to the normal-size ones at our local city hall or at the bank. I've even been inside the postmaster's office once, but it was a shoe box compared to this ridiculous space. He could put a king-size bed in here and still have room to host meetings.

I scan Lister's domain, taking in the huge wood desk, trophies made of crystal, framed diplomas declaring this man spent a lot of money on his education, and shelves and shelves of books. There are floor-to-ceiling windows looking out over the city too. I find myself drawn to them. I stop at the nearest one, but not too close to it. Being thirty-three floors up is suddenly very dizzying.

"I'm afraid I have some bad news for you," he says, walking over and stopping behind his desk.

I forget about the view and turn around. "What's that? Did they change their minds about the settlement?" That would be a bit of a bummer. Saying *We wouldn't have wanted your money anyway* doesn't quite have the same ring to it as *Take your thirty million bucks and shove it where the sun don't shine.*

"No, not that. The problem is that we didn't find out you were going to be here until just a few hours ago, so I didn't have time to call them in. They're out of town right now on a last-minute trip."

I chew my lip. This is very inconvenient. I have a return ticket out tonight and was assuming he could put a meeting together today. *Should I just leave a message with Lister to pass on to them? And who the heck is selling me out?* I can't believe my sisters would tell this guy anything, so how the heck did he find out I was coming here a few hours ago?

I can't leave a message with Lister. It won't have nearly the same impact. And if I'm being honest with myself, I have to admit . . . I really do want to say what I came to say to their faces so I can see their expressions when I deliver the news that their long-lost daughters plan to stay that way. I'm probably going to flip them off too, for good measure, and I doubt Lister would do that for me. From the looks of this office, they pay him too much for him to risk it.

"Where are they?" I ask, even though I don't really care. I'm just stalling so I can think things through more thoroughly. *Can I get a refund on that plane ticket?* I think I remember it being nonrefundable. *Dammit.*

"They're in Toronto." He stops there and just stares back at me. He's apparently not going to offer any more information—like what these men are doing there and when they'll be back—and I'm certainly not going to beg for it.

I walk over to his bookshelves. "Have you read all of these?" The spines on the textbooks tell me that he deals in mergers and acquisitions, contracts, and international taxation. *Boooring.* Why am I not surprised that his reading material is as dull as he is?

"Yes."

I pull one of the volumes off the shelf and open up to a random page. "What is the corporate taxation rate in Trinidad and Tobago?" I turn around and narrow my eyes at him, waiting for his brilliant answer.

He shrugs. "I have no idea. Why don't you have a seat?" He gestures at a chair across from his desk.

I snort as I slide the volume back onto the shelf. I knew he hadn't read all those books. I walk over and take a seat, setting my purse on the floor next to me. It's time to stop stalling and get down to business. There's a hot dog out there in Manhattan with my name on it, and my sisters made me promise I'd try one and describe every last detail of it to them when I get back. Our mothers have never allowed a single processed meat product to enter our home, and we've been dying of curiosity. "When will they be back?" I ask.

"They're taking a flight out first thing tomorrow morning. Their plane lands very early. If you wish, I can arrange to have them meet you at your hotel after they arrive."

I stare at Lister, trying to figure him out. His expression is completely impassive. He doesn't look like he's happy to have me here, that's for sure. You'd think he'd be nicer to the daughter of his clients, though, even if she is here to tell them to kiss her butt.

"You don't like me very much, do you?"

"I have no feelings about you either way."

I swear this man has to be a robot, which really makes me want to push his buttons. "What about my sisters? How do you feel about them?"

He picks up a pen and starts writing on a piece of paper, effectively letting me know that I'm not even important enough to share eye contact with. "I have no thoughts on your sisters either."

"What do you think about these clients of yours who are ready to hand over thirty million bucks to three women they've never met before?"

His jaw twitches. "To be honest, I advised them not to do it."

Now we're getting somewhere. "How come?"

He stops writing and looks up at me. "I'm sorry, but I can't share that information with you. My clients enjoy confidentiality in their conversations with me."

"But you already told me that you told them not to do it, so I guess that rule only applies . . . sometimes?"

He says nothing but his jaw twitches again, several times. I think I'm pissing him off. I also think I don't care.

"How did you know I was going to be here?" I ask.

"I received a phone call."

No way did my sisters sell me out. The whole plan was for me to come in here and do a sneak attack, catch them unawares so they wouldn't have time to play games and come up with reasons that weren't genuine. "Who called you? Because I know it wasn't my sisters."

"It was Barbara."

I knew it. My mother sussed out our plan. She probably put Em under a hot reading lamp and interrogated her. Em can't hold in a secret to save her life. I'm going to give her a serious guilt trip for not texting me and telling me what she did.

Lister looks up at me, and it's possible I see a tiny spark of pity in his eye. Now I'm pissed. Nobody pities my family. Nobody.

"You don't like my mothers much, do you?"

"How I feel about anyone in your family is completely irrelevant."

I shrug, letting my anger fall away. He's not worth it, and like Buddha always said, hanging on to anger is like grabbing a hot lump of coal to toss at someone else . . . or something like that. "You're right. It is irrelevant. I don't really give a hoot; I was just trying to be polite." I look around as I tap my hands on the arms of the chair I'm sitting in. "So, this is your office, eh?"

"Yes." He goes back to writing.

"How long have you been here?"

I think he's about to answer me, but a knock on the door interrupts him. I turn around and find a blond woman in the threshold wearing a white nearly-see-through blouse, beige pencil skirt, and nude stilettos. She doesn't even look at me. "Greg, Mr. Stanz is here to see you."

I sit up straighter in my chair. I'm pretty sure I heard that name outside, but it can't be . . .

"Show him into the conference room. I'll be right there." Mr. Lister stands up and smooths down his tie, buttoning his suit coat. He looks almost nervous, which is really interesting.

Someone shows up behind the woman and then walks around her. Mister Grabby Hands himself! I stand up in front of my chair and back up until my butt hits the edge of Mr. Lister's desk. *What the hell is he doing here?* My mind races to put the pieces of this puzzle together—he knows Greg . . . He was at the airport and knew my name . . . Greg knew I was coming . . . *Uh-oh* . . .

"No, that's okay," Grabby Hands says. "I'll just meet him in here." He walks into the office and turns around, slowly shutting the door right in the woman's face. She has to back up a step to keep her nose from getting smooshed.

A rude dude acting crude. Why am I not surprised? He's the type of man who will grab a girl he hasn't even been introduced to yet.

Lister clears his throat. "Hello, Ty. I guess you missed Amber at the airport."

Ty turns around and hooks his thumbs in his front pockets as he stares at me. "No, I didn't miss her. I ran right into her, actually."

It all falls into place . . . why this turd has been stalking me since I got here. I glare at Lister as I point at the weirdo standing near the door. "You sent this animal to pick me up?"

"Animal?" Ty takes two steps closer, pulling off his sunglasses. "*She* attacked *me*." He points at his eye using one of the little arms of his sunglasses. "I have a bruise."

I laugh. He sounds like an angry toddler. "A bruise? That's not a bruise . . . it's smeared makeup. Please." I know a blob of smeared eyeliner when I see it. My sisters and I have played with makeup since we were tiny. We don't wear it much, but we know how to use it. He's the first man I've seen in person with eyeliner on, but to each his own. Maybe he's a musician too. That would explain a lot of things, like his behavior, hair, and body art. I'm not impressed. Not really.

Ty frowns and rubs at his eye. He looks at his finger, trying to determine whether I'm right or not.

"Okay, I don't know what happened, but obviously things went a little off track." Lister holds up his hands, trying to make peace. "Why don't we just sit down and figure out where we go from here?"

I back away from both of them. "No, I'm not sitting with him." I look Ty up and down. "First of all, he needs a shower, and second of all, he needs to put on some clean clothes. And third of all, he put his hands all over me, and I don't even know who he is. That's assault. I know my rights." I fold my arms and face Lister. "I want to sue him. You're hired."

Ty starts laughing. "Sue me? That's rich. There're about fifty videos on YouTube right now showing you beating the shit out of me *and* that guy with the camera."

Lister frowns at me. "Is this true?"

"No, it's not true." I drop my arms to my sides. The righteous indignation that was riding shotgun with me just a minute ago starts to slip away. "Not really. I mean, they both asked for it. I was just defending myself from their advances."

"Advances? Are you *serious*?!" Ty is yelling now, and the madder he gets, the more his voice sounds like a little old lady's. It makes me laugh. I try to keep it in, but I can't.

"She's laughing." He gestures at me. "Do you hear her laughing?" He uses his glasses to point at his eye again. "This isn't makeup, okay?"

Lister tips his head down and rests the bridge of his nose on two fingers, pinching it. He scrunches his eyes closed really tightly. It looks like he's hurting himself. "How did this go so wrong?" he asks no one in particular.

"Listen, man, I'm no chauffeur, okay? I know you're shorthanded and all, but sending me out there was a bad idea. I told you that, but you didn't listen. The paparazzi were all over me the minute she started yelling."

"You know you weren't asked to go because we're shorthanded," Greg says, shaking his head in disappointment.

"Hey! I wasn't yelling," I say, annoyed that I'm being cut out of the conversation and painted as the weirdo in the situation when I was clearly acting like any normal person would. This isn't about why Ty was sent to pick me up; it's about his assault of my person. "I was just telling you to take your damn hands off me."

Lister stares at the ceiling and hisses out a long breath. "You're right. It was a mistake." He looks at me. "I'm sorry. He was supposed to . . . not put his hands all over you . . . but pick you up at the airport in one of our firm's cars and bring you here. I assumed my office was your destination."

"Man, I'm telling you, I *didn't* put my hands all over her! She's exaggerating!"

Lister holds his hand out at Ty, effectively telling him to shut up, which Ty does.

I look at both of them, and while I can tell they're both angry, I detect no real malice. I believe Lister is telling the truth and that Ty just lacks some manners. But this doesn't change the fact that Ty grabbed me like I was the last gluten-free dinner roll on a Weight Watchers buffet, so I'm not just going to forgive him and forget everything he did.

I cough once and straighten my posture as I address Lister. "Well . . . he apparently needs a few lessons in how to deal with women, but that's not my problem. Your office was my destination because I figured you could put together a meeting with . . . the interested parties. But seeing as how you can't do that right now, there's no need for me to be here anymore." I walk toward the door, hoping Ty will move out of my way before I get too close. I'm so ready to run back home, and screw the whole hot dog and long-lost fathers adventure. I'm not brave. I'm a lily-livered chicken, just like my sisters. Bawk, bawk, bawk!

"Where're you going?" Lister asks.

Ty backs out of my way. I nod at him once, thanking him silently for at least being respectful toward me this time.

"You're not running away, are you?" Ty asks softly.

He knows I'm running and he's issuing a challenge. Or he's mocking me. I can't tell which. Either way, it makes it really hard for me to continue on my current trajectory. When he gives me a poo-eating grin, it makes my decision for me: I cannot run from this.

Taking a notepad from my purse, I write down my phone number, tear off the sheet of paper it's on, and walk over to slap it down on Lister's desk. I pause in the doorway on my way out and face Lister, completely ignoring that other jerk in the room. "I'm going to eat some lunch and find a place to stay, since I'm obviously not going to be able to leave here tonight like I planned. You have my number now. Call me when you can set something up." Screw going home. I'm not afraid of Ty Grabby Hands. I came here on a mission and I'm going to complete it.

"You don't have a room booked?" Lister asks.

"No, but this is New York City. I'm sure I won't have a problem finding someplace." Maybe a youth hostel, since that's all I can afford at this point.

Lister picks up his phone and speaks to the person who answers. "Zoey, I need you to book a room at the Four Seasons for Ms. Amber Fields."

"Aka Jessica Albatross," Tyler says softly so that only I can hear him.

I'm torn between wanting to reach out and slap that stupid hat off his head and laughing along with him. I have never met a more frustrating person in my entire life. I think he could be an interesting person under all that grunge, but rather than indulging in the idea of getting to know him better, I glare at him while he glares right back at me. And now that I'm looking at him in such close proximity, I think he might be right; I may have accidentally bruised the corner of his eye. *Oops.*

A tiny bit of guilt sneaks into my heart, courtesy of the very healthy conscience my three mothers have spent twenty-four years instilling in me. I can hear their voices in my head right now: *You should never lash out at someone in anger, Amber. You need to learn to control your emotions, Amber. Not everyone is going to understand your passion or appreciate your expression of it, Amber.*

Lister nods at his phone. "Thanks." He hangs up the handset. "There's a room for you at the Four Seasons."

I saw an ad for the Four Seasons in the airport, and I'm pretty sure it's out of my price range. "I'm not interested in anybody's charity."

"It's not charity. We have a corporate account there. It's a write-off on our taxes every time we use it for clients." He hesitates, as if he's going to say more, but then he glances at Ty and stops. I'm glad, because it's none of Ty's business who I am or what I'm doing here.

I blink a few times, letting the idea of staying in that hotel settle into my brain. *Am I taking charity from someone if it's giving them a benefit to their business?* I don't know anything about the tax code, but I do know that I just spent ninety bucks on cab fare and I only have $210 left. That's not going to get me very far, especially if I'm going to be stuck here for another day. "Fine."

"You want me to give her a ride over there?" Ty asks.

I look at him like he's insane. "You've *got* to be kidding me. I'm not going *anywhere* with you."

"Why not? I'm a good guy." He points at his face, smiling like he's charming or something. "You're the one who injured me, remember?"

I snort. "Yeah, right." As far as I'm concerned, a 'good guy' doesn't just assume a perfect stranger will get into a car with him at the airport; he takes a moment to introduce himself and be friendly first.

I walk out the door without another word, take a left, and keep on going. Eventually, I find myself in a room full of copy machines. I could've sworn this was where the lobby was. "Dammit."

"Are you lost?" A young girl wearing jeans and a crop top is standing there looking at me as she snaps her chewing gum.

Why lie? If I keep walking, I could end up right back in Lister's office with Ty laughing his butt off at me. "Yes. I am *very* lost." This girl doesn't look like a legal secretary or a lawyer, but she probably knows her way around better than I do.

She smiles as she tosses her messy ponytail over her shoulder. "Come with me. I'll show you how to get out of here. I used to get lost aaall the time."

I follow behind her, enjoying the way her hair swings back and forth as she bounces her way down the hallway. She looks so young and free. I used to look like that . . . before three old men sent their lawyer into my life to turn it upside down.

"Do you work here?" I ask.

"Me? No. Not really. I'm supposed to be filing stuff, but it's super boring, so I just make photocopies of goofy things and send pictures of them to my friends on Snapchat."

I nod. "That sounds like more fun than filing. What's Snapchat?"

She spins around. "Ohmygod, you don't know what Snapchat is? Give me your phone." She holds out her hand expectantly.

I dig around in my purse for the small device, handing it over when I finally locate it.

She looks at it with a funny expression on her face. "What's this?"

"That's my phone."

She scoffs. "No, *this* is not a phone. This is a *dinosaur*." She opens it up. "Oh my big butt, it's a flip phone." She looks at me with more focus, checking out my threads and my purse. "Are you a total hippie, or what?"

"I am." I smile back really big.

She hands me my phone, nodding. "Respect. I like you."

"I like you too. What's your name?"

"Linny Lister." She grins and two dimples sink into her cheeks.

"Linny Lister." The name makes me a little ill. "Does that mean Greg Lister is your father?"

She sighs. "No, he's my uncle. Do you know him?"

"I sure do." I try to smile. I don't want this girl to know that I think her uncle is a dinkus.

"He's pretty much a douche bag, huh?"

I burst out laughing. "I did *not* say that."

"Don't worry, you don't have to. Everyone else does." She turns around and continues down the hall, taking a left and then another right. "But he can be really cool too. You just have to catch him in the right mood."

"And what would that mood be?" I can't picture it at all, but I'm sure she knows him better than I do. I'll try to take her word for it.

"The mood that he's in when he's not in this office." She rolls her eyes as she looks at me over her shoulder. "Which happens very rarely because he pretty much lives here."

"Huh." I file that away in the back of my mind. Where I live, it seems like I get to know who people are right from the beginning . . . who they *really* are. Nobody hides much out on the farm. But I get the impression that here in the city, nobody is as they seem. It's all very strange. I feel like I've taken an airplane to another planet.

We turn a corner and I catch a glimpse of the lobby up ahead. "Okay, this looks familiar."

"Yep. Those are the elevators." She points. "They'll take you down to the lobby." She stops at the edge of the reception area and gives me a quick hug goodbye. "What did you say your name was?"

"Amber. My name is Amber Fields."

"Okay, Amber Fields, hippie girl . . . I hope you have a really wonderful day." She flashes me her dimples again.

"You too, Linny Lister."

She walks off with her ponytail swinging, and I turn around to face the elevators. Everyone at the reception desk is being very industrious, paying me no attention. I don't bother with niceties, since I know they're wasted here. Instead, I stride across the room with my chin held high, wondering how far the Four Seasons Hotel is from this building. I may just have to walk so I have enough money for that hot dog and a ride to the airport.

CHAPTER SEVEN

It turns out that the Four Seasons Hotel is not that far from the lawyer's office, after all. I follow the security guard's instructions and walk for twenty minutes amid the cacophony of blaring horns, yelling construction workers, and quickly accelerating taxicabs, and find myself outside the front doors of another big building. This one looks older in style than Lister's office. It's also not as tall. Yes, it's scraping the sky, but not as much of it. And it's not all glass either, although the front of it has a very tall section that's split in half by a fan-shaped overhang. There are three men standing outside in uniform. One of them gives me a funny look as I enter, but the others ignore me as they chat between themselves.

I enter through the clear doors and make my way across the lobby's geometrically patterned marble floors and up a short set of stairs to the front desk. I feel like I've just entered a palace. I wish I could say I feel like a princess, but when I compare what I'm wearing to everyone around me, I feel more like the court jester.

A woman who looks to be about my age, wearing a black suit with white piping on the collar, greets me with a smile. "Welcome to the Four Seasons. How may I help you?"

I lean over the counter and eye her four-inch-high black stilettos that explain why she looks tall enough to dunk a basketball. "I believe I have a room reserved for me here? My name is Amber Fields." Sweat droplets are popping out on my back, tickling the fine hairs there. I have no idea why I'm so nervous. Maybe because there are more cut flowers in vases around me than I have growing on my entire farm. They must spend a fortune on the arrangements alone. They're doing a good job of eliminating the stink of car exhaust and city stench, though, so I get why they would create a budget for it.

The woman types some things into her computer before responding. "Yes, we have you right here in one of our one-bedroom Manhattan suites. May I have a credit card, please?" She holds out her hand.

"Manhattan suite? Sounds interesting." I'm stalling because I don't have a card, and this is already starting to get embarrassing. I haven't even been here for two minutes yet.

"Yes, the suite is very popular. It offers views of the Chrysler Building, the East River, and the Atlantic Ocean. You also have a great view of the downtown skyline. You can take some great pictures from inside the suite." She pauses. "May I have your credit card, please?"

I frown, nerves making my hands tremble and my heart race. I don't want to have to turn around and beat feet out of here. Talk about a walk of shame. "I thought this room was being taken care of by Mr. Lister's law firm."

She smiles patiently at me. "It is. But we take a credit card impression for incidentals."

I shrug, feeling both slightly relieved and freaked out at the same time. I've never been so confused in my own head before. "Sorry, I can't help you. I don't have a credit card."

The woman gives me a funny look. "We aren't going to charge you anything if you don't eat or drink items from the room's bar."

I'm losing patience quickly. Can't she see this is making me really uncomfortable? "That's really nice, but it doesn't matter. I don't *have* a card."

She pulls her hand back and stiffens her spine. "What do you mean you don't have a card?"

I want to stomp my foot with frustration, but I don't. I force myself to smile instead, trying to heed my mothers' advice to rein in my temper and reactive nature. It probably looks like I'm suffering from indigestion, which isn't too far off the mark; I'm feeling sicker by the second.

"I don't think I can be any clearer than I'm being," I say. "I do not *own* a credit card of any type. I pay cash or I don't pay at all." I wait for her to digest the information, something that appears to be proving very difficult for her. I hate that my face is burning. I know it's beet red, while hers is taking on a nice shade of pink.

"One moment, please, Ms. Fields." She picks up the telephone and rests it on her shoulder as she types some things into her computer. She sighs, letting me know in no uncertain terms that I'm being a royal pain in the ass. I hate that she's able to make me feel both guilty and scummy without a single word being spoken.

When the person on the other end picks up, she speaks very softly. "We have a little issue here. Someone booked in the Lister suite does not have a credit card." She nods a few times and then slides the phone off her shoulder, catching it in her hand and hanging it up.

Her expression changes lightning fast from irritated to easygoing, like she hasn't a care in the world. The difference is no less than stunning. She gives me a cheery smile as she shifts her attention from the keyboard to my face. "Okay, that won't be a problem at all. If you could just fill out this form here." She places a piece of paper and a pen on the counter between us.

I'm shocked at the transformation. Here I thought we were about to roll up our sleeves and throw down, yet now she's acting as though I've handed her eight credit cards instead of just the one she was asking for. She's pretending like not having a credit card is no big deal when before I was some kind of degenerate. I wish I could brush it off, but I can't. I feel . . . bad. Like a person who doesn't deserve to be here. *How ridiculous is this place?*

I shake my head to get my brain back to square one. If she can play this game, so can I. But for the record, New Yorkers are *weird*. I'm so glad I don't live here. I could never fit in and I wouldn't want to. The choice I made two years ago to stay on the farm and live out my life there with my family instead of going out into the world and getting a job is looking really good right now.

I lose myself in the standard formality of the check-in process. The form she gave me is asking for all the normal stuff . . . name, address, phone number. I fill it in slowly, making sure my handwriting is neat and legible, and slide it back to her. The couple minutes it takes me to complete the task helps me calm down.

"Here is your key," she says, slipping a plastic card into a paper folder and writing on it. "The elevators are to your right." She gestures like the flight attendant did when indicating the location of the exits on the plane. "If you have any problems, just give me a call or stop by at the desk here." She puts the little card holder on the counter, folds her hands at her waist, and smiles.

I wish I had a camera because I would take a picture of her right now so I could show my sisters what I'm seeing. She looks like a model on a poster for the hotel. Not a hair is out of place, her makeup is flawless, and her expression is so professionally bland, it makes her look as though she's been molded out of plastic. More New York City craziness. Did we or did we not just go toe-to-toe over a credit card? I say yes, but her face says no. *Weird, weird, weird.* It's like you can be rude here, and it doesn't count.

I begin to walk away, but then I stop and turn around and go back. If she can let bygones be bygones, so can I. The girl lifts an eyebrow, waiting for whatever it is I'm going to say.

"Do you know where I can get a good hot dog around here?"

She hesitates, as though she doesn't quite understand the question. "Hot dog?"

"Yes. A hot dog. You know . . . elongated, phallic-shaped meat byproduct in a bun?" I grin.

Her responding smile is tight. "Any particular type of hot dog?"

I shrug. "A New Yorker hot dog. The kind people talk about."

She nods sagely. "You can get a New Yorker hot dog at any of those carts you see outside on the sidewalk. I believe there's one a few blocks down that way." She points to her right, again like a flight attendant.

"Do you eat hot dogs?" I ask, wondering if she knows what she's talking about.

The girl shakes her head. "No. I'm vegan."

My suspicions are confirmed; she wouldn't know a good hot dog if it jumped down her throat and digested itself. "Okay. Good to know. Thanks. And congratulations on your . . . uh . . . vegan status." I find it ironic that this proud vegan is wearing what looks like leather shoes, but I'm going to let it go. She already seems like she's having a bad enough day.

"My pleasure," she says with a tight smile.

I leave the reception area, hitching my purse higher on my shoulder as I walk over to the elevators. A man in uniform is waiting. *They sure do like their gold buttons around here.* He holds the door open for me when I get in and then steps inside with me.

"What floor would you like, ma'am?"

I open up the little folder the woman at reception gave me. "Forty-ninth floor, I guess." I show him her neat handwriting.

"Yes, forty-ninth it is. Thank you." We ride the elevator up together. After the fifth floor, I can't stand the silence any longer.

"So, what's your name?"

He looks startled. "Jeremy." He smiles awkwardly at me before going back to staring at the buttons.

"Hi, Jeremy. I'm Amber." I hold out my hand.

He shakes my hand, smiling. "Nice to meet you." He looks like he wants to laugh.

"Where are you from?" I ask him.

"Michigan."

"That's a long way from here," I say. "In more ways than one."

"Yes, you're right." He doesn't say it, but I think he gets me.

"What brought you to New York City?"

"A girl." He sighs, looking at the ceiling, losing his happy face.

"How'd that work out?"

"Not so great." He looks embarrassed, shifting his gaze to the buttons. We're on floor fifteen now.

"That's too bad. But there are other fish in the sea, right? And the sea is deep here in Manhattan, I'll bet."

"Yeah. Right. Sure." He doesn't sound convinced.

"How is the dating scene here?"

He looks at me funny. "Okay, I guess."

I sigh wistfully. "I'm only here for a day. Probably not enough time to date anyone."

He pauses before answering. "You could go on Tinder."

I frown. "*Go* on it?"

"Yeah. The app. Tinder." He waits for me to respond, but I'm not sure what to say. "On your phone."

"Oh." I pull out my phone and hold it up for him to see. "This phone?"

He smiles and shakes his head. "No, that's not a smartphone."

I look at it disappointedly. "No, it's not very smart at all. It doesn't even do Slapchats."

"Do you mean Snapchat?"

I have to think about it a few seconds. I could have sworn Linny said *slap*, but perhaps she said *snap*. "Maybe."

He shrugs, trying not to smile. "Don't worry about it. Tinder kind of sucks anyway."

"What is it?"

"It's an app on the phone where you can find dates. Like one-night stands or whatever you're looking for, really."

"Oh my god." I try to figure out if he's serious, but he sure seems like he is. "Are you kidding me?"

"No." He laughs. "You seriously don't know about Tinder or Snapchat?"

I shake my head. "Nope."

"Where are you from?"

The bell to the elevator rings and it slows down. "I'm from central Maine. I live on a hippie commune there."

"No shit." His smile drops away in an instant. "Oh, man. I shouldn't have said that."

I reach out and pat him on the arm. "Don't worry about it. We say *shit* on the farm all the time. I may not know about smartphones and apps, but I do know how to cuss up a storm when necessary."

The doors to the elevator open. "Okay, well, have a nice day, Miss Fields."

"I will. You do the same, Jeremy."

"Yes, ma'am. I will."

As the doors start to close, I put my hand out and make the elevator open again. I hate leaving him thinking about his bad luck with the girl who brought him to New York. "And don't worry about the dating thing. One of these days the right girl will come along, and she'll see you for who you really are. Wait for her. She'll be worth it."

His face goes red. "Okay. I will. Thanks."

I back up and let the doors close. The last thing I see is Jeremy the elevator man staring at the floor. Poor kid. I can tell he's had his heart broken. It's funny . . . we sometimes get people like that out at the farm. They come for a few days, weeks, or months, trying to figure out where they went wrong. So far every single one of them has left with some idea of what they want next in life. Glenhollow brings peace in a sometimes crazy world. That's what our last visitor said. I think I've already met several New Yorkers who could use a few weeks at the farm.

The hallway leading to my room is not overly ornate, but it's still obvious they spent a lot of money making it look classy. It's nothing compared to the elegance of my room, though. It almost takes my breath away. I've never seen anything like it.

First of all, it's big for Manhattan. My sisters and I did some research; the apartments here can be just a single studio with barely enough space to turn around in and still cost thousands of dollars a month in rent. There are floor-to-ceiling windows in the hotel room's living space and bedroom. The carpet is soft and thick. Everything is brand new and modern without looking cold. Whoever designed this place could teach the people over at Lister's office a few things about making a place seem more welcoming.

I check out the bathroom and then walk over to the windows, pushing the gauzy curtain aside. The view is pretty spectacular, maybe even better than the one Lister has. It makes me wonder how much this room is costing his firm. I don't like the idea of owing him something after staying here. I have money in savings, but I have a feeling one night here would cost as much as I make in six months of selling honey at the farmers' market.

I hear a soft knock at the door, so I walk over and look through the peephole. There's another man in uniform waiting. *More gold buttons.* I open the door.

"Hello." I give him a smile. He's older than Jeremy, I think, but not by much. They have a very young staff inside the building, whereas the guys out front looked like lifers in comparison.

"Hello, Ms. Fields. My name is James. I'm here to see if there's anything I can get for you."

"Like what?" He's kind of stumped me with his offer. *Do I need to ask for towels, or are they already in the bathroom?* I can't remember what I saw in there other than eight tons of marble.

"Anything you could possibly want." He smiles big, revealing super-white teeth. "Extra pillows, tickets to a Broadway show, a driver to take you somewhere . . ."

"Wow. You really did mean anything."

"We try to make our guests' stay here as comfortable as possible."

My curiosity is piqued. "How much would a ticket to a Broadway show cost me?" I hadn't considered doing anything like that, but if the band members aren't going to be back until tomorrow, maybe I should.

"It depends on which one you're interested in seeing. Do you have one in mind?"

I shrug, not especially wanting him to know that I have no clue what Broadway shows are playing or even what they're like. "I don't know . . . one of the more popular ones."

"Well, it depends on what kind of seat you want, the day of the week, and the time of the showing . . . but if you want something not too far back and near the center, weekday, eight o'clock, and not one of the hottest shows going, probably about a hundred and seventy bucks."

Well, I guess that settles that. "Okay. That's good to know. I'm not interested in seeing a Broadway show right now, though."

"Okay, that's fine. If you change your mind or if you need anything else, just ring the front desk. You can ask for me directly or the concierge. Anyone will be happy to help you."

I can't believe how nice he's being. After the little scene at the front desk, it's a nice change. "I will do that. Have a nice day, James."

He smiles. "You too."

As he's walking away an idea comes to mind. "James?"

He pauses and turns around. "Yes?"

"How much does this suite cost per night?" I'm still not sure I'm okay with being indebted to Lister. I wonder how long it'd take me to pay him back.

"I'm not sure. I can have someone at the front desk call you and give you that information, if you wish."

I chew my lip, not sure I want that girl down there knowing I'm snooping. "It's probably pretty expensive, huh?"

"Definitely above my pay grade." He smiles, and it makes me feel like we're co-conspirators—two people in this building who could never afford to stay here for real.

His answer reminds me that he's a working man and that he came up here to offer me help. I'm pretty sure I'm supposed to tip him. "James, hold on a second." I dig around in my purse and find that floating ten-dollar bill given to me by the taxi driver. It's a huge chunk of what I have left, percentage wise, but I'm pretty sure I'll still be able to afford a hot dog and a ride back to the airport with what I'll have left. I hold it out. "Here. Thanks for your help."

He walks over and takes it from me. "Thank you. That's very generous of you, especially since I really didn't do anything."

"You can pay me back by telling me the best place to get a hot dog."

"No problem at all. My favorite place is Gray's Papaya on Seventy-Second and Broadway. Times Square is only a ten-minute subway ride from there, if you want to experience that whole thing too."

I mull that over in my head. "Gray's Papaya, huh?" I must look confused because he elaborates.

"Yeah. They serve hot dogs and tropical drinks. Believe it or not, it works. It's not too far from here. You could walk, since the weather's nice, or grab a cab or hop on the subway." He looks down at my shoes. "You have sensible shoes, so . . ."

I look at my ballet flats. "Yeah. I guess I didn't get the memo about the stilettos I see everybody wearing around here."

"Believe me, you're better off. All the women I work with moan and complain about how sore their feet are. I think if they wore shoes like yours, they wouldn't be in so much pain."

"It's kinda silly what women will do to show off their calves, isn't it?"

"Yeah." He takes a couple steps toward the elevators. "Is there anything else I can do for you?"

"Nope. All I needed was the hot dog."

"I could go get the hot dog for you, if you want."

"Really? It seems kind of silly to make somebody take a walk for me just so I can have some junk food."

"Nah, we do that kind of thing all the time."

"Oh. Well, no, thanks. I appreciate the offer, but I need some fresh air."

He laughs. "Then you probably shouldn't go outside."

I grin back at him. He totally gets me. "Yeah, you're probably right. I guess I should've said I need some New York air."

He lifts his hand and waves goodbye as he works his way down the hallway to the elevator. "Have a nice day, Ms. Fields."

"You too, James."

I close the door, smiling to myself. What a nice guy he is. I wonder if everybody who works here is this nice. The girl at the front desk wasn't that bad. She was just flustered because I threw her a curve ball over that credit card. And besides . . . she's a conflicted vegan, wearing those leather shoes and all; they probably don't make many cloth stilettos. Maybe she just needs a nice juicy steak to help her fix her mood.

There's another soft knock at the door. James must've forgotten something. I throw the door open with a big smile on my face. "Hello again, Ja . . ." The word dies in my mouth as I see who's standing there.

"Wow, you're happy to see me for a change," Mister Grabby Hands Ty Stanz says. "That's nice."

I lose my smile and good humor in a flash. "I thought you were someone else."

He looks around, up and down the empty hallway. "Who else would I be?"

I shake my head. "Never mind. Why are you here?"

"Lister told me to come over."

"Is Lister your boss?"

"No, actually, Lister works for me."

"Then it's kind of weird that he's telling you what to do and you're doing it, right?"

He shrugs. "Maybe. I'm just trying to handle things for the band while they're out of town."

I lean on the doorframe and look him up and down. "So, what exactly is it that you do, Mr. Stanz? Because it seems to me that those people outside Lister's office were pretty excited to see you." He doesn't strike me as an errand boy. More like a heavy . . . someone's bodyguard. But if he's a bodyguard, why isn't he guarding someone? And how does that make him famous?

He plays with the brim of his hat, twisting it left and right. "You're not funny, you know."

His response confuses me and puts me on the defensive. "I'm not trying to be funny. I'm asking you a serious question."

He looks up at me and pulls his sunglasses off. Now I can see his eyes and they're squinting at me.

"What?" I say, when I can't stand the tension anymore. "Why are you looking at me like that?"

"Because . . . I'm trying to figure out if you're for real."

"I *am* for real. What is your problem, anyway? I'm just asking a simple question." This man could not be any more frustrating, and I don't think he's even trying to be.

"I just don't believe you don't already know the answer to that question."

"I wouldn't ask it if I already knew the answer, okay? I don't play games like that."

His laugh is bitter. "*Everybody* plays games like that."

I shake my head. "Whatever. Are you going to answer my question, or am I going to shut this door in your face like you did to Lister's secretary?"

He gestures at the interior of my room. "Are you going to ask me in there or not?"

I bark out a laugh. "You've got to be kidding me."

"What? Are you afraid of me or something?" He's smiling like he's funny.

"Oh, I don't know why I would be," I say sarcastically. "I mean, you approach me at the airport and manhandle me, dragging me around by the arm—not once, but twice—and then you try to accost me in my cab when I have my money out. Why on earth would I be afraid of you?"

He hisses out a quick sigh. "Oh, give me a break. I'm no threat to you. You're the one who smashed me in the eye, remember?" He points at his face again, ripping off his hat so I can get a good look. The spot he's indicating is a little more purple now than it was before.

Without even knowing me, he's sensing exactly what buttons he can push to get me to react. I hate that he's labeling me as some kind of abuser. My mothers have preached peace and kindness to our fellow man every day of my life, and here I am . . . one day in the big city and I'm already giving people black eyes. "Stop saying that. I didn't hurt you on purpose. You stuck your face in the cab and came after me. I was just defending myself."

He puts his glasses and hat back on and sticks his hands in his front pockets. "How about we make a deal . . . I won't tell anybody how you messed up my face if you let me in there so we can talk for a few minutes. Clear the air before the band gets back in town."

I back away from the doorway a little bit, almost ready to concede. "Not that I agree that I messed up your face . . . but fine. We don't need to tell anybody about our previous interactions; that would be perfect with me. But if you lay a single finger on me, I will Mace the shit out of you." I don't care if he's Lister's client or whatever. If he tries to take liberties with me, he will pay the price.

I reach into my bag that's still over my shoulder and pull out a tiny aerosol can of water that I bought in the airport to help keep my skin hydrated and protected against this polluted environment. It's pretty much the opposite of Mace, but he doesn't know that. I wrap my fingers around the label so he can't see it as I hold it up. "This will make your eyes burn like the fires of hell, so stay far away from me."

He holds up his hands in surrender. "Don't worry, I have no intention of getting anywhere near you, trust me."

"Fine." I back away, opening the door wider. "Come on in."

He walks through the door and into the living-room area, settling down in a chair. I shut the door behind him and turn around to face the music. When I join him in the living room, I find him with one leg crossed over the opposite knee while he looks around. "Nice digs," he says as he pokes the top of the couch cushion with a stiff finger.

I take a seat across the coffee table from him. "It's not what I would've picked, but it's free, so whatever."

He nods. "I guess you like the simpler life?"

I get the distinct impression from his tone that he doesn't believe what he just said. "Actually, I do."

"Sure. Right." He looks around some more.

Rather than continue to be insulted by him I push to get an answer to my question. "So? You're here now. You've reached the inner sanctum." I hold up the fake Mace so he knows I'm not messing around. "Tell me what your situation is."

He leans back and laces his fingers behind his head, tipping his cap up off his forehead. "Sure. What do you want to know?"

"Who are you and how do you fit into the puzzle? You said you don't work for Lister but he works for you. But you wear eyeliner, you were conscripted to pick me up at the airport, and you look like a baggage handler who works for the airlines, so I'm at a loss as to who you really are."

A slow grin spreads across his face as he stares at me. "A *baggage* handler?"

I shrug. I'd tell him that he has the muscles for it, but I don't want his ego getting any more involved than it already is.

"Man, that's cold. I've been called a lot of things in my life, but I don't think I've ever been called a baggage handler before."

When he laughs, it takes the edge off my anger. And when he takes his sunglasses off and his hat with them, the rest of my negative emotions disappear almost completely. I have to admit . . . he is pretty cute, even though his eyeliner is smeared and his hair is sticking out all over the place. I'm actually interested to know the answer to my question now, when before I was only mildly curious.

He stops laughing and looks at me, his expression softening. "You really don't know, do you?"

I shake my head and sigh. "Don't make me Mace you."

He tips his head back and laughs loud and long. When he finally stops he grabs his hat, twisting it in his lap. "I am . . ." He pauses and seems to go into himself, no longer totally with me in the room. His voice lowers and loses all emotion. His expression goes dark. "I am . . . a replacement for an irreplaceable man."

CHAPTER EIGHT

What does that even mean?" I ask. *A replacement for an irreplaceable man?*

Ty still seems lost within himself when he answers. "It means that I took over the job of lead guitarist for Red Hot after Keith James died, but according to pretty much everyone in the entire world, I'm not up to the job."

Now the makeup, hairdo, and tattoos are starting to make sense, along with the fact that he was in Lister's office. "You're not up to it because you can't play their songs well enough?" I find it hard to believe that a band as experienced as Red Hot would accidentally hire someone unqualified.

"No, that's not it."

After trying to imagine my mothers' reaction to him being onstage, knowing how much they cherish Keith James and all the rest of the band members, I nod. "Okay, I get it. You're thirty years too young, you're not sporting a teased mullet, and you don't yet have a beer gut, wrinkles all over your face, or hanging jowls."

He looks up at me slowly, his expression at first suspicious but then more relaxed as the lines of worry ease away. "No, that's not it either." His smile is barely there, but it's charming, nonetheless.

"Oh, trust me, I'm sure it is." I roll my eyes and shake my head, lowering the fake Mace to my side. "The women who fell in love with these guys thirty years ago or whatever are all the same; they're lost in the past. They see these guys who haven't changed their clothes, hair, or music, and they picture their own pasts, imagine they're still living in them—still young, still vibrant, still wild and free. I'm sure when you walk out onstage you destroy the illusion. It won't matter how well you play . . . you turn the clock forward just by being you."

I can picture my mothers going to one of their concerts and complaining about how there's a baby up onstage where he doesn't belong. It's probably why they never mentioned there being a replacement for Keith; they figured if they said it, it would make it real. They can get really weird about Red Hot. I made fun of one of the band's album covers once, and I got sent to my room for half a day, and was only allowed out when I apologized to all three of my moms for being disrespectful.

"Maybe." He's studying his fingers as he rubs his knuckles. He doesn't sound convinced.

It's possible he sucks. That could explain why people aren't excited about him being there. "Are you good?" I ask.

He looks up at me. "What do you mean? Good about what?"

"Not good *about* something. Are you good *at* something . . . playing guitar? You must be, otherwise they wouldn't have hired you."

"I think I am."

Maybe it's a genuineness issue. "Are you a fan? Were you a fan before you got the job?"

"The biggest." He sounds very confident about this part of his story, and his mood becomes more animated. "I've been listening to their music since I was a kid. I know every single one of their songs backward *and* forward."

I smile at his silliness. "I think I might like to hear one of their songs backward." This situation is obviously bugging the hell out of him, but at least he can joke about it.

His smile disappears. "I wasn't kidding. I really can play them backward."

I laugh. "Why on earth would you want to do that? Their songs are boring enough going forward."

"Boring? Are you kidding me?" He sounds offended now, like my mothers would be if they heard me say that.

I'm taken aback by his strong reaction. "Are you also the president of their fan club?"

He looks confused, which softens his angry expression. "I don't get it."

I smile to put him at ease. "Your feathers got a little ruffled there. I was starting to think you've been running the fan club since high school or something."

He shrugs, relaxing back into the couch. "I am a fan. Hardcore. I have been my whole life."

"Well, I've been listening to the music my whole life too, but I have to be honest . . . I don't get it."

He throws his arms over the top of the couch and drops his head back. "Yeah, well, it doesn't matter."

His comment shouldn't hurt, but it does. I'm way too sensitive today. "No, I don't suppose it does." I look around the room, trying to come up with a conversational topic that will get us past the awkwardness, but I'm coming up blank. I wonder why he's here when the band can't see me until tomorrow. I'm also curious about why he's not with them. But knowing that he's not exactly welcomed by the fans, I figure it's probably a touchy subject, so I decide not to bring it up.

"So what's your deal?" he asks. "How do you fit into the puzzle?"

Now it's my turn to look at him suspiciously. "You must already know that, seeing as how you're Lister's errand boy and the lead guitarist for the band."

He lifts an eyebrow. "If I already knew, why would I be asking you?"

My own words thrown back at me. "Touché." I guess he is paying attention. "If you'll answer a question for me, I'll answer your question," I say. My curiosity is getting the better of me.

"Shoot," he says.

"Why did you offer to pick me up at the airport?"

"I didn't."

"Oh."

"Greg asked me to do it."

"Why did he ask you and not a taxi?"

"He told me you were a VIP who was too important to the band to trust with a taxi, and I was curious enough about what that meant to say yes."

I shouldn't be flattered by being labeled a VIP. I know this, and yet . . . "Why are you here now? Did Greg ask you to come?"

"That's two questions. No, three. That's three questions."

I frown, confused. "What?"

"You said you had one question for me. I answered it, so now it's your turn."

"Okay, fine," I concede. "What's your question again? I forgot."

"What's your deal? How do you fit into the puzzle?"

I sigh, staring at him. He really doesn't know; I can tell by the expression on his face. "It's kind of personal."

"I gathered that." He's still waiting, expecting me to answer.

For some strange reason, I have this idea that it would be nice to tell him the Big Secret. Then I wouldn't be the only one in the city besides Lister who knows what I'm doing here. Besides . . . he's in the band; he has every right to know their business.

"Well, as it turns out, I may be a love child of one of your fellow band members." It sounds so weird hearing myself say that out loud. I said it in a joking way, but this isn't funny. The emotions I tried to keep tamped down come flooding out. I have to grit my teeth to keep from crying over how mad it makes me.

Tyler's grin slowly dissolves and he lifts his head as his arms slide down to rest at his sides. "Who? Which one?"

I shrug. "Beats me. I have no idea." My nostrils flare with the effort of keeping my emotions in check.

His hands curl into fists against his legs. "If you don't know, how can you possibly be making that claim?"

A claim? Oh my god, he thinks I'm a gold digger! "I'm not making *any* claim. They're the ones making claims." I'm fully prepared to be mad at him for his senseless attack on my motivations, when he flops forward and rests his face in his hands, his elbows propped up on his knees.

"I think I had too many beers last night. None of this is making any sense, and I have a monster headache."

I dig through my bag, dropping the fake Mace inside. *A headache I can fix.* "Don't worry. I have a remedy in here somewhere."

"I'm clean, don't bother."

I look up at him. "Clean?" *Is he saying I'm a dirty hippie?* "What's that supposed to mean?"

He lifts his head. "It means I don't take narcotics, so don't bother."

He sounds angry, which is nothing but confusing to me. "I'm not a drug dealer, geez. I have homeopathic stuff in my bag." I stop digging around. "But if you're not interested, never mind." *Screw him.* I'm not going to waste my proven home remedy on him if he can't respect it.

He's staring at me like I'm the enemy.

"What is *wrong* with you? Are you angry at me now?"

He shrugs. "Nope."

"I guess you're a moody guy or something, then, because a minute ago you were smiling, and now you look like you want to punch me in the eye."

He looks over at the wall. "The only one punching anyone in the eye is you."

I narrow my eyes at him. I think he's deliberately trying to piss me off at this point, and this New York rudeness is really not my cup of tea. "If you don't quit saying that, you're going to be really sorry."

"Oh yeah?" He looks over at me, his grin a bit on the devious side. "What are you going to do about it? Beat me over the head again?"

I snort. "As if."

He stares at me and I stare right back. We're at an impasse, it seems, the conversation played out and the mood . . . confusing. Sometimes it almost feels like he's flirting and then he turns into a teasing older brother type. I prefer the former to the latter, but he's decided to be cranky now, so as far as I'm concerned, he can just go fly a kite in the street.

I stand up because I can't think of what else to do. I let this guy into my hotel room because he was a tiny bit charming and I knew he wasn't dangerous once I saw him in Lister's office, but now he's ruined it. For a few seconds there I thought we could actually get along, but now I know we can't. He's got a chip on his shoulder the size of a boulder, and I don't have the patience for that kind of nonsense. It does not matter to me how good-looking a guy is; if he's high-maintenance, I am *not* interested.

"So, what's your plan?" he asks.

I have no idea what he's talking about, but it doesn't matter. "None of your business."

"Going to try to cash in?"

I'm not really sure what he means by that, but his tone isn't nice. "Excuse me?"

He stands, walking out of the living room and heading toward the door without a word.

I'm so confused. "Where're you going?"

"I've got somewhere else to be that's not here." His insult is clear.

"Good!" I shout out behind him as he opens the door. "It was much nicer in this room without you in it!"

He looks over his shoulder at me as he's leaving. "Enjoy your free ride while it lasts."

He slams the door behind him, and I'm left staring at it with my jaw falling almost to the floor. I was a nice person and invited this guy into my room, engaged in what I thought was a meaningful conversation, and yet somehow he ends up insulting me and I end up being the asshole.

I really, really do not belong in this city, and after interacting with the new lead guitarist for Red Hot, I am now more certain than ever that I don't belong in the rock 'n' roll world either.

CHAPTER NINE

I'm too upset by the way Ty treated me to stay in the room any longer. I'm a nice person, I know I am, but he made me feel like I wasn't. He insinuated that I'm a gold digger and that I came all the way down here to New York City to fleece the man who claims to be my father. I am not going to lie down on that bed and cry over something some guy who doesn't deserve a single one of my tears said. I'm way stronger than that.

I throw my bag over my shoulder, drop the card key inside it, and leave the room. I'm going to have one of those damn papaya hot dogs before I leave here, no matter what. I need to have something good to tell my sisters when I get back instead of all this bad-news garbage.

I walk to the corner and look at the street signs. I'm pretty sure the roads in Manhattan are numbered, and if I just head in the right direction, I'll eventually hit Seventy-Second. According to what I'm seeing here, I'm at least ten blocks away from my destination, but a long walk is exactly what I need to clear my head and assuage my bruised heart.

I adjust my purse over my shoulder and wait for the lighted-up man to tell me it's safe to cross the street. My ballet flats make no sound on the sidewalk as I work my way through the crowds of people, most of whom are wearing business clothes. There are tons of people out, and even though there's not a lot of space between us, everyone manages to move in the direction they need to go without bumping into each other. It's like a precisely timed, choreographed dance we're all involved in, and yet we've never practiced it before and none of us are listening to the same music.

I experiment with walking straight ahead, without veering left or right, to see what will happen. People move to avoid me without even sparing me a glance. It's like they're on autopilot and they have internal anti-collision devices working to keep them from smashing into another human. It's fascinating.

I walk by boutiques, restaurants, and cafés, offices, and places that might be residences because I see people walking in with children who look like they're home from school at lunchtime. There are hotels and kiosks offering pizza by the slice for a dollar. I could eat several slices and barely make a dent in my budget, but as tempting as that is, I'm going to have that damn hot dog if it kills me. Something has to go right for me today.

I'm really glad I'm not wearing any silly high heels right now. I probably wouldn't make it two blocks. The longer I walk, the more the mood of the city starts to sink in. It feels like this place is alive—not just the streets that are crawling with cars every single second, but even the unmoving concrete and steel and glass that surrounds me . . . the sounds and the smells and even the rumbling I sometimes feel under my feet from the cars and subways going by . . . it all adds up to a palpable vibrancy.

The atmosphere here is so different from back home. There I often feel isolated and alone, even when my family is standing right there next to me. It's so quiet, and every day is just like the next and the one before it. Nothing excites me there or makes me want to jump out of bed in the morning, because it's always the same, same, same. It makes me sad to think I might actually prefer the vibrancy of New York City to the calmness of Glenhollow Farms, for two reasons: one, I decided when I finished college that I would go home and stay there to help support the family—and nothing about that situation has changed; and two,

I've already seen that I don't really fit in very well here, so even if I did want to come back, it wouldn't work. It makes me think there isn't a place for me in the world.

The sun glints off shiny skyscraper buildings. A breeze sometimes bumps against me as I reach a cross street. Different odors assault my senses, depending on whether I'm walking past a hole in the ground with steam coming out of it or a Chinese restaurant. This place is crazy, and yet there's a big piece of me that understands why someone would want to be here, to live here and call this place home. The energy—I've never felt anything like it, and I work with fifteen bee colonies all year long, so that's saying something.

It feels like I have an electric current running through my body—and that current is being fed by other people, cars flying past, neon signs, horns, the wind . . . Where Glenhollow Farms offers me peace and tranquility, this place offers the opposite, but not in a bad way. It reminds me of the difference between being young and being old, and for the first time in my life I'm thinking that being out at Glenhollow Farms is like being old before my time.

I understand why our mothers moved us out there and why they went so far from this city when they became pregnant and were ready to start their families together. I can't imagine what it would be like to raise a child here after having lived in open green spaces my whole life; I think it wouldn't be half as good or healthy. But it must've been so hard for them to leave, if this was the life that really excited them.

For the first time since learning the truth of my origins, I feel bad for my mothers . . . guilty that I was one of the reasons they walked away from their lives. They gave up a lot to become our parents and to do right by us—as opposed to our fathers, who made zero changes and went on with their lives without us. Did our fathers know that was what they were doing? For a moment I wonder, and a hint of compassion toward them tries to sneak in, but then I remind myself that if they didn't know about us and our lives, it was because they didn't bother to go after our mothers when they left . . . and there's no excuse for that. If they cared about our moms enough to be with them for two years and get them pregnant, they should have cared enough to ask why they left. Our mothers wouldn't have been hard to find, considering the band's manager and original bassist both knew their whole story.

I arrive at Gray's Papaya in a melancholy mood, just as the big lunch crowd is heading out. But the place isn't empty by any means. Awash with shades of red and orange and signs of every shape and size advertising their menu options, the café welcomes me in and tells me I'm about to have some fun. My mood lifts just the tiniest bit. They must rake in the bucks here, because there's a line I have to wait in for five minutes before I can place my order.

"I would like one of your most famous hot dogs, please." I smile at the girl across the counter.

"Which one?" She's practically zombie-ish, staring at me with empty eyes.

"Your most popular one. Whatever it is, I'll have that."

She sighs. "We have a lot of popular ones."

I try to keep smiling. "But you must have one that is the *most* popular."

"Not really."

My temper flares. What really makes me crazy about this city is that just as I start to like it again, somebody has to act like an asshat and blow it for me. I turn around and face the ten or so people who are in line behind me and raise my voice so all of them and everyone sitting at the various tables eating their lunch can hear me.

"Which hot dog should I order?!" I yell out into the restaurant. "Tell me the best one!"

There's no hesitation; I get fifty answers shouted back at me, and I pick the one that I hear the most. I turn around and smile at the girl. "I'll have one of your Recession Specials with chili, cheese, and onions."

Her expression never changes. “Okay, fine. What do you want to drink with that?”

“I’ll have your most popular tropical drink.”

She stares at me and I stare back at her. In my head, I hear the whistled theme music that plays in every western movie depicting a gunfight.

“May I suggest the papaya drink?” she asks, no inflection in her voice.

I grin. “That’s the spirit! Yes, I’ll have one of those.”

A tiny hint of a smile appears on her lips as she pushes some buttons on her screen. “That’ll be $3.99.”

My eyes bug out of my head. “That’s it? For a hot dog and a drink?”

“For *two* hot dogs and a drink.”

“Damn. Talk about budget friendly. I hope it doesn’t mean I’m getting discount dogs. Like yesterday’s wieners. You’re not giving me old wieners, are you?”

“No. They’re today’s stock.” She’s back to being a zombie.

I fish out my money. “Okay, if you say so. But I came a long way for this, so I hope it’s good.”

“It will be. Best in the city.”

I hand her a fifty-dollar bill. “That’s what I want to hear.”

My hot dogs and drink are ready in a jiffy, so I sit down at a table where I can watch everyone in the room and feast my eyes on the meal before me. I close my lids and inhale as deeply as I can. I want to be able to describe what I’m seeing, smelling, and tasting to my sisters in as much detail as possible. There’s a hint of something spicy and something sweet reaching my olfactory nerves . . .

A guy’s voice filters into my private thoughts. “Are you gonna eat it or have sex with it?”

I don’t know why this weird stranger’s conversation is entering my brain right now, but I’m going to ignore it because whoever he is, I know he’s not someone I want to engage with.

"Did you hear what I said?" The voice is closer. And louder.

I open one eye. There's a strange old man standing in front of me who I've never seen before. "Are you talking to me?" Maybe I should be scared, but I'm surrounded by at least fifty people, and they're acting like what he's doing is totally normal. *When in Rome . . .*

"Yeah. I asked you if you're gonna eat it or have sex with it." He smirks.

I am now no longer in the mood to eat this hot dog. "You're a jerk, you know that? You just ruined my lunch."

He laughs and shuffles off, leaving a strange odor behind.

A girl sitting next to me with a nose ring and blue hair nudges me on the arm. "Ignore that guy. He's a creep. He comes in here all the time and bugs people."

She's digging into her hot dog with abandon, leaving globs of sauce on either side of her mouth. She looks like she's about fifteen or sixteen years old. I think of Linny Lister and wonder if the two girls would get along.

"He ruined my appetite."

"Meh. You can't let it bother you. He's just one of those people who tries to shock other people. Lowest form of life. Not worth worrying about."

"Yeah." I stare at the hot dog. I really want to try it, but now that this guy has introduced the idea of sex around my meal, I'm worried it's going to look like I'm eating some guy's dong when I insert it in my mouth. I'm no prude or anything; I've had sex with a few guys and enjoyed it . . . but still . . . I gaze around the room. Nobody else seems to mind what they look like when they're eating *their* hot dogs. *Can I be bold like a New Yorker?*

"You could ask them to wrap it up and take it and eat it somewhere else if that'll help," my neighbor suggests, using a handful of napkins to wipe her mouth mostly clean.

I think about it and decide against it. If I do that, it'll be admitting defeat, and I'm tired of feeling like crap about things that aren't my fault or have nothing to do with me. Screw that guy; I can be bold like a New Yorker. Hell yes, I can. I come from down on the farm, dammit. I walk into bee territory and steal their honey, and I even get stung sometimes, but does that stop me? No, because I'm fearless. I've cleaned out stinky possum cages without barfing and I've milked goats and suffered my share of kicks for it, too, because I'm tough. The taxicab driver tried to rip me off, and while he mostly succeeded at that, it was only because I was in a hurry. I feel confident that I could have given him the tip I wanted to instead of the one he chose for himself if I'd had the time and wasn't distracted by Mister Grabby Hands trying to accost me again. The lady at the Four Seasons acted like I was a degenerate for not having a credit card, but here I am, kicking ass all over this town anyway, not letting her judgment slow me down. And I tried to tell Ty the story of why I'm in the city and he treated me like I'm some kind of shithead, but I'm still standing, proud of who I am and where I come from.

I don't get these people or how they operate, but that doesn't mean I'm going to let them take me down. I grab my hot dog and take a giant bite out of it, eating that thing like a boss as I try not to choke on all the little bits of onion and chili bean that fall into the back of my throat.

"There you go," my friend says, bits of bun flying out of her mouth as she gives me a thumbs-up. "You're a hero now. Deep-throat that thing."

I get caught up in the mood, grinning as I try to chew around the massive mouthful of garbage I have in my mouth. I am quickly finding that hot dogs are salty and do not taste like any identifiable meat that I am familiar with.

I take a second bite of my dog and then sample the juice drink, hoping it'll help quench the fire of fresh onions and chili. Surprisingly, it does the job and goes together pretty well with the mix of spicy flavors

I have going on. *Who would've thought?* Processed meat and fruit . . . there's a veritable party going on in my mouth right now.

I finish the hot dogs even though I know it's way too much food, and stumble out of the restaurant feeling bloated and sick. I'm probably going to leave out this part of my story when I recount it to my sisters; I don't want to ruin it for them. And honestly, even though they're giving me indigestion right now, the hot dogs were pretty darn good, and the juice is something I want to try to re-create when I get home.

When I return to the Four Seasons I'm in a much brighter mood than I was when I left. As I'm walking over to the elevator, somebody at the reception desk waves at me. I recognize the man sporting many gold buttons and walk over.

"Hi, James."

"Hello, Ms. Fields. I have a message for you." He hands me a piece of paper over the counter.

"Thanks." I open it up and read what is written inside on Four Seasons notepaper. *Please call Greg Lister at blah, blah, blah . . .* I pull my cell phone out of my purse and dial the number, taking a few steps away from the reception desk so I can find some privacy.

"Lister-Spector-Harvey," says the person answering the phone.

"Hello. I received a message that I need to call Greg Lister. This is Amber Fields."

She patches me through and another female voice answers. "Hello, Greg Lister's office."

"You don't sound like Greg Lister," I say, trying to be funny.

"How may I help you?" she replies, no humor in her voice at all. I can totally picture his secretary in her sexy outfit with nude, uncomfortable high heels. I wonder if Lister knows she's gunning for him.

"This is Amber Fields. I'm just returning a phone call."

"Please hold." Some classical music comes over the line, and I'm about to hang up after I hear five minutes of it, but then the line is picked up again.

"Ms. Fields, this is Greg Lister. Thanks for calling me back."

"You have news for me?"

"Yes. I've talked to the band. Is there any chance they could meet with you tomorrow morning over breakfast?"

A little bit of panic seeps into my heart, and the hot dogs churn uncomfortably in my stomach. Now that the actual meeting is being set up, the stress is back, full force. "I'm not sure. I need to get back to you." I'm worried about missing my flight tonight. I need to talk to my sisters and figure out a Plan B in case I can't get reimbursed. Not having a credit card makes it really difficult to buy plane tickets. We had to drive into town and use a travel agent to pay cash and get the one I have.

"Okay, let me give you my cell phone number in case you call back after hours."

I scramble around in my purse and find a pen. "Go ahead." I write on the note James gave me as Greg recites the numbers. "Got it. I'll call you back later. Bye." I close my phone and look around. Although it seems like everybody's going about their business and ignoring me, I worry that people are listening in on every word, so I take the elevator up by myself—Jeremy is nowhere in sight—and let myself into my room. I position an armchair so it faces the window. I'm going to enjoy the New York skyline while I call my sisters down on the farm and figure this thing out.

CHAPTER TEN

Rose picks up the phone immediately. "What's going on? What happened? Tell us everything. I'm going to put you on speakerphone."

Just hearing her voice makes me feel better. A wave of homesickness washes over me and gives me goose bumps. I can't believe how much I miss my sisters. I haven't even been gone a whole day yet.

"Is she there?" It's Em, sounding a little panicked.

"I'm here. Can you guys both hear me?"

Their chorus of voices sounding extra cheerful as they yell, "Yes!" creates a stabbing feeling in my heart.

"Okay, cool. So here's what's going on right now . . . I need your help."

"Anything," Rose says in her confident voice. "Whatever it is, we're here for you. And we feel really bad about letting you go down there alone, by the way."

"Yeah," Em chimes in. "We should've gone with you. We totally chickened out, and we're butts for doing that."

"No, it's fine. It's better you aren't here. Not everybody is very nice. It's been a little depressing, to be honest." More like a roller coaster, but I'm going to spare them the details; they're already worried enough as it is. "The hotel is nice, but that's about it."

"Really? A hotel?" This is from Rose. She's the most compassionate of the three of us. "I'm so sorry."

"Yeah, it's going to take an extra day. Don't worry about it, though. It's not a big deal, I promise." I take a deep breath so I can tell them the story. "I need to change my plane ticket so that I come back tomorrow instead of tonight, because they aren't here until tomorrow morning, but they do want to meet."

"I was afraid that was going to happen," Rose says. "Maybe we should've called ahead."

"Well, somebody did call ahead. Barbara." I roll my eyes, still irritated about that. It's because of her that Ty and I got off on the wrong foot like we did. If he hadn't known about me coming, he never would have shown up at the airport, and I never would have used my kung fu moves on him.

There's a long silence. "I'm sorry," Em says. "She asked me too many questions about why you were spending so much time in town, and I couldn't keep it in." She sounds overly sad.

I totally called it. Em is the weak link in our chain, *always*. "It's not a big deal, I swear. The lawyer only found out I was coming a few hours before I arrived, but by then the band was already in Toronto." I can't say 'our fathers' because it makes me feel sick to my stomach to admit we have parents out there who've ignored us all our lives. My gut is burning with the need to tell them off again. It's either that need or the hot dogs . . . I'm not sure.

"So, you're going to meet them tomorrow?" Rose asks.

"Yes. That's the plan. A breakfast meeting."

"Did you talk to their lawyer?" Em asks.

"Yes, I did a little. And I also talked to the guy who plays lead guitar in the band now too." Bitterness rises up in me. Another jerk in New York City. Why does he have to be so cute, though? That doesn't seem fair. Rude people should be ugly and nice people should be hot.

"Oh my god, don't tell our mothers," Rose says. "They'll squeal like teenagers. You know I hate that."

"Don't worry. He's nothing special." I say this and try to sound convincing, but it makes me feel bad to have voiced those thoughts aloud. He's a human being like anyone else, and even though he acts like a jerk sometimes, I'm sure there's somebody out there who thinks he's pretty special. He sure did get some crowds gathered around us at the airport and in front of Lister's office.

"Why would you say that?" Em asks. "Was he rude to you or something?"

"Maybe a little. I don't know. I can't really figure him out. He's weird. Everybody here is weird."

"Huh," Rose says. I think she's going to say more but she doesn't.

"Huh? What's that supposed to mean?"

I can imagine her shrugging. "Oh, nothing. I just expected you to get along really well out there."

It feels like she's saying I'm a jerk too, but that's not like Rose. "Why?"

"Because . . . of the three of us, you're the most outspoken and direct. I hear that's what New Yorkers are like, so it just seemed like you would speak their language better than we would."

"I've met some nice people here and had some good conversations, sure, but anybody associated with the band kind of rubs me the wrong way, I guess you could say."

"Well, that's not surprising," Rose says. "It's an uncomfortable situation. Maybe nobody really knows how to handle it properly."

What she's saying makes sense. "I know *I* don't know how to handle it properly. It seems like every time I open my mouth I get into a disagreement with someone."

Em laughs. "Just try to remember to stay calm. And don't let them mess with your head. You know who you are and what the plan is. We don't need their guilt money or their charity. All you have to do is stick to the plan."

"Right." I nod and stand. I'm feeling stronger already. "I'm going to meet with the band members, and I'm going to tell them we are not interested in their payoff and that our hearts are not for sale. They can take their money and *shove* it up their butts!"

"You may want to leave off that last part," Rose says.

I can hear Em mumbling in the background. "I think she can leave it how it is."

I smile big, my faith in humanity fully restored. "Don't worry, sisters; I've got your backs."

"We know you do," Rose says.

"We'd better go now," Em adds. "I think this phone charges us for every minute that we talk."

"I think it does too." *Stupid tiny rip-off phones.* "And by the way, we're really missing out. Apparently, those really expensive phones we didn't buy are smartphones, and they have all these apps on them, and you can get on the app and find a one-night stand."

"We can just go to the local bar and do that, so why would we need to do it on our phones?" Em asks.

She has a point. "I really don't know. I'm still trying to figure all this stuff out." I brush my hair back from my face. "I had a hot dog, but I'm going to wait and tell you about it when I get home." Hopefully, the stomachache will pass by then and I'll be able to offer up a better description than 'gut bomb.'

"Cool," Rose says. "I hope you go do some more fun stuff before you get back, because we're living vicariously through you right now."

"I will, I promise." I have no idea what that thing is that I'm going to do, since I can't afford anything, but I'll find something, even if it's just wandering around Central Park. "I need you guys to do me a favor, though."

"Name it," Rose says.

"Could you figure out if my plane ticket is refundable? And if it's not, how am I going to get back tomorrow?"

"I'm on it," says Em. "I'll take care of everything, and I'll send you a text when I have answers."

"Thanks, sweetie pie. I love you."

Both girls chime in together. "We love you too!"

"I'll call you before I go to bed. Kiss, kiss. And since our moms apparently know what I'm up to, give them a hug for me. And tell them not to worry . . . I'm fine."

"We will," Em says.

"Don't talk to strangers," Rose trills with a smile in her voice.

"I would never." I'm still smiling when I hang up the phone.

CHAPTER ELEVEN

I'm used to doing a lot of hard work at the farm, but for some reason, simply walking to and from the hot dog place has exhausted me. I think New York is draining the energy directly out of my body and feeding it to the surrounding environment. I don't like this nearly as much as the city giving me its energy like it was earlier. For this reason, I decide a nap should be my next big adventure, but I'm not fifteen minutes into it when there's a sound from the other room waking me up.

I sit up straight as a board and look around, momentarily confused as to where I am. I take in the tasteful wallpaper, the paintings, the expensive furniture around me, and the brightly lit New York City skyline at the foot of my bed, and I realize . . . I'm on a mission. But instead of enjoying my one and only trip to Manhattan, I am sleeping off a hot dog stupor like a senior citizen.

A knock at the door reminds me of what woke me up in the first place. I get up and wipe the drool off the side of my mouth, straightening my hair as best I can as I walk over to look through the peephole.

"What are you doing here?" I say at the messy-haired fool standing out in the hallway.

"I have a message for you from Lister."

"What are you, his errand boy?" I'm finding it really hard to believe that a high-powered lawyer like Lister and a highly paid famous musician like Ty Stanz can't find a more convenient way to contact me . . .

like using a telephone maybe? Obviously, there's something going on here. Lister's probably trying to get some inside information by using Ty as his spy. Too bad Ty sucks at it with his bad attitude and that chip on his shoulder.

"No, not an errand boy, just a good Samaritan."

I pull open the door and stare at Ty Stanz, the dummy who thinks he's going to get a warm welcome after what he said when he left here last time.

"What's the message?"

"Can I come in?" He doesn't look apologetic but he also doesn't look angry or mean either. More than anything, he looks tired. I guess we have that in common.

I back out of the way and open the door, because I'm curious enough about his motives for being here that I'm willing to chance another unpleasant encounter. "Fine, I'll let you in . . . but if you're here to insult me again, you're wasting your time. I'm not interested in your garbage, and all it'll do is earn you a one-way ticket out into the hallway."

"Noted." He walks into the living room and takes the same spot on the couch that he was in before.

I follow him into the room and stand in front of him with my arms folded over my chest. "What's the message?"

He looks everywhere but at me. His eyes roam the room, glancing up at the windows and down at the rug before he answers. He speaks directly to the coffee table. "The message is that you are cordially invited to attend an event this evening that's being hosted by one of the band's sponsors."

"What kind of event?" I wasn't expecting this at all. *An event?*

"It's a publicity thing." He sounds less than enthusiastic about the idea.

"Publicity for the band? Why on earth would I be invited to that?"

He finally looks up at me. "I thought you said that you were related to someone in the band."

"I did say that, but it doesn't mean I'm somehow involved with their publicity issues."

"Well, you're invited. I'm not the one making decisions around here. I told Lister that I would discuss it with you, and that's what I'm doing." He slaps his hands on his jeans as he looks around. His body language is telling me that I'm not getting the whole story.

"There's something else going on here." I start tapping my toe. "Are you going to tell me what it is, or am I going to call Lister and get it out of him?"

Ty leans forward and starts punching one hand into his other palm. He's not doing it in an angry way; I think he's just trying to figure out how to say what he's got on his mind.

I stop tapping my toe and wait for his mouth to catch up to his brain.

"He wants me to get you to go. I'm not supposed to just tell you about it, I'm supposed to *convince* you." He hisses out a sigh of annoyance and throws himself against the couch cushions, lifting his arms up behind his head again.

"Why you? Why not Lister himself or someone else who works for him?"

"Because," Ty says, "it's a sensitive situation that he doesn't want spread around his office, and I volunteered to help out, since I didn't go with the band to Toronto." He tips his head back and closes his eyes. He actually looks like he's sleeping, so I just watch him for a while. Then one of his eyes opens. "You're staring at me."

"I'm staring at you because I wasn't sure if you were asleep or not, and if you were sleeping, I didn't want to bother you."

He sits up and shakes his head. "No, I'm wide-awake. Wide-awake in this nightmare that is my life."

I sit down on the chair as I try to figure him out. I don't think I've ever met a more confusing person. He definitely could use some time down on the farm, preferably when I'm not there because I'd be too tempted to throw manure at him or something equally disgusting. He is so *very* annoying.

I already have enough complications in my life right now; the last thing I need is to be involved in his issues . . . but I find myself being dragged down into the rabbit hole anyway. It has something to do with that sad face of his and that hair sticking out all over the place. He's freaking adorable is what he is.

"You told me that you're the new lead guitarist for Red Hot. Why are you calling your life a nightmare? You said that you're their biggest fan. It seems to me like you've got a dream come true on your hands. And why didn't they have you go to Toronto?"

"Sometimes things that look like dreams can turn into nightmares before you know it." He's staring at me intensely. I have to look away when my emotions start to run a little too warm for comfort. Is he talking about himself? Does he know I find him attractive? Is he warning me away?

"It sounds very complicated," I say, forcing myself to stay engaged in the conversation rather than let my libido run away with me. Using Ty's perspective to examine my own life, I'd have to say I agree with him. Some girls would be thrilled about the idea of inheriting millions of dollars from a famous relative, but for me, it seems more like I've been invited into a nightmare where I have to face people who never gave me a chance to love them or to be loved, who didn't love my moms enough to ask them why they walked away without a word. It makes my heart ache too much to bear. I'm definitely not thrilled at the idea of standing in front of the band tomorrow morning and telling them how my sisters and I feel about their payoff attempt.

"It is complicated," he says, sounding very tired. "Are you going or not?"

"I don't know." I shrug, feeling more exhausted now than before. "I don't know why I should."

"Neither do I."

We stare at each other, a challenge in the air. "You don't want me to go, do you?"

He shrugs. "It doesn't matter what I want. It matters what the band wants, and it matters what Lister wants."

"You don't want to be there either, do you? At the event, I mean."

He shakes his head very slowly. "No, I do not. I don't like being a monkey who has to dance on command, being told one minute I should do one thing and the next that I need to do the opposite, but right now, that's where I'm at."

I don't need to know exactly what he's talking about to understand the sentiment or the concept. "I don't like that either. I don't blame you for being upset about it. Why don't you just quit and walk away?"

"Would you walk away from the one thing you've wanted your entire life? Even if it meant paying dues and sucking it up when things got tough or unpleasant?"

His words make my heart feel sick. "I don't know. I guess I never wanted anything that bad." I walked away from the one thing I ever wanted—a life off the farm—and up until this very moment I never seriously questioned whether that was the right thing to do or not. I convinced myself it was the best thing for everyone concerned, and my family was so happy with my choice. But maybe it wasn't the right thing to do. Maybe I should have fought harder for myself instead of settling for what was right for the family.

"Maybe one day you will want something that bad, and then you'll know what I'm up against."

I know there's a darker side to fame. Our mothers talked about it a lot when we were growing up, but we always assumed they were talking in a generic sense and not speaking from experience. So many things they said about selling one's soul to the devil are floating in my mind. *Did Ty do this? Did he trade fortune and fame for his soul?*

I'm more convinced than ever that turning down these inheritances or whatever they are is the right thing to do. Just being in the room with someone who's only remotely involved in the whole scenario—a band member, no less—has me questioning my decisions about my life path. My life and my sisters' lives are perfect exactly the way they are, and the evidence to back that up is sitting right in front of me. Here's a man who got his dream job with the band and he couldn't be more miserable about it. I made the right decision to go back home and settle down there, to walk away from something I considered "bigger." The only thing I'm missing out on is pain.

Pity softens my heart. Ty and I really aren't that different. We're both frustrated with the band, and we both want something from these men of Red Hot. Of course, he wants to live in peace with them and I want to tell them to get bent, but still . . . it's a common interest. What would be the harm in spending a little more time together until the band is available to meet with me?

"How about this . . . , " I say, a germ of an idea taking root. "How about if we both go to the event together, two monkeys in somebody else's zoo. Maybe it won't be so bad if you're not the only chimp in the room." This way I'll also have something to tell my sisters besides the fact that I got a stomachache from eating processed meat and had to sleep it off.

His jaw twitches and his lips press together. He rubs the palm of his hand with his opposite thumb. Then he picks at his nails. "Maybe that could be cool."

"I promise I will leave my Mace in my room."

He starts to grin but still doesn't look at me. "It's a relief to know I'm not going to be sprayed with a can of water."

I huff out a sigh. "Rude." All that time I thought I was being a badass and he was laughing at me.

"What's so rude about that?" He's finally looking at me again.

"You could've just played along."

"I'm not really good at playing along."

"Neither am I." I feel an inexplicably strong connection to Ty right now. He's sitting there looking tragic and messed up, the exact model of a man my mothers have been warning me against all my life—apparently in an effort to stop another generation from making the same mistakes they did—and yet I could no more deny him than I could say yes to another hot dog. The last thing I want to do tonight is sit in this hotel room and fret over my meeting with the band tomorrow morning. I could use a distraction.

"Good." He stands. "I'll pick you up at six. Make sure you have your ID with you."

"All I have is a passport. Is that okay?"

"Yep. Perfect."

"Okay." I stand up too, suddenly feeling energized again. *Nap? Who needs a nap?*

He starts heading out of the room but hesitates at the door, looking over his shoulder at me. "It's kind of a formal thing." He looks me up and down.

I look down at my skirt and blouse. "So, what you're saying is . . . my current outfit isn't going to cut it?"

He lifts a shoulder. "It's fine with me, but I have a feeling you'll be more comfortable if you upgrade a little bit."

"And by upgrade, you mean sell out?"

He nods and lifts his hand, shooting me with an imaginary finger-gun as he winks. "You got it, sister."

"Are you going to upgrade?" As the door is swinging shut behind him, I hear his answer faintly.

"We'll see."

I run to the hotel room telephone and pick it up, hitting zero. When the person answers I blabber into the phone, speaking so quickly I hardly understand myself. "I need to talk to James right away. In your concierge department."

CHAPTER TWELVE

I am so glad I went to James with my problem. He knows everything about this city and its shopping situation. Now that I know I can get pizza by the slice for a dollar and that I'm going to an event tonight that probably will have food, plus the breakfast tomorrow that will probably be paid for by the band, I know how much I can afford to spend on clothing.

I soon learn, however, that all the stores I might have gone to without James' guidance would've only afforded me a pair of socks on my shoestring budget. But thanks to the concierge of all concierges, I'm learning everything I need to know about thrift stores—which ones have the best stock, when they get shipments in, and who has the best deals. I've also had a full training session from a friendly stranger on how to navigate the complicated subway system. I have visited three stores, located all over the city and in Brooklyn, and I now have a complete outfit that does look pretty damn hot if I do say so myself.

I'm back at the hotel room by five o'clock. While I was out kicking ass all over town, the other concierges were busy in the hotel being miracle workers. They not only located a curling iron for my hair, but they also managed to find someone to press my dress and buff the scuffs out of the used shoes that I bought. For the first time in my life, I am going to be wearing stilettos. I hope I don't fall down a flight of stairs and kill myself.

I'm just putting the finishing touches on my hairdo, letting a few pieces of curled hair frame the sides of my face while the rest of it sits in a messy bun atop my head with chopsticks holding it in place, when there's a knock at the door. I make sure there are no deodorant stains on my deep-green, sparkling gown and practice walking in front of the mirror a few times with my heels before I answer it. I don't bother with the peephole; I just grab the handle and pull it open.

He's there and I'm struck speechless. This is a big deal for me because I'm rarely at a loss for words. *Heaven is here on my doorstep.* I think the man standing before me is Tyler Stanz, lead guitarist for Red Hot, but I can't be sure because he's wearing a suit coat and a tie; and even though the tie isn't knotted very well and it's slightly askew, and even though he's still wearing jeans, at least they're clean this time, and the black dress shoes he's got on go perfectly with his dark hair that looks a little more artfully arranged than it did earlier today. And his black eyeliner is amazing—not a smear in sight. He looks like pure trouble and it starts my heart beating way too fast.

"Where did the hippie chick go?" he asks. I can't read his expression. Maybe he's feeling uncomfortable? It's hard to say. Things are getting awkward quickly.

I poke my thumb out behind me. "She's down on the farm. Do you want me to invite her out with us tonight?"

He holds out his elbow. "She can tag along," he says gruffly. "I wouldn't want her to disappear completely."

Right answer. From the small table by the door, I grab the little clutch purse that I got for a buck fifty, slide my key card and phone into it, and step out, shutting the door behind me. Putting my hand in the crook of Ty's elbow, I walk on tiptoes down the hallway to the elevator, worried I'm going to fall over if I take a normal stride in these shoes. I feel like I'm going to the prom, which is something I've never done before. Being homeschooled made that pretty much impossible. Ty is about two inches taller than me since I have these ridiculous heels on, which is perfect as far as I'm concerned.

"I feel like I should've brought you a corsage," he says when we get to the elevator.

"I was just thinking that we look like we're going to the prom together."

We both chuckle nervously. When the elevator door opens, Jeremy is inside. He glances at me and smiles before going back to staring at the panel of buttons in front of him.

Ty and I step inside and the doors shut behind us. "Jeremy, we'd like to go to the lobby."

"Yes, Ms. Fields."

Ty leans in and whispers in my ear. "You know him?"

I whisper back. "I know everyone."

He stares straight ahead, slowly shaking his head but wearing a smile. I like this new vibe we have between us. Most of the frustration is gone, and whatever bit is left is on the back burner on a slow simmer. I don't need to deal with it now.

I'm glad I've got this monkey-man with me, because I'm pretty sure I'm not really prepared for this event, whatever it is. I might look the part with this killer dress, but I've never been to a gathering of more than thirty people. The biggest one I've ever been to was down on the farm, celebrating the summer solstice, and clothing was optional—a totally different atmosphere and set of expectations for sure.

There's a driver outside the hotel waiting for us. He's holding the back door of a limousine open so we can climb in. After buckling up, I grip my purse with two hands. I'm so freaking nervous, I'm feeling sick to my stomach. Those chili hot dogs are killing me. I want to text my sisters and tell them what I'm doing, and I will, as soon as I can trust that I won't barf in this vehicle.

As the car enters the early evening traffic, I wonder where exactly we're going. Ty says nothing. For fifteen minutes the car is totally silent, save for the horn honking the driver sometimes uses to communicate his feelings to the other drivers and pedestrians we encounter.

I use the time to text Em and Rose. *I'm going to an 'event' tonight with Ty, lead guitarist. Wish me luck!* I don't get a response. I'm ready to scream from the buildup of tension when the car pulls over in front of another building and comes to a stop.

I try to get a look at it through the window, but the building is too high. "The event is in here?" It looks like another office building.

"Not exactly." Ty gets out of the car and comes around to open my door for me before I can do it myself. I'm the country girl, too stunned by the big city at night to act like a normal person. *Duh.*

I get out, relieved to feel the cool air on my overheated skin, sliding my arm through Ty's without a word. We walk to the building together, enter through turnstile doors, and get into another elevator.

"This looks like an office," I finally say.

"It is an office building on some of the floors and others have residences. We're going to the top."

A penthouse party. *Cool. I think.*

We get out on the top floor, but then he takes me through a door that has stairs behind it. I follow him up, wondering if I'm doing the right thing. He hasn't said a word, and this is really weird. *A big event on the roof? Is that safe?*

When he opens the door at the top of the stairs, a stiff breeze hits me and throws my ringlets around my face. One of the clumps of hair sticks to my lip gloss, so I have to peel it off before I can speak.

"What are you doing?" I ask.

"I'm taking you to the event." There's a really loud noise outside, like a giant air conditioner unit running. How on earth could they possibly have a nice event out here with that noise going on in the background? *They can't. It's a setup.*

I hesitate with my hand on the stair railing. "Are you planning to throw me off the top of this building?"

He frowns at me. "Why on earth would you even *think* that?"

"Because I can't imagine that there's an event on the top of a building that's this loud, that's why."

"Come on," he says, waving me up. "Be brave." He winks at me so quickly I'm not even sure he did it.

Seize the day. My mother's voice echoes in my head. Barbara has told me often over the years that she regrets each time she failed to seize the day or to take the chance to do something that she was too afraid to do. I can do this . . . whatever this is, this loud party on a roof. I don't need to know how the hosts are going to pull it off; I just have to walk out there and be fabulous in my green dress. Easy peasy, lemon squeezy.

I walk up to the top of the stairs and take Ty's outstretched hand. *We're just two monkeys playing in a zoo together. Just for one night. I'm not alone.*

"Keep your head down," he says, and when I step out onto the roof of the building, I realize why he said that—there's a helicopter waiting, and its blades are spinning.

CHAPTER THIRTEEN

"Whoa! Wait a minute! What the hell is that?!" I shriek. I reverse through the door onto the landing at the top of the stairs. "You never said anything about a *helicopter*, for Pete's sake!"

Ty has to yell to be heard over the sound of the flying machine whose blades are moving faster and getting louder. "If I had told you, would you have come?"

"No!" Riding on a regular plane was difficult enough. This would be akin to dangling myself over the city on a string.

He lets the door close so we can hear each other better. "It's perfectly safe. I've been on a hundred of them by now."

"But it's going to be dark out soon."

"They fly using radar. It's safe, I promise. And you're not gonna believe what the city looks like from up there. I swear, it's something you'll never forget."

I'm panicking as I envision my fiery, painful death. "But what if it crashes?" *Fire. Twisted metal. Smoke. Blood.*

He gives me a scolding look. "Come on, hippie chick. People ride in helicopters all the time. They're safer than airplanes."

I can't tell if he's lying or not. "Who told you that?"

"I read it on Google. Come on." He holds out his hand, expecting me to take it. "I don't want to be late. It's better to get to these things early so we can leave early."

I stare at his hand. Do I want to take it? Do I want to get into a helicopter that could crash into a building and kill not only me and him but many innocent people? *No, I don't.* But my hand goes out anyway and latches on to his.

"Come on," he says. "Just keep your head down. And hang on to your chopsticks." He's staring at the back of my head.

I pause in the doorway. "Don't you like my chopsticks?"

He grins. "Love the chopsticks. If they run out of forks on the buffet you're going to be all set."

I smack him lightly in the gut as we walk through the door together. "You're going to pay for that later."

"I hope so. It'll give me something to look forward to."

We half-walk, half-run across the dark surface of the roof to the waiting helicopter. It's a lot smaller on the inside than I imagined it would be. There's a single seat in the front for the pilot and two seats in the back for us.

"Where are we going?" I ask anyone who will answer.

Ty gives me a hand up into my seat and helps me figure out how to put on the safety belt, which is a lot more complicated than the one on the airplane. He settles himself into the spot next to me and makes sure we both have on headsets before he answers my question. His voice comes into my ears through the little speakers. Much of the helicopter noise is now blocked out. I have no idea if the pilot can hear us.

"We're going over to the airport," Ty says.

"Why didn't we just take a cab?"

"Because." He looks at me as the pilot shuts the door next to us, closing us into the tiny capsule. "It's not nearly as fun or as fast. We have a flight to catch."

"A flight?" My mouth drops open and stays that way.

"Yeah. Didn't I mention that?" He's got the biggest shit-eating grin on his face. He's enjoying himself way too much.

Unbelievable. I totally fell for his nonsense. Two monkeys in a zoo? *Please.* I may be a monkey, but he's a fox. "You are in so much trouble right now," I say, trying to be appropriately mad but failing miserably.

He smiles harder. "Really? And that's a bad thing?"

I shake my head. "You just wait and see." I fold my arms over my chest, but when I realize how much it pushes my boobs up, I stop. Out of the corner of my eye I see him staring.

"Keep your eyeballs in your head where they belong," I warn.

His head turns to the front. "My eyeballs aren't doing anything wrong."

I battle a smile as I try to chant away the attraction I'm feeling. *He is not charming. I will not flirt. He's not going to wiggle his way under my skin or my skirt.*

The helicopter moves, tilting slightly to the left. Both my arms fly out involuntarily. One of them slaps Ty in the chest, and the other one hits the door next to me with a bang. A scream escapes my lips.

Ty folds my hand into his and holds it at his chest. "Don't worry. Takeoff can be a little wobbly, but it'll be fine in a minute."

My laugh is very shrill. "Ha, ha! A little wobbly? That sounds awesome!"

He squeezes my hand more firmly. "You're safe with me. I promise."

I really don't think I'm safe with him at all. He convinced me to go to this event and didn't give me the whole story, which ended up with me in a tiny helicopter that feels like it's dangling from the end of a yo-yo string.

We lift up from the top of the building and move over to the edge. I don't want to look, but I have to. If I'm going to die, I want to see it coming so I can mentally prepare myself. I start to scream as we get too far over the edge to stop. *Too late! Too late! We're going to die! We're going to plummet to the earth and explode! God, please let me die an instant and pain-free death!*

Next to me is Ty, laughing his butt off with his headset in his lap.

"What's so funny?" I yell, breathing so fast it sounds like I just finished a 5K.

He puts an earpiece of his headset up to his ear. "What?"

"I said, what's so funny?"

"Your screaming!" he yells. "It's hilarious! Your mouth is open and I can tell you're freaking out, but all I can hear is the copter." He puts his headset back on. "Mic check, mic check . . . can you hear me now?"

I yank my hand away and hold on to my seat belt with an iron grip. "Shut up. It's not funny. I'm scared."

He stops laughing and goes completely serious. "Don't be scared. I swear to God, I would never let you go up in a thing like this if I thought it was going to hurt you."

I glance at him and then go back to looking over the edge of the building. The helicopter moves slowly past the office building next to the one we entered from the street. This is real. I'm actually dangling in the air in the middle of Manhattan. I think it's magic that's keeping us up. *I believe in magic. I believe in magic. I believe in miracles. Please, God, don't let us fall.*

My speakers crackle and then Ty's voice comes into my ears. "Honestly, if I'd known you were going to be this freaked out, I wouldn't have done it. I thought you would think it was cool."

Was he trying to impress me by bringing me on this thing? I'm charmed and pissed at the same time. These are two emotions that should never be trying to work together. I shake my head at this Ty Stanz craziness.

We pass another building and then one more. My heart is beating so hard it feels like it's going to cramp up and stop. But lights are coming on around us, making it look like the city's twinkling, and that's not entirely awful. "Well, it's not cool. Not really."

He leans in closer to me. "Are you sure? Because you don't sound very convinced."

I shove him away. "Be quiet. I'm busy praying that I don't die. Don't interrupt me, or God might not hear me in time to stop this death trap from falling out of the sky."

He chuckles and takes my hand again. "Just hold on to me. You're going to be fine."

We both stop talking and stare out the windows. I have to admit, the scenery is pretty amazing. This is nothing like riding in the airplane, where I only got a tiny window that offered very little view of what was below me. I can see everything from where I'm sitting now. The edge of the city becomes visible and then a big river appears. Several bridges span the water; they're loaded with cars that have their headlights on.

I'm glad it's not the middle or end of summer yet because then the sun would still be up this late and I would miss all of these lights coming on. The tension slowly eases out of my body as the helicopter levels out and flies in a straight line. The stress isn't gone completely, but I don't feel like I'm about to have a heart attack or a stroke anymore either.

"How long until we're at the airport?" I ask.

"Fifteen minutes."

I look at Ty's profile as he stares out the window to his left. He is so damn handsome. I wish he were ugly; maybe it would be easier to stay mad at him. "And where is this flight going, exactly?"

He turns, his expression pained. "Can I plead the Fifth on this one?"

I sigh. "No, you cannot."

"How about if we just make it a surprise?" His eyebrows go up and he nods, trying to sell me on the idea.

I'm torn. I want to say no and insist he tell me what's going on, but something about his reaction makes me think he's nervous. Maybe he's worried that I'll dig my heels in and say I'm not going if I don't like his answer about our destination. And I think the only reason he's going is because I am. *How bad could it be, anyway?* He knows I have to be back in the morning for the breakfast meeting.

"How important is this event to you?" I ask.

He thinks about it for several long seconds before he gives me an answer that sounds like a confession. "I want to say it's not important at all, but that would be a lie."

"Why would you want to lie about it?"

"Because. I don't care about all this PR garbage . . . this bullshit. I just want to play music, that's it."

I nod because I get it. I get *him*. "But these events are part of the deal. Part of being a member of the band."

"Exactly. They're uncomfortable and stiff and full of fake people, but it's something I agreed to do when I signed up."

"Why do you hate it so much? Is it just because of the fake people?"

He shrugs and looks out the window. "That's part of it. I don't know. You'll see when we get there. Maybe."

"What do you mean, *maybe*?"

"I don't know." He looks at me, his expression almost sad. "Maybe you'll like it."

I look out my window, a little hurt that he thinks I'm the kind of person who likes hanging out with assholes. I speak before thinking my words through. "I doubt it. I can't imagine me liking something that you don't."

Neither one of us says anything else until we get to the airport, but the mood between us is heavy. It's possible I made some sort of declaration with my last statement, but I didn't mean to. I just feel a really close connection to him right now since we've had this helicopter-induced near-death experience together, and I also sense a great deal of pain coming from him that I want to ease as a friend if I can. He's stuck with the band because he loves the music, but I'm not getting the impression he really loves the band *members*, which is super inconvenient since they're in this big-time relationship together. I wonder again why he's here while they're in Toronto. Hopefully, I'll find out by the end of the night.

Whatever their relationship is, it's definitely weird. I think these band members have too much control over both Ty and us Glenhollow girls. All they have to do is snap their fingers and they turn people's lives upside down. That's probably why I sense some sort of kinship with Ty. I think my sisters would like him too, if they could get past his abrasive exterior. I'm finding it easier and easier to do, the longer I'm with him.

My thoughts are interrupted by the helicopter arriving on the tarmac at the airport. It's not a perfect landing, but I think our scary takeoff prepared me for anything, so I hardly scream at all when we bounce down on the ground and finally come to rest. A black town car takes us from there to a private jet.

Ty stands next to me at the bottom of the stairs leading into the plane. The wind batters my hair and almost knocks my chopsticks out. I stick them more deeply into my 'do as he watches.

I give him a warning look. "If you mock the chopsticks, you're not going to be allowed to borrow them when we get to the buffet."

"I would never mock the chopsticks. The chopsticks are cool."

"Maybe I'll buy you a pair someday." I wink at him.

He looks up the stairs, his good humor melting away in an instant. "You ready?"

Not that I'm okay with the mood swings, but I am starting to get used to them. My plan is to ignore any emotions of his that I don't like, so I will be disregarding his sudden party-pooper attitude. I straighten my posture and hold my purse with both hands in front of me. "Not until you promise me this thing isn't going to crash."

"I promise." He gestures at the stairs so that I'll go up first. I begin my ascent but then turn around to look over my shoulder at him. "Don't look at my butt."

His eyes are dark. He's not smiling like I expect him to be. "No promises."

I fight to hide my smile as I go up the stairs to the entrance. I hope he does look at my butt; I sure didn't buy a dress this tight to be ignored.

A woman in a navy-blue pantsuit is waiting, smiling at me. "Welcome aboard."

"Thanks. Where're we going?"

She opens her mouth to answer but looks confused. She stalls out, probably because it's weird to be taking a passenger somewhere who doesn't know where she's going. *Yes, I'm a kidnap victim. Save me!*

Ty shows up behind me. "Don't tell her. It's a secret."

The girl gets a load of my fellow monkey and a huge grin lights up her face, her eyes practically twinkling with merriment. "Oh, okay, Mr. Stanz. Your secret is safe with me."

I watch her go all googly-eyed at Ty and it reminds me how cute he is. I've been so busy being annoyed with him, I've not really appreciated that about him. If you go for rockers, and I'm not sure that I ever have before, he's definitely got all the things groupies like: the hair, the tattoos, that I-don't-give-a-shit-about-the-world attitude. But I think deep down he's sad. He doesn't fit in. He wants to but he can't. Maybe that's part of the attraction for me. I feel that way often myself.

I wonder if this event will shed any light on who Ty Stanz really is and what's behind his angst. Just picturing it makes me feel compelled to get involved, fix what's broken. Protective instincts toward a near stranger? *Huh. That's weird.*

Normally, Rose is the healer of wounds in our house, both physical and psychological, so I must be channeling her energy. I'm only going to be here for another twelve hours or so and then I'm leaving, so feeling responsible for Ty's happiness could be mighty inconvenient. Plus, he's in a band and I live on a hippie commune, and I've made my choice to stay there to help my family. There is no future for me anywhere else or with this man except for this single, friendly outing—or whatever this night is.

I vow to just enjoy my time with him and see him as a friend, despite the attraction I feel toward him. I can definitely do this. I'm a down-to-earth, well-grounded person, and I've never been one for flights of fancy. I make hard decisions all the time. A New York City romance is not in the cards for me, but that's okay. There will be other men and other situations more convenient than this one, for sure. I feel so powerful right now, totally in control of my destiny. I'm only feeling the tiniest smidgen of regret. Minuscule. Microscopic. It's hardly even there. What regret? I don't know. See, it's gone already.

I sit down in a plush leather seat and am handed a glass of bubbly wine by the flight attendant. Ty takes the seat next to me and touches his glass to mine. "Bottoms up." He gulps his back, draining the entire thing in five seconds. His bad-boy image is in full effect, and my powerful, I-don't-need-this-man confidence falls away a little as my heart skips a beat and then goes mushy.

"Aren't you supposed to sip the stuff?" I have to lighten the mood to keep myself from being stupid.

"Trust me . . . you'll want to get liquored up for this." He signals the woman for a refill and she comes over with the bottle.

Without thinking, I take it from her hand and nod at her. "We're just going to keep this here with us." If my friend wants to get liquored up, who am I to stop him? Maybe it'll help him relax.

She gives me a tight smile and walks away, leaving us alone. I set the bottle down in front of me on the small table that sits next to the window.

"I like your style, hippie chick." His voice carries true admiration.

I tip my glass toward his face. "I like yours too. Nice job on the eyeliner tonight, by the way. No smears."

"Thanks." His grin is wide and very infectious as he takes the bottle from the table and fills his glass to the rim.

I sit back in my seat, slowly sipping my drink as the jet takes off to parts unknown. I'm hardly scared at all as the flying machine that's held up by magic and a ton of highly flammable jet fuel races toward the end of the runway and begins tilting toward the sky. I really want to call my sisters and tell them about the crazy adventure I'm on right now, but I think it'll be better if I can tell the entire story from start to finish. I cannot wait to call them later tonight.

CHAPTER FOURTEEN

What Ty calls a little event, I call a monster party. A limousine takes us from the small executive airport in a city I haven't yet managed to identify to a club that's been rented out specifically for the thing we're here for . . . whatever that is. The place is packed, and the minute Ty enters, he's swarmed by fans. Two large men step up and take positions on either side of him. He quickly grabs my hand and pulls me in close.

He speaks to the guy on his left, yelling to be heard over the music. "She's with me. Don't let her get lost."

I look at the two guys who appear as though they could be professional fighters and realize they're acting as bodyguards tonight. They keep the crowd at bay as we move through the throng to the bar.

"This is insane!" I yell. People are shoving one another, trying to get near Ty. Women are practically crying when they look at him. Guys don't seem concerned whether they're assaulting these women or not . . . they just want a piece of the man who's holding my hand.

"This is my life," he says over the music playing in the background. I recognize the song right away; it's one of my mother's favorites: "Red Hot Love."

We get to the bar, and the bodybuilders clear us a space. We stand next to each other while our protectors turn their backs to us, facing the crowd and keeping people away. Flashes are going off all around us.

I can't tell which ones are coming from the disco balls and which are coming from cameras.

"They're taking pictures of us." I hope my chopsticks are where they should be. I resist the urge to check, though, because I fear someone will take a photo of my armpit; it's not my best feature.

"I know. You get used to it."

I shake my head. "I could never get used to that. It's going to give me a headache."

"Why do you think I wear those sunglasses all the time?" He gives me a sad smile.

"You don't have your glasses right now."

He pats his chest. "They're in my pocket." He mumbles something I don't hear.

"What did you say?"

He speaks really loud, blasting me in the face. "My mom says I shouldn't wear them all the time . . . that I should let people see my eyes." He seems to realize when he finishes that he spoke too loud and turns away, embarrassed.

I put my hand on his shoulder and shake it a little. "She's right. You have nice eyes. You shouldn't hide them all the time."

He glances at me and looks like he's going to respond, but the bartender comes over, pulling his attention away.

"What can I get you, Ty?" he asks.

I lean in close to speak directly into Ty's ear. "Do you know him?"

"Nah."

It's weird to me that perfect strangers will call him by his first name, acting as if they're buddies. How would I feel if the entire world started calling me Amber? I think it would be very unsettling; I'd wonder if I should remember their faces from previous meetings.

"I'll take a scotch, rocks." He looks at me, nonplussed by the bartender's easy familiarity. "What would you like?"

I shrug. "More champagne?" My sister Rose is an authority on anything having to do with chemicals. She's been an organic chemistry buff since we were kids, way before she majored in it in college. She told Em and me that mixing drinks is not a good idea, back when we were fifteen years old and sneaking booze we found in our mothers' cabinet. I went for what I called the suicide—a little bit of everything mixed together. She stuck to whiskey, and Em went with rum. All three of us were vomiting our guts up the next morning, so I'm not sure if her advice was solid or not, but I'm following it anyway.

"I need to make sure certain people see my face," Ty says.

"And who would those people be?"

The drinks come, interrupting our conversation. He hands me mine and then lifts his. "Cheers," he says, tipping his glass toward me.

"Are you going to answer my question?"

He lifts a brow. "Are you going to touch my glass and toast to our continued good health?"

I guess we're entering another battle of the wills. I stare at him over the rim of my glass. "I will if you will."

He nods, sending a jolt of what feels like electricity through me. *Those eyes . . .*

I touch my glass to his.

"The band," he says.

His words do not compute. "The band?"

"Yeah. They need to see me here. So do my manager and my agent."

Did I mishear something because of all the noise in here? "I'm not sure I understand. Are you telling me the *band* is here tonight?"

"Yeah."

"But . . . they're in Toronto, I thought."

He looks at me with his face all scrunched up in confusion. I'm not sure if he's really lost or just mimicking my expression.

"Yeah," he says. "And we're in Toronto right now, too."

Say what? My brain is spinning. I was so busy drinking the champagne and chatting about nothing in the car on the way over, I wasn't paying attention to any of the signs we must've passed. "We're in *Toronto* right now?"

"Yeah. Didn't you see the sign at the airport? Wonder why that woman took our passports?"

"No. Oh my god." I look around at everybody. "These people are *Canadians*?"

He laughs. "Some of them, probably."

"The *band* is here?!" I smack him on the chest.

He jumps, startled but still smiling. "Yeah. The band is here. I think I've said that, like, three times already."

I slap him on the chest again. "Why didn't you *tell* me?!"

"I just did!" He's laughing outright now.

I smack him one more time. "You know what I mean. You sneak-attacked me!" Panic fills my chest and makes me feel like I'm choking on it.

He has the grace to look ashamed as his mirth fades. "Would you have come if I'd told you all the details?"

I'm so desperately sad that he deceived me like this. I totally trusted him. "Of *course* I would've come. That was the whole point of me being in New York in the first place. I thought I wasn't going to meet them until tomorrow morning."

"Because nobody thought I could get you here."

When I see the look on his face, my heart plummets into my stomach. "Are you telling me that this was some sort of little game for you? Some sort of challenge?" I feel like the world's biggest fool. All those moments of camaraderie—or what felt like it could be something else, something special—were just an illusion. *God, I must be desperate to have been so easily fooled.*

"No. It's not like that," he says, his expression losing all humor and tenderness.

I'm so angry I can't even stand to look at him anymore. "Yeah, right. I bet this was really funny for you . . . trick the hippie chick into coming on a plane with you. Put her on a helicopter and scare the shit out of her. Fool her into coming to see the men who are trying to manipulate her." I slam my glass down on the bar so hard the stem breaks. "Well, you can go make toast in a bathtub for all I care, Ty Stanz. I'm out of here."

Without another word or care for what he has to say, I slide out between the bodyguards and push my way through the crowd. There's no way Ty can follow me because the minute I make a hole in his little barrier, fans rush in and plug it up, which is perfectly fine with me.

I can't believe I was feeling sorry for him and his poor nightmare of a life before. *Boo hoo.* Please. He has women with their boobs falling out of their shirts worshipping the ground he walks on and men ready to mow these ladies over just to exchange a hello with a guy they think is cooler than life itself. He could probably get a blowjob right there at the bar if he wanted to. His life sucks like my life does. *NOT.* I'm so much better off on the farm than with any of these jackasses who don't value honesty or forthrightness. My decision to remain there is looking better and better every second.

I'm fuming, weaving through strangers, trying to get as far away from Ty as I possibly can. I am such an idiot. I let myself believe there was something of substance to that man, something worth getting to know. *Ha, ha. Joke's on me! The big city gets another one over on the hippie chick.*

At least I still have my telephone. I could call my sisters and whine and vent about what an idiot I am, but that's not going to help me right now. How am I going to get out of here without enough money to pay for a bus ticket? Rose and Em don't have credit cards either, and I'm pretty sure it will cost more than what I have left in cash to get from Toronto back to New York.

"Amber!" Somebody grabs my arm and yells in my ear. "Amber, you're here."

I glare at this person who wants to die, otherwise known as the man grabbing my arm. It's Lister. *Asshole number one.*

I yank myself free. "*Don't* talk to me."

"What's wrong?" He's stunned.

I face him, so angry I want to jab one of my chopsticks up his nose. "What's wrong? What's *wrong* is this little game you guys are playing. I don't appreciate it one bit."

His face turns into a mask. "I don't know what you're talking about."

"Yes, you do. You challenged Ty to get me to this place? Why didn't you just be up-front with me and invite me yourself? You knew I wanted to meet with them as soon as possible! I would have said yes!"

He looks lost. "I didn't challenge him to get you here. I asked him to *invite* you. What did he do?"

"Well, he did what you asked him to, all right. And he tricked me into getting onto a helicopter and a jet so we could fly here without him telling me where we were going or who was going to be here." I poke Lister in the chest with my finger. "You told me that I was going to meet the members of the band tomorrow *morning*, not *tonight*."

"Yes, that's true, but this thing came up at the last minute. It wasn't even supposed to include a performance, which is part of the reason why Ty wasn't here."

Those terribly inconvenient feelings of protectiveness toward Ty rise up again. "Why wasn't he invited? Regardless of whether there was supposed to be a performance or not, he's in the band. He should have been here."

"It was supposed to be an old-school fan hangout with just the original members, but then it morphed into something more involved. Things changed and we needed Ty to participate. And since he was coming, I figured you might as well tag along too. I was trying to make the meeting between you and the band happen sooner because you didn't look too thrilled about having to wait until tomorrow."

My anger is starting to fade in the face of his explanation. "You should have said something to me instead of letting Ty pull all those shenanigans on me."

He shakes his head. "I'm sorry you got dragged over here without the full story. I should have handled it myself, but Ty assured me he'd take care of it. Normally, he's completely responsible and serious. I don't know what's gotten into him lately."

I look around at the huge crowd, imagining the amount of time and planning that obviously went into this event. "This party does not look like it came together in the last few hours."

"No, you're right about that, but the fact that Ty had to come and the idea that we could get you here to speed things along, that came up very recently. I swear it." He holds up a hand like he's making a pledge.

He seems like he really wants me to believe him, but it makes no difference whether I do or not. What's done is done. I don't belong here, and I don't belong around people who couldn't tell the truth to save their lives. "This is not my scene. I'm leaving."

He puts his hand on my shoulder much more gently this time. "How are you going to get back?"

I seriously want to cry, not only at the fact that he has a point but also because he's feeling sorry for me, and I hate being pitied. "What do you care?"

His mask slips away and his face twists angrily. "Are you kidding me? Do you have *any* idea how upset my clients would be with me if you took off and nobody knew where you were?"

The ferocity of his response takes me aback; he's always been so mild-mannered. "You people don't own me." He's somehow managed to make me feel like the bad guy in this scenario. *How does he do that?*

"Yes, that's true. Nobody is saying that they do. That doesn't mean they don't care about you and your welfare."

I nearly scream at that load of bull. "*Care* about me? Are you *kidding* me?! We *are* talking about the same men who blew off my moms and didn't bother to find out about me and my sisters for twenty-five years, aren't we?"

He stiffens and his jaw pulses out several times before he answers. His mask is back in place. "You haven't heard the entire story. I suggest you give them a bit of your time so that you can hear it before you start judging like that."

Alarm bells are jangling in my head. I don't want to hear this. I don't want to see him and I don't want to know what he's hinting at. But anger builds in me so strongly, it won't let me back down. "You'd better not be suggesting what I think you're suggesting."

"And what would that be?"

"That my mothers have lied to me."

"I'm not suggesting anything of the sort. But you know as well as I do that there are always two sides to every story. I dare you to listen to the other side."

I can't believe he's actually daring me. This guy has a really big set of balls on him. "Fine. Where are they? I'll hear them out right now." *Not that I'll buy the bullshit they'll be selling.*

He looks over his shoulder. "I don't think now is a good time."

As if on cue, lights suddenly come on and illuminate a stage. It's got instruments and microphone stands poised and ready.

"What's going on?" I ask, as the crowd surges forward in unison, carrying me and Lister with it.

"Free concert," he says, trying to resist being jostled around. It's messing up his precious suit. "Some of our sponsors put it together. It's for a special cause."

I'm torn; I want to get the hell out of here and tell all these people, including Ty, to screw off, but I've come all this way, and I even flew on a damn helicopter to get here. And I'd be lying if I said I wasn't a little bit curious about seeing Ty, that jerk, onstage.

I shrug in defeat. "Fine. I'll watch, but then I'm leaving."

He takes me by the elbow, trying to lead me away from the stage. "Come on. We have a private viewing area. It'll be more comfortable for you than standing in this crowd." He looks around distractedly, like all of these people dancing, jumping, and screaming are annoying him. He's probably worried they're wrinkling his clothes.

I pull myself from his grip. "No, thanks. I think I'll be happier down here." I turn my back on him and face the stage.

I want to stay angry and offended, but it's really hard not to get caught up in the moment with all these people smiling, cheering, and holding up their beers, phones, and lighters. I was never a Red Hot fan, but my moms sure were, and I know they would pee their pants and possibly pass out if they were standing next to me.

My moms aren't here physically, but they are here with me in spirit. I wish more than anything they and my sisters could be here sharing this moment with me, because even though there are at least two sides to this story, I know our mothers did everything they could to give us a wonderful life—and Red Hot is their favorite band by a mile.

It's too dark to see details of the people walking out onstage, but they're picking up instruments and chatting among themselves. *It must be them.* My heart is beating wildly at the idea that one of these men could be my father. I see outlines of teased mullets in the mist that's being pumped out from the sidelines. People are starting to cheer loudly, voices already going hoarse. I'm both thrilled and sickened in equal measure. I've never experienced such opposing emotions together before. It's literally making me dizzy.

The last person up onstage is Ty. Unbelievably, there are some who pause their cheers to boo. But then someone strums a guitar, the drummer taps out a short but complicated rhythm, and the spotlights pop on. The lead singer takes center stage. I know who he is: Redmond Wylde, otherwise known as Red *Hot* Wylde, according to my mother. For the first time in my life, I'm staring at this man and wondering if he's the one—the man I've always wondered about. *Talk about surreal.* I look for clues that might tell me he and I share DNA. He's tall and lanky, his long, teased hair brown with reddish highlights. There's no way for me to tell if it's dyed, though. His face is thin and his nose hawkish. I almost reach up to touch my own face but stop myself. My nose isn't that big. His cheekbones are high and his chin strong. I sense he's a stubborn person by the set of his jaw; my sisters would say he and I have that in common.

"How're y'all doing tonight?" he asks, his aged voice sounding nothing like the one that sang the songs I've memorized.

The responding screams are deafening, drowning out my thoughts about shared facial features and personality traits. Everyone forgets that they're not thrilled by the fact that Ty is standing on the stage with his gorgeous hair, his jacket off, and his sleeves rolled up so you can see his tattoos with a guitar slung over his shoulder. They scream for their idols, who are about to play a song that dates back over twenty years, probably about the time that many of these people here were living their glory days, just like my moms.

I don't really care what these old buffoons onstage are going to do. All my attention is on the lead guitarist. To be honest, I go a little faint seeing Ty standing there. I think I'm getting a small taste of what my mothers felt when they watched this band rocking out all those years ago.

The music starts, and it's so loud, it feels like it's playing inside my chest, forcing my heart to pump blood through my body with the rhythm they're setting. Something sneaks in under my defenses and settles into my bones. The opening lines of the song wash over me.

"Hello, lady, dangerous lady, have I got a song for you . . ."

As the song progresses, Ty's fingers move across the strings, his instrument practically a part of his body. The complex fingerings seem like child's play for him. The sound is pure and perfect, every note crystal clear and sharp. His guitar rests on his thigh, and he bends and flexes his body to the beat, the music and his passion taking over his expression. The emotion he feels for the band and the music is right there for everyone to see. I wonder if they know what it means when his face goes all dark like that. No wonder my mothers followed these guys all over the place. I get it now. I totally get it.

Oh shit . . . what?

CHAPTER FIFTEEN

I want to say that the band sucks, but I find myself singing along to every song they play. I've probably heard each one of them over a hundred times . . . maybe a thousand times or more in total, so it's no surprise that I can. I picture my moms dancing around the house and singing at the top of their lungs, hugging one another and collapsing into giggles on the couch. Red Hot music always made them so happy. It makes me sad that they had to leave that relationship behind for my sisters and me.

I stare at each member of the band, trying to pick up clues as to who might be my father or Rose's or Em's. I don't see any resemblance to any of us, but maybe it's because they have so much makeup on and that hair . . . Oh my *god*, that *hair*. What on earth are they thinking?

I know big-hair bands are coming back in style, but these guys are *not* pulling it off. I don't think my critical feelings are coming from the fact that they're family-abandoning jerks either, especially when some girl standing next to me is pointing and laughing at them.

When the band pauses between songs, I heed the call of my bladder and go to the bathroom. I'm in a stall listening in on people's conversations to pass the time.

"Did you see that guy singing?" one girl says.

"That's Red Hot Wylde," another girl says.

"But his hair . . ." She giggles. "He needs some extensions or something."

"I know, he's thinning on top." They both laugh and then snort in synch. They sound drunk, but the alcohol is working as a truth serum; the guy is definitely going bald, and his attempts at teasing his hair to hide it are bordering on pitiful.

"What about that guy on lead guitar?" the first girl says.

"I know. Who *is* he?" her friend replies.

Another woman speaks up. She sounds older than these two I've been listening to. "That's Keith James' replacement, and not much of one if you ask me."

My hand hesitates on the door of my stall. I'm ready to unlock it and have a conversation with this woman. I mean, I'm no expert, but I know good guitar playing when I hear it, and I know all the band's songs by heart; he didn't miss a single note.

"What do you mean?" one of the girls asks. "He's *totally* hot."

"He may be hot, but he doesn't belong in the band." The woman is clearly angry about this.

"Because he's too hot." The two girls laugh again.

"No, because he doesn't get it. He wouldn't look like that if he got what we were here for."

"I'm just here for the free booze," one girl says.

"And I'm here for the music," the other younger girl says. "I *like* the music. But I could care less who's playing it. They sound better on the radio when you can't see their faces."

"Word up," her drunk friend says. I hear two hands hitting together—probably a high five.

"You don't know what you're talking about. You missed out when they were playing in their heyday. There was nobody better. They could pack an entire stadium in ten minutes of ticket sales, and that was before we had the Internet. We camped out for days to get those tickets."

"Yeah, but that was then and this is now," says the drunker of the two girls.

I can't sit there and listen anymore. I leave the stall and find all three women checking themselves out in the mirror. I was right—two of them are younger and the last one looks to be about the same age as my mothers.

The young girls leave and it's just the two of us outside the stalls for a few moments. "So you really love the band, huh?" I ask the older woman.

She applies lipstick very carefully to her bottom lip. "Yep. Have most of my life."

"My moms too."

She looks at me funny. "Moms? Plural?"

"Oh, I meant my *mom*. Singular." I usually remember not to do that when I'm in public. Not that I'm embarrassed, but it usually requires an overly long and awkward conversation with a stranger that I'd like to avoid tonight.

"They were amazing," she says, sighing as she puts her lipstick away.

"Aren't they still, though?" I smile, trying to cheer her up. Those idiot girls harshed her mellow big-time. I could imagine my mothers going off on someone saying that stuff about their favorite band.

"Yeah, they're still great. But that kid they hired . . ." She shakes her head in disappointment.

I turn to face her a little bit, leaning on the sink. "What's wrong with him? He seems like he's a pretty good guitarist."

"He is. He's just not . . . Red Hot material."

"I hear he's been a fan of the band his whole life. He knows all their songs backward and forward." Apparently, I'm a saleswoman for Tyler Stanz now. *Yep . . . a glutton for punishment.*

She shrugs, taking out a comb to tease her hair up even higher than it already is, which is several inches off the top of her head. "That may be, but he just doesn't have the look."

"You mean the mullets?"

"What's that?"

"You know . . . the haircut. Short in the front, long in the back?"

"Oh. Yeah. Maybe." She shrugs, teasing more hair. "I mean he really does stick out, don't you think?"

Yeah, he does stick out. He's the only one who looks halfway decent up there. "He does, but shouldn't it be about the music and not what he looks like? I mean, if they hired him, obviously they believe in him. They think he's good for the band." Yes, I am still trying to sell this woman on Ty. I'm obviously desperate for conversation and missing my mothers.

She shrugs. "Maybe. But they haven't said anything about it."

"What do you mean? Who hasn't said anything?"

"The band. They go on interviews all the time, and they know people are saying this stuff about the guy, but they never say anything about it. They never defend him. It's like they agree with us."

Now I'm starting to get the idea why Ty is so upset. "Oh . . . well . . . that's weird. You'd think they would defend their choice."

"Exactly." She puts her comb back in her purse and snaps it shut. "Which tells me that they don't want him there." She arranges her bangs on her forehead. "He's probably there because some lawyer or some band manager said he had to be, and they don't even want him. They're being forced to use him. I hear he wasn't even supposed to be here and then he just suddenly showed up. He doesn't even have the respect to get here with the band."

"Is that fair?"

The woman looks at me like I'm crazy. "What do you mean, *fair*?"

"To guess what their reason is without knowing for sure. To assume he showed up late in a disrespectful way."

She stares me down. "Listen, little girl . . . I've been following Red Hot since I was twelve years old, and I'm not going to tell you how old I am right now, but trust me . . . I've been a fan for a *long* time. I know them like they're my brothers."

"Really?" She makes me want to smack that smarmy smile off her face. "How many kids do they have?" *Ha! She'll never pass this test.* If she doesn't say at least three, then she's wrong.

"They have no children because they never got trapped by any women and they never got married."

Trapped. That's what people are going to say about my mothers . . . maybe even about my sisters and me too. It makes me sick to even think about it. "Maybe they're gay," I say, hoping I can plant a seed of doubt in her mind.

"Please. They are *players.* But they're smart, not like those other idiots."

She walks around me to leave the bathroom.

"What other idiots?"

"Those idiots like Mick Jagger and Steven Tyler who didn't use birth control and got girls pregnant and then got stuck with kids they didn't want hanging around with their hands out."

I'm so shocked I don't know what to say at first. But as she opens the door and walks out, I yell at her back. "That's a pretty harsh judgment on those innocent kids, don't you think?"

"All I know is what I see in the news." And then she's gone, taking her nasty judgments with her.

The door is shut for half a second before it opens up again and lets in noise from the band playing their next tune and two more women old enough to be my mother. I'm trembling with anger and something that feels like fear. *What if people find out that the band members have three daughters? Will they say horrible things about my sisters and me? About our mothers? Will they think that we're all assholes with our hands out?* It's the conclusion that Ty jumped to, and he knows the band personally. *Oh shit.*

We've lived completely anonymous lives down on the farm. Nobody has ever said anything rude to us except the occasional town council member who didn't like our horse manure piling up or us using a barn as an animal clinic. But this is a whole other ball of wax, that a stranger who knows nothing about me would judge me or someone in my family so cruelly.

I wash my hands slowly, contemplating the change that could be occurring in my life right now, a change that I have little control over. *This is nuts.* I really need to talk to my sisters, but I don't want anyone in here overhearing my conversation.

More groups of women pour into the bathroom laughing and talking, some of them tripping over themselves because they're so drunk. I dry my hands off and leave, staying on the outskirts of the throng. The song comes to an end and Ty turns his back to the crowd.

Red clears his throat and speaks. "The band's going to take a break, but we'll be back for another set in about twenty minutes. Booze is on us and so are the snacks, so eat and drink up, and don't forget to tip your bartenders. All profits from tonight's event go to the Children's House Charity. Make sure you stick around, because we've got some exciting news to share with you soon."

Lister shows up at my elbow, scaring the crap out of me. "Are you ready to meet them?" he asks.

I look up at him, angry and annoyed, the conversation in the bathroom still fresh in my mind. "They actually want to meet me on their break? They think this conversation is just going to take a couple minutes?"

"It can take as long as you want. They don't have to go back out in twenty minutes if they're not ready or you're not ready."

I snort in disgust. "That's just what I need. All these people hating me more than they probably already do."

"What are you talking about?"

I shake my head. "Never mind. Just bring me to them and we'll get this over with." I don't need to worry about the twenty-minute deadline. What I have to say isn't going to take any longer than two minutes, tops. I rub my stomach as we walk, worried I just might vomit when I meet the man who claims to be my father.

CHAPTER SIXTEEN

I want to say that I'm feeling brave and confident as hell, but that would be an utter lie. I'm shaking and breaking out in a cold sweat, and my heart is hammering away big-time. I think the chopsticks in my hair are clicking together to the same beat as my chattering teeth. It feels like I'm walking in subzero temperatures when I know good and well that the body heat collecting in here is warm enough to steam up the front windows of the club.

"They're in a private room upstairs," Lister says. "There are lots of people up there with them, but we'll ask them to leave."

We climb a steep set of stairs and go down a long, dimly lit hallway. He stops outside a door that has two bodyguards on either side of it.

"Are you ready?" he asks, looking down at me.

"No. Definitely not." I grit my teeth together so he won't see they're chattering.

His expression softens. "If you don't want to do this, just say so. I can send you back to New York on the jet, and you can see them in the morning when you're ready."

I imagine myself telling my sisters this story, including the part where I chickened out two seconds before meeting the men who claim to be our fathers. I shake my head. "No. Let's just get it over with." I smooth down my dress even though there are no wrinkles in it and grip my purse like it's a live bomb that I need to keep from hitting the floor.

Lister opens the door and gestures for me to go in ahead of him. I do, but stop just inside.

There are several people milling around. Some of them are dressed like they're roadies, and others are decked out like I am. Most of those in finery are women. There's a lot of big hair in the room, regardless of the gender of the person sporting it. One side of the space has several long tables covered in linen tablecloths and platters of food. It looks like a wedding reception buffet. There's even a four-tier cake in the middle. I've been to exactly three non-hippie weddings, and none of them had food as fancy as what I'm seeing here.

In the back of the room are several members of the band, lounging on couches and plush armchairs. To the left, over in the corner, is Ty with three women standing in front of him very closely, enough to make it appear very intimate. It annoys me, even though I have no right to feel that way. He's holding what looks like a scotch in his hand and is nodding, but his eyes are roaming the room. When they land on me, they lock on mine and he stiffens and stands up straighter. Another electric jolt hits me.

I look away. I'm still a little mad at him for the way he handled things earlier, but I know this emotion will fade. He was just trying to have fun with me, but he didn't fully appreciate the pressure I was under with meeting the band members. I believe he would have done things differently if he'd been more fully informed. I also feel bad about the things that the woman in the bathroom said about him, but that's not anything I'm going to worry about right now or probably ever. I have only one mission to complete tonight: I need to have this horribly awkward and painful conversation with these men before they go back out onstage . . . and then I need to go.

I wish I knew how my mothers would feel about this, if they'd be proud of me or disappointed. This is such a foreign situation for me to be in; nothing in my life has prepared me for being the spokesperson for my sisters, making declarations and assertions to perfect strangers that reach back into our history and out toward our future. I miss my family. I miss Glenhollow Farms. I really don't want to be here.

One of the band members with big hair, I think it's Red but it's kind of hard to see from here, raises his hand and speaks loudly.

"Everybody . . . can I get your attention, please? Could everyone but the band step outside and go back downstairs, please? We need to have a short meeting." He pauses, looking at some of the guys wearing black jeans and black T-shirts, all of them sporting beer bellies. "Crew too. You guys can head on down."

People look surprised and not very happy, whispering among themselves as they move to comply. Many set their glasses on nearby tables on their way toward the door. I walk over slowly to the buffet, trying not to be obvious about the fact that I'm staying while they're leaving, but I can sense these strangers staring at me. My ears start to burn as whispers float over.

I turn my back and focus on the cake. It's beautiful—a wedding cake fit for a princess. It's covered in white icing with pink and yellow roses, little purple violets, and orange begonias too, wrapping around each layer and flowing down the sides. They all look so real, I reach out and touch one to find out what it's made of—*sugar, maybe*. I look over my shoulder to see if anyone's watching, and when it seems that everyone's attention is elsewhere, I grab one of the small purple flowers and pop it into my mouth. This is exactly what I need. With a little sugar rush, I can get this over with easy peasy, lemon . . .

"I saw that," says a voice over my shoulder.

A shiver runs through me. I know who it is but don't look back.

"So what?" *Crunch, crunch, crunch.*

"You nervous?" Ty steps around to stand next to me.

"No. Why would I be nervous?" *Crunch. So sweet . . . unlike this guy next to me.*

"You just look kinda nervous to me."

Crunch, crunch, crunch-crunch-crunch. "Go away." I lick the sugar off my teeth. I hope they aren't purple now from the food coloring.

"But I hear we're about to have a meeting."

"Whatever. Just get away from me."

He sighs, sounding annoyed. "Listen, I just want to apologize."

"Too late. I'm here to have this meeting and then I'm leaving. It's been nice knowing you." I feel like I just jammed an ice pick into my own heart. I know I'm being rude, but I can't have him stand near me like this. I'm too tender right now, too on the edge—and Ty is the one person who I think could easily push me over, with only a few simple words. It doesn't make a whole lot of sense considering how little we know each other, but there's no arguing with this heart of mine.

Suddenly, Lister is there in his place. "Okay, the room is clear if you want to come on over."

I stare at the cake. I'd rather sit down and eat this entire thing than talk to those men.

"Amber?"

"Yeah. Just give me a minute."

I've got to get this done, I can't back out now. Rose, Em, and I talked about it for days on end, weighing the pros and cons, coming up with lists and lists of reasons why accepting their money would be the end of everything as we know it, an event we could never undo—a big, fat mistake. I have no choice but to go forward.

When I recount the story to my sisters tomorrow, I won't tell them how long I stood here hesitating. I won't tell them that I was second-guessing everything and strongly considering running out the door without saying a word.

I turn around and don't even bother with a fake smile. What's the point? I'm not happy and I sure don't want them to think that I am. This is seriously sad business. We're about to discuss how much my sisters and I despise them . . . these men we don't even know because they never bothered to get to know us . . . these overrated, potbellied has-beens who put their adoring fans over their girlfriends and children.

I walk with Lister over to the couches where the band members are all sitting. There are five of them in total. The only one I know by sight is Redmond . . . Red Wylde, lead singer. They look very different from their pictures on the album covers in my moms' collection. As I stand in front of them, Lister gestures to each one in turn.

"Amber, may I introduce to you the members of Red Hot . . . We have Mooch Gyllenhaal here on drums . . ."

A gray-haired man with a barrel chest and thick tattooed arms waves, grinning awkwardly.

"Cash Stagger over here on rhythm guitar."

The pudgiest one of the group lifts a finger without expression.

"Paul Goldman on bass . . ."

This very short band member gives me a thumbs-up and a smile that looks relaxed.

"You've already met Tyler Stanz, their new lead guitarist who took the place of Keith James, who passed away six months ago."

Ty just stares at me with his trademark dark expression.

"Then we have Red Wylde, lead singer."

Red is the most enthusiastic. He takes a couple steps toward me with his long, lanky frame. His arms are out, as if he expects me to hug him or something. "Amber. Welcome."

I take a step back and look away, successfully halting his forward movement. I'm relieved when he stops his advance and slowly lowers himself to the arm of the couch next to the drummer. Everyone is staring at me expectantly.

"Thank you," I say, wishing I could sound assertive instead of shy.

"Hello, Amber," the drummer—Mooch—says. He's wearing a big smile. "It's a real pleasure to finally meet you." He stands up and holds his hand out.

I grip my purse and stare at his fat fingers and wide palm. I really want to tell him to screw off and keep his dirty hands to himself, but he has such a nice smile and he looks so happy, I don't have the heart to do it.

I'm totally failing at being righteously angry, dammit. I release the grip I have on my purse, and even though my palm is clammy, I shake his hand anyway. "Hello."

The other band members jump to their feet and follow his lead. Red wipes his hand off on his pants before he offers it. I wish I could do the same because mine is sweating like crazy, but I don't want to leave a big sweat mark on my dress.

I mumble greetings to each of them, finding it difficult to look them in the eye. I wanted to hate them. I wanted to stare them down and be disgusted with what I saw. But they all appear so hopeful, it's making my heart ache. This isn't at all what I thought it was going to be like. I expected to face monsters, but all I see are middle-aged men hoping for a miracle. And I don't think I can be the one to bury their hopes in a grave so deep they'll never see the light of day again.

The room goes quiet when Lister puts his hands together. "So, I guess we all know why we're here."

Mooch speaks up. "Actually, I'm not really sure." The other band members smile and laugh a little.

I don't think it's very funny, though, so I don't.

"I have no idea what we're doing here," Ty says. "And I'm not sure I really should have been invited to this party, to be honest."

At least he and I agree on something.

"You're a member of the band now, so you're invited," says Paul in a gruff voice.

I roll my eyes at that one. They'll say it in here, but they won't admit it out in public? That's just wrong. I mean, even if Ty is a moody butt-head a lot of the time, a deal is a deal; if they asked him to play guitar for them, they need to welcome him with open arms.

Red gives me a funny look but doesn't say anything.

"Well, from what I know," Lister says, "Amber flew down from Maine to talk to you about the legal papers that I dropped off at her house a couple weeks ago." He looks at me for confirmation.

"Yes, that's true. I'm here representing myself and my two sisters. They . . . couldn't come." They were the smart ones. I, however, am a glutton for punishment. It wasn't bad enough that they insulted us long-distance; I'm here to be insulted to my face.

The band members move to the edge of their seats, looking at me expectantly. Respectfully, maybe. I hate giving them that credit, but I know these are men who are used to running the show, getting what they want, and never hearing the word *no*. But they're being patient with me, and the only one who seems to be in a hurry to get it over with besides me is Ty; he's tapping his foot softly and strumming on his thigh with his head down.

I can't meet their eyes, so I look over their heads at the wall behind them. "We got the papers from your lawyer . . . Lister . . . and the message that I have from my sisters and me in response is . . ."

My mind is racing, short-circuiting, suffering instant-onset Alzheimer's. *What do I say? How am I going to say it?* Telling them to stick the money up their butts sounded so awesome before—we're going to stick it to The Man!—but now it just seems rude and disrespectful. My mothers raised me better than this. *Dammit! Go away, conscience! You're ruining everything!*

I open my mouth and let the words fall out, because no amount of inner conversation is going to make this easier; I just need to get it over with. "The message is that we appreciate your offer, but we're not interested. So thanks very much and have a nice life."

Okay, so I panicked.

It feels like the walls are closing in on me. I move to go around Lister because I need to get the hell out of this place *right* now. Unfortunately, my stupid stiletto heel catches in the area rug and I start to go down. I reach for the closest thing, which happens to be Lister's arm.

I grab his jacket, but he wasn't expecting my weight on him so he falls backward with me on top of him. He catches himself just before he's dumped into an armchair and onto the lap of the rhythm guitarist. Everyone jumps to their feet to help, hands going out.

Once Lister steadies himself, he assists me with getting to my feet again. *Holy hell, how embarrassing!* Now I have another walk of shame to look forward to. As I try to right my dress that's somehow become twisted, my purse swings out and whacks Lister in the face, making him wince with pain.

"Oh shit!" I reach out to fix it somehow, but don't know what to do exactly, so I end up just patting him on the forehead. "I'm *so* sorry. There, there."

"Yeah, watch your face, man," Ty says from across the room. "She's got a killer right hook."

I refuse to rise to the bait, but, oh, how I wish I could have another ten minutes in this room with Ty's sorry butt so I could make him regret the shit he's giving me right now. I don't know exactly what I'd do with those ten minutes, but I know I wouldn't waste them.

Red is at my right elbow, distracting me from how annoying Tyler Stanz is. "Are you okay? Did you hurt yourself?"

"It looks like you broke your shoe," Mooch says. He bends down and picks up the heel of my stiletto, which has indeed separated from the sole. I hadn't even noticed, since I've been trying to stand on my tiptoes this whole time.

I could not possibly be more embarrassed. I take the piece of my shoe from his hand and shove it in my purse. "That's okay. No big deal. I have lots of other fancy shoes." That's a lie now and for the future; I will never buy a pair of these kinds of shoes again! I gather up the bottom of my dress to keep from tripping on it and try to walk out, but there are too many people in my way.

"Excuse me," I say, trying to breathe through the panic.

"Please don't leave." Red is standing in front of me, pleading with his eyes and his words. "We'd really like you to stay."

"It's getting late," is all I can say without exposing what's actually going on, which is the fact that I'm about to have a panic attack. It's just too overwhelming for me to be here. I expected to be full of one emotion: righteous indignation. But instead, I'm dealing with loss, sorrow, regret, curiosity, frustration, and any number of other feelings that were never a part of my plan.

He points at the food. "We have cake. We had it brought in just for you. Even the flowers are edible. Would you like to try it? Have a little slice? What do you think?"

What I'm thinking is that there's no reason for me to stay. Not even for cake, as beautiful as it is. This is the beginning and the end of our relationship . . . game over. It's not going to happen, so why prolong the agony? It's not like I'm going to ask them why they never reached out to us, why they didn't care enough to ask after us, why I never had a cake like that for one of my birthdays, or why they let our mothers disappear from their lives when they were carrying babies in their bellies. What's the point? I've already got a crack in my heart over it . . . no need to break it wide open and destroy it. Like Rose said on many occasions, it's better to let sleeping dogs lie. Our lives are good now. We should be happy with the blessings we've been given.

I shake my head. "No, thank you."

"Are you sure? Because we're not going to play for very much longer. Once we're done, we can just sit down and have a conversation." He pauses. "About whatever you want."

It's so tempting to say yes, especially when he's practically begging—and I don't think this man ever begs—but this wasn't a part of our plan. Rose, Em, and I decided that keeping it simple was best . . . that raising ghosts by reliving the past was only going to bring us trouble with not only our lives but our mothers'—the women we love more than anything on this earth, even though they're human and made mistakes in their pasts that are causing me endless amounts of grief right now.

Now that I see with my own eyes how much our mothers sacrificed—walking away from this life of luxury, fame, and fortune—it makes their dedication to us even more amazing, and I couldn't be more grateful to them for it. My need to stand up to these men and tell them to their faces how my sisters and I feel seems like a horrible mistake now. I've opened the door to something that should have stayed closed.

I shake my head more vigorously. "No. There's really nothing for us to say to each other."

"But there is," a voice says from across the room. We all turn around and find Ty standing there, his hands shoved in his front pockets.

I instantly start to fume at his interference—I was almost out of here—but he keeps talking, effectively stalling my escape.

"I don't know what's going on here exactly, but Amber told me earlier that she thinks she's the daughter of one of you guys, and you made her some kind of offer . . . but now she's leaving and telling you she wants nothing to do with you. But it's obvious the feeling isn't mutual, so I'd say you have a lot to talk about."

I feel like my head is going to explode. *How dare he!* The best thing for me to do right now is leave, but my temper won't let me. I have a little unloading to do first.

"Oh, *really*?" I glare at him. "So now *you're* the authority on what people need to be talking about, is that it?"

He looks at me funny. "Not really."

"Well, how about this . . ." I point to him and the band, circling my finger around to include all of them. "How about *you guys* have a conversation between *yourselves* about why everybody outside this room thinks Ty doesn't belong in the band while you guys are in here saying he *is* a part of the band—so much a part of it, in fact, that he gets to listen in on a conversation about three illegitimate children you abandoned twenty-five years ago. Why don't you guys talk about *that*, huh?"

"What is she talking about, Ty?" Paul asks, turning to face his new guitarist.

"I have no idea." Ty's expression is stormy. He sure as shit does know what I'm talking about, though, and so do they. They can't possibly be this clueless. I know they read the gossip magazines; surely their egos need feeding.

I point at him when their attention starts to move back in my direction. "Yes! He does! He knows *exactly* what I'm talking about. He walked out on that stage tonight and people started booing, and I know this isn't the first time. He loves the band and he knows all your music forward and backward." I pause, still kind of blown away by that level of dedication. "Did you know that? Did you know he can play your songs backward? And yet, all you guys do is blow off this bullshit from your faithful fans, bullshit I *know* you hear and see, and you don't stand up for him in public. So what do you think everybody believes about him?"

"I would really love to know," says Cash, looking a little astonished.

I'm on a roll, and I have all of them staring at me in rapt attention, so there's no turning back now. *Two barrels, trigger—click! Boom!* "I'll tell you what they think . . . they think that Ty has somehow blackmailed you into letting him be in the band or that someone is forcing you to let him in but you don't really want him there. And I don't blame them for thinking that, because that's exactly how it would look to me too if I'd never talked to him. It's only because I *did* that I know any different."

My heart is beating so hard it's aching in my chest. I have to get out of here or I'm sure it's going to be permanently damaged by all the stress I'm putting it under. "Anyway, I have to go. It's past my bedtime." I look at Lister. "Can I get a ride to the airport?"

He nods after checking with Red, who gives his silent assent. "We have a car for you outside. We can go right now if you want."

I keep all my focus on him. I can't face the men I just verbally body slammed. Ty will have to live on in my memory because I'll never be able to look at him again after what I just did; I'm sure he'll see it as a betrayal. "I do want that. Thank you."

I leave the room without a backward glance, trembling and covered in cold sweat. I want nothing to do with these people. They have serious issues. I don't, however, because my issue is now dealt with. *I did it! Mission accomplished!* I just wish I didn't feel so defeated and sad. I thought I was going to feel a lot more powerful and satisfied in this moment.

I walk through the door and Lister follows. He puts a hand on my shoulder to stop me. "Wait a minute." He faces the bodyguards in the doorway. "I need you to escort Amber out to our car and then go with her to the airport and make sure she gets on our jet that's taking her back to JFK tonight. And then make sure someone from the security team gets in the car with her at JFK to take her to the hotel. Nobody bothers her, understand?"

"Yes, sir," the taller one says. "We'll call ahead and set it up."

He turns his attention to me. "I'll leave a message at the hotel about breakfast if you're still interested."

I shake my head. "No, thanks. I've said what I came to say. I'm leaving tomorrow morning." *Even if I have to hitch a ride home.*

He nods, looking grim. "Are you going to be okay?"

His concern—his *fake* concern—annoys me. Why is he pretending to care? He told his clients not to give us money, so he should be happy with our decision. And he was part of this scenario, partnering with Ty in getting me here and surprising me with the band. *Just walk away, Amber. Walk away. He doesn't matter.*

But I could no sooner walk away than I could invite him to my wedding. "What do you care?" I put a hand on my hip and stare at him. "I mean, really . . . *what* do you care?"

"I know this must be difficult for you."

"No, you don't. You have no idea what this is like. But I have a suggestion for you . . . Don't worry about me." I point at the door. "Go worry about that band in there, because they've got problems. And if they don't deal with them, you're going to have bigger issues than three illegitimate children on the payroll."

"What do you know about all this? About the things you said in there?"

"I know what I know. I hear things. I'm not wrapped up in your cozy little world where everybody kisses your butt and says yes, yes, yes. I live in the real world where people tell it like it is." I leave him with that little nugget of hard truth and walk away. I'm not interested in conversations with Greg Lister, the guy who thinks it's a good idea to make Ty his errand boy where I'm concerned.

The wall of muscle that's been assigned to ensure my safe travel and delivery gives me a big sense of relief. With them at my sides, nobody is going to stop me from getting out of here—not that anybody would want to.

Feeling like a stranger in a strange land is not familiar or comfortable for me. I need to get home where I belong. It makes me sadder than sad to know that the big city is not where I was meant to be. I always imagined it could be an option one day, if things on the farm changed and my mothers didn't need me so much anymore, but now I know I was just fooling myself. I could never fit in with these kinds of people, and I wouldn't want to.

The two big shadows follow me, their heavy boots clomping loudly on the floor. I'm up with one step and down with another because one of my shoes is missing its too-tall heel. It becomes embarrassing pretty quickly, spoiling my cool exit.

"I can help you with that if you want," one of the men says.

I stop, looking up at him, confused. "Excuse me?"

He points at my shoe. "I can help you with that."

Does he have a miniature shoe repair kit in his pocket? Looking more closely at him, I find that very hard to believe; his pants are waaay too tight. *This should be interesting.* "Have at it." I hand him the broken stiletto and start digging around in my bag for the heel.

"No, the other one," he says.

Oh. That makes more sense than a shoe repair kit. I take off the good one and hand it over. In two seconds, he rips the heel off and gives it back to me.

I take the shoe from him and smile, slipping both of them onto my feet. Finally, something is going right. I test them forward and back a few steps. "Sweet. Now I have ballet flats. Kind of." These are much more my speed. They're a little awkward, but they're better than the up-down thing I was doing a minute ago.

"I have a sister," he explains.

"Lucky girl." For a moment I wonder if my sisters and I could have half siblings, other kids created with other women while the band was roaming the world and living like kings. But then I sweep that idea under the stairs where it belongs, dark and dusty, never to see the light of day. Our lives are already complicated enough with these men; no need to make it worse.

My temporary bodyguard nods at my comment and we move forward, making our way through the crowd to the car. His friend rides in the front seat and he rides in the back with me. As the town car pulls away from the curb, I put the window down a little bit so some of the night air can hit me in the face. I can't believe how sweaty I am.

The bodyguard next to me nudges me on the arm, and I look over to find him offering me a handkerchief. It's not until this moment that I realize I've been crying.

CHAPTER SEVENTEEN

As soon as I get inside my room, I shut the door and lean against it. I'm so exhausted, my brain actually hurts. The band's music is still inside there, thump, thump, thumping against my gray matter. I search through my bag as I limp over to the bedroom, looking for one of my homeopathic remedies for headaches. For the first time in my life, I'm not confident it'll work. I think the problem is that the pain in my head is originating in my heart.

I use the kettle in the tiny kitchenette to steep the herbal concoction from my bag before taking out my cell phone. It's late, but I know my sisters are wondering what's going on. I finally got a text back from them that told me to call when I returned to the hotel, and Em is a night owl, so she'll be waiting up for sure.

What am I going to say to them? Are they going to be disappointed that I didn't give those men a piece of my mind? There's only one way to find out; I dial their number and put the phone to my ear.

Em picks up right away. "Hi, how did it go? Did you have fun? Who did you meet? Was there anybody famous there?"

I can't help but smile. I haven't tasted the tea that I'm making yet, but I'm already feeling a little bit better. "Yes and no. Is Rose awake?"

"Yes. She's sitting right here with me. We were hoping you'd call. I'm going to put you on speakerphone."

There's a beep and then I hear Rose speaking. "Hi, sweetie. Are you okay?"

Leave it to Rose to know before she even hears my voice that there's something wrong. "I'm okay. Not great, but I survived." There's a hitch in my voice so I stop to gather my emotions.

"Are you crying?" Em asks. "It sounds like you've been crying or you have allergies or something."

"I may have done a little bit of crying, but it's also possible that I'm allergic to New York City." I try to laugh but it doesn't come out right so I quit.

"Tell us everything," Em says. "Leave nothing out."

"Honestly, there's not a lot to say." I'm going to omit the parts that concern Ty because they're totally irrelevant. "The band was supposed to meet me tomorrow morning for breakfast, but at the last minute they invited me to this event they were having in Toronto."

"Toronto? The band was there? What?" Em pauses. "Wait a minute . . . Don't tell me you went to *Toronto* . . ."

"I actually did. I rode in a helicopter and a jet to get there, too." Hearing myself say it makes it seem way more exciting than it actually was.

"No way!" Em exclaims. "That is so amazing. Were you totally excited?"

"More like scared out of my wits, at least during the helicopter ride. We flew off the top of a building in Manhattan, and I felt like we were going to drop right to the ground as soon as we went over the edge."

"Oh my god. I would've peed my pants," Rose says.

"Me too," Em adds. "I practically am right now just hearing the story. What happened next?"

"Well, we took the helicopter to JFK and then got on a private jet."

"We?" Rose asks.

"Private jet," Em says before I can respond. "Sounds swanky."

"Yeah, it was swanky. I was with the lead guitarist, Ty. He replaced Keith James about six months ago. He's the one who's kind of been hanging out and letting me know what's going on with the band."

"Oh, he's cute. I remember seeing a picture of him," Em says.

"Yeah, he's cute, but he's also difficult, so . . ." My heart hurts saying that.

"So, what happened next?" Rose asks. "After the swanky jet."

I relate the details of our plane ride and arrival at the club.

"Wow, that's kind of romantic, actually," Em says. "This Ty person picks you up in a helicopter and a jet and takes you to a show he's playing in without telling you where he's taking you? Sounds like a romance novel."

"It sounds a little kidnapper-ish to me," Rose says.

"It wasn't that romantic. More like annoying." I pause, not wanting them to hate Ty without meeting him first. "But not kidnapper-ish. I agreed to go everywhere we went, pretty much. I just didn't know I was agreeing to Canada." It sounds so ridiculous telling it like this.

"You never felt unsafe, I hope," Rose says.

"No, not at all. Other than being scared during the first part of the helicopter ride, I didn't feel like I was in danger or anything. There were probably five hundred people at the club, and believe me, they were all psyched to be there. Everyone was in a great mood."

"What were the fans like?" Em asks. "Were they our age or older?"

"It was a mix . . . maybe half and half. Everyone there was a fan of the band, although not all of them were fans of Ty. Some people don't really like him, I guess."

"How come?" Rose asks.

"I'm not positive, but I think maybe it's because he's so much younger and cute, and he doesn't fit in with the band visually. But also the band hasn't done a very good job of welcoming him into their lives in a public way." I don't like talking about it, because I feel guilty that I unloaded all my bad feelings on them in that room, stepping into something that's definitely not my business. *Time to change the subject.* "That's not really important. The important part is that I actually met the band and talked to them."

"Oh, boy. I'm not sure I'm ready to hear this part," Em says.

"Here, take my hand, sweetie," Rose says. "We're ready. Just tell us. We can handle it."

"Well, they were very nice." I'm not going to tell them about the cake they bought especially for me. I don't want them to have the feelings and regrets I'm living with now. "And, like we agreed, I told them that we weren't interested."

"And they were cool with that?" Rose asks.

"Yes and no. They didn't get mad, but they also asked me if I could stay and talk some more . . . but I told them no." I wait to get their reaction. There's a long pause before Em speaks.

"Is that it?"

"Yeah, pretty much. Oh . . . and . . . the best part—on my way out the door, I tripped and broke the heel off my shoe. I made a very graceful exit, as I'm sure you can imagine."

"Oh, you poor thing," Rose says, laughing in commiseration. "That must've been totally embarrassing."

"Yeah, definitely. But I'm over it." *Mostly.*

"So, what does this mean?" Em asks. "Are you coming home tomorrow?"

"I don't know. What did you find out for me about a plane ticket?"

"Well, you were right . . . ," Em says, sighing. "That first plane ticket was not refundable. But we're going to the travel agent's office tomorrow morning to get you a new one. I think the earliest we'll be able to get you out, though, is four o'clock. There aren't many flights coming up here."

"That's fine. I've got this hotel room I can stay in. I'll probably walk over to Central Park and check that out before I leave." I'm hoping all the greenery will help calm my nerves.

There's another long pause before Rose speaks. "Okay, well I guess we'd better go to bed and save the minutes on these phones." She sighs.

"I hope you're going to be okay. I wish we were there to give you a cuddle."

"Me too, but I'm going to be fine. I'm just really exhausted. This was emotionally draining."

"I can imagine," Em says. "Just take care of yourself. You'll be home soon, and then we'll give you the biggest group hug you've ever had."

"Sounds perfect." I can picture it already, embraced in the warmth of my sisters' love. There's nothing like it. "Good night, girly-girls. I love you so much."

"We love you too," Em says.

"Big hugs. See you tomorrow." Rose makes a kissing sound before she hangs up the phone.

I put the cell on the dresser and slowly remove my clothing. The dress I wore tonight is so pretty, but I'm not going to keep it. Every time I see it, I'll think of this night, and it'll make me sad all over again. I fold it up into a small square and put it in the dresser drawer, intending to leave it there when I depart tomorrow. Maybe the chambermaid will be able to use it.

After removing my underclothes, I climb into bed naked. I don't even take the time to brush my teeth; I'm too exhausted. The last thing I see in my mind as I fall asleep is the dark expression that Ty was wearing during that meeting. I shouldn't give a hoot about that man or what he's going through, but I do. It seems like such a simple problem they could solve so easily. It's too bad they're all so clueless. Regardless of how rude he was to me, I hope Ty manages to come out in a good place at the end. I can't imagine how devastating it would be for him to get kicked out of the band when being with them is his dream come true.

I had a dream once, of leaving the farm and living in a city, being an important businessperson, putting my marketing degree to work. The choice to stay didn't break me, but after being here and seeing the crowd at the club and all the things happening around me in Toronto and Manhattan, I wonder if my life isn't a little *too* tame . . . if I haven't accepted a life meant for a person winding down instead of a girl just getting started.

If I could do anything in the world, what would it be? The only thing that swirls around in my head is that damn band and Ty's problems. Their manager really sucks if he can't see this situation, or if he sees it but doesn't prioritize resolving it. If I were in charge, things would be different.

I realize all of a sudden that I'm imagining being involved with the band. I shake my head, getting it out of the weird place it has ventured into. Obviously, I've had too much champagne to think straight.

I fall asleep and dream of the farm, of New York City streets with their loud blaring horns, and two hot dogs that I can't seem to finish. The creepy old man from the restaurant is looking at me again, asking me what I'm going to do with my hot dogs, leering at me. In my dream I stand up and slap him across the face and tell him to mind his manners. It feels good sticking up for myself. I wish I could do it more in real life, be bold like that and brave.

My dream then shifts into a hazy place where I can no longer identify people, places, or things . . . just an overwhelming sense of unfinished business that leaves me restless and uncomfortable.

CHAPTER EIGHTEEN

I wake up with a hell of a hangover. All I had were three glasses of champagne, so this situation isn't one bit fair. I clean my teeth using the toothbrush and toothpaste supplied by the hotel and put on the clothing that I was wearing yesterday, slipping into my real ballet flats—not the hastily constructed ones—as I head to the door.

I need to eat some breakfast. I'm going to put it on my tab here at the hotel and send Lister some money for it when I get home. Screw going out to Central Park. After that terrible night's sleep, all I want to do is hibernate until it's time to leave. I'd order in room service if it weren't so expensive.

The phone on the small table by the door catches my eye because there's a blinking red light on it. I pick up the handset, pressing the message button. A recorded voice plays.

"Good morning, Amber. This is Red. I hope you don't mind me contacting you at your hotel. I was just wondering if you might have time for a cup of coffee this morning. I'm going to be down in the lobby waiting. If you want to join me, come find me. If you don't, don't. I'll understand either way. But I want you to know that I'd really like to see you, and I'd like to talk to you about Ty, also, if you have time. You said some things yesterday that got me and the others thinking, and I'd like to discuss them with you."

The message stops and the line goes dead. I slowly lower the handset to the cradle. Is this some sort of trick? Does he really want to talk to me about Ty or is this just a way to wrangle another meeting with me? Is he going to try to convince me that he's a good father and that he never meant to ignore us for twenty-five years? I'm quite sure I don't want to have *that* conversation, especially with this damn hangover throbbing in my skull.

I can't make this decision on my own; I don't trust myself not to be overly influenced by Red's use of the name Ty. I open up the little flip phone and call my sisters.

Em answers. "What's up? We haven't gone to the travel agent yet. We're leaving in a half hour."

"No, that's not why I'm calling. I just got a message from Red Wylde. He wants to meet me for coffee."

"Oh," she says abruptly. "Why?"

"He says he wants to talk to me about Ty, the lead guitarist."

"Are you going?"

"I don't know. That's why I'm calling. I wanted to see what you guys thought."

"Well, I can't speak for Rose, and she's not here right now for you to ask her directly, but I would say that I don't see any harm in having a conversation about Ty, if that's what you want to do."

"But I'm not sure that it's what I want to do," I whine. "Make the decision for me." I no longer trust myself where Ty is concerned. His situation tugs at my heartstrings a little too strongly, making me think I'm not being rational when I imagine fixing all his problems.

"I think . . . you should go. It sounds like you had a really short conversation last night and . . . I don't know . . . maybe you didn't get a chance to say some of the things you wanted to say."

She's hinting at something, but I don't know what it is exactly. "What do you mean?"

"Well, it sounds like you said a couple little things to the band and then left. Did you get a chance to ask them why they've been gone for twenty-five years? Did you tell them how angry we are?"

My heart sinks. *Mission failure.* "No. I was going to before I got in there, but then when I met them, it didn't feel right. They seem to be very nice—not great fathers, obviously, but decent enough people in their old age. I just . . . I don't know. I dropped the ball." Neither my emotions nor my words are making much sense right now. These men deserve to be called out for what they did, but I let them slide.

"You didn't drop the ball. We trust your instincts, you know that. If it didn't feel right, that's fine. But maybe this morning in a different environment, just one-on-one, things could be different. Maybe it would make you feel better to say some of the things that are going on in your mind."

"Would it make *you* feel better?"

"I would be happy with you going in either direction. I promise. You're the one who took the responsibility of going down there, keeping us from having to deal with all that heavy emotion. You're taking care of us like you always do. We trust you to do what you think is right."

"No pressure."

"Absolutely no pressure," she says with a smile in her voice. "Seriously. Just go in there and let him have it. Or don't. Just do what feels right."

"You do realize that my first instinct is not always the best avenue, right?"

She laughs. "I do know that whatever your first instinct is, it's usually pretty entertaining. And I think the situation is so heavy, it could use a little bit of that lightness."

"Fine. I'll have coffee with the guy. What's the worst that could happen, right?"

"Right! That's the spirit. Just call me back and let me know what happened. And I will call you as soon as I know about your airline ticket."

"It's a deal. Give Rose a hug for me."

"I will. She's busy with another sick animal. I think this time it's a porcupine. She came back earlier looking for her big gloves."

"Ugh. Porcupines. I don't know how she does it."

"I know, me neither. Love you. Bye-bye."

"Bye."

I go back to the bathroom and work at fixing my hair and putting on a bit of makeup. Some of the waves are still there from my curling iron adventure yesterday. My 'do could do with a washing along with the rest of me, but I'll wait until I get back home and have some fresh underwear.

I'm nervous again, and starting to sweat. I throw on a little extra deodorant from the sample-size bottle I keep in my purse, before I leave the room with my key card. I try to talk myself out of being nervous all the way down to the lobby, but it's not working.

CHAPTER NINETEEN

At first I don't see Red. There are several people in the lobby, but I finally find him hiding behind an open newspaper. He's wearing a cowboy hat, Western boots, and dark glasses, with rings on almost every finger. If he wanted to be incognito, he should have tried harder; he's easily identifiable from a hundred yards as an aging rocker. But at least his hair is tied back in a ponytail and not teased up to the sky. The lines on his face are deep, and when he stands up to greet me, I can see he's stiff by the way he moves.

"Good morning, Amber," he says in a gruff voice. "Don't you look beautiful." He reaches toward me and I stiffen, not expecting the warm welcome or the contact. It doesn't stop him or even slow him down, though. His arms go around my shoulders and he gives me a short hug, patting me on the back. He smells like aftershave. There's a man who used to stay at the farm who wore the same scent. He looked like Santa Claus and always made us laugh. It's a point in Red's favor that he's conjuring up those warm, happy memories.

"Did you sleep okay?" he asks, pulling back and reestablishing some comfortable distance between us.

What do I say to that? That I had weird dreams and thought way too much about Ty? No. Of course I'm not going to say that. But the bed was big and the sheets were soft. "Yes, it was fine. The room is nice."

"Good. I hope they're taking good care of you here."

"They are. Almost everybody's been pretty nice."

"Almost?" He lifts a brow.

I shake my head. "It was nothing I couldn't handle."

He smiles, chuckling to himself. "Good for you." He looks around and notices a couple people staring at us. "Why don't we go grab that cup of coffee?"

I turn sideways so he can walk past me. "Sure."

I follow him through the lobby over to the restaurant, my nerves jangling as my mind races. What will we talk about? What does he want to say to me? Is he going to try to pressure me?

He walks up to the person standing at the front of the restaurant and removes his glasses. I see the recognition dawn on the face of the employee instantly. "Do you have a private area where I can have some coffee with my friend alone?"

"Of course, Mr. Wylde, please follow me."

We walk behind the man past several occupied tables. He puts us in a far corner of the restaurant, an area that appears to be closed to other guests. Moments after we've settled into our seats and put our napkins in our laps, a crew of four waiters comes out with room dividers and closes off our section from prying eyes. It's impressive, I have to admit. The comparison of this to my Gray's Papaya experience is laughable.

Red smiles, placing his hat and his sunglasses on the chair next to him. He smooths his hair down with two hands and then rests his forearms on the table. One of his rings is a big silver skull with red ruby eyes. It's funny to me that he'd wear jewelry like this. Shouldn't he be more sedate in his old age?

"Would you like to get some breakfast?" He looks around the restaurant. "Seeing as how we're here in one of the nicer places in town."

I shake my head. "I don't have much of an appetite."

"All right, then. Good enough." He raises a hand and signals someone.

A waiter comes over, bowing slightly at our table. "How may I help you?" he asks.

"I'll have a cup of black coffee, as strong as you can make it." He looks at me. "And how about you, Amber?"

"I'll have some herbal tea, please."

The waiter nods and leaves us alone.

I can't think of a single thing to say. I examine this strange man, searching for clues on his face, trying to decide if he looks like me or one of my sisters. His eyes are blue, but that's not helpful because both Rose and I have blue eyes. The problem is that he's too old; his face has changed a lot from how it looked on his first album cover, and I think the hard living he's been doing has taken a steep toll on his complexion. He has age spots and more wrinkles than someone his age should. I see no resemblance to any of us.

"So, here we are." He smiles. I can tell he's had a lot of expensive dental work. I wonder how much it cost him. I wonder how much good my mothers could have done with that money. I try not to be bitter about all the times we fought city hall on our own because the lawyers were too pricey.

"Yes. Here we are." I try to smile but my lips are trembling too much to make it work.

"I'm sorry everything was so uncomfortable for you last night."

"No need to apologize." I shrug. "There's no way it could have been comfortable."

"We should've waited to have breakfast with you this morning. It's just that we were so anxious to meet you, and when the idea came up that we could fly you to Toronto, everybody just jumped right in and agreed with the plan."

"Whose idea was it?"

"It was Mooch's, actually."

"He's the drummer, right?" I know this already, I'm just trying to participate in the conversation.

"Yes. Since day one." He chuckles.

"Hasn't everybody been with the band since day one? . . . Except for Ty, of course."

"No, actually, Paul joined us in our third year. He replaced a guy named Darrell who we didn't get along with very well in the end."

"He's on your first album, right?"

"Yeah. We bought him out a long time ago, though. We don't hear much from him these days. Haven't in a while."

They bought him out like they want to buy us out. *How adorable.* I wonder if Darrell is as bitter as we are.

"You have no idea what he's doing these days?" I wonder how Red can so easily dismiss a fellow musician who helped his band find the fame and fortune they yearned for. Their first album was one of their best, according to my moms.

"Nope. Not interested." He plays with one of his rings, twisting it around and around. "So, how are your sisters doing?"

"They're fine." I hope he doesn't think I'm going to sit here and start telling him about our life at Glenhollow Farms. He has no right to know about that.

"That's nice. I was hoping we could meet them too."

"That's probably not going to happen."

"*Probably* not?" He's sounding hopeful again. I'll give the guy one thing: he sure is determined. I wonder if I inherited that gene from him.

"They're pretty busy," I explain, for some reason sparing him the truth that they just weren't interested enough to bother.

"Really? What do they do?"

I guess I walked right into that one. Now I'm stuck giving him some private details I would have rather kept to myself. I sigh. "Rose runs an animal rescue clinic, and Em helps with our farmers' market business."

"Fascinating. So Rose actually runs her own clinic? Or is she partners with someone else? A manager?"

"She runs her own clinic. She's not exactly a veterinarian, though; it's a nonprofit organization."

"But she does medical care on animals? That's excellent."

"She does quite a bit, yeah. She doesn't do surgery; she has a vet who comes in to do that for her."

"Good for her. That's pretty cool. I love animals."

Now I'm wondering if Rose got her love of animals from him. *Are we both his daughters? Is she my half sister for real and not just in spirit?*

"Yeah." It strikes me that maybe he's seeking a connection to us like I keep catching myself doing with him. I'm sure he wonders if any of us is his daughter. Maybe that's what the big interest in hanging out with me is; he's just trying to solve the mystery for himself.

"You were going to pay each of us ten million dollars," I say, the words popping out of my mouth.

"Yes. We're *still* willing to do that." He turns very serious.

"But you don't even know if you're related to us. Who's paying the money?"

"We're all chipping in and paying equal parts. All of us, even-steven, except for Ty and Paul, of course. Keith's estate is participating; it was in his will."

"But that means somebody could be paying money out to a child or children who aren't even his."

He nods slowly, leaning back in his chair. And then the waiter arrives to bring us our drinks, so the conversation stops for a little while. I move the tea bag around in the teapot while Red sips his coffee.

"We are aware that because of the situation, some of us may be paying money into an inheritance that we really have no connection to, but it doesn't matter."

"Why doesn't it matter?" I can't help but be fascinated, especially when the concept of parting with millions of dollars for a stranger is so alien to me. Hell, I can't even afford another plane ticket right now.

He looks at me, and I swear his eyes start to fill with tears. "Because we all loved your mothers equally."

"I . . ."

I stop right there because I don't know what to say to that. I never considered our situation from this perspective before. My sisters and I always figured this offer was some sort of apology for being shitty fathers—a payoff. None of us ever connected it to our mothers directly.

"I hope you believe that," he says. "They were very special to us."

I try not to get bitter and angry over his words, but it's impossible. I have to clench my jaw shut to keep from saying anything rude. Instead, I pour some of my tea into the waiting cup.

"You're awfully quiet. Are you this way all the time?"

I shake my head, almost laughing. *If my sisters could see me now.* "Not really."

"Ty told us that you were pretty talkative with him."

I shrug. "I suppose you could call me that on a normal day."

"But today is not a normal day," he says softly.

"Not even close." I take a sip of my tea, suddenly not able to look him in the eye.

"I wish I could say something to make this easier for you."

I put my cup down and face him. "With every word you say, you make it more difficult."

"I get it." He drinks more of his coffee and looks around the room. "You know, when you get to be my age, you look back on your life and you think about the things you did and the choices you made . . . and you wonder how many of them were the right ones and how many of them were wrong."

"I'm sure everybody does that." I'm just trying to be nice, because I don't think most people made as many bad choices as these men did. They've had all the money they could possibly need and then some for a long, long time, so they can't claim financial hardship as their reason for not being involved in our lives. It was a clear and present choice they made: *We don't want kids or women in our lives. The end.*

"One thing I do know that wasn't a mistake . . . ," he says, stopping and waiting for me to respond.

I'm being led down a path but I can't see the destination, and I'm not sure I want to either. But to not respond would be rude. "What's that?"

"Spending all the time we did with your mothers. We had them with us for two years, and it was the best time of our lives." He stares at me earnestly. "If you look at our music, at the things that we wrote in that two-year period, you can see it . . . hear it. Everybody can. It was our best stuff."

"That was a long time ago."

"Yeah. Twenty-seven years."

"I'm sorry things didn't work out between you guys." I mean it, too. I think my mothers are as sad as he seems to be.

His smile is wistful. "Yeah, I wonder what today would look like for me if I had done things differently back then."

"Well, I can't imagine you'd be happy living on a hippie commune in central Maine."

He smiles sadly. "Don't be too surprised. I seriously considered it a few times in my life."

I don't know if he's joking around, but I can't help but stare at him, trying to read his expression. "Yeah. Sure."

"You don't believe me, do you?"

"No, not really."

He shifts in his chair, leaning toward me. "How much do you know about our relationship with your mothers?"

I squirm in my seat, uncomfortable with the direction this conversation is headed. But I can't *not* answer him. My sisters would kill me if they knew I got this close to actually finding some answers and chickened out.

"Not a lot. I know they were with you for a couple years, having a great time, and then they got pregnant and had to leave."

"That's it? That's all the detail you have?"

"Pretty much. And this is the story we just got recently, mind you. My entire life, I never knew that they had *any* kind of relationship with you at all. You were a face on an album cover; that's it." I was mad at my moms for keeping the Big Secret from us for about a day. Then my sisters and I realized . . . they had no choice. They did the best they could at the time. They were told moms and kids weren't a part of the plan, and they believed that to be true too.

I watch as several emotions cross over his features. He looks surprised at first, then angry, and finally . . . sad. He stares down into his coffee mug. "I get it. That was probably the smartest thing for them to do."

"I think so too."

He looks up at me. "Why's that?"

"Because . . . could you imagine what that would've been like for us? To grow up knowing that we had fathers out there who were touring the world, having a big party, and believing they were ignoring us the entire time?"

He grips his coffee mug hard enough to make his fingers go blotchy white. "That's not how it was. We didn't do that."

I sit back in my seat and stare at him. "I'm pretty sure it *is* how it was . . . or how it would have been if our moms had tried to stick around. But it's all water under the bridge now. We're fully grown women, and it doesn't matter." I want to say, *You can't hurt us anymore,* but that would be a lie, as I'm finding out in this moment.

He stands up and rubs his hands on his jeans and turns sideways. I think he's going to take off, but then he changes his mind and sits down. He runs his hands over the top of his head and scratches his scalp a little bit. When he looks up at me, he seems tortured.

"I'm telling you the truth when I say that I loved your mothers. All of them. Still do. And I wouldn't say a negative thing about them because I respect them. I know how strong they are, and I know how smart they are too, and that they did what they thought they had to do as mothers. But I want you to know that you don't have the whole story. You don't know some things that maybe you should know."

I shake my head. I will not be manipulated into forgetting the truth—and that is the fact that, after twenty-five years, these men had no trouble finding us. If they did it two weeks ago, they could have done it twenty-five years ago too. There's no excuse for staying away. "I know everything I need to know. I'm sure of it."

He smiles sadly. "You're stubborn, just like your mother, Barbara."

I consider that a compliment. "I've heard that a few times in my life."

"She was such a hoot." He relaxes into his chair with a faraway look in his eye. "She always made everybody laugh. And nobody gave her any sass either, because she'd shut them down in a second."

"She's pretty much the same now." I'm proud of my mom. I love who she is.

"I'd give anything to see her," he says wistfully.

"She'd probably give anything to see you too." I shrug. It's not a lie. She cries over his stupid album covers, still to this day.

He looks down at his hands in his lap. "I wouldn't want to mess up your life by showing up out of the blue."

"I wouldn't want you to do that either." Finally, we agree on something. It's so very sad.

Our conversation dies out, and we just sit there in silence sipping our drinks. I pour more tea from my teapot, even though I'm not going to drink it. I just want this to be over, but I don't have the lady balls to stand up and walk out. Either that or I'm too curious about what's going to happen next to miss out on it.

"You said something last night about Ty," Red says. "And I talked to Lister after, and he said that you mentioned knowing some things about the band and what's going on."

He waits for me to respond, and I'm not going to be a child and give him the silent treatment. "Yeah. So?"

"Do you feel like sharing any of that with me?"

I shrug. "Yeah, sure. That's an easy conversation." I'm actually relieved to know this is what we're going to talk about now. That dream I had with Ty looking so dark is still haunting me. Maybe I'll be able to exorcise that ghost before I leave New York.

"So, what do you have to tell me?"

"Well . . ." I square myself in my seat, preparing to deliver my potentially unpleasant ideas. "I just met Ty yesterday, so it's not like I'm an authority on the subject, but it seems pretty clear that he's not fitting in with the band from your fans' perspective."

"But we have no control over that."

I frown at his naïveté. "Of course you do. You have complete control over it. The problem is you're doing all the wrong things."

He seems amused. "And what would those things be?"

I don't care if he's mocking me; this is my chance to tell him some hard truths that he needs to hear. I'm doing it for Ty. And my moms. They'd want Red Hot to be the best it can be.

"To start with, when your fans boo him when he goes out onstage, you don't say a word about it. That's not helping at all."

"We found out a long time ago that giving in to hecklers or troublemakers only makes it worse."

"When was the last time you tried it?"

He thinks for a few seconds and shrugs before answering. "Twenty years ago, maybe."

"Well, hello . . . it's 2017. Times have changed. You guys . . ." I laugh, unable to continue, because this is a totally pointless conversation. I'm talking to a man who has a mullet, for god's sake.

"What? Finish what you were going to say. Please."

This is not as easy as I thought it was going to be. I'm about to hurt his feelings. I should be happy about this, but I've lost a lot of the scorched-earth fervor I had before I came out here. "You guys don't change with the times. And I know that this is your *thing* or whatever, but there are some things that shouldn't stay stagnant."

"What do you mean we don't change with the times?"

I look at him closely to see if he's messing around, a ghost of a smile haunting my lips, but when he seems totally serious, I stop grinning. "You *do* realize that you still wear your hair and clothes the same way you wore them twenty years ago, right?"

"Yeah, but that's part of our image."

"No, that's you living in the past. Being stagnant."

He shakes his head and sits back. "You don't understand how the rock 'n' roll business works."

"You're right . . . I don't know how the industry works from the inside, but I sure as heck know what it's like from the *outside*, from a fan's perspective. I am part of the listening public, you know."

"You listen to our music? Are you a fan?"

I let out a long breath. "I've been listening to your music since I was *in utero*. It's not like I had a choice. But honestly, no, I'm not really a big fan. You guys are just too . . . old-school."

"But old-school is *cool*." He gives me a charming smile.

"Yeeeaaah . . . And sometimes old-school is *outdated*." I can see my insult hit its target because he flinches.

Now I feel bad. "I don't mean to be rude. I'm sorry. My moms didn't raise me to be like that. But you asked, and I'm just being honest with you; you guys could use a serious update."

He nods absently, finishing off his coffee and pushing the mug away. His body language tells me he's totally disregarding everything I just said. *Oh well.*

"I have a proposition I'd like to put your way," he says after a few moments of quiet contemplation.

"I already heard your proposition, and I told you . . . we're not interested."

He waves his hand, brushing away my comment. "No, not that proposition. Something else."

"Oh. Well, what is it?" I know for sure that I'm going to say no thank you to whatever it is, because I want no further contact with these people, but curiosity has me listening anyway.

CHAPTER TWENTY

Red leans in, resting his bejeweled hands on the tablecloth, fiddling with the silverware by his plate as he delivers his proposition to me. "As you mentioned before, we have a bit of an image problem and some issues with integrating Ty into the band. This is not news to us. But what you don't know is that we've got a new deal on the table with another label that we're real happy about for the most part, but they've mentioned some of the things that you have."

"The need for an update?"

His mouth twists before he answers. "Pretty much. We're not exactly comfortable with the idea, but that's not the worst part of it. The worst part is that the person they've assigned to handle that updating process is a complete wanker."

I almost laugh but manage to keep it in. "What does that have to do with me?"

"There's room in our contract for negotiation. What would you think about helping us out? On a temporary basis, of course. Very short-term thing."

"I don't think I'd be interested in that." I'm not even sure what he's talking about, but it doesn't matter. No way am I working anywhere near these guys.

"Maybe not, but hear me out." He sits toward the edge of his chair, quickly becoming more animated. "Like you said, you're part of this new generation. You're younger, and you're not really into the old-school thing. Add to that the fact that you know our music. You said you've been listening to it since you were born."

"Since *before* I was born," I clarify. Our mothers are fond of telling the story of using Walkman headphones on their bellies so we could learn the lyrics to Red Hot's songs before we could form words.

"Yes, exactly. And that's cool, because we need somebody who really knows our music, backward and forward, like you said Ty does. And I know your moms are fans."

I roll my eyes. "To call them fans would be the understatement of the year." If they found out I turned down a job with the band, they'd probably shoot me.

"Cool. So, you've grown up in a household that had Red Hot playing, right?"

"Always in the background of my life. Always."

"See? You get us. I mean, you get the music, anyway. You don't get *us*, which makes sense because we're just these old guys, you know, hanging on to the past. *Stagnant.* So you could do us—and Ty—a real solid, help us out, just, you know, update our image, get our gigs going again for the younger generation."

Now I understand what he's trying to say. But I still don't see why *I'm* the one who's receiving this proposition. I've already told him I'm not interested, and surely there are a hundred other more qualified people than me out there in the world.

"Why on earth would I want to do that?" I ask.

"Well, you'd be helping your friend Ty out, for one."

I snort by accident, laughing and inhaling at the same time. "He's not my friend." He's annoying, confused, and sneaky. And hot, but that part doesn't matter. And sometimes charming, but that also doesn't matter.

"Really? He always seemed like a pretty cool guy to me." Red's smile is slow. I think he's teasing me.

"Well, he can be cool, sure. But he can also be a jerk. Trust me."

"Maybe he's just frustrated because of the stuff that you were mentioning. Because he doesn't feel like he belongs."

Red is plucking those damn heartstrings of mine again. *Sprong!* I've been a homeschooled hippie living on a commune all my life; I know a thing or two about not belonging. And I most certainly know what it's like to have a dream and watch it slip away.

"Maybe," I concede, "but that's not my problem." *It's not my problem, it's not my problem, it's NOT my problem!*

"But aren't you at all interested in the story?" I can tell he desperately wants me to understand him, but I'm lost.

"What story?"

"The story about the time before you were born, and then the time you were conceived, and then the time after. Don't you want to hear our end of it? Don't you want to get to know the man who's your biological father, and the fathers of your sisters?"

Click, click, pull! Boom! Both barrels! He saved the big guns for last. *Smart man.* His words have sent my emotions warring inside me. I would be a complete empty-headed numbskull to not wonder about those things, but I fear the price I'd have to pay to get to know them would be too high.

I sigh, letting my frustration out in a long stream of hot air. "Of *course* I'm curious, Red, but not knowing has kept me protected my whole life . . . and I kind of like how uncomplicated and simple my world is." Being in that club in Toronto just that one night taught me all I need to know about the crazy life of a rocker and anyone attached to one.

"I *get* it, I do . . . I really do." He reaches out to take my hand, and I let him because I'm temporarily caught up in his enthusiasm. "And I know that this rock 'n' roll lifestyle is not something you want. But you don't have to be a part of that. You can be in the background as a consultant. Nobody even has to know who you are to the band, know your background or how we're connected. We can keep it totally professional to the outside world. They won't even *see* you."

For a nanosecond I wonder what it would be like to have the freedom to say yes. But then that moment passes and I ask myself: *Who would manage my hives? Who would help Rose in the clinic? Who would take my place and do all the things I do to keep our family business running?*

"I don't know. I have work on the farm I have to do." I pull my hand from his grasp.

"It wouldn't be for long. Just a couple weeks. And if you need to go home to do some work, you can go back whenever you want. You'd be in complete charge of your schedule. It's a hundred percent flexible. The jet would be at your disposal. It can even fly into smaller regional airports, you know."

I can't believe it, but he's actually tempting me. There's no denying that the idea of pointing this man and his bandmates in the right direction so that Ty can have a satisfying career with them would make me feel good. Ty's not always a jerk, and I think the times that he was, he was suffering from a broken heart or misinformation. The band that he loves more than anything in the world isn't reaching out to him like they should, but I could show them how.

Two big questions remain, though: Do I want to learn more about these men who are fathers to my sisters and me, or am I better off not knowing? And do I have a moral obligation to help another human being—Ty—when he needs it, even though it may harm me in the process? Maybe. But I'm not convinced.

"I'd need to talk to my sisters about this. And I'm not saying yes at all. Just that I'd need to talk to them before anything could ever happen differently in my life." My heart is pounding hard and fast. This conversation is forcing me to pull out decisions I made in the past for closer examination . . . choices I made that could now be altered as a result of what I do with Red's proposal. If I were given another chance, would I still choose to stay on the farm with my family, or would I choose something more exciting for myself . . . something focused on my own happiness and not the happiness of others?

"You and your sisters are pretty close, huh?" he asks.

"Closer than anyone in the world. I won't do anything that would hurt them, and I make decisions only with one hundred percent of their support."

"That's fine with us. I'll tell you what . . . Take the day. Hell, think it over for as long as you need to. And then, when you're ready to give us a decision, get in touch through Lister. He always knows where we are. How's that sound?"

A tingle runs along my entire body, as if my life somehow fundamentally changed in that moment. "That sounds . . . fine."

"Excellent." He stands and I follow suit. "Thanks for meeting me for coffee," he says, digging into his front pocket.

"Sure, no problem. Thanks . . . to you too. For meeting me." Thirty minutes with the man and I'm still an awkward nerd. And yet, he's as cool as a cucumber in a freezer. We can't possibly be related.

He throws two twenty-dollar bills down on the table. "Are you all set for your stay here?"

I look at him, confused about what he means. "I think so."

"You have enough money for your travel and accommodations?"

He thinks I need his money. I go cold at the insinuation. "Yes. I don't need anything from you."

His arms drop to his sides and he stares at me for a long time. It makes me uncomfortable.

"What? Why are you looking at me like that?"

He slowly shakes his head. "I'm looking at you like that for so many reasons. I'm wondering if you're okay. I'm wondering if you're happy. I'm wondering if there's anything in this world that I could do or give to you to make your life better. I'm wondering if you're my daughter or the daughter of one of my best friends. I'm wondering if you know how much I loved your mother. I'm wondering if you know how sorry I am for not being a part of your life all these years."

Gut punch. Tears rush to my eyes, and I don't want him to see them. "I have to go." I leave the restaurant at a run and don't stop until I'm at the elevators. I slap the buttons trying to get the damn thing to come faster. When the doors finally open, Jeremy is standing there, smiling with his silly gold buttons in two rows down his chest.

"Hello, Ms. Fields." As soon as he sees my tears, though, his face falls. "What happened?"

I rush into the elevator. "Just bring me to my room, please. I'm sorry for being rude."

"You're not being rude, ma'am. Just sad. I get it."

I cry silently all the way up to my floor and pat Jeremy on the shoulder as I leave the elevator. It's all I'm capable of right now.

CHAPTER TWENTY-ONE

As soon as I'm in my room, I call my sisters, but the phone just rings and rings, and neither of them answers. I think about my next move and realize there's only one for me to make. I can't just sit here in this hotel room wondering what I should do. I'll walk around in circles and wear a hole in this expensive carpet. I call the house phone at the farm and wait for someone to pick up there.

"Yello."

"Is this Barbara?"

"No, this is Carol. Amber?"

I nod. "Yes, it's me."

"What's wrong? You sound like you're crying."

"I am." I take a deep, shuddering breath, trying to control my emotions.

"What happened? Tell me what's going on."

"I'm not sure that's a good idea."

She instantly goes tough on me. "I know you're in New York City, and I know you've met with the band, so *out* with it."

"They told you?" I didn't think to instruct my sisters to keep our conversations to themselves. *Is everyone going to be angry at me when I get back?* All that thought does is make me cry harder.

"Yes, they've told us. And while we're not thrilled with the idea that you went down there without saying anything to us, we understand."

The load weighing on my heart lightens just a bit. "Okay, well that makes me feel a little better."

"Are you upset because you thought we'd be mad at you?"

"No, it's more than that."

"Do you want to talk to me, or do you want to wait for your mom?"

"Is she around?"

"No, she went out to the store, and I don't know when she'll be back."

"I guess I can talk to you."

"So, I'm sloppy seconds, is that it?" I can hear the smile in her voice.

"No, it's not like that at all. You know I love you just as much as I love Barbara."

"I know, I was only teasing. Talk to me. Maybe I can help."

"Well, I just had coffee with Red Wylde."

"Really?" Her voice becomes all breathy and high-pitched. "How is he doing? How does he look? Does he look good? I'll bet he does. What was he wearing?"

"Carol, if you're going to go all fangirl on me right now, I'm not going to be able to have this conversation with you."

Her tone becomes more subdued. "That's all right, I get it. Just ignore me. I'm having a little moment, that's all."

"Well, if it makes you feel any better, he was very silly about you girls too. He said he really loves you. His memories of you are . . . fond."

She doesn't respond, but I can sense her intense emotions over the telephone line. I keep going so she won't start crying.

"We were talking about the inheritance or settlement . . . whatever . . . that they've offered, which we turned down, but he said there's more to the story than what you told us."

A long sigh comes over the line before she responds. "Maybe there is."

"What do you mean, maybe?" I'm not liking the feeling that's welling up in me. I want to believe my mothers are innocent of any wrongdoing in this situation, that they did what they thought was best and weren't being intentionally cruel to anyone involved.

"Well, there always is, isn't there? There're always two sides to every story. But we have never lied to you. Maybe by omission, but not directly."

"I know that." A piece of Red's story leaks from my brain. "But maybe *you* don't have the whole story."

"What did he say about it?"

"I didn't want to hear his baloney, so he didn't say anything. But he did make me feel crappy about painting him as the bad guy."

"Don't they all?"

"All?"

"Yes. All men. In my experience they tell you the story that makes them look as good and innocent as possible. There's a reason we chose to leave and not involve them in that decision, but it doesn't make them bad guys, per se. It's just . . . the way it had to be."

"Maybe." Carol's responses leave me with the sense that I still only have part of the story, but this is not the time to dig deeper. "Anyway, he made me a different proposition."

"Is this going to make me upset?" she asks, suspicion lacing her voice.

"I don't think so. They're having a bit of an image problem with this new band member they have, and they've asked me to help them out with it."

"And how would you go about doing that?" She sounds surprised.

"Well, I would work as a consultant, I guess. It's just for a couple weeks. I'm supposed to help them update their look."

"You mean change the way they look *physically*?"

"Maybe. I haven't really thought it through."

"Are you sure that's a good idea?"

"Which part? Changing their look or taking the job?"

"Either one. I mean, do you really want to leave here and live in New York City?"

"No, I don't think so." I feel like I'm lying to my mother. Do I want to live in New York City? Part of me is saying yes. My pulse quickens. I couldn't. Not permanently. They need me on the farm.

"Hmmm . . . You just said *think* so," Carol says.

Busted. "So? What does that matter?"

"You're not a person to do anything by half measures or to waffle. When you say you don't *think* so, that means you're considering it."

I sigh loudly, so frustrated with my confused brain and a mother who can read my mind better than I can. "Maybe I am. I don't know. I'm very mixed-up right now."

"Does this have anything to do with that lead guitarist, by any chance?"

"No," I scoff. *Ridiculous*. "Why would it?"

Her voice takes on a teasing tone. "I don't know. I hear he's pretty cute. And I hear he's been spending some time with you, too."

"Listen, I'm not a groupie, okay? I'm not going to fall in love with the lead guitarist for Red Hot, unlike *some* people."

"That's not funny."

"And neither is you teasing me about falling in love with some guitarist I don't even know."

"Is he really that bad?" She sounds sad about the idea.

This conversation is exhausting. "I don't know. No. Maybe. I don't want to talk about it anymore."

"Okay. Well . . . did I help you at all? I'm not sure I have."

"I don't know. But I need to make a decision soon about what I'm going to do. If I'm going to help them out, I don't want to go all the way back home and then come back here again. I'd like to just get it done and then fly home after."

"You said it's going to be a two-week thing. We can certainly handle anything that's going on here for that period of time, so don't worry about the farm. If that's what your indecision is about, it's a nonissue."

"No, it's not just my work on the farm or the hives or the market."

"Tell me what it is, then. Just come right out and say it."

I blurt out the thought that keeps trying to hide from me. "I don't want to get attached."

"To whom?"

"To anyone!" I yell. "I get it, okay? I can see how you and my mom and Sally got wrapped up in this stuff all those years ago! They're nice guys when they want to be. And they're interesting. And they're talented." I hate admitting that. I don't like their music now any more than I did before, but after having met them, it has more meaning to me. And knowing that my moms were around when they wrote their best music that Ty plays so well only enhances that emotion. I can still picture him up on that stage, and the image makes my heart skip out of rhythm.

"I know, I know," she says wistfully. "I get it."

"But these men didn't want us," I say, close to weeping again. "They let all of us go."

Carol says nothing to that.

"So why should I give them the time of day? Why should I help them out? I *should* spend two weeks trying to destroy their band, not help it."

"Come on, Amber," she scolds softly, "we didn't raise you to be like that."

"I know. And that pisses me off too."

She laughs. "Why?"

"Because. That would be justice, for me to do something mean like that . . . and I like things to be fair."

"Oh, come on . . . First of all, two wrongs don't make a right; we've always taught you that. And second of all, since when is life ever fair?

Life is *never* fair. In fact, if life starts being fair, you'd better watch your backside because karma is coming for ya."

"Why does it have to be like that?"

"Because . . . if life were fair all the time and you never had any obstacles or things to surmount, it would be incredibly boring and you wouldn't want to go on anymore."

I let that sink in for a few seconds. She's probably right. She always is. And even if I disagreed, I don't have the juice left in me to argue about it. "You've given me some things to think about. How about I call you guys later?"

"Just don't forget one thing," Carol says.

"What's that?"

"Remember that we love and support you, which means we trust that whatever decision you make is going to be in your best interests, because you're smart, you're strong, and you're nobody's fool."

"Thanks for the vote of confidence. I wish I shared it."

"You do, though! You know what you're all about. You're not going to fall for any big-city nonsense. And you're not going to fall for the groupie bullshit either. You're smarter than we were."

I almost don't want to say this, but I need to be up-front with her. "What if I do think the guitarist is really cute?"

"Big deal. So he's cute. Love is not just about looks, and you know that. Remember, life on the road is not easy. These men sacrifice a lot. And anyone who's going to be with them on a permanent basis is going to have to sacrifice a lot too. It's why we left. If you go into this thing with your eyes open and you know what's what, then you're less likely to get hurt. Your moms and I were very naïve when we were your age, and we were younger than you are when we were with them. We didn't know our assholes from a hole in the ground back then. We're older and wiser now, but we did a lot of stupid shit back in the day."

"Do you think me staying here and working with them for two weeks is a stupid thing to do?"

"No. Honestly, I think it will be good for you and a lot of fun. You've spent way too many years here on the farm, and you almost never get out. Since college, anyway, and even then, you were so close and always came home on breaks and did nothing off the farm. It's not natural for someone your age."

"Hey! Whose fault is that?" I'm a little offended that my sacrifice is being painted as me being unnatural.

"Yes, I know we raised you here and we homeschooled you long before it was the hip thing to do, but you're twenty-four years old now. You could've left a long time ago."

"I would never." I can't believe I'm hearing her say this. I know I *could* have left, but I didn't because of them . . . and because of my sisters and the animals and the farm. It felt like the whole world was against us sometimes, and it was only through our shared strength that we made it. What kind of person would I be if I'd left them behind just to make myself happy?

"Well, maybe you should think about taking a break from Glenhollow so you can see how the other half lives."

My head is spinning. It's like she's giving me a permission slip to abandon the family. "I don't want to be a part of the other half. People who have a lot of money are assholes."

"Not necessarily. You can do a lot of good things with money. And I'm not telling you to take the money they're offering, because I'm sure it comes with strings, but stay there for a couple weeks and do your thing. They're going to pay you something for your work, right? Maybe do a little shopping. Eat in some cool restaurants. And make sure you send us pictures."

"I'm not sure I'm going to take the job."

"Okay, but if you do, then do everything I just said." She laughs.

"Would you tell Rose and Em that I called?"

"Yes, I will tell your Siamese twins that you called, and I will fill them in on what you said. I know they're working on getting you a ticket. I told them to get one that's open-ended, though, so don't worry about what date you decide to come back. It'll all work out."

"Oh. Wow. Okay." I pause, one more thing on my mind that I need to fix. "Are you mad at me that I left without talking to you first?"

"Not at all. It's about time you guys got your own lives and did what you needed to do without asking your mommies for permission."

I'm more than a little stunned by her answer. They've been so protective of us all our lives, and I'm positive they were grateful when I decided to stay rather than start my life elsewhere. "Why the change of heart? Why are you suddenly so willing to let us go?"

She lets out a long sigh. "Your mothers and I have had several long talks since that lawyer visited. We realize that we've made some mistakes. I think we're ready to own up to that now. You and your sisters have been pretty sheltered, and we thought we were doing the right thing raising you that way, but now, we're thinking maybe we should have done things a little differently."

"Because of the money?"

"No, it has nothing to do with the money. But it has everything to do with your attitude about men and your fathers."

"The abandoners, you mean."

"Yes, but I don't think it's fair, for the record, that you call them that. Remember, we left without saying a word to them. Ted and Darrell knew, but not the others. Who knows what would've happened if we'd had a conversation with them first, before we decided to leave. We thought we knew how they'd react based on things they'd said about kids and wives before we got pregnant, and we thought we knew what the consequences of staying would be for all of us, but how could we have? We were so sure back then, so full of our vision for our lives . . . so ignorant . . ." She sighs heavily. "It's too late to wonder about the what-ifs now, but do me a favor and keep this stuff in mind. Twenty-five years ago, we made a decision that impacted everyone, and at the time, it seemed like the right one. But as you get older, you look back on the things that you did and the choices you made, and you wonder if they were the right ones."

"That's funny you say that . . . Red said the exact same thing to me this morning."

"I always did love that man," she says almost sadly.

That's it. If I do take this job, I'm going to make sure my mothers see their groupie crushes at least one more time before they die. It's ridiculous that these longtime fans and old-fart musicians think about one another with such fondness but don't even bother picking up the telephone.

I'm a little closer to making a decision, thanks to Carol, but I really need to speak with two more people who I pray will try to talk me out of it. "I'll wait for Rose and Em to call me before I make any decisions."

"You are your own woman, Amber. You don't need to get permission from them any more than you need to get permission from your mothers."

"I know. Thanks, Carol. I love you."

"Love you too, kid. Chin up. Life is meant to be exciting. Go live it."

I pull the phone away from my ear and disconnect the call, imagining the look on Carol's face as she hangs up on her end of the line. She's tough, but she has a very soft center, and I'll bet she's crying.

Regret sucks. I can't even imagine how much of it our mothers are living with right now. I don't want to end up like them—in my forties and wishing I'd made different choices when I was younger.

CHAPTER TWENTY-TWO

I can't wait around in this hotel room all morning for my sisters to get back from wherever they are—probably talking to the travel agent about a new ticket for me. I need to clear my head.

I leave the room with my bag over my shoulder and take the elevator down to the lobby. I wave at James and Jeremy on my way out and stop just outside the main doors. I look left and right, trying to figure out which direction I should take.

"May I help you find something? Would you like me to call you a cab?"

I smile at the older gentleman who works as a doorman for the hotel. "Actually, if you could tell me how to get to Central Park from here, that would be great."

He points up the street. "Just head in that direction for two blocks. You can't miss it."

Now that I look in the direction he's pointing, I think I can already see it. *Duh.* "Thank you very much."

"Don't mention it."

I walk with purpose, glad to be out. The fresh air is bracing. My mood has shifted considerably; today's a *great* day to be alive. A half hour ago it felt like everything was hopeless, that I was stuck between a rock and a hard place. But after talking to Carol, something inside me has changed. I don't know what it is. *Did I just become an adult instantaneously after one conversation?* It kind of feels that way.

Before I arrived in New York, I never really questioned who I was or where I came from. It didn't matter. I had the farm, I had my sisters, and I had my mothers. We also had the occasional housemate or people pitching tents on the farm, and they always kept life interesting. The farmers' market is always fun. We have our regulars and new people who pass through. For me, that was almost enough; it wasn't that difficult taking my dream of another life and locking it away in the dark recesses of my mind. But as I head down to Central Park amid the noise and the fumes and the smells of cooking food and brewing coffee, I wonder if it really *is* enough. *Am I hibernating out there? Am I hiding from the real world and from what I really want to be doing?*

I'm not sure that's the case. It sounds a little melodramatic when I hear it echoing around inside my head. But I think it would be wrong to dismiss the idea that maybe I should get out more and try new things once in a while . . . just to be sure that the life I'm living is the one that I'm choosing to live and not the one that I ended up in by default.

My phone rings and I pick it up without looking at the number. "I am so glad you called." I need to get Rose's and Em's opinion on all this stuff.

"Well . . . okay . . . that's not the hello I was expecting, but I'll take it."

I stop immediately, causing someone behind me to bump into my back. A man dressed in leather pants and jacket, his hair teased with a few feathers hanging in it, apologizes and goes on his way. *Wow. There are all kinds of people in this city.*

"Where did you get my number?" I ask the troublesome man on the phone. I can't believe Ty is calling me.

"Lister gave it to me. I just stopped by your hotel but you weren't there." He sounds funny.

"No, that's right; I'm not there." I cock my hip and rest my elbow against my ribs.

"Can I ask where you are?"

"Sure, you can ask . . ." I start walking again, more slowly this time.

"But you might not tell me?" he says, finishing my sentence for me.

"I don't know. I'm really not sure what to say to you, Ty, I have to be honest."

"Just tell me you're not at the airport."

"No, I'm not at the airport." My stupid heart soars with the knowledge that he doesn't want me to leave town.

"Good. So where are you?"

There's no way I'm going to get out of this, but I'm not sure that I want to anyway, so . . . "I'm walking to Central Park." It's a half a block ahead.

"Oh. Are you there yet?"

"No, not quite." I'm waiting for another light to cooperate. A crowd of tourists with cameras slung around their necks surrounds me. They're speaking animatedly in a language I don't know.

"Cool. Wait for me. I'll catch up."

I panic. "No. Don't catch up."

He laughs. "Why not?"

"Because. I'm taking a walk. Alone." I'm not ready to see him. I have too many big life decisions to make right now, and seeing him is only going to make things more confusing.

"You can't possibly be walking alone. This is New York City."

He thinks he's charming. I scowl. "You know what I mean."

"Is it that you don't want to take a walk with *anyone* or you just don't want to take one with *me*?"

This man is so exasperating. "What difference does it make?" He made it perfectly clear how he feels about me last night when he threw me under the bus. Why is he trying to be cute with me now?

"I just thought we could have a little chat. A friendly conversation, no big deal."

"I was going to Central Park to clear my head. That's going to be pretty hard to do if I'm having a chat with you."

"How about I escort you down to the park and we can chat on the way . . . and once we get there, I'll leave you alone?"

"I'm almost there."

"So? I can be short and sweet when I need to be."

He's being so reasonable, I'm finding it hard to deny him. At some point I'm just going to sound bitchy, and that's not who I want to be with him. Besides . . . I'm only a half a block away . . .

"Fine. But I'm not stopping. If you can catch up to me, fine." I hang up the phone without another word and slide it into my purse. The light hasn't even turned green yet when I feel somebody tapping me on the shoulder. I turn around and find Ty there.

"Hey," he says, completely out of breath, heaving and holding his chest.

He's wearing a dirty baseball hat, big aviator sunglasses, and the same gross jeans he was wearing yesterday, with a really old, faded Red Hot T-shirt that has the band's first album cover on it.

"Did you just run all the way from the hotel?"

"Yeah. As soon as you told me where you were headed, I started. Saw you from down the block." He massages his chest and winces. "Man, am I out of shape or what?"

He could've fooled me. He may be out of breath, but the muscles in his arms make me think he goes to the gym every day. To distract myself from further evaluation of his hot body, I turn toward my destination and start walking with the tourists as they move out into the street. "Try to keep up."

"I hear you had a meeting with Red this morning," he says, easily keeping pace with me.

"I might have." I want to know so badly how much he knows about that meeting and if he was included in their plan, but I don't want to give him the satisfaction of having something over me.

"That's cool. I hope you guys can work something out."

Clearly, he wants to know more, and I would really love to share details of my life with this man, because it almost always feels good to have a conversation with somebody and get another opinion on it—but I don't like the idea of becoming vulnerable to him. He's already shown me that he'll turn on me in a second. It makes me cranky to think of how well we get along sometimes and then how *not* well we get along when one of his moods strikes.

"You said some things that really got the band talking last night," he says.

"Oh yeah? That's great." We reach the other side of the street and the entrance to Central Park.

"Are you mad about that?" he asks.

"No, I'm happy for you. I really am." I need to calm my attitude down. He's just trying to be nice, even though he's also attempting to dig information out of me. He thinks he's so sneaky, but he's not *at all.*

"I think they're ready to make some changes. I'm actually pretty surprised. I never thought I'd hear them say some of the things they said."

He just keeps dangling carrot after carrot in front of me. *How am I supposed to resist this?* "Cool." I'll just try to keep the conversation going with as little commitment as possible until I reach the interior of the park.

"Do you mind if I ask you a personal question?" he says.

"Yes, I do mind."

"Good, because I'm really curious."

I pause to stare at him. "I just said I *do* mind."

His grin is lopsided. "I know. But I'm going to ignore that part."

I shake my head and continue walking. "You are so nosy." *And charming.*

"I am. But only with you."

My heart skips a beat. Even though I know he's making a joke, for a split second, he made me feel special. "What do you want to know?" I ask, willing to at least hear him out. We've reached the park, but I'm not yet ready to tell him to leave me alone. Hopefully, he'll push one of my buttons soon and make it easy on me.

"I don't have all of the story, but from what I understand, you have two sisters, right?"

"Correct. Rose and Emerald."

"Emerald. Cool name."

"We call her Em."

"Yeah, that's probably more manageable than Emerald."

If he could see my sister's eyes, he might second-guess that idea. Our mothers call her Emerald almost all the time, and it suits her; I'm just lazy with names.

"And you guys all live together on a hippie commune, like you said, right?"

"Yes. In Maine."

"And you all think that somebody in the band is your father?"

"No, that's not correct."

"See? I'm confused. Help me figure this out."

I stop and put a hand on my hip. "Why? Why does it matter to you?"

He stands there looking at me for the longest time. All I can see is the reflection of my own face in the lens of his sunglasses.

"I wish to hell I knew," he finally says.

"Curiosity killed the cat, you know."

"I know." He smiles. "What can I say? I like to live dangerously."

I roll my eyes at his ability to be both charming and annoying at the same time. *How does he do that? Am I the only one who notices this skill he has?*

"What?" he asks.

"Nothing." I shake my head to rid it of these silly thoughts and continue our walk. We're moving farther into the park, but the idea of him leaving makes me sad, so I keep talking to keep him at my side. "We were *told* that our fathers are in the band. *We* are not saying anything about it."

"Who told you? Was it Lister?"

"It started with Lister when he visited our house two weeks ago to tell us. But our mothers have since confirmed it."

"So, before Lister came to your place, you had no idea?"

"No. No idea." I shake my head. I still can't believe it when I seriously think about it. *Me? A daughter of someone in Red Hot? Naaahhhh . . .*

"That is really hard to believe."

My blood starts to heat up at the tone in his voice, and not in a good way. "Believe it if you want or not, I don't care."

He continues, oblivious to my rising temper, if his tone is anything to judge by. "I mean, how can you not know who your fathers are? Especially when they're famous like that? Why would your mothers keep that from you?"

I try to walk faster, but hoping I'll be able to leave him behind is pointless. He has longer legs than me and he definitely can't take a hint.

"I mean, I've known who my father was since birth, but if I didn't, I sure as hell would be looking for him until I found him. Did you look for them?"

"No, we did not."

"Why not?" he asks.

I want to leap to my mothers' defense and tell him we had no reason to look for men our mothers couldn't even identify, but now I know better—they knew all along where to find the men who helped bring us into the world. Regardless, I'm not going to let Ty's careless words cause me to be angry with my mothers. They did what they felt they had to do, and I do not doubt for one second how much they love my sisters and me. I don't need to justify their actions to this guy.

"Because . . . we're not like you, I guess," I say. "We're happy with our lives." Sure, maybe that was an insult, but so what? He's being rude, so I can be rude too. Carol's mention of two wrongs not making a right burns in my brain. *Shut up, conscience!*

"What are you planning to do here in the park?"

"Be alone."

I feel his hand on my arm and it slows me down.

"I'm pissing you off again, aren't I?"

I pull my arm out of his grasp and take a step away to put more distance between us. "Yes, you are. You're very good at it, and I don't think you're even trying this time."

He hisses out his annoyance but doesn't say anything. He shoves his hands into his pockets and starts walking again with his head down. I go too, not wanting him to wander off without me. Our business together isn't finished yet, but I sense it's about to come to a close very soon.

Every once in a while, somebody will stop and glance at us or do a double take, but so far we've managed to walk through this part of Central Park without being molested. But I'm pretty sure if we slow down too much or stop, people will start taking a closer look at him, and then my plans of having a calming walk will be over.

"I think you'd better leave me alone now," I say, coming to terms with the idea that it's for the best if he goes his way and I go mine.

"You're that mad at me?"

"No, I just want a little bit of privacy, and I know if I walk through this park with you, people are going to start bothering us."

"You don't like that attention, do you?"

"No. Do you?"

"I don't know. It's not bad all the time. Before I was with the band, I thought it was what I wanted more than anything. I couldn't wait for people to recognize me, so I'd no longer be a nobody."

"I highly doubt you were *ever* a nobody." Men like Ty don't just walk through life unnoticed or unloved. He's hot, he's amazingly talented, and he's charming . . . and he knows it. Guys like that get attention.

Out of the corner of my eye I catch him smiling sadly. "Maybe you'd be surprised," he says. "But anyway, now I've got all the attention I ever wanted and then some; and sometimes, yeah, it's a pain in the ass."

"Like when you're trying to harass a woman on a walk?" I smile so he knows I'm only kidding.

"No . . . when I'm trying to have a conversation with her and get to know her better."

I halt immediately and face him. "And what is it you're doing right now?" I'm not sure I can believe him. I want to . . . for sure it makes my heart go a little mushy to think that he wants to be with me because he finds me interesting . . . but there's a risk in believing something that's not true. Ty could easily hurt me.

He stands there with his shoulders hunched forward and his hands jammed deep into his front pockets. "What do you mean, what am I doing? I'm taking a walk. With you. Trying to talk to you."

I shake my head. "No, you're not. You're interrogating me. There's a difference between a conversation and an interrogation. You're saying you want to get to know me, but why do I think you're just doing that so that you can gather information for your own purposes or to use it against me in the future?"

"I don't know . . ." He sounds annoyed and maybe a touch guilty. "Because you have a very negative outlook on life?"

"No, I really don't. If you could see me outside of New York City, you would know that I am a very positive person. When people have problems, I find solutions. But every time I'm around you, things turn ugly and dark. Do you know why that is?"

"I could guess," he mumbles.

"You don't need to guess because I'm going to tell you. You have a crappy attitude. You're moody and you're suspicious of people you don't have any reason to distrust." *People like me.* I move closer to him and drop my voice, because I'm afraid some of the people looking at us are starting to recognize him. "I'm not the bad guy here, okay? I'm trying to help you out."

He pulls his hands out of his pockets and stares at me. "You're trying to help me out? How are you doing that?"

"Never mind." He won't understand. He'll see it as me causing him problems when I'm actually solving them. I start walking again, but his hand on my arm stops me.

"What did you do?"

"I didn't *do* anything. You heard what I said to the band last night, though." Now the idea of working for them as a consultant seems like a really bad idea. Ty doesn't want my help; that much is clear. I can tell by the expression on his face. *Distrust. Fear. Anger.*

"What you said was nice. I was a little surprised you said it, actually."

I wasn't expecting this reaction. The weird expression on his face quickly disappears, making me wonder if I imagined it. "Why did it surprise you?"

"Because." He shrugs. "I didn't think you gave a shit about me being in the band or about how people treat me."

I wish I could see his eyes behind those stupid glasses.

"What's the matter?" he asks.

"I can't see your damn eyes. It's making me crazy."

He pulls his glasses off. "Better?" His eyelids are swollen and his eyes red-rimmed. He didn't put new eyeliner on, but there's plenty of the old stuff smeared around.

"You look like hell," I say before my manners have a chance to stop me.

He gives me half a grin. "Thanks. You don't look so bad yourself." He points at my face.

I sniff and lift my chin, resisting the urge to rub any errant mascara out from under my eyes. "I may have been crying earlier this morning, okay? I can't help it if my eyes are puffy from that."

He looks down at the ground, kicking at a small stone on the pathway. "Yeah, I get it. Things are kinda heavy right now."

I let out a long sigh. "I feel like I'm riding a roller coaster whenever I'm standing next to you, Ty."

His smile is sad as he looks up at me. "You too?"

We stand there staring at each other for the longest time. And then a few people stop near us, and then more people stop, and suddenly we're being surrounded.

Ty grabs me by the hand and pulls me along the path. "Come on, let's go. We're gathering a crowd." He starts to jog, and I run with him, gripping my bag against me so it doesn't bang on my leg.

"Where're we going?" I ask breathlessly. This is exciting in a way, running from strangers into the darker areas of the park.

"To my favorite spot."

I give in to the moment and let Ty lead me. I don't know where we're going, but I'm looking forward to getting there. Something is happening between us, and it doesn't feel all bad for a change.

CHAPTER TWENTY-THREE

We take several winding paths through the trees and over little hills. It's beautiful in the park. There are lots of people walking with their dogs, with friends, with family members, or alone. There's even a man with a tiny pup using a little wheelchair for the dog's back legs. I wish I could take a picture to show Rose. I make a mental note to tell her about it later.

"It's just up here," Ty says.

We reach a small clearing with something embedded in the pathway in the shape of a circle. Ty points to a building across the street at the edge of Central Park. "That's where Yoko Ono lives, at the Dakota. It's the same place where John Lennon was shot and killed."

I look at the building that seems very much like many of the others I've seen. But it isn't. Of course it isn't. It's where a music legend, known for preaching about tolerance and love, had his life taken by a madman. I feel very blue all of a sudden. Before, when I heard of a musician being killed, it was sad, but now it feels much more personal. *What if someone wanted to kill Ty because they didn't think he belonged in the band?* The idea chills me to the bone. Wanting to help him becomes an urgent need.

"Such a tragedy," I say, trying to get my thoughts back on the sane track where they belong instead of veering into Crazytown. "Why are people so awful?"

"Sometimes the music affects people in strange ways." He stares down at the ground, his jaw muscles twitching over and over again. I know he's talking about himself, but should I ask him for specifics? I can tell it's something that really bothers him.

"Is that what's so special to you about this place? Are you a John Lennon fan?"

"No. I am a fan, but this is why I come here." He points at the ground.

The word *Imagine* is embedded in the sidewalk, a mosaic of tiny tiles.

Ty explains. "There were so many fans and people in mourning always gathered around their apartment building, it was causing problems for the residents. So, Yoko Ono donated a million bucks to this area of the park—it's shaped like a teardrop—to create this memorial for him. It's called Strawberry Fields. A lot of times when I come here, people have it decorated with rose petals in peace signs and stuff." He shrugs. "I don't know . . . It just kinda makes me think."

"What do you think about when you look at this?"

He folds his arms across his chest, appearing to cave in on himself. His body language is screaming pain. "I don't know."

I lower my voice. "Sure you do. Just tell me."

He looks up at me. "If I tell you this, will you answer a question for me?"

I shrug. How bad could it be? I have no big secrets anymore. "Sure."

"When I stand here and look at this, I think about the cost of fame. I wonder if the choices I'm making now are going to hurt me later, or hurt people I love later. And I wonder if it's going to be worth it. I mean . . . if someone I love gets hurt, am I going to look at what happened and say it was still worth it? Still put my happiness before theirs?"

"That's pretty dark." I laugh a little, trying to lighten the mood.

"But it's valid. People make choices all the time, but they don't realize how much those choices can affect somebody else. Maybe we're wired to be selfish. Maybe we're supposed to just do what we want to do, and if somebody's hurt in the process, so be it." His words reflect almost exactly the thought process I went through after coming home from college. I had a choice, and I made it based on avoiding causing pain to the people I loved. I wonder where I'd be right now if I'd been more selfish . . . if I'd put my own happiness ahead of the good of my family.

"It doesn't sound like you're wired that way," I say. "You seem to be very concerned about how your choices are going to affect other people." It makes me like him more than I already did, to know we feel the same way about people who are important to us. How can he be like this *and* be a jerk at the same time? He can't . . . not deep down, anyway. This man has a conscience. I think in this industry it's rare. The men who are fathers to my sisters and me don't have one—or at least it's a very belated anomaly that they do.

"My life is dark sometimes," he says. "I guess it's appropriate for me to have dark thoughts once in a while."

This sounds too much like a pity party for me to indulge anymore. "Come on . . ." I punch him lightly in the arm. "What's so dark about your life? You're playing lead guitar in your favorite band, the band you love more than anything in the world. So people boo you once in a while . . . Who cares?"

"You'd be surprised how much it hurts, even for an asshole like me." He smiles bitterly as he slides his sunglasses back on.

I think about it for a little while and nod. "Maybe I wouldn't be able to brush it off so easily if it were me either."

"I don't know. You seem pretty tough."

"I can be tough. But I don't think I'm nearly as hardcore as some of the people who live in this city."

"I don't think either one of us is."

We stand there staring at the memorial for a long time. I lose track of how many minutes go by, and I like it; I like getting lost in time with him. He's two feet away from me, and it's not like we're holding hands or anything, but it feels intimate and I don't want it to end.

"So . . . I get to ask you a question now," he says.

"That was the deal." I try to sound bright and unconcerned, even though I'm worried about how deep he's going to try and dig. I don't want him to know that he's affected me so much.

"Who is your father?"

Phew. That's an easy one. I shrug. "I have no idea."

"Can you explain that to me?" He pulls his sunglasses off. "It's a personal question. If you don't want to answer it, that's cool. But I really wish you would."

I get the impression he wants to be closer to me. That's all the motivation I need to tell him my secrets. "The story is actually pretty simple and short. My mom and her two best friends were groupies of the band. They followed Red Hot around for a couple years. They all got pregnant around the same time, with someone or some*ones* in the band, and then they left. End of story."

"Why didn't they bother to find out who the fathers were, though? Didn't they care?"

"Of course they cared. That's our mothers' problem, actually . . . They care too much. They wanted to protect us. Knowing who our fathers were was a lot less important than keeping us out of their crazy world . . . keeping us safe."

"So the band set them up in some commune in Maine?"

I shake my head. "No. The band was not involved in that. Not directly."

"What do you mean?"

I sigh. "I don't really want to talk about this. It makes me upset, and I would rather stay chilled out." Every time Ty asks for more details, I feel anger toward my mothers, and I know that's not right. The ones I should be angry with play in a band called Red Hot. I gesture at the mosaic. "This memorial is really nice and this last half hour with you has been nice too." I look up at him, pleading. "Let's not ruin it, okay?"

He nods curtly. "I agree. So, what are your plans after this walk?"

"That is a great question. One I don't have an answer to." My mind swims with options. I could call my sisters again. I could go have another hot dog. I could try a slice of one-dollar pizza. I could take a nap in my hotel room and try to get rid of the rest of this headache. But none of those options sounds very appealing. If I'm going to be honest with myself, I would say I want to spend more time with Ty, but that would be crazy. A mistake. Inviting trouble.

"I have some shopping to do," he says. "You want to go with me?"

"Shopping?" That doesn't sound too awful. "What are you looking for?"

"I've got to get some clothes. All I have for hanging around are these dirty jeans and a couple T-shirts." He looks down at himself. "I need some new stuff. Nicer stuff, maybe."

"I thought the grunge thing was part of your look."

"No, not quite. I don't usually look quite this rough. I lost a lot of my stuff recently."

"You lost your clothes?" I'm trying to imagine how he could have managed to lose all but a few items of clothing, but I'm not coming up with any ideas.

"Kind of. More like they were stolen." He looks embarrassed.

"What was stolen? Your whole wardrobe?" I laugh. He can't be serious.

"Yeah."

"No way. How?"

He lowers his voice, looking left and right suspiciously before he answers. "There's this group of kids who like to break into celebrities' places and steal their clothes."

"Seriously?" I stare at his face, trying to determine from his expression whether he's pulling my leg, but I can't see his eyes through those damn glasses. He sure sounds like he's telling the truth, however.

"Yes. It seriously happened. I don't like to talk about it, though."

"Why? Because it's still an open investigation with the police?"

"No, because it's embarrassing."

"Why is it embarrassing? I'd think it would be more angering than anything else."

He whispers, "Because they took my drawers too."

Now he's talking crazy. "The *drawers* from your *dresser*? Like the actual drawers? What did they do . . . bring a moving truck?"

He smiles awkwardly. "No, not those drawers. The other kind. *Underwear*."

"Oh." I can't help it; I giggle and whisper probably way too loudly, "They stole your *panties*?"

He pushes on my arm. "Shush. Men don't wear panties."

"But . . . You must have a huge wardrobe, though." I can't imagine how someone could steal the entire contents of a person's closet and not get caught in the middle of the act. "I heard celebrities never wear the same thing twice."

"My wardrobe wasn't that big. There's a person with us on the tour who's responsible for buying all my clothes, and after I wear what they buy, we usually just get rid of it. It's too hard to find Laundromats on tour. So there wasn't much there . . . just jeans, T-shirts, other stuff . . ."

"Your *drawers*." I wink at him.

"Yeah." He tries not to smile but fails.

"Okay . . . well . . . I guess you're starting from scratch, then. Do you have any idea what you're looking for?"

"We're going to be working in the studio for a while, so I can afford to put a little bit of a wardrobe together."

"Any special style?" I'm getting into the idea of helping him shop. I know for a fact he looks good in both casual and formal clothes. I wonder if he's wearing *drawers* right now . . . I swear I try not to look down . . .

He shrugs, the movement forcing my eyes upward.

"I don't know," he says, oblivious to my ogling. "I figure I should upgrade my look a little bit. I could use a second opinion, so I don't make a wrong move."

"And you think I'm qualified to do that?"

He looks at my outfit. "Well . . . not exactly. But you're better than me all by myself."

I reach out and gently slap his shoulder. "You are so rude."

"Hey, I like the hippie chick look. But it's not the look I'm going for, for myself. If you tell me you're more than a one-hit wonder, then maybe I can trust your judgment."

"I don't know if I'm more than a one-hit wonder. I'm into natural materials and I'm not going to apologize for it."

"Hey, yeah, me too. That's cool. You don't see me wearing leather pants, do you?"

I look him up and down. "No. And you get points for wearing canvas shoes, too."

"See? I can be a hippie dude."

I laugh at that. There's no way he could ever be a hippie dude. He smells too nice for that. "Okay, fine. I'll shop with you for a little while, but at some point I'm going to need to have a conversation with my sisters, so if they call I'm going to abandon you and leave you to your own devices."

"No problem. Come on." He reaches out and takes my hand.

I'm in too much shock to fight him off. His fingers interlace with mine, and I try to act like it's the most casual, normal thing in the world to be holding hands with Ty Stanz. It means nothing. We're just two people going on a normal, casual, no-big-deal shopping trip together.

My heart is not buying that nonsense *at all.* It's hammering wildly in my chest, telling me that this is no casual thing and that of course it's a big deal. People don't hold hands with their acquaintances or friends; they hold hands with people they feel close to, people they want to touch.

I'd really love to not get overly girly about this, but it's impossible. In my experience, handholding leads to kissing and then sometimes to a whole lot more. *Oh God, don't let him try to kiss me!* I think about that for a few seconds and then alter my request: *Okay, God, maybe let him kiss me once, just to see what it's like.*

CHAPTER TWENTY-FOUR

The first store we go into is way too foofy. There are turtlenecks on every mannequin and so much plaid I feel like I've been teleported to Scotland. I check out one of the price tags on a cashmere sweater and nearly choke on my own tongue. *Fifteen hundred dollars? Are they insane?*

Ty is looking around with a pained expression.

"You look constipated," I say, trying not to laugh.

"I think I am getting constipated looking at these things."

"Why are we even here?" I giggle.

"Because our style consultant told me this is where I need to shop."

"Your style consultant needs surgery."

"Surgery?" he asks, looking at me all confused.

"To get the stick removed from her butt."

"That's what I'm thinking." He grins. "You want to get out of here?"

I nod. "Please." This clothing is hurting my eyes. Everywhere I look there's another dead animal: a fox fur collar on a suede coat; leather jackets; crocodile bags; snakeskin shoes. *Ugh.* It's no better than a taxidermy shop.

We head out into the cool air, Ty's hand easily sliding into mine. My heart soars once more. *It wasn't a fluke before!* I thought he was going to ignore the handholding thing and pretend it never happened, but now it's becoming a *thing*; we walk outside, we hold hands. *Whee!*

I'm in high school for the first time, living the dream! I will my palms not to get sweaty.

He uses his free hand to point across the street. "What about that place?"

I check out the mannequins in the window. They don't seem nearly as pretentious as the others. "That looks promising."

We jaywalk, causing several cars to honk at us. We run and I squeal a little, freaking out that I'm breaking the law and doing something dangerous. Ty drags me along and then jumps up to the curb, laughing maniacally.

"That was crazy," I say, out of breath. "Don't do that again."

"Too much living on the edge for you?" he asks as he pushes the door open.

"Yeah. Too close to the edge. I like to be more in the middle."

"Living life in the middle. Hilarious." He smiles at me so big, it makes my insides turn to jelly.

I have to look away to keep from saying something stupid. *Time to get serious and stop all this girly-girling around.* I drop his hand and search through the racks to find a few things that I like. I hold items up and he either nods or gives me a thumbs-down. By the time I have five of them gathered, he's ready to leave.

"Aren't you going to try them on?"

"No. I hate trying clothes on."

"But we don't know if they fit."

He quickly looks at the tags. "They're my size. Come on, let's pay for them and go."

I don't understand his big rush. "Don't be silly. You need to try these on." He could waste his money in here so easily, and nothing is what I'd consider cheap.

He moves in closer and whispers in my ear, "We're starting to get more attention than I think you want. People are taking pictures."

My heart drops as I look around and realize he's right. There are no fewer than three camera phones pointed right at me. It really pisses me off, and I head for the closest one without thinking. "Do you mind?" I demand in a harsh voice.

The camera slowly goes down. "What?" the young woman says. She looks to be about the same age as I am.

I say it louder because maybe she's hard of hearing. "I said, *Do you mind?* We're trying to have a private moment here."

"Sorry . . . I was just . . ."

"I know what you were *just* doing. You were taking pictures or video of complete strangers, thinking you have the right to do that. But you don't, okay? We're allowed to shop without people taking pictures of us."

Poor Ty. No wonder he's always cranky. I have never appreciated the gift of anonymity more than I do now. It makes me realize how smart our mothers were for taking us so completely away from this scene. My sisters and I would have been so messed up, especially Em. Just imagining her being pinned down by a stranger like this infuriates me.

The woman turns and walks away, and I shift sideways to see the other person still filming me. The third person has turned her back and gone the other way, but lady number two is still at it. *Oh, this is so not happening.*

I walk over to her and put my hand right over the phone and shove it down. "Put it away."

The girl gives me a look to kill. "Bitch, you have no right to touch my phone!"'

I'm taken aback by her anger. "Did you just call me a bitch?" I turn to look at Ty, to ask him if he believes this craziness, but he's at the register, putting a wad of cash on the counter.

"Yeah, I called you a bitch. You don't touch my stuff without my permission, you hear?" She moves in closer, her boobs just inches from mine.

I play this game with my sisters all the time. It's called chicken, and I never lose. "How about you stay out of my private business, and then I won't have to touch your stuff. How about *that*?" I bump her with my boobs. *Chicken? Are you chicken yet?*

"There ain't no such thing as private business here. This ain't *your* store." She lifts her arm and waves it around her, effectively wafting her body odor up into my nose. "You're out here in public, just like me. I can take pictures of whatever I want in public." She smiles in full satisfaction of her knowledge of the rules of photography. She backs up a step, but her head is bobbing and weaving something awful. Her cranium looks like it could get disconnected from her spine at any moment.

I stare at her, not sure she's right about that "being in public" thing. Maybe that is the law, but it sure isn't very polite. "You know . . . people like you are the reason why people like Ty don't want to leave their houses anymore."

"Oh, yeah?" she laughs.

"Yeah. Why don't you just give him a break? Let him live his life?"

"What's it to you? You his new girlfriend?" She looks me up and down and snorts. I don't think I passed her inspection.

"No." I scowl at her, wishing I were wearing a cleaner patchwork skirt. "I'm a friend. And I'm worried about him, so why don't you just mind your own beeswax."

"Beeswax?" She snorts really loudly, waving her hand between us as she slowly backs away. "Fine, bitch. I'll mind my own *beeeeswax*. And I'm gonna take some more pictures too. Ha!" She quickly throws her camera up and takes a picture of my face, the flash going off in my eyes.

I stand stock-still, gritting my teeth together and slowly closing my eyes, white lights ghosting against the inside of my lids. I'm going to count to five, and if that *person* is still here when I open them again, I'm probably going to have to slap her.

Five . . . four . . . three . . . two . . .

Somebody touches my arm gently, making me practically jump out of my skin, but then I hear Ty's voice in my ear and I calm down about the idea of giving someone a kung fu chop to the throat. I open my eyes. The woman is gone and my idea of heaven is standing next to me, but he doesn't look any happier to be there than I am.

"Let's go. I've got what I need."

I look down at my hand. I'm still holding a denim jacket. "What about this?"

He grabs it and hangs it on the nearest rack. "Too nineteen eighties. Come on, let's go."

"You're probably right." I leave the store wholly depressed, Ty having to practically drag me now because holding hands doesn't seem nearly as fun as it did before.

"You can't engage with those people," he says after a few blocks. "It's pointless."

"But she was so *rude*. I don't know why people have to be so damn *rude*."

"Believe me, I know." We stand at the corner waiting for the light to change. "But they're fans, so you just have to deal with it as best you can and move on."

I look up at Ty, feeling so bad for him and anybody else who has to go through this. "But you should be allowed to go out in public and live your life without people stalking you."

"It's the price we pay." He's not looking at me.

I tug on his hand until he does. His eyes are bloodshot, redder than they were before. Is he sad? Mad? I can't tell.

"But you deserve better than this."

"This is what I signed up for. I knew if I became associated with the band that I was going to be sacrificing my private life. We all know this. You make a deal with the devil and you've gotta live with the consequences. Payment always comes due."

I'm silent all the way to the next store. It's a lot like the first one we went into—very chichi, as Carol would say. Foofy is what I call it.

"Are we going to be able to find something in here for you?" The whole idea of shopping is no fun for me anymore, and the wall-to-wall cashmere certainly isn't making it any better.

"Probably not, but I don't think they let people with cameras in here."

I scope the place out and realize he's right. There is a guard at the door and anybody who looks like the camera-carrying type isn't allowed in. "Maybe that's why your style consultant sent you to that first place." I can't think of anything more depressing right now than being forced to buy clothing made of animal skins and fur because of strangers who refuse to respect another person's privacy. No wonder our mothers moved us out into the middle of nowhere.

"Maybe. Or maybe she's just really out of touch. What do you think about this?" He holds up a jacket that looks really nice. I walk over and touch it, then look at the label. "It's real suede. If you don't mind wearing animal hide, I guess it's cool." I feel like crying.

"I've worn plenty of them before." He looks closer at it.

I shrug.

He puts it back on the rack. "Maybe we can find some synthetic suede instead."

My heart lifts the tiniest bit. *He cares what I think.*

He turns around, catching me smile. "You are such a hippie chick." He smiles too.

I sigh. "Guilty."

"It's cool. I'm not giving you shit for it." He unexpectedly grabs me by the side of the head, leans in, and kisses me on the forehead before he walks away.

I instantly go warm from my scalp to my toes. *He kissed me!* It wasn't on the lips, but it doesn't matter—it was tender and caring, qualities I don't think Ty shows the world very often. We're growing closer.

I don't know why or how it's happening, but for this past hour, he has ceased being a jerk. I feel like I'm finally getting to know the real Ty.

There's something behind those sunglasses, hidden in those eyes of his, that makes me believe he's incredibly sad. Something that made him so desperate to get away from wherever he was, he sold his soul to the devil to get out . . . because I don't believe it was just his love for Red Hot that spurred his ambition.

I wonder if I'm going to find out what that thing is. Or if I even want to. My inner conscience that has a voice very much like my mother's tells me I'm probably better off not knowing what fueled his rise to the top. I have a feeling that the more involved I become with him, the farther I'm going to fall down a rabbit hole of my own. I just hope the devil isn't waiting at the bottom, ready to offer me a deal I can't refuse.

CHAPTER TWENTY-FIVE

As we're leaving the store, I hear my phone ringing in my bag. I stop immediately and dig around until I find it. I look at Ty apologetically. "I have to grab this."

He nods and takes my hand again, guiding me while I answer the call.

"Hi, it's me," I say. I have an attack of the sillies now that I'm finally talking to my sisters. I have so much to tell them. *I'm holding hands with a rock star!*

"Hi, Me," Em says laughing. "You sound happy."

"I might be." I can't give her details because the man behind my happiness is standing right next to me, guiding me toward a coffee shop.

"Yay! Tell me about it."

"What's going on with you guys?" I say, trying to direct her away from the subject of me and the crazy emotions that I can barely control.

"Well, we went and got you another plane ticket, but now I'm thinking that was a mistake."

"Why?"

"Because I talked to Carol. It sounds like maybe you have other plans now?"

"I'm not sure. I really need to talk to you about it, but now is not exactly the time."

Ty signals a time-out with his hands using a *T* formation.

"Hold on a second." I put the phone off to the side. "What's up?" I ask him.

"I'm going to run in here and grab us a couple drinks. Why don't you sit down at the table there and talk to whoever that is?"

I nod and take a seat, not wanting to waste any more time. I watch as he walks into the café, mesmerized for a few moments by his sexy swagger, and then put the phone back to my ear.

"Okay. I'm back. I have a few minutes to talk in private."

"Who are you with? Is it that Ty guy again?"

"Yes. He's going into a café to get us some coffee."

"Does he know you don't drink the stuff?"

"No, probably not." This is crazy. The lead guitarist for one of the hottest bands in the country is buying me a coffee I won't drink in Manhattan. If someone had told me a month ago that this is what my life would look like, I would have told them to take another hit off their bong.

"Okay. So what's the deal?" she asks.

"Is Rose there?"

"No. She still has that porcupine at the clinic. I guess he got hit by a car pretty bad. She's waiting on the vet to show up."

Standard-issue Rose emergency. "Okay, well, I may have already made up my mind, but I would really like to know your opinion anyway."

"Okay, shoot. Tell me all the details, and I will be perfectly honest with you."

"Okay . . . Where do I start? . . . This morning at breakfast, Red made me an offer. He wants to know if I can stick around here for a couple weeks and help them update their image a little bit."

"That's what Carol said. And how do you feel about it?"

How do I feel about it? When I try to concentrate on that question, my head starts to spin with what-ifs and wherefores. "I have mixed feelings."

"I'll bet. But which is the overriding feeling?"

"I don't know . . ." I bite my lip hard. My pulse is racing. This is so nuts. I was supposed to come here, tell those men to screw off, and go home. *Easy peasy, not so lemon squeezy.*

"Yes, you do. Don't be coy with me. I can hear it in your voice. I know you're thinking something crazy. *And* you're being silly. It has something to do with this Ty guy. Don't pretend it doesn't."

"Fine." I let out a long breath, blowing the air up into my hair. I'm sweating with nerves again. "I hate that you can read my mind like that."

"I've been reading your mind since we were six months old."

"I know, don't remind me. Anyway, it's true . . . He's intriguing."

"Is that all?"

"Well, he's talented. He's also pretty insightful. And he's . . . a little tortured."

"Okay, now we're getting somewhere. So this guy is a tortured genius and you're going to help solve all his problems."

I lose my smile. "Don't say it like that. That sounds mean."

"I'm not being mean. But you *are* the solutions girl. Whenever there's an issue, you're the one who's going to resolve it."

"Is there a problem with that?" I don't want to remind her that this is why I'm here in New York in the first place, dealing with all of *our* issues, and it's also why I live on the farm instead of somewhere else.

"There's nothing wrong with it at all, unless you run up against somebody who will take advantage of it."

"What do you mean?" Her comment sounds ominous.

"What I mean is, I don't know this guy Ty. Is he a good person? Maybe he sees that you're somebody who can be taken advantage of."

My heart sinks as her words penetrate and start to make sense. It is kind of strange that Ty was rude to me . . . *until* he found out exactly who I am and what I mean to the band. *Could it be that he's using me? Being nice to gain something for himself?* I want to jump to his defense, because I really don't think these things are true, but that wouldn't be fair to my sister. She's just telling me how it is, being dead honest, and I appreciate that.

"I know what you mean. But I don't know."

"What don't you know?"

"I don't know if this is a situation I need to avoid or one that was tailor-made for me."

"Well, huh . . . Are you getting any vibes either way?"

The seed of doubt she planted has taken root. *Why exactly is Ty holding my hand now?* "I'm getting vibes, but I don't know if I can trust them."

"Because it's coming from that guy, right?"

"Some of them, yes. We held hands, and I felt like I was in high school."

"Except that we were homeschooled," she says wryly. "So what does that even feel like?"

"You know how often we talked about high school and how cool it would be if we were walking down those halls and had a locker and a book bag. Believe me, my imagination was very vivid back in those days. I just *knew* what it would feel like to hold a boy's hand and walk down the hallway with everyone watching."

"Me too," she says sadly. "I get it." After a pause she continues. "You said some of the vibes were from him."

"Yes. And the band, of course. I mean, I was supposed to come here and tell them off, but now I'm thinking about working with them? I know Red wants to talk to me about our lives and about our moms. I know I should just walk away from that, but he says there's more to the story and I can't help but be curious."

"Of course you can't. That's totally natural. We're curious too, Rose and I."

This is part of the reason my sisters and I are so close; we suffered the same dreams lost or never realized, and we're surrounded by the same history, upbringing, and outlook about the world. We get each other on a level no one else could. I'm so glad I'm talking to Em right now. She'll help me make the right decision, untainted by silly girly emotions.

"When Red was talking about this job, my first instinct was to say no; but I think this is something I *could* do. I think it might be fun. And it's only for two weeks."

"Listen, you don't need to sell me on it. It sounds like you want to do it, so I think you should."

"But what if something goes bad with Ty?"

"What does it matter? It's either going to go bad because you leave, or it's going to go bad because something terrible happens between you and him because you're there. But it could go well too. And he's not the only reason you're staying. He's just a minor character in your world right now. The men in the band are part of our history, like it or not, and knowing our history might do you and us a lot of good. We won't know until we hear it, though."

"But I'll only know what will happen with Ty or our fathers if I stay."

"Yes. Only if you stay. So, how important is this guy to you? How much do you care about him?"

"I just met him. I don't know if I care about him at all."

"It sounds like you do, though. Even though you've only known him for a little while." She's mocking me, but I deserve it. I sound like a total wiener. Does that stop me from seeking validation? No.

"Maybe it's because I'm that problem-solver person that you claim I am. Maybe I see that he has problems and I want to resolve them."

"I don't know. I think I was too hard on you earlier. We meet people with problems all the time, and you don't try to solve them. You do it for people who intrigue you in some way or for people you care about. Does it mean you're going to fall in love with Ty or he's going to fall in love with you? Probably not. But you could have some fun in the meantime."

"Are you suggesting what I think you're suggesting?" I smile. Now my mind is going places it probably shouldn't.

"Hey, you're a single woman in New York City. I hear that's *the* place for romance. I don't think you should have too many rules assigned to your situation. And even if there were rules, you should probably break them."

"Maybe you could come up here and join me." My fear is getting the better of me. Having one of my sisters by my side could make all the difference.

"Maybe another time," she says, going a little cagey. "I'm in the middle of a project right now."

"A project?" I get excited for her. "Are you painting again?" She hasn't created anything in a long time. She only works when the spirit moves her, and it doesn't move her very often anymore.

"I don't know. Maybe. I think you going down to New York has really stirred some things up for me."

"You are preaching to the choir, sister." I laugh. Yes, our lives have become very stirred up, and nothing much has even happened yet. *If I work for the band, will it get worse or better? Will I regret it? Will it be terrible enough to cause bad blood between myself and my mothers?* I don't believe that this could happen. I love those ladies more than life itself, and whatever I learn about their pasts is not going to change that fact. I feel like I'm about to embark on a journey of self-discovery, learning about how all these people made decisions that impacted the direction my life has gone in since the day I was born.

We sit for a moment in companionable silence. My mind wanders and only comes back when Em speaks. "So, what are you going to do, sister of mine?"

"I think I'm going to do it." I nearly have a heart attack hearing myself say those words. "If it doesn't work out, I can always quit and come home, right?"

"Yes," she says cheerily. "Because this time I got you an open ticket, and all you have to do is go to the counter at the airport and show them your ID and you're good."

This feels like an amazingly good omen. "An open ticket? Is that even possible?"

"If you pay a little extra, it is."

"I hope you didn't use up too much of your savings."

"What am I going to do with my savings? I never leave here."

"You really should come down here sometime." I look around the city, at all the people hustling and bustling. It's starting to feel more familiar to me now. I'm not looking at it in disgust anymore; now I see . . . possibilities. "Manhattan really is something else. It's electric. You can feel the energy humming all the time. It gets into your body."

"Sounds completely nerve-racking."

I laugh. "It is a bit at first, but you get used to it. It might actually be a little addictive." My blood is racing at the idea that I could actually fit in here. I imagine myself as a big-city businesswoman and it makes me almost giddy with excitement. This is the perfect situation; I'm going to live this other life for two weeks. I'm not abandoning my family; I'm just here temporarily. I'll be back at the farm in no time.

"I think I'll be happy to just see some pictures and get a report about what's happening once in a while," Em says. "Will you keep us posted?"

"I will for sure. I guess I need to go talk to Lister and tell him what I'm thinking about doing, and see what he says. Maybe he'll be a jerk again, and then I won't want to work with them anymore and my problems will be solved."

"And what are the chances of that?" she asks, laughing.

"I know, right?"

Ty opens the door with his elbow and comes out balancing two cups in his hands.

"I have to go; Ty is back."

“Okay. Don’t do anything I wouldn’t do.”

“Well, that doesn’t leave me with very many options, does it?”

She laughs. “Be good. I love you. And I’m going to tell Rose everything, okay?”

“Go ahead. And call me anytime you want.”

“I will. Love you, love you, *love* you. I’m so proud of you too.”

I pause for a minute before hanging up. “Proud of me? Why?”

“Because . . . you’re being bold and brave and beautiful. And I wish I could be more like you.”

“And I wish I could be more like you: artistic, sensitive, sweet, and kind.” I lower my voice to confessionary levels. “I have been so mean to people since I got here.”

“No, you haven’t. You’ve been standing up for what’s right, like you always do. I know who you are, and you don’t have a mean bone in your body.”

She makes my heart melt with her kindness. “Love you, sister.”

“Love you too.”

I fold up the phone and reach up to take the cup from Ty.

“I thought I remembered you don’t like coffee, so here’s a green tea.”

My heart goes as warm as the beverage in my hand.

CHAPTER TWENTY-SIX

The walk back from the café to my hotel remains mostly a blur, but the part where Ty comes up in the elevator with me to my room and then stands outside my door . . . *that* will be burned into my memory for the rest of my life.

"What are you doing tonight?" he asks.

He's playing it cool, so I'm going to try to do the same. "I'm not sure. I have to talk to Lister and see what he says about all this stuff."

"All of what stuff?"

I don't know how much the band has shared with Ty about this job they proposed to me; it can't be much because he hasn't mentioned it, and now he's wondering why I need to talk to Lister. Outside my hotel room doesn't really seem like the place to talk about it either. *Best to be vague.*

"Just some things I discussed with Red this morning."

"Oh. So . . . are you going back home today?"

"Maybe. It depends on what happens with Lister."

"Cool." He looks over his shoulder down the hall and then at the floor between us. "If you're going to be around, maybe . . . you want to come over to my place for dinner?"

"Maybe. I mean . . . sure. Will you be the chef?"

"Nah, I'll get takeout. I'm not much of a cook."

My heart is beating rapidly. This sounds like a date. And I shouldn't be surprised he's asking me out or over to his house, because we've been holding hands for hours it seems and we've done nothing but share goofy grins. I'm nearly twenty-five years old and this should be a no-big-deal kinda thing, but try to tell that to my heart, cuz it ain't buying it.

"How about if I call you and let you know after I meet with Lister?" I reach into my bag and find my phone, pulling it out and opening it up. "I think I have your number in here."

"Sure. Give me a ring. Let me know."

"What will you do if I can't make it?" I'd hate for him to be waiting around all day for my call.

He shrugs. "I don't know. Order in. Drown my sorrows in a bottle of whiskey."

I push on his shoulder. "Stop. Don't try to make me feel guilty."

He grabs my hand and holds it between us. "I'm just kidding. But I would like to see you again before you leave." He steps toward me, closing the space between us.

I've never been this near to him before. My pulse is racing. His face is messed up from his smeared makeup and earlier sadness, but he's still the most gorgeous man I've ever seen. He moves closer still, and his breath puffs across my lips as he whispers, "I really want to kiss you right now."

Oh, what the hell . . . why not? "Go ahead and do it then," I whisper back.

Suddenly, our lips are touching. And then his hand is on the side of my face and the kisses get deeper. Our tongues slide against each other, hot and wet. My hands go up to rest on his shoulders as my body catches fire. His free hand slides down to my waist, sending chills all up and down my spine. That bed is so close . . .

There's a *ding!* and the elevator doors slide open. It takes a few moments for the sound to penetrate my brain and connect, telling me what's going on. I quickly pull away, just in time to see a man turn left out of the elevators and walk down the hallway rapidly. He's hunched over and I can't see anything but his rear view, but he looks . . . *so familiar.* He turns a corner and I lose sight of him. Trying to place his form and body language is an exercise in frustration.

Ty looks over his shoulder. "What's going on?"

"I don't know . . . There was some guy. He looked familiar, but I don't know why."

"Was he wearing a uniform?"

"No, he wasn't. He was wearing a leather jacket."

Ty looks at me and grins teasingly. "Like nine out of ten people in New York City right now."

I smile too, realizing how silly I sound. "Yeah, pretty much." He must think I'm so naïve.

That kiss was really amazing, but now that my blood pressure has calmed down and my brain is back to working at full capacity, I don't think we should repeat the experience. I'm standing too close to a hotel bed that could easily fit the two of us, even if we were rolling around having crazy sex. Now is not the time to enter into that kind of relationship with Ty, especially if I'm going to be working as a consultant for the band for two whole weeks. A lot can happen in that period of time, which could seriously overcomplicate things that are already crazy.

"I'll wait for your call, then?" he asks, pulling back.

"Yep. Maybe if Lister can meet me soon, I'll be able to call in the next couple of hours."

"Great." He walks backward all the way to the elevator, giving me a thumbs-up after he presses the call button.

I don't want to act like I'm mooning and fawning over him—even though I have the very strong urge to be that desperate, nutty person—so I take out my key card and use it in the door before he gets onto the elevator. Once inside, I pause a moment to take a couple breaths.

Damn, damn, damn-damn-damn. He is so hot. Even just imagining Ty in my hotel bedroom makes my face and other more intimate parts of my body grow warm. Leaving him out there was a great decision; I just wish it didn't bring so much regret with it. Trying to be good when I want to be bad is so hard!

Once I'm more or less under control, I use the bathroom really quickly and then wash my face. My cheeks are flushed and overly warm. I'm pretty sure I'm not sick, though . . . unless falling in lust with somebody is an illness. It kind of feels like it is. I'm embarrassed over how easy it would have been for me to fall into bed with Ty. All he would've had to do was ask. I should be grateful that he was gentleman enough not to do that, but part of me is disappointed. I am one confused and sexually frustrated woman, that's for sure.

I'm tempted to call my sisters and talk to them about it, but I don't want them to know how easily I'm falling for this guy. They'll remind me of how little action we get out at the farm and how it's obviously me being desperate. I don't want to hear that right now. I want to believe there's a spark between Ty and me and that he senses it too.

I walk over to the chair that's facing the windows and sit down, contemplating my day. It started out with a bang, having tea with Red, and then just got better and better from there. And now here I am ready to commit to two weeks of working with the band, something I would never have imagined I'd do. *Surreal.* My life is officially crazy. But there's no point in delaying the inevitable, so I grab my phone from my bag and call Lister's office. Surprisingly, he comes on the line within minutes instead of making me wait or having his gatekeeper tell me he's not available.

"Amber. What can I do for you?"

"I had a conversation with Red this morning, and he said I should contact you after I made a decision about what I wanted to do."

"Yes. He mentioned something to me about it this morning. Apparently, he's made you some kind of offer? Some sort of paid position?"

I can't tell from his tone whether he approves. I really shouldn't care whether he does or not, but his lack of readable emotion is making me nervous and cranky. *How is this man always able to make me feel less than adequate?* "Yes," I say, soldiering on. "It's a two-week thing. Nothing permanent."

"Okay."

He's not going to help me out in this conversation at all. *Jerk.* "So, if I'm going to accept his offer, what do I need to do?"

"We can start by you coming to my office to sign a contract, or I can send a courier over to where you are—at the hotel I assume—and you can sign there and send it back with the courier when you're done."

I wasn't expecting this answer. "A contract? You want me to sign a contract?"

"Yes. It's standard procedure. Anyone who works with the band signs one."

This sounds a lot more serious than what Red and I were discussing. But after I think about it for a few seconds, I realize I don't want to interfere in Red's business any more than I already will be by telling him and the rest of the band what I think they should do to update their look. If this is their standard practice, I'd better just wrap my head around it and get it done.

"Okay. I don't have anything better to do, so maybe I'll just come there to your office now?"

"I'll have it ready for you. Would you like me to send you a car?"

I hate saying yes to that, because it seems like I should be able to walk from here, but my feet are killing me from all of the wandering around I've already done with Ty. "That would be nice. My feet are sore. I went all over Central Park today."

"The hotel receptionist will call you when the car is there."

"Okay. Thank you. I guess I'll see you soon."

"It won't be me you'll be seeing. It'll probably be an associate."

"Okay. Thanks. Bye." I close my phone and think about what he said. *A contract.* It sounds very official. I guess I can understand why a band would need to have one. There's probably something in there saying that I'm not allowed to tell any of their secrets. That makes sense. I can sign something like that, no problem. I have no interest in sharing anything I know about those men with anyone but my sisters and maybe my mothers.

I pace back and forth in front of the windows of my room until I get the phone call telling me that Lister's car is downstairs. I check my watch—thirty minutes from the time I hung up with him. Not bad, considering the traffic out there.

I head downstairs, walking past people sitting at various tables set up in the lobby. Some of them look like businessmen having impromptu meetings and others could be groups of friends, celebrating and laughing. There's a man sitting all alone in the farthest corner with a newspaper open and his one leg crossed over the other, just like Red was doing this morning.

I pause for a moment and stare at him, but when I see his fingers more clearly, I realize it's not Red; this man doesn't have any rings on. He is wearing leather pants, but he has different boots—like the kind a person wears if he's riding a motorcycle. *Is it the guy from the elevator? Maybe he's staying on the same floor as I am. Maybe it's just chance that has me seeing him all over.*

As I walk to the car, I shake off the paranoia that suggests I'm being watched. Red is not stalking me and neither is his evil twin. The man is not that desperate. When he wanted to see me, he left me a message and let me decide whether we met or not. And he sent a lawyer to make contact the first time, right out in the open. There was no sneaking around or weirdness to it. Red strikes me as a very respectful person, so I know he wouldn't spy on me. I'm almost positive. I shake off the chill that comes over me. *Does everyone walk around this city seeing ghosts?*

The car ride to the lawyer's office is uneventful. This time when I reach the lobby, there's a young woman waiting for me, and she smiles and approaches with her hand out. "You must be Amber. I'm Jennifer. I'm here to help you with your contract."

I shake her hand. "Okay, that sounds good."

"Please follow me." She's walking on her three-inch heels like she was born in them. I have to move fast to keep up with her long strides. Her platinum-blond hair hangs straight down her back, not a strand out of place. All the women in this office are really well put together. It must take them forever to get ready in the morning. I have to imagine they're busy in the bathroom ten times a day, too, checking to make sure everything is still perfect. Lister probably sleeps in a suit and polished leather shoes. No wonder he always seems uncomfortable around me. He's probably worried I have cooties. I smile at the thought of chasing him around this office maze with my finger out, threatening to infect him with hippie-itis.

Jennifer leads me into a conference room with a long table. It seems silly for me to be in here just using up one chair; the place is big enough for a board meeting of a Fortune 500 company. There's a folder on the table and it's open with a stack of papers inside.

Jennifer stands next to me and moves the papers around, pointing to them as she explains. "This is our standard NDA . . . a nondisclosure agreement. In this, you're agreeing not to discuss any personal details of the band members or their business with anyone outside of the band. That includes the press but also any of your friends or relatives."

Poo. I had serious plans to tell my sisters every single tiny little microscopic detail. I guess that's not going to happen. At least not until I have their blood oath that they won't tell other people.

She slides another paper out. "This is a contract for services. This is where you agree to provide certain services to the band over the specified period of time indicated here, and to accept the compensation that's being offered here." She points to the number and I nearly choke.

"They're going to give me twenty thousand *dollars*?" I look up at her to see if she's laughing.

"Did you want to negotiate for more?"

I shake my head. "No, twenty is fine." *Negotiate?* Hell, I would have accepted a tiny fraction of that.

"Good," she says, turning the page. "And here is where the band agrees to give you an advance. Once you sign this, I can cut you a check because we have all the money here in our trust account."

According to this paper, they're going to give me half of the money up front. I look up at her. "Does this mean I need to pick up my hotel tab now?" Not that I don't want to, but I'm pretty sure even with this big paycheck, affording the digs I'm in will be pushing it. I'll have to move to another place in a less ritzy area.

"No." She turns a page and points to another paragraph. "Here is where it says that your accommodation and meals are included as part of the deal. And your accommodation is the Four Seasons. I believe you're already staying there?"

I nod, part of my brain going numb at the extravagance. "Uh-huh."

"Fine. You can stay in the same room or you can move to another; it's your choice. Just keep all your receipts for anything you pay for on your own so we can reimburse you. The hotel room and hotel restaurant bills will be paid for directly by the firm."

She turns another page. "Here is the paragraph that provides for you to have transportation."

My eyes skim the page. Apparently, I'm going to have a car and driver. I feel so important.

"And here's the last part where you agree that this is the entire agreement between all of you and that you are not going to seek other compensation from the band or anything else." She hands me a pen.

I take it from her and then flip through the pages so I can get back to the front. This thing is ten sheets of extra-long pager in length. I should probably read it more thoroughly, but I don't want to be rude.

I look up to meet her eyes. "Is there anything else I should know about this contract?"

She tilts her head. "Like what?"

"I don't know . . . I'm not a lawyer. Is there anything in here that's going to bite me in the butt later?"

Her smile slides away. "If you'd rather pay another attorney to review it for you, that's within your rights. In fact, we encourage you to do that." She presses her hands together, one on top of the other.

"No, I don't need to lawyer up or anything like that. I just want to know if you've told me everything that's in here."

"Yes. There are . . . you know, some legalese-type terms that probably won't mean much to you—they're just standard contract provisions—and you can see inside the other paragraphs I pointed out, more detailed explanations of what I've already told you, but it's all there. Why don't you take a moment to read through it? And when you're ready to sign, pick up the telephone there and dial 8-4-1-9."

I nod. "Okay."

She leaves me alone in the room and I stare at the papers. I try reading the first few paragraphs but I keep zoning out and have to reread the same sentences over and over. The only books I like reading are novels—books that have a story that keeps my brain humming along. Nothing could possibly be duller than this document in front of me. My brain isn't humming, it's going blank. I don't think I've had enough sleep to absorb the information.

I turn to the last page and find the line where I need to put my signature. With a flick of my wrist, it's done. I sign the nondisclosure agreement too and look at the other items inside. They're asking me for my Social Security number and other personal information. I guess since they've already found me, it's not like I need to hide my address or anything like that. I fill in all the necessary details and close the folder. Then I wait.

I can't remember the number of the extension she gave me, but surely she'll come check on me any minute. After ten minutes go by, I realize she's probably going to be happy to leave me here all day. I walk out into the hallway, glancing right and left. Everything looks exactly the same and there's nobody around. *Ghost town.*

I head left, assuming this is the way I should go in order to get back to the reception desk, since it's the direction I came from. Unfortunately, my sense of north, south, east, and west proves to be very consistent, and I end up once again in the copy room. The familiar scent of warm paper and chemicals hits me.

"Hi, Linny Lister." I smile at the girl whose back is to me.

She mumbles something under her breath.

"I'm sorry, I didn't catch that."

"I *said* I'll be out in a minute."

I should probably walk away because she doesn't sound happy, but she's just a kid. And she's stuck in this stupid copy room when I'm sure there are a thousand other places she'd rather be. I walk in farther and stop when I'm standing next to her. When I glance sideways at her profile I can see that she's been crying.

I know kids are sensitive about their emotional lives, so I try to make a joke out of it. "Did you get busted for making a copy of your butt?"

She slowly turns her head to look at me. "What did you just say?" She doesn't believe she heard me right. I doubt Uncle Lister would ever ask her a question like that.

I try not to smile. "Are you crying because you got busted for making a photocopy of your butt?"

She looks confused at first. "No?"

I frown. "You didn't do your boobs, did you?"

She starts to smile. "No. I've never done anything like that in here."

I shrug. "I don't think I'd be able to work here without trying it at least once."

She looks back down at the copier and wipes her face. "I'm just having a bad day."

"Yeah. I hear you." I rub her back a little. "I get those from time to time." I tap my finger on the top of the machine. "You know, though . . . Fun with copiers could go a long way toward cheering you up. Regardless of what's getting you down, nothing is more cheerful than a nice photocopy of a set of bare buns." I know this because I saw one once in college and swore to myself if I ever had the chance, I'd make a copy of mine one day. *I think today might be that day!* I'm ridiculously excited.

She chews her lip. "I did used to make photocopies of my hands at Thanksgiving and turn them into turkeys."

"Into turkeys?" Now it's my turn to smile.

"Yeah. You know . . . how you make the fingers look like feathers and the thumb look like the head and you color it in?"

"Ah, yes. I did those at home when I was little." Sadly, our mothers still have them hanging on the fridge every November.

She loses her smile. "Yeah, well, after you do about twenty of them, it gets boring."

"It's time to up your game." I don't know what wild hair gets up my butt in that moment, but making Linny happy becomes tops on my priority list. And although I'm about to walk away from this place with ten grand in my pocket and another ten grand two weeks from now for what I'm sure will prove to be a shit-ton of work—I mean, why else would they pay me so much?—I still feel like I can afford to be generous with my time.

I elbow her gently. "Okay, step aside. Show me how to work this thing. I'm going to show you how to make a really cool photocopy. Better than hand turkeys by a mile."

She stares at me with her jaw open, excitement dancing in her eyes. She points. "Just press the green button, and it'll make one copy of whatever you put on the glass."

I search the machine. "Show me where the glass is. Is it here?" I lift part of the lid on the machine but I don't see anything but more plastic.

"No, you have to grab this part here." She lifts a big section of the machine up to reveal the glass. I'm not quite tall enough to make this happen, so I race over and grab a footstool that I saw in the corner of the room and bring it back. I step up on it and pause to look down at her. "Are you ready for this?"

She nods vigorously, making her ponytail swing around. Her tears are forgotten. "I am totally ready."

I lift my top and take my bra along with it, exposing my breasts. "You'll have to excuse me; I grew up on a hippie commune. We're kind of free with nakedness."

She starts giggling. "Don't worry. I have a pair of my own."

I lean over and place my boobs on the glass, my head to the side. "Whoop! Whoa, that's cold."

"Ohmygod, ohmygod, ohmygod, you are so crazy." She's laughing so hard, she starts to fold in half.

"Where's the green button?" I look to my right but I'm bent too far over to see it.

Linny runs around the other side of me, still laughing and gasping for air. "I got it, I got it. Are you ready?"

"I am ready! Five—four—three—two—one! Hit it, sister!"

She presses the button and a bright light flares up in my face and then slowly scans across my chest.

"Oh my god, you are so crazy," she says between giggles. She runs back to the other side of the machine.

As soon as it's done, I stand up and pull my shirt down. "Behold. The awesome boob shot." I step down from the stool and lean my arm inside the copier over the glass, using the sleeve of my shirt to rub any prints off the surface. Lord knows this firm doesn't need the ghost of Amber's boobs haunting their precious legal documents.

Linny pulls the paper from the tray. She holds it up and giggles, dangling it in front of her. Her eyes are sparkling. "Oh my big butt, *look* at your boobs. They look huge."

I take it from her and look down at them, smiling. "They do. Like two giant headlights." I snag a pen from a nearby counter and quickly sketch the grille of a car around the headlights before handing it back to her. "There. Now that's something you can hang on your fridge at Thanksgiving instead of the turkey hands."

"Are you done?" says a voice from the doorway.

My heart drops into my shoes. Linny's smile disappears and her complexion goes stark white. We both turn at the same time to face the man in the doorway.

Lister's face looks as though it's been carved out of granite.

Holy hell . . . how long has he been standing there?

"I think so," I say with false cheer. I give Linny a quick hug and whisper in her ear before I let go, "Burn that. And no more crying today."

She hugs me back stronger than I expected her to as she whispers her response. "Thank you for cheering me up."

I walk out of the copy room with my head held high, following Lister down the hallway. *Mission accomplished.*

CHAPTER TWENTY-SEVEN

I cannot *believe* I just put my *boobs* on the glass of Lister's copy machine. Am I insane? I think Em was right about me; when I see problems, I feel like I need to solve them, regardless of whether it's a good idea or not. I need to learn how to control myself, because I'm in a city loaded with people who have issues.

Lister goes into the conference room where my papers are still sitting and waits for me to take a seat. My face is burning so hot, I know it has to be flaming red, but he doesn't say a word about it.

"I see that you signed all the documents."

"Yes. I couldn't remember the telephone extension Jennifer gave me, so I went looking for her and ended up . . . in that other room." I finish weakly, knowing that this does not explain why my breasts were pressed up against the glass of his copier.

"Wait here and I'll have a check brought to you for the advance." The jaw muscles on his face are clenching and unclenching.

I look up at him as he towers over me. He's staring at the papers, but I know he sees me. "Are you upset about me taking this job or about the copy machine?" I cringe, waiting for his answer.

"How I feel about anything with regard to you is irrelevant." His voice is as cold as ice.

"Maybe to you, but not to me."

"Let me give you a little tip." He finally looks at me. "You're not going to get very far in this business if you're always worried about what other people think about you."

"What business?"

"The business of working in the music industry."

"But I'm not working in the music industry."

He stares at me with his eyebrows scrunched together.

"What? Why are you looking at me like that again?"

"What did I tell you just a minute ago?"

"I don't know. I don't remember." This is a test and I'm clearly failing it.

"Don't worry about what others think about you. Just do what you need to do." And with that he leaves the room with the folder of papers in his hand.

Ugh, what a jerk. I'm so glad I'm not going to be working with him every day. It's then, as I think this, that I realize I don't even know who I'm going to be working with or how I'm supposed to contact that person. Whoever brings me that check better have some answers for me, or I'm going to have to go hunting for Lister again, and who knows where I'll end up this time. I can't promise there won't be more naked boobs involved, because he's annoying the heck out of me, and I need to release the stress somehow.

I wander around the room, circling the big table for a full ten minutes before Jennifer comes back. She has a big check in her hand, which she slides into an envelope and hands to me along with a copy of everything I signed.

"Thank you," I say, taking it from her and putting it in my bag. "I have a question for you. Who is my contact person for this project?" I feel very official asking this question, like a real businesswoman. I've got plenty of sales experience from my many years running a stall at the farmers' market, but this is the first time I've ever felt big-time.

"I don't know. I think you'd better ask Greg."

"Could you bring me to his office? Every time I try to find my way around here, I get lost."

"He's not available right now."

"Oh. Well. This is very inconvenient." I really don't want to hang around in this office any longer than I already have. "Can I leave a message for him to call me?"

"You certainly can."

I wait for her to say something else, but she leaves me hanging. I have to ask the question or I'm going to wonder all day long. "Did I just leave a message for him or not?"

"With me? Yes, you did. I will tell him that he should call you at his earliest convenience."

I sigh in relief. She gets me. "Okay, cool. Thank you very much." We both walk to the door together, but I hesitate at the threshold when I realize I have a somewhat worthless piece of paper in my bag.

"Is there something wrong?" she asks when she realizes I'm not right behind her.

"I don't have a bank account here in town, and the one that I use back home is a credit union for farmers . . . so I don't know how I'm going to cash this check or whatever." I sure as heck don't want to walk around with ten grand in my bag, but my room has a safe; I could stash most of it in there if I could only cash this thing.

"Wait here for a minute; I'll be right back." Jennifer leaves me alone again.

I expect another ten-minute pause in my day, but she returns in less than half of that, handing me a business card.

"Call this person and make an appointment. He'll help you open an account and give you access to the funds right away. They work with our firm all the time."

I look down at the business card and see that I will soon be dealing with HSBC Bank in their Fifth Avenue branch.

"Thank you. I really appreciate your help. I just need one more thing."

"What's that?" She folds her hands in front of her.

"I need you to show me how to get the heck out of this maze. Every time I try to do it on my own, I somehow end up in the copy room."

She smiles. "Follow me."

I go behind her and don't bother trying to memorize my way out. I don't expect to ever be back here again, so there's no point. I wave at Linny as I go by, and she waves back, no tears in sight and a smile on her face. If I can turn a teenager's mood around, I can certainly consider my day a win. I know when I was her age, my emotions were not that easily swayed.

Jennifer gets me to the reception area and I wave goodbye to her as I step into the elevator to ride it down to the lobby. The same driver who dropped me off is waiting at the curb, and he signals stiffly to me and points to the open back door of the dark vehicle.

"Are you going to take me to my hotel?"

"Yes, if you wish. I am at your disposal for the next two weeks." He doesn't crack even a hint of a smile.

"Cool. What's your name?" I hold my hand out.

His handshake—delivered with an expression that shows he's less than thrilled with the physical touching—is brief and limp. "My name is Mr. Blake."

"Nice to meet you, Mr. Blake. Would you mind doing me a favor?"

He stands at attention, not meeting my eyes. I think he's staring at my earlobe. "What do you need?"

"Before I go back to the hotel, I'd like to go to this bank." I hand him the business card.

He takes a look at it and nods briefly before handing it back to me. "Very well, ma'am."

I rest my hand on the top of the door before I get in. "Please don't call me ma'am. I prefer Amber."

"I'm more comfortable with formality," he says, putting his hand on the door. I think he's hinting at me to get inside and stop bothering him.

I frown. I'm riding around with the fun police. This isn't going to be cool at all. "Okay, whatever you say, Mr. Blake."

I climb into the car and he shuts the door behind me. I sigh. This should be exciting, but being with him is a downer. Still, I can't believe I'm actually here in New York City and staying for a full two weeks with my own driver, and that soon I'll have ten big ones in a new bank account. I feel like Cinderella—Cinderella with a cranky pumpkin-stagecoach driver.

The idea of being a princess makes me think of that cake in Toronto, and my excitement over this new opportunity turns to worry. *Did I just fall into a trap by signing those papers? Am I going to regret this? Did I just sell my soul to the devil?*

CHAPTER TWENTY-EIGHT

I thought the bank was going to be a hassle, but the people in there were really nice. An hour after arriving, I'm walking out the door with a thousand dollars cash in my purse and a brand-new debit card. They also offered me a credit card, but I declined. My mothers have told my sisters and me for years and years that living on credit is a bad idea, so I'm paying cash wherever I go. And the first place I need to go is the underwear store.

After the driver opens the door and helps me get settled in the car, I lean forward, holding on to the front seat. "Mr. Blake, I need to get some clothes. Do you know a good place where they have everything, including underwear?"

He clears his throat, staring straight out the front window. "Yes."

"For regular clothing, I like the vintage stuff. I already went to a few stores around town I liked. My favorite was over in Brooklyn. But they don't really have underwear, and even if they did, I probably wouldn't buy it because it's used."

"Understood."

"Can you take me to a place that does *just* underwear? Not used, but brand-new?" I look at the side of his face. His right eyelid is twitching. "You do know a place that specializes in new underwear, I assume . . ."

"Yes, ma'am."

Gosh, he is so uptight. He really should loosen up. "Good." I pat his shoulder. "Let's go there. But *first* let's also go get some hot dogs at Gray's Papaya, because I'm starving." I scoot back to settle into my seat belt. *Who can say no to a hot dog?* Mr. Blake and I can bond over a papaya drink. Maybe then he'll let me use his first name.

He moves out into traffic.

"Do you like Gray's Papaya? I discovered them yesterday, and even though the dogs gave me a stomachache, I decided it was worth it."

"No."

Dammit. "Oh. That's too bad. I was going to buy you a Recession Special." I look at his reflection in the rearview mirror. I get nothing from him—no reaction whatsoever.

"And a papaya drink. They're really good. Packed with vitamins."

Still nothing.

"There's a guy there who asked me if I was going to eat my hot dog or have sex with it."

Finally, I see a twitch. It's his right eye again.

"Are you a bodyguard too? Because you might need to go in with me and make sure that guy doesn't harass me again."

"No."

"No bodyguarding?"

"No."

"That's too bad." I think about that for a few seconds. "But what if you drop me off somewhere and someone rushes up and attacks me?"

He says nothing.

"Will you try to save me or just get back in the car?"

He sighs but says nothing. He just drives.

I'm getting the distinct impression I will be screwed in the event of a physical altercation.

"When I buy my hot dogs, will I have to eat them in the restaurant or can I eat them here in the car? I don't know the driver/drivee protocol yet."

"I prefer that you not eat them in the vehicle."

"Are you allergic?" I ask in a caring voice.

He frowns but doesn't respond.

"To hot dogs. Are you allergic to hot dogs? Or chili maybe? Or is it the papaya? Because I can skip the papaya if you need me to."

"I'm not allergic."

We weave our way through traffic, and the silence inside the car weighs on me. "So . . . how long have you been driving for Lister?"

"Two years."

"Do you like it?"

"Sometimes."

I smile. "Is now one of those times?"

He doesn't answer.

"Of course it is. I don't know why I even asked. I'll bet it gets boring sometimes, though. Driving around all these people in their stiff, starched shirts."

He says nothing.

"If you were driving a taxi, you'd see lots of people from all over the world. Now *that* would be interesting. Don't you agree?" I lean forward, staring at his profile.

"Sure," he says absently as he takes a right turn.

I do a fist pump. *Yes!* I got him to give me a voluntary answer. I'm going to see if I can get another one before we reach the restaurant.

"Yeah, but you also get held up sometimes, if you're a cabbie, huh? And nobody from the law firm has probably ever held you up."

"No."

"So, there's *that* benefit. Boring passengers, but none of them want to rob you."

"No. Yes."

"Well, you don't have to worry about me. I'm not going to rob you. But I may have to eat my hot dog in your car because I don't want that old guy perving out on me again."

"Do what you have to do."

I smile the rest of the way over to Gray's Papaya. I'll get Mr. Blake to warm up to me eventually. I'll wear him down like drops of water eventually drill holes in boulders.

When I see the sign for the restaurant, I point out the front window. "Would you mind going around the corner over there? I don't want anybody to see me getting out of this car."

He does it without comment.

"I love your car, don't get me wrong. I just don't want anybody thinking I'm stuck-up."

I wait but get no response. I tap him on the shoulder and speak in a hushed tone. "This is the part where you say that I'm not stuck-up."

He pulls around the corner and parks the car. After he lets me out, I pause on the curb, standing next to him. He's several inches taller than I am. "So, you want a Recession Special?" I ask.

"No, thank you." He folds his hands at his waist and stares at my earlobe again.

I reach up and tug at it, just to be sure there's nothing on it. "Okay. But if you change your mind, just shout." I leave him and walk up the sidewalk to the restaurant, taking my place in line. I order like a pro, not even batting an eyelash when she asks me what I want. I already feel like a New Yorker. When I tell her it's to go, she packs it up for me. I'm on my way out when I see that weird old man again. My stomach clenches into a knot.

"Don't even try it," I say as he makes eye contact and looks as though he's about to move in my direction. He's just outside the door and I'm ready to run if necessary. "I am *not* in the mood for your rudeness," I add.

He starts laughing, tipping his head back and opening his mouth really wide so I can get a good view of all the holes where teeth should be. Then I look at where he's standing and see that there's a bunch of belongings and things piled up next to him. *Is he homeless?* I've heard homelessness is a big problem here, but he's the first person I've seen who looks like he might be. I have seen quite a few people here who would look very at home at Glenhollow; on the farm, we often have visitors who don't use soap—they think it's toxic or something. It makes this man suddenly seem less threatening.

I walk over and stop in front of him.

His laughter subsides. "What are you looking at?" he growls.

"Nothing. You. Not to say that you're nothing or anything. I'm just looking at you for no reason." Leave it to me to have an uncomfortable conversation with a homeless man.

"Well, you can just move along. I don't like people staring at me." He's coming off as slightly aggressive now. I should probably be scared of him, but he looks so pitiful, I can't muster the emotion.

"Are you hungry?"

He sticks his bottom lip out at me. "What?"

"I asked you if you're hungry." I raise my voice and enunciate in case he's hard of hearing. *"Are you hungry?"*

"No. I don't need your charity."

"Okay . . ." I hold the paper sack up in my hand so he can see it. "But inside this bag, I've got a chili cheese dog with onions. Are you sure it doesn't sound interesting to you?"

His face loses some of its angry wrinkles. "No. I can't eat onions or chili. Gives me gas and bad breath."

I have to bite my lip not to smile. His teeth are brown, and I can smell his breath from here; I don't think onions are his problem. "How about a dog, no chili, no onions? Would that interest you?"

"Maybe." He shrugs with effort, as if he's carrying a heavy weight on his shoulders. "Who's asking?"

"Me."

"Who's me?"

I roll my eyes. "Amber. Amber Fields is asking if you would like a hot dog without chili or onions."

His voice lowers. "Well, if Amber were offering that hot dog with ketchup and spicy mustard, then I might say yes."

I wink at him. "Stay right here."

I rush back over to the line and get another order going, this one with a cup of coffee and a papaya drink added to it. Maybe I can get some vitamins into this guy with the fruit drink, but if not, at least I'll help him get his caffeine fix. I also get a third hot dog to add to my bag, this one with the same fixings as the old man's. Maybe Mr. Blake will change his mind.

I get out the door as soon as I can, worried my original hot dogs are going to get soggy. I hand the old man his bag. "Bon appétit. What's your name?"

He looks inside. "What's all this?"

"Hot dogs, caffeine, and a fruit drink with vitamins. Eat it, drink it, and stop being so grouchy . . . whatever your name is."

"It's Ray," he says gruffly.

"Okay, Ray. I hope you have a wonderful day." *I totally just pulled a rhyme out of thin air. Sweet.* I walk away with a bounce in my step. It feels good to be nice to people.

He starts laughing as soon as I start walking, and then he shouts at my back loud enough for the whole block to hear. "What are you going to do with your hot dog, Amber Fields? Eat it or have sex with it?"

I know I should be disgusted at his rudeness, but all I can do is giggle. "I'm going to *eat it*, Ray!" I yell over my shoulder. When I look back at him, he's giving me a thumbs-up and laughing enthusiastically enough to arch his back.

This guy's got nothing better to do than to scare the shit out of people with sexual innuendo outside a hot dog store. *There but for the grace of God go I.* I'm going to think of him every time someone makes me want to pull my hair out, because he's a great reminder that life could be a hell of a lot worse.

When I reach the car, Mr. Blake is waiting. He opens the door for me and I slide inside. He gets in too and sits there with his hands on the steering wheel.

"I know you said you didn't want anything, but I got you a dog anyway." I put the wrapped package over the seat into the front with him. "Save it for later. Maybe you'll get hungry and you won't want to stop somewhere for food." I unwrap my first dog and take a big bite.

"Don't spill on the seats," he says.

"Okay, geez, lighten up. I know how to eat a dog without spilling." The moment the words are out of my mouth, a giant blob of chili hits my chest. I quickly clean it up, hoping he won't see me, but then I catch his gaze in the rearview mirror. I roll my eyes and sigh. "Can we go to the underwear store now, please?"

He puts the car in gear and turns out into traffic without a word.

What is it with these New York people? Everyone's so grouchy. I chew on my food, wondering what it will take to cheer up this particular grouch. I smile. Maybe his name is Oscar and he can't help himself. *Oscar the Grouch.* "Is your name Oscar by any chance?" I ask him, secretly giggling inside.

"No."

I can't hold the laughter in anymore. "Okay. Just asking." It cheers me up way more than it should to tease him like that. *What else can I ask him that might loosen him up?*

"Do you have any kids, Mr. Blake?"

"Yes."

"How many?"

"One."

"Cool. I have two sisters but no kids of my own yet. How old is yours?"

"Seven."

"Wow." The word is out before I can stop myself.

He looks at me critically in the rearview mirror.

I cringe. "Sorry. It's just . . . you look like you might have older kids."

Yep. I'm a jerk. I should probably just shove this last hot dog in my mouth and leave it there.

"I married late in life."

I'm relieved and surprised that he's not holding my social gaffe against me. Words pop out of my mouth unbidden. "The confirmed bachelor is wooed away by his one true love." I catch his expression softening in the mirror. *I'm in!*

"What's your wife's name?"

"Mrs. Blake."

I snort. "Good one."

He might actually smile a tiny bit. Either that or he's getting a leg cramp.

"And what does Mrs. Blake do for a living? Does she work outside the home, or is she a stay-at-home mom?"

"Yes."

"Both?"

"No."

"Which one?" I have to force a smile this time. He's really making me work for this.

"She stays at home."

"So your child is in school during the day?"

"No. She's at home. With my wife."

"Homeschooling? I was homeschooled." I sigh and shake my head. How I wish my story were different. "My whole life. From birth to age eighteen. I took an equivalency exam and officially graduated with the local school, but I never spent a single day there."

At the next traffic light he stares at me in the rearview mirror.

"What?" I ask, wiping at my face. "Do I have chili on me?"

He goes back to looking at the road. The car is silent for a while, and then out of the blue he says, "She's not homeschooled."

"Oh." I have to think about that for a little while. She's seven and at home with his wife, but she's not being homeschooled.

"What's her name?" I ask, knowing I'm probably going to regret asking more questions, but also knowing I can't quit here. We just got to the scary part of the conversation, and what kind of asshole backs out when it gets scary? Not this one.

"Elizabeth." The sound of her name on his lips is like a weird antidote to his coldness. His shoulders slump a little and his arms get a bend in them.

"Do you call her Elizabeth or does she have a nickname?"

"We call her Lolly."

"Like Lollipop. That's cute."

He grips the wheel hard, over and over. I can tell he's stressed, so I leave it alone for now. I don't want him to hate me so much he abandons me in the underwear store and tells Lister he's refusing to drive me anymore. All Lister needs is another reason to dislike me.

Now that I have my clothing situation figured out, it's time to deal with the Ty issue. Do I want to go to his place? Yes and no. We have a connection that's undeniable, but that doesn't mean I have to act on it. I'm working for the band now, so it could get really complicated. But then again, I'm only here for two weeks, and wouldn't it be silly not to have fun too? All work and no play makes Jill a dull girl. I decide to throw caution to the wind and have some fun for a change. My life doesn't always have to be about responsibility and doing the smart thing.

I pull out my phone and press the button that is Ty's phone number, waiting for him to pick up. I end up in his voice mail.

As I listen to his voice instruct me to leave a message, I get nervous. Should I hang up or speak? What if this is a mistake? What if he's changed his mind and he doesn't want to go out with me anymore? If I hang up without saying anything, he'll be forced to call me back and it'll be all up to him. That'll be the easiest way to handle it. Unless he doesn't call. Then I'll sit there all night wondering if he even knows that I called or what I did to make him change his mind.

I hate that I'm being so indecisive and non-confident. What would a New York City girl do? A girl who knows who she is and what she's all about? I decide not to give in to weakness. I don't need to impress anyone or play games. Like Lister said, I shouldn't worry about what other people think of me. If Ty wants to go out with me, he'll call back; if he doesn't, he won't. I can always go back to Gray's Papaya and buy my pervert friend Ray a dinner dog.

I speak after the beep. "Hi, Ty, it's me. Amber. Turns out I'm going to be in the city for a little while longer, so if you still want to do that dinner thing tonight, call me back with your address. I have somebody who can drive me over." *I think.* My heart feels like I strained it, the way it's aching right now. *Please call me back.*

I close my phone and slide it into my purse. I watch the scenery go by and smile up at the big buildings. They don't seem nearly as intimidating now as they did yesterday. *Am I already integrating into the Manhattan culture? Am I starting to fit in?*

Part of me wants that to be a yes answer, to know that I can handle myself here. But then the other part of me remembers that some people here shoot cabdrivers and sit outside hot dog stands and yell insults at people. Do I really want to belong in a place like that? I wonder what my sisters and mothers would think. I hope I haven't bitten off more than I can chew.

CHAPTER TWENTY-NINE

I'm glad I decided to go shopping and buy some new things. Now I can finally have a nice hot shower and use all these new products I bought to make my hair and skin smell delicious. In the vintage shops I directed Mr. Blake to, I was able to find some fabulous clothes for not a whole lot of money, and if I wear every outfit three times, I have enough clothing for my entire two weeks here and I won't have to go shopping again. I even bought a new purse that goes with everything. It's totally wild—sporting every color of the rainbow with sparkles sewn onto it. I love it so much, it's my favorite thing about New York so far. *Except for Ty . . . and my new job.*

I drop my new wallet, my key card, and my telephone inside the purse along with a few odds and ends, and put it on the front table near the door of my hotel room. Ty left me a message with his address, but I still have a half hour to kill before I leave. *All dressed up and nowhere to go.* I stare at myself in the mirror for the fifth time and decide it's time to do something other than pace the floors and listen to Ty's message on my phone for the hundredth time. *Love his voice so much.* I don't need to hang out here in the room. There's a big bar in the lobby.

I ride the elevator down, chatting with Jeremy the entire way.

"I'm glad you're feeling better today," he says.

"Yeah. That was horrible this morning. My eyes were so puffy afterward."

"Is everything okay now?"

"Yeah, I'm good. Just a momentary setback."

"That's a good attitude."

"And how goes the hunt for the girlfriend?"

"Pretty good. I met a nice lady last night."

"Good for you," I say, cuffing him gently on the shoulder. "I hope it works out." After the doors open, he reaches out and holds the edge of one door for me so it won't close too soon.

"Thank you, Jeremy."

"My pleasure. Have a good evening, Ms. Fields."

"I plan on it. You too."

I walk over to the lounge—the Ty Bar, of all places—and pause in the entrance, taking in all the red chairs and the glowing yellow-orange muted light that shines out of etched glass panels behind the bottles of liquor. It's very pretty in here. I take a seat at the end of the bar, not wanting to be too conspicuous. When the bartender comes over, I smile at him.

"What would you like?" he asks, his red tie cinched up tight to his neck, a gray vest and starched white shirt making him look like he could be a businessman taking a turn serving drinks to customers.

"How about some wine?" I have no idea what a good or bad wine is, so I hope he'll suggest something for me.

"We have a nice house red. It comes from the Médoc region of France."

"That sounds perfect. I love the Médoc region." That's a lie. I wouldn't be able to find Médoc on a map if you paid me. But he leaves me alone to fetch my drink, and I take a moment while I'm waiting to look around.

People are sitting in small groups of two or three at short tables in deep-red colored upholstered chairs. There are a couple of women sitting together with jewelry pieces so big I can see them from across the room. I wonder if they're having a silent competition between themselves to see who can be the most sparkly. I look down at my own hands and arms and see my bangle bracelets and that's it. I was never much for wearing rings.

Somebody walks up and takes one of the high leather chairs on my other side, so I turn around more fully to see who it is. An older man in leather with long hair stares the bartender down, like he's willing the man to come over using the power of his mind. He doesn't even look at me.

He reminds me of someone. Could it be . . . maybe . . . *Was he in that room in the club in Toronto before Red kicked everyone out?* I need to find out or it's going to drive me crazy not knowing.

"Do I know you from somewhere?" I ask.

He glances at me. "I don't think so."

I'm racking my brain trying to remember where I saw this guy. It's not his face that's familiar; it's his clothing. Paul was wearing something similar, but I don't think that's what it is that's triggering my brain.

When the bartender comes over with my wine, the man next to me orders a Budweiser. I take a sip of my drink and look around the room, pretending to be interested in what's going on out there. But the only thing I *really* care about is my neighbor here. The chairs are pretty far apart, so it's not like he's intruding on my personal space, but it's just *weird* that I'm pretty sure I know him from somewhere even though he's pretending like I don't.

I look at him again. "Have you ever been to Toronto before? Or central Maine maybe?"

"Nope. Never been to Canada or any part of Maine." He keeps staring at the bartender, who's all the way at the other end of the bar getting his beer.

"I swear you look very familiar to me."

When his beer arrives five seconds later, he takes it from the bartender and puts a ten-dollar bill down on the bartop before straightening up. He tips his bottle toward me and winks. "Have a nice night." He walks away and leaves me sitting there alone.

I watch as he makes his way across the room and sits down at a small table, choosing a seat that faces away. Now all I can see is the back of his arrogant head.

I hate when stuff like this happens. I really don't like unsolved mysteries. This is going to bug me all night. Knowing me, at two o'clock in the morning, I'll suddenly remember where I know him from. He's probably someone who came to a retreat at the farm and spent his entire time wandering around naked and high. That would explain why he doesn't recognize me or remember the fact that he's been to Maine. Seeing him in clothes is probably throwing me off. People often deny they've come to the farm after they leave; it's not easy for some people to admit they tried out the hippie lifestyle.

I sip my wine as my mind wanders, wondering what's going to happen tonight with Ty. He's invited me over for dinner. Does that mean sex is on the menu? Will I sleep with this man who gives me chills by just looking at me? It would undoubtedly be a mistake for us to sleep together. I've just signed a contract saying that I'll work for him and his partners for two weeks. Sex would absolutely complicate everything. But I picture Ty's face in my mind and his hands on my body, and I think that I may not have the strength it will take to say no. Maybe I'll get lucky and he won't even broach the subject.

By the time I finish my wine, it's time to go. I sign a paper saying that the drink will be put on my hotel room tab and leave the bar. I find Mr. Blake in the car outside waiting for me. I hand him a piece of paper that I wrote Ty's address on. "This is where we're going tonight."

He opens the door for me and I get in.

The drive over there only takes ten minutes. When I look up at the building that is our destination, I almost feel like there's been a mistake. "This is where he lives?"

"Yes. Up in the penthouse." Mr. Blake gets out of the car and opens my door. "Do you need my assistance getting into the building?"

I look at him in surprise. I don't think this is something he normally does. "You mean like a bodyguard?"

"No. Not like a bodyguard."

I shake my head as I try to count the floors from the outside. "No. It's okay. I guess I'll see you tomorrow?" I look at him for confirmation.

"You don't need me to wait for you?"

"Don't you have to get back to your family?"

He stands military straight and stares off into the night. "I'm on call twenty-four hours, seven days a week. If you need me, I'm here."

I wave him away. "No, go. Go be with Lolly and your wife. I can get a cab home if necessary."

He looks at me as though I'm trying to trick him. "Are you sure?"

"Of course." I walk away and wave at him. "Have a good night."

He stands outside the car staring at me as I walk away. I look over my shoulder three different times, but he's still there when I go inside. *Whatever. Stay or go, I don't care.* Mr. Blake is a mystery, but not one I'm going to solve tonight. My priority right now is hanging out with Ty and somehow finding a way to broach the subject of me working for the band. Hopefully, he already knows, but if he doesn't, I need to talk to him about it. I don't want him to think I'm blindsiding him when I show up for my first day.

There's a doorman at the entrance who wants to know all of my particulars before he bothers to call up to Ty's residence. Once I pass the security protocols, he brings me to the elevator and comes inside to press the button for me. There's a little card he has to slide into a slot on the button panel so that I'll be able to access the floor that I want. *Wow. Swanky.* I nod my thank-you and fidget all the way up to the top of this really high building. Normally, I don't worry about elevators falling, but if this one does, I'm going to be as flat as a pancake. I start to stress out, watching the numbers change way too slowly.

Forty-five . . .

Forty-six . . .

Forty-seven . . .

I can't look anymore. I close my eyes and wait, praying for my safe delivery. A ding and a slight bump let me know I've arrived. I open my eyes and look at the ceiling. "Thank you, God, for not letting me die before I see how this ends."

The elevator doors open right into his apartment. Ty is waiting for me in the marble-floored foyer.

I step off and look around, trying to calm my racing emotions. This place is amazing, and he looks incredibly hot. He's freshly scrubbed and doesn't have any eyeliner on. It's just him, simple and clean. He's wearing one of the outfits I picked out for him today. He gestures to himself with arms outstretched. "What do you think?"

I nod, smiling. "You wear it well."

He points at me. "New threads for you too?"

I turn in a slow circle with my arms out so he can admire my purse too. "Yep. I went shopping today. I even got new underwear."

He laughs. "Excellent. I love new underwear."

I realize I've revealed too much, but it's too late now. *Quick! Distraction!* "Want to give me a tour of your bachelor pad?" Too late I realize I've just invited myself into his bedroom right after telling him I have new panties on. *Wow.* You can take the girl out of the hippie commune, but you cannot take the hippie commune out of the girl. *Sigh.*

He holds his hand out to take mine. I walk over and we connect. A warm current buzzes up my arm. I'm already sweating. I'm super glad I bought that scented lotion from that smelly-stuff store and slathered it all over my body.

"Follow me." He takes me from room to room, covering what must be five thousand square feet at a minimum and a million bucks' worth of interior decorating. There are four bedrooms, a huge kitchen, and not just a living room and a family room but a movie room too. Everything is furnished with stuff that looks really expensive.

"This is like a real theater," I say, running my hands over the back of the blue velvet chairs. "You should see the cinema where I live. It's pitiful compared to this." There, my feet stick to the floor. Here, they glide on silk carpets. No way could I trust myself to eat a chili dog in here.

"I'd like to see your cinema someday," he says.

I check to see if he's joking, but his expression is serious. It makes my heart skip a beat.

"Maybe you will . . . someday." I don't believe it, of course. Ty Stanz is never going to come up to central Maine, and to wish otherwise would only end up with me breaking my own heart. I've got to be smarter than that.

"I hope you like Chinese food." He leads me back to the kitchen.

"I do. I don't eat it very often, but when I do, I always enjoy it."

"Cool. Do you know how to use chopsticks?" He reaches into a drawer and pulls out a couple pairs and drops them on the counter. "Other than for putting up your hair, I mean." He smiles.

"A little bit. But you may want to give me a fork so I don't completely embarrass myself."

He opens up another drawer and grabs a handful of silverware. "You got it." He picks up the chopsticks and points them and the forks toward the other room. "Dining room is through there."

I lead the way into the other room, where there's a large table with several paper bags on top of it. I look around the room expecting to see other people. "Are you having a party?"

"What do you mean?" He puts all the silverware down on the table with a clatter.

I gesture at the table. "That looks like a lot of food."

"Yeah." He sounds a little embarrassed. "I wasn't sure what you'd like, so I ordered a lot of stuff. Whatever we don't finish, I'll just put in the fridge and eat another day."

"Cool." Maybe he was as nervous about this date as I was. The thought should calm me down, but it's having the opposite effect. *What's happening, what's happening, what's happening?*

I help him unpack the bags. It was very sweet of him to think of me and order so many things to make sure I would be happy. Ty can be thoughtful when he wants to be, which is nice to know. My mothers would approve. *Holy hell, where did that thought come from?*

Okay, so trying to convince myself that this whole thing is no big deal isn't working; it feels like I have a Fourth of July sparkler lit in my chest. I really need to find a way to calm down, because if I'm this agitated over him ordering Chinese food, I'll end up having an orgasm when he kisses me.

As we serve the food onto the plates and sit down to begin eating, guilt starts to nag at me. He's being so thoughtful, but all day long I've been focused on my new job. Ty and I haven't had a conversation about what I'm still doing here in New York City and what I'll be doing for the next two weeks. I'm trying to figure out how to bring up the subject without ruining this peace we've found together when he speaks over my thoughts.

"So, when're you going back?"

His question tells me he doesn't know about the deal I cut with the band; either that or he's pushing me into telling him what he already knows. But I have no idea why he'd play games like that. I push the food around my plate with the chopsticks. "In a couple weeks." I can't look him in the eye. As it turns out, guilt is the perfect antidote to the lovesickness that was ailing me. Will he be mad at me for making deals without his knowledge? He is part of the band after all. Will he be mad at Red? Am I causing problems for the band already? What if he thinks I stayed just for him? Will it scare him away?

"Really? I thought your plan was to leave really soon. I had no idea it was going to be in two weeks." Okay, so he's not playing games; he definitely doesn't know about the job offer. Great. *Way to go, Red.*

"Yeah, well, something came up." I push the food around some more, quickly losing my appetite for all things noodle.

He stops eating. "And what would that be?"

I look up at him to find a strange expression on his face. "What?" I don't know why he's looking at me like this.

"I'm just wondering why your one-day trip turned into a two-week trip, is all."

He's definitely not happy about it, which makes no sense. Is this not a date? And don't dates mean you want to spend more time with a person and not less?

My temper starts to flare. I have no patience for games. "Why? Does it make you upset that I'm going to be here longer?"

He shakes his head and shrugs at the same time, telling me he's either confused about how he feels or he's about to lie. "No. Doesn't bother me at all."

I put my chopsticks down and fold my hands in front of me. "Why don't we make a pact, right now."

"A pact?"

I nod. "Yes, a pact." My sisters and I are big on pacts. When you live with two other sisters the same age, it's pretty much required. "Let's agree not to lie to each other anymore. Let's just be straight up. All the time, no matter what, we tell the truth. I think it'll help us avoid a lot of misunderstandings and miscommunications."

"Sure." He holds out his hand, looking as though he's accepting some sort of weird challenge I didn't realize I was issuing. "I can agree to be straight up, if you can do the same."

I shake his hand, surprised by how firm his grip is. "Deal."

I pick up my chopsticks, hoping I'm not making a mistake by asking my next question. "So . . . tell me why you're either confused or angry about the idea of me staying here for two weeks." I take a single noodle and put it in my mouth, sucking it up until the end. It slaps me in the cheek, leaving behind something wet. I quickly wipe my face with my napkin, hoping Ty didn't notice.

He shovels a bunch of food into his mouth right after I ask the question, which effectively delays me hearing an answer for a solid two minutes. I raise my eyebrow and sip my glass of water while I wait, relieved to know I'm not the only nervous piglet at the table.

"Well," he says, taking a sip of his beer before he continues, "I was just wondering if you're staying because of me."

I instantly feel sick to my stomach. If it makes him angry that I'm staying, that cannot be good. What a fool I was imagining us having a connection . . . imagining us having *sex*! But I can't let it drop. I need to know everything—what he's thinking and feeling. It'll make it easier for me to walk away if my heart is thoroughly battered rather than just bruised.

"In what way would I be staying here for you?" It sucks that he wasn't in on the conversation with the band about why I'm extending my stay, because it means he's going to hear it from me first—another sign that he's really not a part of the group. Not to mention the fact that right now he thinks I'm staying for him, and it's making him angry. I must have completely misunderstood the handholding and kissing today. I am such a hippie chick dweeb. No way am I cut out to live in this city. Thank goodness I only agreed to two weeks!

He stares at his plate. "What I meant was, are you staying here for two more weeks because you want to be with me, or is there another reason you're doing it?"

"Just so I'm clear . . . do you mean in a *romantic* way?" Apparently, the knife in my heart isn't enough; I need him to twist it, too.

He shrugs and then takes a huge bite of food, making it impossible for him to actually answer. But I think he already has with that shrug. Time to be a big girl and salvage what I can of this situation.

"Hmmm. Okay then . . ." I fold my hands and put them on the edge of the table. "Because I've agreed to be honest with you, I'm going to go ahead and tell you not only what my plans are, but how I feel about what you just asked me. Because, ultimately, I think trying to guess what each other's emotions are is a recipe for disaster."

He stares at me while he chews his food.

"I was offered a position by Red and the other members of the band—apparently not you, though—to work as a consultant for them for two weeks."

He stops chewing and his eyebrows go up.

"I'm realizing now that they didn't discuss it with you, and I'm sorry about that, but I want you to know that I wasn't aware of it until just this moment, and I certainly had nothing to do with that part of it."

He starts chewing again, only very slowly now. He takes another sip of his beer.

"This is a temporary job, and it will not be repeated. I'm going to help with a few things, and then I'm going back home again, and I will not return." Hearing myself say this makes me sad. Have I decided this for real, or am I just saying it to Ty because that's what he wants to hear? Two seconds pass . . . Then the moment of craziness passes and I confirm for myself in my mind that I am telling the truth. Nothing has changed for me; I'm still needed at the farm and I'm still the kind of girl who doesn't let my family down.

He finally swallows the rest of his food. "So, you're not staying here for me."

I twist my mouth around as I try to figure out how to answer that honestly. "Yes and no."

"Clarify." He takes another long sip of his beer. He's almost done with the bottle.

"Well, do you remember what I said the other night in front of everybody? When I pointed out that the fans were booing you and not accepting you?"

He pushes away from the table a little bit and folds his arms across his chest as he nods. "Yep. I remember it."

"Well, apparently that got Red and the others talking, and they decided they wanted to try to do something about it."

"What's that got to do with you?"

"I guess they think I can help them update their look a little bit and find a way to help you integrate into the band from the fans' perspective." *There. I said it.* I feel so much better getting that off my chest. Now I'm not in the know while he's in the dark. I search his face for signs of how he's taking the news, hoping he's not angry. Unfortunately, his expression is unreadable.

"And how are you going to do this?" he asks.

"I'm open to suggestions. I don't have a solid plan yet. Part of it, I guess, includes updating their physical look a little bit. Maybe getting rid of the teased hair and the mullets."

He glares at me. "What? That's a *terrible* idea."

I look at him like he's crazy, which he must be, because he was born in the same generation as I was; he doesn't get to claim senility as his problem.

"Why do you say that?" I ask.

"Because . . . that look is what the fans are in love with. You take that away, and you're going to have a revolt on your hands."

This is the first time I've ever doubted this idea for the band. I figured Ty would be totally on board with it. I also believe, though, that Ty will always have the best interests of the band in mind, so if he's against it, what hope do I have of selling the rest of them on it?

"Are you sure about that?" I ask. "Are you sure it's the look and not the music?"

He leans over, pulling his chair closer with his butt as he dumps more food from one of the boxes onto his plate. "It's both. They're wrapped up together. You can't separate one from the other."

"Sure you can. You just need a hundred percent buy-in."

He pokes at his food. "You can't force fans to buy into stuff."

"No, but if the band is all-in, you could ease the fans into it and make it more palatable for them. And then you can make them like it."

"You've got pretty high hopes for this idea of yours." He jabs at his food, filling up his chopsticks with another pile of noodles.

"I just want things to be good for you guys."

He lets out a long sigh and stops jabbing his noodles. Then he gets up to retrieve another bottle of beer and sits down as he twists the top off. I watch as he downs half of it in three long gulps.

"I didn't mean to upset you. That was never my intention."

He's looking off in the distance, his beer suspended in midair. "It doesn't upset me. Not for the reasons you think."

Thank goodness. "Well, since we've decided to be honest with each other, maybe you can share that with me. Tell me what's going on." I'm so relieved I haven't upset him by taking this job. There's still hope. Hope for what? I don't know and I'm afraid to hope.

He puts the beer down and slowly rubs his stomach with his free hand as he stares at his plate. "It's kind of a long story."

"I don't have plans to go anywhere this evening other than here," I say softly. I sense a new vulnerability in him that I haven't seen before.

He looks up, his eyes smoldering. "How late?"

"Do you mean how late am I going to stay here?"

"Yeah."

I shrug, my heart hammering away in my chest. *What is he asking me, exactly?* I cannot make assumptions where this man is concerned; he's too confusing. "I don't have a curfew. I can stay as late as I want."

"And how late do you *want* to stay?"

This is a really frustrating conversation with neither of us ready to say what really needs to be said. "I guess I'll stay as long as I'm having fun. But the minute this isn't fun anymore, I'll leave."

He nods and stands. "Fair enough." He holds out his hand. "Have you had enough to eat yet?"

I get on my feet, putting my napkin on the table next to my plate. "Yes. That was really delicious, thank you."

He's still waiting there with his hand out. I don't know why he wants to hold my hand now when just two minutes ago he looked like he wanted to kick me out of his penthouse.

"This could become really complicated if we let it," I say.

"You're right; it could."

"Isn't your life already complicated enough?" I have to be sure that we're both thinking the same thing.

"It absolutely is." He looks down at his hand and then meaningfully at me.

You can't win if you don't play. I take his hand and let him lead me into another room. I'm worried he's going to take me into his bedroom and make a big move on me; I don't think I'm ready for that. But he doesn't. We end up in his home theater.

"Are we going to watch a film?"

"Of sorts." He points to a plush blue velvet chair in the back row. "Why don't you have a seat while I get the computer up and running. I want to show you a few things."

"Sure." My sense of curiosity takes over and makes me forget that I was worried about those looks on his face and his defensiveness toward my decision to stay. I take a seat and settle in, inhaling the scent of new wood and rich upholstery. This thing was either built recently or it's rarely used.

What's about to happen? I have no idea what tricks Ty has up his sleeve, but I know it's going to be interesting, whatever it is. *Will this explain things to me or make them more confusing? Or will it have absolutely nothing to do with him or me or why he's so upset right now?* The only way for me to find out is to just be patient, which is not my strong suit.

I really wish I could call my sisters and gossip with them about the possibilities, but I resist that urge. There will be plenty of time later for us to analyze every moment of my day and come up with the wisdom of the ages. For now, I have to fly solo.

CHAPTER THIRTY

Ty is back in just a few minutes, and he takes the chair next to me. He's holding a remote control, which he aims over the back of his head to start a film rolling. The lights dim with another touch of a button.

"What is this?" The film that starts to play looks very amateur in style.

"These are some home movies I had put together from some old films my parents had."

The first few minutes of the show are of a little boy. He's holding a guitar. His hair is messed up and long. It makes my heart go soft.

"Is that you?" He's pudgy, running around in the backyard with the plastic instrument, his body covered in dirt. Next to him in a baby seat is an infant with a blue blanket over him.

"Yeah. That's me and my brother, Sam."

"I didn't know you had a brother. Is he your only sibling?"

"Yeah. It's just the two of us."

A big man comes in and fills the screen, beefy with a large gut. He grabs Ty by the wrist and swings him up into his arms, causing the little boy to drop his guitar.

I cringe at the harsh, physical nature of it. Our mothers never picked us up like that. It looks almost painful. I glance sideways at Ty, but his face looks as still as a corpse's.

"That's my dad."

"Did you get along?" I ask in a hushed voice. The movie is silent, so I don't need to be quiet, but I sense there's something strange going on here.

"No. I wouldn't call us close."

A woman enters the scene. She's so thin she looks like a skeleton. Her head appears too big for her body. She picks up the baby and rocks him, smiling at the camera. Whoever's filming is standing very still or they're using a tripod.

Ty's father goes in and out of the frame, dropping little Ty on the ground near his instrument. Ty has his back to the camera as he picks up and plays the plastic guitar again. He's wearing scrappy shorts and no shirt. His feet are bare. He looks neglected. *Is that a bruise on his back or dirt?*

Then his father is in the shot again, setting up what looks like a miniature microphone on a stand. When Ty doesn't turn around, he uses the microphone to hit him on the back of the head to get his attention.

Ty spins around with his eyes wide open, but when he sees the microphone now attached to the stand, he walks right up to it and starts singing his little heart out. It's a silent movie that tells me so many sad things.

I have to say something to let Ty know I'm watching, that I see what he wants me to. "You've been playing guitar since you were really little." I'm battling tears of pity and sadness. No child should ever be treated this way.

"Yeah. I was six in this film." He reaches over his head and presses a button on his remote. The screen goes dark and then it lights up with several little boxes that show a single frame inside each one. He moves a cursor over one of the vignettes and presses another button.

Another film comes to life. Now I'm watching an older version of Ty. He looks like he's in his early teens, maybe. He's playing guitar in a garage, and his father is on a ratty couch, watching with a beer bottle in his hand. The camera moves around a lot. Now it's not just Ty with a guitar but another boy also.

"Is that Sam?" I ask.

"Yeah. He's amazing." Ty's voice is softer. Calmer. "I wish I could play as well as he does."

I twist sideways to look at him. "What are you talking about? You're amazing. I heard you, remember? I saw you onstage. You were fantastic."

He doesn't look at me. He seems mesmerized by the images on the screen. "Yeah. I can play Red Hot stuff, but not a whole lot else. Sam writes his own music, and it's killer. He's gifted."

I stare closer at this brother of his. He's darker than Ty but not by much. Maybe a little more broad-shouldered. "Where is he now?"

"I don't know."

I want to ask him why he doesn't know where his own brother is, but the next scene captures my interest and I forget to ask. Ty's father seems to be losing his temper. He's waving his arms around, the beer bottle still in his hand. Some of the liquid inside splashes out and hits Sam in the face, causing the boy to throw his arm up reactively. The teen pauses and then uses his forearm to wipe off the beer. The look he has for his father is pure murder.

Ty stands up all of a sudden and shoves his father back, his guitar flying out to the side. His father stumbles and falls back onto the couch, dropping his beer bottle where it smashes on the ground.

My jaw drops open. I'm now watching a horror movie.

The camera goes crazy, jerking and flipping around, but I catch glimpses of the father getting off the couch and then the boys and him getting into some sort of wrestling match. Pieces of equipment fall over and then the screen goes black.

Ty reaches over his head with the remote, but I take it from him and hold it in my lap. The room is dark except for a faint glow from the screen. I turn to face him. He looks tortured.

"Why are you showing me these things?" I ask softly.

His jaw pulses in and out, the only indication I have that he's heard me.

I gently stroke the back of his hand. "You're very angry right now."

"I'm not angry." His voice is flat.

"Then you're sad. And I can see why you would be, after watching those videos. But why do you have them in digital files like that? Why do you torture yourself and watch them like this?" I want to weep for him. A mothering instinct I didn't know I had in me is rising up to take over my heart and brain. I need to help him . . . ease his pain. I can't do that as a girl who would love to kiss him again. He needs someone who will just listen and hold him.

"So I never forget," he says.

"Never forget what? The things that make you unhappy?"

"Where I come from."

I'm moving on instinct now. I stand and hold my hands out. He looks at me, anger simmering in his eyes. I reach down and take his hands, pulling on them until he can do nothing but either yank his hands free or stand. He chooses to stand.

I step closer to him and put my arms around him, resting my head against his chest. I rub his back. "That stuff is in the past. You need to let it go."

He stands as rigid as a board, but I keep caressing. I know how to soothe a mom or a sad sister. With all the estrogen in our house, I've become something of an expert at calming down emotionally distressed people. I don't know if my techniques will work on a man, but I'm sure going to try.

I try to find words that will help calm him. "Some people aren't meant to care for kids. Some people screw up a lot more than they do things right. And some people have temporary moments of insanity. I don't know what the deal is with your father, and I don't know what the deal is with your mother either, but I can see there was a lot of unhappiness there in your family."

His hands come gently to my back. He's not giving me a full hug yet but I'm getting him there, so I keep talking. "Your past does not determine who you are today. *You* make that choice. You do not have to be an angry person. You do not have to be sad about what happened to you when you were a kid. You can choose a different life for yourself."

"Sometimes I feel like my life was chosen for me."

I rub more vigorously. "These people may have influenced you, but they did not make your choices for you about how you were going to react to what they did. It seems to me you took a bad situation and turned it into a really good thing." I look up at him. "You played music all that time, and it looks like you had a garage full of instruments. That tells me that somebody was supporting the idea of you being a musician. Somebody who was important to you."

"My father. He supported us playing. For the most part." He doesn't seem very happy about that.

"It's all about the music, isn't it?" I say, quoting back some of his words. "It does things for people, doesn't it? Sometimes good, and sometimes bad."

He nods, his chin trembling the slightest bit. "For me it was an escape, I guess."

"And maybe a way to connect with a man who wasn't that easy to get along with?"

He doesn't answer. He turns sideways and drops his head, pinching the bridge of his nose.

I move my hands up to go around his neck so I can pull his head down to my shoulder. "I guess that's a good thing that music was your escape and that you spent so much time escaping with it. I never would've met you otherwise."

That's when his arms go around me tightly and hang on. "You must think I'm the biggest weirdo you've ever met in your life," he mumbles into my shoulder.

I laugh. "Are you kidding me? I live on a hippie commune. Do you have any idea of the weirdos I've come into contact with in my lifetime? You're seriously small potatoes in comparison, believe me."

He laughs a little. "I'd like to hear more about that, actually. Maybe then I wouldn't feel so bad about bringing you in here and showing you my horribly depressing home movies."

I pull away and put my hands on either side of his face, staring up at him. "I would be happy to tell you all about my upbringing, because I guarantee you, it will cheer you up and make you feel completely normal. But why don't we go into the other room where it's not so dark and depressing and do something else for a little while first?"

"What did you have in mind?"

"I don't know." I shrug, searching for an idea that's a lot less heavy than telling each other all of our dark secrets. "Do you have any board games or cards?"

He searches my eyes for a few long seconds and then takes me by the hand and leads me out of the movie room. "I have something that you might enjoy. Better than a board game."

I follow him through his penthouse wondering if we're going to be playing strip poker, glad I'm wearing my brand-new, never-worn-before matching bra and panty set.

CHAPTER THIRTY-ONE

I follow Ty through the apartment, and he brings me into his family room. He flicks on the television and messes around with something in a nearby cabinet and then comes back over to hand me a small black box.

"Go ahead and have a seat," he says.

I look down at what's in my hands. "Are we going to play video games?"

"Yeah. Do you like 'em?" He presses some buttons on his controller as he aims it at the TV. Several screens flash by.

"I've never played one before."

He pauses. "You're not serious." He's looking at me and smiling like a little kid.

"No, I am serious. I almost never watch TV either."

He walks over and flips a switch on the wall, leaving just the dim glow from the television to light the room. "I'll try to take it easy on you, since this is your first time."

"I am a video game virgin." The words come out before I think too hard about what they could mean for us.

He smiles devilishly. "Is that so?"

"Can we forget I just said that?"

"Not on your life." He takes me by the elbow and guides me over to the couch. "Sit. I'm going to give you a quick primer and then I'm going to school you."

I'm enjoying his sense of competitiveness. He's much more cheerful now that he's imagining winning than he was a few minutes ago reliving his past. It makes me want to be good at this . . . whatever it is.

He presses a button to start the game, and we're presented with a scary scene of a bombed-out or abandoned city. "This is called *Apocalypsis*," he says. "It's set in a post-apocalyptic world and you have to survive against your enemies."

I settle into my seat and point my controller at the screen. "Oh, I'm gonna be totally good at this. I live on a farm. If the whole world comes to an end, you should come to my house. We'll live like kings."

He starts showing me the buttons on the controller and pointing to things on the screen. I'm not sure I totally understand everything, but it's fun having him sit here by me and lean over and give me a chance to sniff him without him knowing what I'm doing. He smells amazing—like a boy, which isn't something I get to experience much at my house . . . the place otherwise known as Estrogen Central.

"Okay, so you're that character there—Bryn. She's a girl and she's really tough, so I figured you'd like being her."

"What makes you think I'd like it so much?" I look at him, enjoying the blue glow from the TV that makes him seem otherworldly.

"Because she reminds me of you." He turns to face the screen and points at it with his controller. "I'm her buddy, Bodo. He's a foreign exchange student from Germany who got stuck in the US after the war. I'm about to start the game . . . Get ready."

Our two characters are walking around a devastated city. It's pretty depressing, but when zombies come out and try to get us, I instantly get carried away with the game. Sometimes Ty nudges me to try to distract me from my strategy, but I'm getting the hang of it quickly.

"No fair," I say after he shoves me sideways on the couch. I keep pressing buttons even though I'm on my side, delivering a karate chop and a roundhouse to a zombie whose head falls off, effectively earning me fifty points and some more ammunition.

He does it again.

"No fair! You can't cheat just because you're losing."

He laughs. "I'm not losing. Check out the score." He points at the screen with his controller. As soon as I realize he's distracted, I shove him and then grab several more points with some really cool karate moves and a grenade I had handy.

"Hey. Now *you're* cheating," he says.

I shrug. "What can I say? I learned from the best."

He grabs my controller out of my hand and quickly gathers some points for himself.

I go after him, trying to get my controller from his outstretched hand. "Hey, give it back! This is out of bounds. This is worse than cheating. You're using your manliness to take advantage of me." I'm straining over him, trying to get it, and then suddenly his lips are on mine.

I pull back, a lot of my excitement over the game gone, quickly replaced by sexual attraction to my zombie-fighting partner. "Hey. That's cheating too."

"My manliness? What does that even mean?" He's laughing.

"Your long arms, dummy." My face is burning.

He puts his controller and mine down on the coffee table and places his hands on either side of my head. He stares at me for a couple seconds and then leans in, kissing me softly.

I vaguely hear the sounds of our battle continuing on the screen to my left, but I'm done with that silly game. Screw killing zombies; I want to do more of what we're doing right now instead.

Our tongues tangle together, and our breathing speeds up. He pushes against me and I lean to my left, my back pressing against the soft cushions. He's on top of me, raising himself up on one arm to keep from crushing me.

My mind is racing. *What exactly are we doing? Is this a good idea? Should I stop things from going too far?* I know the right answers to my questions; I should stop kissing him and get up and leave right now. These are the smart things to do, but I'm not always smart.

He moans, his hand enveloping my right breast and squeezing it. I can't believe how good it feels to have him touching me like this. Ty's body sinks down more fully against mine. He's hard and I want to touch him between his legs, but I also don't want to lead him on. I'm still not sure this is a great idea, even though everything in me wants to keep going—everything but that one tiny part of my brain that's trying to remind me how this is going to play out in the days to come.

His kisses leave my mouth and travel down my neck to my chest, leaving a trail of heat everywhere they touch. I'm on fire, and my hips surge up involuntarily, trying to bring my body closer to his. Ty's hand slides down and grabs my rear end. He presses his body onto me more completely, sinking his hard parts into my soft ones. I moan. I can't help it; the sensations are too much. They're blocking out all my common sense.

He's kissing my chest again, unbuttoning my shirt. He draws the edge of my bra to the side and pulls out my nipple, gently sucking on it. I moan loudly. I've never been so turned on in my life.

"Ty," I say, breathless.

"Yeah?" He slides his scratchy chin across my skin and pulls the other side of my bra over, releasing my other breast.

"Are you sure this is a good idea?" My eyes are closed and I'm straining up toward him, begging for the touch of his mouth on me. My body is not okay with me questioning what's going on.

"No," he says, sending a shock through me. Why does doing the wrong thing feel so right sometimes?

I bury my fingers in his hair, kneading his scalp as his tongue and lips make electric shocks flow through my body from my breasts. My nipples are so hard, and thankfully, he knows exactly what he's doing.

He puts his hand between my legs, rubbing against me, his finger sliding up and down, drawing more heat from inside my body. He's doing something at his waist and then his hand is on mine. He draws me down to his hardened cock that he's released from his pants, silently begging me to touch it.

Of course I do. How could I not? All I can think about is having sex with this man. Who cares if it's the stupidest idea I've ever had in my life? Right now I'm the one with the problem and he's the one with the solution. I need to feel him inside me.

I stroke his hard length up and down, loving when he moans and presses against me; it makes me feel powerful and in control.

That sensation is just an illusion, though. I'm no more in control of this than I am of the weather. Lightning flashes outside the window, causing me to pause. The faint sound of thunder follows and drops of rain streak across the large windows behind the couch. Ty strains against me, his swollen hardness pushing through my hand. I stroke it again, forgetting about the storm raging outside and instead focusing on the one raging in here.

"You want to go into my bedroom?" he whispers, sucking on my neck.

"No." There's a silly, naïve piece of me that thinks if we don't go into the bedroom, I'm going to be okay . . . I'm not going to go through with this. But I'm a fool, because I know better.

I help him pull his shirt off and then we take mine off too. My bra is not far behind. Within minutes, we're fully naked and he's lying on top of me on his couch. I squirm around, barely able to contain myself. My instincts are screaming—*get him inside!*

He pushes up and grabs his pants off the floor, pulling something from a pocket. I hear a ripping sound and realize that he's putting on a condom. Thank God one of us has a functioning brain.

He looks down at me, the glow from the television and then a lightning strike nearby lighting up his face. He is so gorgeous, and he looks hotter than ever with his giant erection standing out in front of him.

"You sure you want to do this?" He comes down over me, his hands on either side of me. I can feel the tip of him pressing against me.

"I think it's a terrible idea, but I don't want you to stop."

He reaches down to position himself and then slowly pushes inside me.

I pull him against me at his hip, helping him sink all the way in by opening my legs and lifting my feet off the couch. I cry out from both pleasure and pain.

He waits a moment until I settle down and then slowly begins to move again. It's like he's pouring liquid fire into me. Every stroke sends another wave of it through my body from between my legs. He kisses me and rolls my nipple between two fingers. Everything is connected and I can't get enough. He really knows what he's doing. Every other sexual encounter I've had before this one was amateur hour in comparison.

He picks up the speed of his strokes and I join him. Our bodies move together perfectly. He seems to know exactly what I need, changing his approach and his rhythm to suit my needs. Something is building in me that I've never felt before. I've always enjoyed sex, but not like this.

"Ty?"

"Yeah, babe."

The word *babe* makes me want to cry with happiness. "Something's happening."

"Yeah, okay . . ." He grunts. "Oh, shit . . . I'm going to come."

"I think I am too," I gasp.

Hearing me say that does something to him. All the muscles in his body go rock hard and he starts moving really fast. I have to hang on because I worry if I let go, I'll fall to the floor at the side of his couch and lose all these delicious feelings that are coming at me from every angle.

Things are quickly getting out of control. I hear strange sounds and moments later realize they're coming from my own mouth. "Ty!" At this point I'm hanging on to him for dear life. This is crazy. What are we doing? He's inside me and he's filling me, pushing me over the edge into a very dark place. It's like I'm falling into the damn video game where there are zombies waiting to get me.

He's sweating, droplets falling down onto my face and chest. He's grunting now and yelling. His body stiffens and jerks several times.

It triggers something inside me, something primal. I scream and grab ahold of him, scoring his skin with my fingernails.

His back arches for several long seconds as he yells like a caveman. Then he drops on top of me, still stroking in and out, holding me in both arms and squeezing tight. I cling to him, fearing what will happen if I let go.

And then suddenly I'm overly sensitive down there, and I feel something being pulled from me. I'm riding waves of sensation coming from the place where we're still connected. I yell and then I cry. And then I have to stop moving because my body can't take it anymore. Tears run down my face into my ears.

We both go quiet. All we can do is breathe and sweat. I can feel my pulse in my neck and his heartbeat against my breasts. We're covered in slippery wetness.

Ty lifts his head after a while and starts kissing me all over my face—my forehead, my temples, my eyelids, my nose, and my cheeks. He finally stops at my lips. And then he smiles against me.

"What are you looking at?" I say, my words slurred from fatigue and the mind-blowing sex we just had. Our lips are softly touching, his breath tickling me.

"You."

"I can't believe we just did that." My smile is lazy. My mouth doesn't want to work anymore.

He pulls back a little. "Are you kidding? I've wanted to do this with you all day today."

I can't stop smiling. "Really?"

"Yeah, really." He kisses me on the lips one time and then leans to the side, pulling out. He messes around with the condom, leaning over me and dropping it somewhere on the floor. "Are you okay?" he asks.

"Yeah. I'm fine. Are you okay?"

"Yeah, I'm cool." He reaches up and moves some hair off my forehead. The air on my overheated skin feels great.

"I could really use a glass of water, though," I say.

"Me too." He does a push-up over me and jumps off the couch, standing up in all his naked glory. "I'll go get us some."

I watch him walk away, his butt hard and round, his legs and back thick with muscle. He has more tattoos than I realized. They cover his back and arms and part of his chest. I hope I'll get the chance to see them in better lighting one day. The idea makes me go warm all over again.

Maybe I should feel embarrassed, lying here stark naked on his couch with our clothing discarded all around us, but I don't. Being naked for me is a very natural thing. What's not natural is me being here in this apartment carrying on a sexual relationship with a man I'm about to start working with. I hope this doesn't overcomplicate things. I'm pretty sure that's about as naïve a wish as they come.

When he comes back with the water I sit up next to him and we look at each other over our glasses.

"So . . . where do we go from here?" he asks.

I shrug. "Beats me."

"Do you want to stay the night?"

I think about it for a few seconds and then shake my head. "No. I have to go to work tomorrow. I'd better get back to my hotel and try to get some sleep." I know if I stay here there will be no chance of either of us getting any rest.

"Are you coming to the studio tomorrow?"

I hadn't even thought of my first day, but the studio sounds like as good a place as any to get started. "I probably should. Just to say hi to everybody and maybe find out how we're going to get things going."

"Want me to pick you up?"

I nod. "Yeah. That would be nice." Especially since I have no idea where this studio is. I feel happiness glowing inside me, knowing that I'm going to see him in the morning.

I put my glass down and start gathering my things, slowly getting dressed as I locate different items. He pulls his jeans on and zips them up. Standing next to me, he reaches over and lifts a chunk of my hair, holding it up so that his fingers draw through it before his hand drops away.

"Why do you look so sad?" I ask.

"No reason." His expression is shuttered now.

I don't want to ruin the moment by forcing him to talk about something he's not ready to talk about yet. But one of these days, I'll figure out his mood swings and the way his mind works to turn a fun moment into a sad one. In the next two weeks, I'll make it happen. I'll get to the bottom of Ty Stanz, and then we'll see where we can go from there, if anywhere at all.

CHAPTER THIRTY-TWO

This is my first time in a recording studio. Before arriving, I had only a vague idea of what to expect. This one, being in Manhattan, is pretty small, though, I think. There's a booth with a large window at the end of the long, narrow room. It has a collection of things inside it, mostly instruments and microphone stands with headphones hanging next to them.

Outside the booth on one side of the room are couches, chairs, and small tables, plus a few mini fridges, and on the other side, across from the furniture, are various mixing boards and computer screens with two seats in front of them. There are windows above the furniture, making it possible to look out at other brick buildings in this more industrial area of the city.

Ty and I walk in together, but we're not holding hands. That would be totally weird. The car ride over here was strange enough. There's nothing like that awkward day after unplanned sex together when you can't really talk because somebody else is with you. Ty's driver is nicer than mine. He was happy to chat about the weather and what he had for breakfast, at least.

Ty points at the sofa. "Why don't you go have a seat over there, and I'll see what's going on." No one has noticed that we're here yet; they're all gathered at the far end of the narrow room near the booth, chatting with their backs to us.

Rather than take a seat, though, I follow Ty. When he reaches the other members of the band and two other people I've never met, the conversation stops. Ty begins to speak with them but soon realizes all of their attention is elsewhere—on me. He turns around, and when he sees me standing there, he scowls.

The angry look on his face pierces my heart like a needle. His expression falls away pretty quickly, but not fast enough. I frown back at him for an instant before turning my attention to the others. "Good morning."

"Hey! You made it," Mooch says. He comes over and stands in front of me looking excited, happy, and confused. I wait for him to explain his emotional state.

"You look so much like your mother, it's just blowing my mind."

I hold out my hand. "Thank you. I consider that a compliment."

Instead of taking my hand, he leans in and gives me a hug. My arms drop to my sides in surprise. He pats me on the back. "Thanks for staying," he says quietly in my ear.

I nod and back up as he lets me go. The attention is overwhelming. He probably imagines he's my father. It makes me sad to think that so many years have passed without either of us knowing the truth. Not that I *want* to know the truth. I couldn't care less which of these men is my sperm donor. What does it matter, really, in the long run? It won't change the fact that for twenty-five years, I had no father. My heart aches just thinking about it.

Paul comes over next and shakes my hand. "I'm going to spare you the hug." He laughs, making me smile.

"Nice to see you again." I actually mean it when I say that. This man was never part of our mothers' past and he's definitely not my father or Rose's or Em's either. Like Ty, he's innocent in this mess.

Cash is next, looking completely different from how he did in Toronto, wearing a pair of jogging shorts that really should be a size bigger and a T-shirt that has seen much better days. He shakes my hand too. "Aren't you a sight for sore eyes."

He moves away when Red comes over. Red looks like he always does, his fingers full of rings, wearing a well-worn leather jacket, his rocker status on full display. He shakes my hand with both of his together. I'm enveloped in warmth and skulls made of metal. He smiles. "I can't tell you how excited we are to have you here today."

"Do you give all of your consultants this warm a welcome?"

He thinks about it for a couple seconds and shakes his head. "Nope. Can't say that we do."

A couple of the guys chuckle behind him.

"You should probably treat me like you would anybody else." I withdraw my hand from his grasp. "I don't want you acting different just because . . . well . . . because you know my mothers." *Awkward moments galore! Well done, Amber!* I want to keep this as businesslike as possible. I want to prove to them and myself that I'm up to the task of updating their image. I always wondered after I chose to stay at the farm if I could have made it out in the big world, and now's my one and only chance to find out. I'm not going to spoil it by letting our personal issues get in the way.

Nobody looks at me after that slick move on my part. Some are staring at the ceiling, others at the floor.

Red turns sideways and holds his hand out, gesturing to the other men in the room. "Amber, allow me to introduce you to our sound engineers. This over here is Pete Ramey, and that over there is Jed Hessler. Best in the business."

These men are as old and grizzled as the original band members. "I recognize your names from the liner notes on one of the albums," I say, walking over to shake their hands.

Pete holds his out first. "I guess you know the music, then?"

"I was born and raised on it." I take Jed's hand to shake it after finishing with Pete.

"Normally, our manager, Ted Swanson, would be here, but he's on a long and well-deserved vacation in Tahiti. We don't expect him back until next month," Red says.

"Yeah, he's always given time off when we're in the studio," Paul says. "There's not much for him to do when we're in here."

I nod, wishing I knew what was supposed to happen next. I pull back and stand near one of the armchairs, staring at the group of men. Everybody seems happy to have me here except one of them.

I'm sorry, Ty. I wish I could say it to him out loud, but I don't need to create any more awkward moments than I already have.

Ty speaks up. "I was hoping we could have a private meeting before we got started today." He's looking at Red as he makes this suggestion.

Red shrugs. "Go ahead, man. I don't mind."

Ty looks furtively at me before he speaks again. "Band members only."

My heart sinks. He's mad about me being here. Or he's not happy with the fact that I was hired without him knowing. I'd be upset too, so I don't blame him. I just wish I weren't in the middle.

Red looks at Pete and Jed, gesturing with his head over to the door. "Sure. We can spare five minutes. Pete and Jed, do you mind?"

They both nod silently and leave the room, stepping outside the door to the foyer and reception area that is currently unoccupied. I couldn't tell when I passed through it earlier if it's ever manned with a receptionist.

I start moving toward the door too, even though Red didn't say anything to me, but the bandleader's voice stops me. "Not you, Amber. You stay."

I hear Ty mumble something behind me but can only make out the words that Red responds with. "She's not going anywhere. Whatever you have to say, you can say in front of her."

I continue toward the empty chamber. "No, that's okay. I need to grab something anyway." I leave the room and shut the door quietly behind me. I lean against it for a few seconds with my hand behind me on the door handle.

That was awkward. Not a good way to start the day or the relationship.

"So, I hear you're the new consultant," Jed says. He's sitting in a low-slung chair. I walk over and lean against the reception desk.

"Yep. That's me."

"And the guys knew your mother, is that it?"

"Yes. Many moons ago, my mother hung out with the band while they toured for a couple years."

The other guy nods his head slowly, narrowing his eyes at me. "I thought I recognized you."

I smile at him. "That would be pretty difficult, since I wasn't born until after my mother and the band parted ways."

"No, I recognize you because you look like your mother. What was her name . . ." He squints and looks off into the distance.

"Barbara?" I offer.

He points at me and winks. "That's it. Barbara Fields. You look *just* like her. Spittin' image."

My ears start to heat up. This conversation is not going in a direction I want it to. *Quick. Think of something else to talk about.* "So . . . you guys do the sound mixing for the band now, eh?"

"Yep," Pete confirms. "We've been here since the beginning, pretty much."

"Cool. And what about new material? Will they be working on something new today?"

"That's the goal," Jed says. "I'm not sure how far they've gotten with anything, though."

"Great. Who's writing the music?" I'm happy to be off the subject of my mother and the circumstances of my birth. "And who's writing the lyrics?"

"We're not really sure," Pete says. "They've been practicing on their own, but we haven't been in on it. This will be our first day working as a team."

"Yeah," Jed says. "Don't expect to be impressed today. First days are never very productive. The band hasn't been working on any new material since Ty started with them, so it's bound to be a little bumpy."

"Okay, I'll set the bar very low."

They both chuckle politely.

The door opens behind me and someone sticks his head through the crack. It's Mooch. "You guys can come back in. We're all done."

"That didn't take very long," I say, happy that it wasn't a long, drawn-out argument.

"Yeah, we've got work to do. No time to be messing around with nonsense."

Uh-oh. I think this means Ty got shut down. That's not going to be good for his mood. Now I'm feeling as frustrated as he probably is. He came in here with something to talk to them about and they're blowing him off. They must know that he found out about my new job from me rather than them. It's pretty disrespectful, as far as I'm concerned.

If I'm right, this is something that needs to be dealt with ASAP, and I think it's my job to do that. But the question is whether I should be doing it with them individually or together as a group. Unfortunately, since I'm mostly unqualified for this job, I have no idea which is the right answer.

Mooch pushes the door open farther so we can come back in. When we're halfway across the room, Ty buzzes right past us without a word and goes out the door, slamming it behind him.

I turn around in shock. *Holy shit. He's really gone.* When I turn back to the band, nobody looks particularly happy.

"Where's he going?" I'm praying they'll tell me he's off to the bathroom for a quick break.

"Don't know," Red says. "Just let him cool off."

I sigh and roll my eyes. Day one and I already suck at this job. This is terrible! Who knows, maybe by the end of two weeks I can totally break up the band and destroy their entire futures. I'll be worse than Yoko!

"Don't worry about it," Cash says. "We'll get started without him. He'll show up."

I hold out my hand. "Wait." Everybody stops to look at me, even the sound engineers.

"I think I need to chat with you before you get started playing anything." I gesture at the furniture. "Please have a seat. I'll stand over here." I set myself up near the mixing boards while everybody finds a place on a couch or chair. Jed and Cash sit on the arms of couches because there isn't enough furniture for everyone.

I begin pacing in front of them, my mind racing with what I'm going to say. I don't want to sound like their mother or somebody they can't respect. I need to be an adult about this, and I also need to lay down some ground rules. *And* I have to do whatever I can to fix what's already been broken by me simply being here.

"I had a nice conversation with Ty last night," I say, walking back and forth in front of them. I keep my eyes glued to the carpet for now so that I can keep my brain on track. "He really is completely and totally dedicated to this band. I'm sure you already know that or you wouldn't have hired him. And obviously he knows his stuff. He's been playing your music since he was six years old." I pause and look at them. "I'm serious. I saw some of his home movies. He's been playing since he was *six*."

A couple of them laugh, while the others exchange glances. I think this impresses them. I'm kind of surprised they don't already know it. *What kind of interview process did they use, anyway?*

"But as you can see, he's not very happy." I start pacing again, imagining him in my mind with that scowl on his face. "And I understand why he's upset. First of all, you guys hired me after you had a discussion among yourselves, but you didn't include him." I pause and look at them. "That's not cool. Not cool at all."

"We didn't exclude him on purpose," Paul said. "He just wasn't around."

I stop pacing, hands on hips. "If Red happened to *not be around*, would you have made the decision without him?"

Paul shrugs. "No. But he's Red."

I look at Red. "If Paul wasn't around, would you have made the decision without him?"

"No. But it's Paul. He has to be in on every decision."

"Exactly. So I'm guessing that if any one of you in the band here—who's in the room right now—were absent, you wouldn't have made the decision. But it's okay to make those decisions without Ty?"

"Yeah, but there's a reason for that. A legal reason." Mooch looks at Paul. "Right?"

Paul nods. "Exactly."

I look at them in confusion. "You mean he's legally not a member of this band?"

Everybody looks at Red, expecting him to answer. He leans forward and rubs his hands together, his rings making clicking sounds as they hit one another. "Yes and no. He's with us on a trial basis. So, yes—on one hand, he's a member of the band. But if he doesn't do certain things, or if certain things don't work out the way we want them to, he won't be a part of the band anymore."

I feel sick for Ty. "And he knows all this?"

"Absolutely. He signed a contract. He had plenty of time to review it, and we've discussed it on several occasions."

I bite my lip, thinking it over. It makes sense that they would want him to do this. They would have no idea what some guy's baggage might be until they spend time with him, so a contract would protect them.

I nod. "Okay. This makes sense." I pace the floor again. "But the problem is, you want to find out if you can integrate him into the band and make him a true member, somebody you can get along with, right?"

They all nod.

"Well, that's great. But the problem is, you're never going to figure that stuff out about him if you don't give him a chance to *act* like a true member of the band." I look up to see if any of this is penetrating.

There's a slightly stubborn expression on Red's face and a blank look on Mooch's, but Cash and Paul seem to get it. They're nodding and glancing at each other meaningfully.

"I don't know Ty that well—probably a whole lot less than you do," I say. "But I've spent some time with him over the past couple days, and I've had some great conversations with him. I watched him onstage with you guys the other night, too, so I think I can say in all fairness that if you don't act like he's a permanent member of the band starting *right now*, you and he are not going to get along, and you guys are going to have to get rid of him."

"If he can't hang, that's the way it needs to be," says Red.

"It's not that he can't hang." I stand there and stare right at him, this stubborn mule who might be related to someone I love . . . or me. "It's more like you're sabotaging him."

Red sits back on the couch, his legs spread and his hands resting on his thighs. "Nobody here is sabotaging the kid."

I point at Red. "There it is. Right there. Again, you're calling him a kid. There's something you've got against him. What is it?"

He hisses out a breath, looking left and right and then at the ceiling. "You're way off base."

I fold my arms and shake my head. "No, I'm not off base at all. I just pressed a button. Trust me . . . I'm an expert at it, so I know when I've done it."

Mooch has a small smile on his face, but all he does is look at the ground. I'm reading body language all over this room, and what it tells me is very clear: Red is in charge, but if Red has an issue, nobody's going to confront him on it; they're going to tiptoe around him and wait for the issue to disappear on its own.

Well, that's just too bad. I'm not the type to tiptoe or let sleeping dogs lie. I'm more the type to strap on a pair of elephant shoes and clomp around until someone wakes up and starts paying attention to me.

"Red, I need to talk to you alone." I glance to my right. "Why don't we go into the booth over there?"

Red looks left and right. "Everything we talk about should probably be said in front of everybody."

"I don't mind," says Mooch, shrugging.

Somebody, I can't tell if it's Cash or Paul, starts singing under his breath. "Someone's in trouble."

"Just give me five minutes," I say, practically begging while trying to ignore the juvenile senior citizens in the room. "I promise, you won't regret it."

Red stands, taking a moment to straighten his spine. Cracking sounds come from his bones. "Okay. Five minutes. And then we need to get to work."

I enter the booth ahead of him and wait for him to shut the door behind us. I take a seat on one of the stools and he does the same. We sit there and stare at each other for a couple seconds. It's really weird looking at this man and wondering if I've seen his eyes before, either in the face of one of my sisters or in the mirror. I have to force myself to think about why we're in here and not the genetic mystery still waiting to be solved.

"I know you're not trying to be difficult, but your attitude and the things you're saying are having the same effect."

"I don't know what you mean." His voice is roughened by years of singing and hard living.

"You hired me to help you, right?"

"Of course. And I appreciate you coming in here to do that today."

"Good. Then I need you to work *with* me and not *against* me."

"But I am." I detect a note of guilt in his voice that gives me hope.

"But you're *not*." I stand, unable to sit still on that stool. The booth is tiny, but I still manage to get three steps in one direction and three steps in the other. Pacing helps me gather my thoughts. "You signed Ty up as a temporary band member and you keep treating him like he'll always *be* a temporary band member. If you continue to do that, he's never going to be anything else but that."

"It just takes time," he says.

"Time, sure. But it also takes *effort*. Effort means you can't have meetings without him, you can't make decisions without him, you can't keep calling him a *kid*, and you can't keep him out of the loop anymore. It's just not fair."

"Life is unfair, and nobody ever said it wasn't going to be."

I stop and point at him. "Don't. Do *not* quote my mother's words at me."

He pulls his head back a little. "I wasn't aware that I was."

I stop and stare at the ceiling, letting out a long sigh. "God, give me strength to deal with this man."

He chuckles, pulling my attention away from the ceiling.

"What?" I ask.

"Gosh, you remind me so much of your mother. I really miss her. How is she doing?"

"Today is not about my mother, Red. If you want to know about my mother, then you and I can have a conversation about her that has nothing to do with the work I'm doing here. That's not going to happen until the workday is done, though. So are you going to cooperate with me or not?" I fold my arms over my chest and glare at him.

He looks down at his knuckles as he rubs them, spins his rings around his fingers a little bit, and then his shoulders slump. "I'm going to help. I will try my best to help."

I feel like I'm talking to my future son. "You are the successful lead singer of one of the most amazing bands that ever played a note of music in the entire world. I don't need you to *try*. I need you to just *do it.*"

He looks up at me with an eyebrow lifted. "Have you ever served in the military?"

I huff out a breath. "No."

"I think you would've been good at ordering people around."

I smile. "I do have two younger sisters I like to boss around, and I've been doing it for over twenty years, so I guess you could say I have some experience." *Hey, maybe I am qualified for this job.*

"So, that's where it comes from." He smiles, his eyes crinkling at the corners. "Guess you have a knack for herding cats."

"Pffft. More like herding eels, I think."

He laughs, his eyes sparkling.

I take a step closer to him, hoping he can see that I'm practically begging. "I can't do this without you, Red. If you're not in it with me a hundred percent, it's going to be a wasted effort. Everybody follows your lead. If you aren't all-in, you might as well just let me pay you back the money that I got out of the bank yesterday and say goodbye. And we can just call this thing a failed experiment and go our separate ways."

He stands and puts his heavy hands on my shoulders as he stares me in the eye. His voice is gruff. "You're not going anywhere, Amber. I finally got you to hang around for a little while, and I'm not gonna screw that up. You just tell me what you need me to do, and I'm going to do it."

I look up at him, seeing the dedication in his expression and the desperation in his eyes. "This is not going to be painless, you know."

"I'm starting to realize that now."

"One of the first things I plan to do is talk to the band about your hair and clothes."

He lets go of my shoulders and looks down at himself. "What's wrong with my clothes?"

I shrug. "Actually, right now, nothing. But this is not the stuff you wear onstage."

"Well, yeah. We have costumes."

I shake my head. "No, you don't. Because you're not actors in a Shakespearean play. You're the real deal and you need to start dressing like it."

He rolls his eyes. "Oh, boy. I hope I don't live to regret this."

As I walk by him to open the door to the booth, he grasps me by the wrist, making me stop. I look up at him.

"I didn't mean that. There's nothing you could do to cause me to regret you being here. I mean that."

"Better hold on to that thought. I have other things I'm going to need you guys to do for me too."

He follows me out, chuckling. And then over the back of my head, he raises his voice and makes an announcement to the group. "Buckle your seat belts, boys. Hurricane Amber is about to make landfall."

CHAPTER THIRTY-THREE

I'm standing in front of the group of men again, still without Ty, but I have a lot more confidence now and newfound hope that things just might work out. "Okay, so that was a good little meeting."

Cash looks over at Red. "And he's only missing part of his ass. You failed to chew it all off."

I smile. As if I could ever chew these guys out. "Ha, ha. Very funny. But seriously . . . let's talk about Ty while he's not here."

"He's gonna love that," Paul says, rolling his eyes.

"No, he probably won't if all he hears is that we talked about him behind his back. But when I have a chance to tell him *what* we discussed, I don't think he's going to be too upset."

"I'm not sure if you know him well enough to say that," Mooch says. "The kid is pretty sensitive."

"Maybe because you keep calling him a kid and treating him like one." I give him the look that my mother gives me when I'm being sassy.

He presses his lips together and nods slowly.

"From my perspective, which is totally coming from the outside looking in, I think the problem is that you guys are treating Ty like he's just a temporary member of the band, when what you *should* be doing is treating him like he's going to be here for the next twenty years. It comes across in everything you do and say, and your fans are absolutely picking up on that, and so is he."

"I'm not even sure *we'll* still be here in twenty years," Paul says, getting a laugh from the rest of the band.

"Well, my job is to make sure that you are, or that you have the option to be."

Now I have their attention. "So . . . the first thing to do is to fix this rift in your relationship. I really think Ty is good for the band. Not only is he talented and completely dedicated to the music, he's got the look that you need."

Cash uses a falsetto voice. "Oooh, somebody's in love."

I glare at him. "If I had something to throw at you right now, I would." I look behind me at the mixing boards.

Jed holds up a hand like a stop sign. "Don't even think about touching my stuff."

I turn back to the band. "Okay, fine, no projectiles. But seriously. He has the look women like and men wish they had. Old or young, his appeal is undeniable. The problem is that there's too big of a gap between what he's got going on and what you've got going on." I try not to squirm, because here comes the big truth.

Cash frowns and looks at his buddies. "I think we just got insulted."

They all laugh.

"No, it's not an insult. It's just an observation. You guys have the same look that you had over twenty years ago, but you're not in your twenties anymore. I get why you're doing it; it's your thing. But the problem is, you're enjoying a resurgence of popularity and there's a whole new generation of people out there." I point to myself. "I'm a part of that generation, and I know how these people think. I know what they're looking for."

"And we're not it?" Red asks.

I'm no idiot. His question is a challenge; I can see it clear as day. And I can also see everyone hanging on his words and my future answer. *It's make-it-or-break-it time.* Okay, no more playing around. I'm going to handle these men like I handle my bees. I'm going to blow a little smoke in their faces, mesmerize them, and then take what I came for: one hundred percent cooperation. *I'm gonna get the honey, baby.*

"Listen . . . You can keep doing what you've always done, and you may pick up some new fans here and there because they like the music and they heard it when they were younger. But face it . . . your existing fan base is getting older. And maybe nostalgia keeps them hanging on to the music, but if you want this new generation of people to be singing your songs and buying your albums for another twenty years, you need to give them what they're looking for. Something they can identify with."

"Maybe we should've hired a different guitarist," Cash says. He looks at his friends. "Remember? We could've had . . . uh . . . that *other* guy . . ." He looks nervous, like he's said too much. I think he's avoiding making eye contact with me.

Red shakes his head. "No, not that guy. Never that guy."

I brush off the part of this conversation that's interfering with me meeting my goal. "If you don't want to make a complete change, I get it. That's cool. I don't want you to become different people. I just want to update the look a little bit. Like Bon Jovi did. He doesn't wear the mullet anymore, right? There's still some hair-teasing there, maybe a little product . . . but he keeps it at a bare minimum."

Mooch looks over at Cash. "You realize this means you're not going to be allowed to wear your jogging shorts to work anymore."

The engineers snicker. Paul hides a smile behind a cough.

I shake my head with my eyes closed. These guys are impossible. Maybe I should be mad that they're making fun, but all I want to do is laugh at them. God spare me from middle-aged rockers hanging on to the past.

"No, wear whatever you want," I say, coming back to the conversation. "I mean, if you don't mind your fans seeing you look like that."

Cash looks down at himself. "Looking like what? I went running this morning."

Everyone else smiles behind their hands, but I don't bother hiding my reaction. "Where did you run from, the donut shop?" I point. "You've got some powdered sugar right there." I point to his chest.

Everybody bursts out laughing except Cash. He looks down and brushes it off as he frowns. "Hey. That's not nice. It's not powdered sugar . . . it's dust from my apartment. We're remodeling."

I walk over and put my hand on his arm and shake it a little bit. "I'm just kidding. Sure it's dust. But honestly, Cash, you're wearing what I would wear when I'm lounging at home with a pair of fuzzy slippers to match." I place my hand on my chest. "Even I, hippie chick extraordinaire, wouldn't be caught dead outside the commune in that outfit."

He looks down at himself. "But these are my favorites."

"And you make enough money to buy a big estate somewhere with a tall wall all the way around it where you can walk around in whatever short-shorts you want to. But you really shouldn't do it in downtown Manhattan."

Mooch looks over at him. "She has a point, man."

Cash makes a face at him. "Traitor."

Red takes charge. "So, other than no short-shorts, what exactly are we talking about here?" He looks at his fellow band members. "You know the new label wants us to do this stuff. Do you remember what that wanker said?"

"Yeah, but we're never going to do *that*," Paul says.

"What did the wanker want you to do?" I ask, super curious. Hopefully, he wasn't pushing for a Ziggy Stardust look. There's no way I could stick around for that.

Cash looks like he's in pain, which, when paired with his current wardrobe choices, is enough to make me nearly kill myself trying to *not* laugh. "He wanted us to do the punk thing. He was talking about mohawks and fauxhawks and stuff like that."

Mooch frowns and shakes his head. "I will not be wearing a fauxhawk in this lifetime."

"Oh, Jesus. Fauxhawks?" This guy, whoever he is, really is a wanker. "No. I agree with you guys. A fauxhawk is a bad idea for anyone over the age of thirty. But may I remind you that you all walk around with teased mullets?" I wait for them to make the connection, but all I get is confusion on the faces around me.

"What's your point?" Paul asks.

"I'm just saying . . . you have no problem with the mullet but you're complaining about the fauxhawk . . . This illustrates my point exactly."

Cash slumps down on the arm of the couch. "I'm starting to feel like I'm in school again and I've pissed off my teacher."

I walk over and give him a hug, patting him on the back. "I'm not that mean, I promise. I want to make this as painless as possible." I stand up with my hands on his shoulders and stare him in the eye. "Do you trust me?"

He nods wordlessly. I think I surprised him with the physical contact. Heck, I surprised myself. Not in a bad way, though. I actually like these guys, and back home, we're always hugging and stuff, so physical contact is just a regular part of my day. I'm happy that I've brought that piece of me to the city.

I back off and look at the group with my hands together. I'm on the edge of victory; I can feel it in my bones. "My first act as your official consultant is to suggest that you get haircuts."

I wait to see what they say. They all look at one another, mystified and maybe a little afraid.

"Since none of you are Sampson, I promise that cutting off some of that long hair in the back is not going to cause you to lose your strength *or* your musical talent."

"How much are we going to cut off?" Paul asks.

"How about we let the professionals decide?" Surely there's someone here in Manhattan who knows how to cut hair and do it well. That will be my next mission after I leave this place . . . to find that magician.

"As long as I don't look like Lister when you're done," Cash says, pouting.

Everybody laughs and nods, even Jed and Pete.

Victory is mine! "Okay, I got it. I promise you, nobody is going to have to walk around looking like Lister. Except Lister, of course. Poor guy."

We all have a good laugh at that. The more I picture them wearing suits with business haircuts, the harder I giggle. By the time Ty walks back through the door, we all have rosy cheeks and the mood is much lighter.

Ty stops just inside the room and stares at us suspiciously. I'm trying to decide if I should go over to him in front of all these men, when Red stands and does it for me. He walks over and puts his hand on Ty's shoulder, forcing him into the room in a friendly way. "We're sorry, man. We weren't laughing about you. Come on in. We owe you an apology."

The rest of the band stands and the engineers go over to their mixing boards, quietly turning their backs to the group.

"What're you talking about?" Ty asks. He still hasn't lost his suspicious air.

"We haven't been fair to you since you joined us, and that's on me." Red holds his hand out. "I'm sorry. You didn't deserve that bullshit."

I almost feel like crying watching this happen. Ty is getting exactly what he deserves—an apology and some respect. I'm so proud of Red for being a bigger man than he was being before. He actually listened to me and now he's following through on a promise he made. It's pretty heady stuff, knowing how powerful this guy is in the music industry and that he trusts me enough to act on my advice. I know if I weren't a blast from his past, he probably wouldn't have, but still . . . I'm going to take my successes where I can get them.

Ty slowly reaches up and shakes his hand. "Thanks. But you don't need to apologize for anything."

"Yeah, we do," Cash says, walking over and shaking his hand too. "We were assholes. We should've done better."

It's Mooch's turn next. "Yeah, you can thank your girlfriend over there for setting us straight."

I stare at the ceiling, wishing Mooch hadn't called me that, but loath to bring any more attention to it. Ty is probably going to hate me forever for being labeled his girlfriend. I can't even look at him right now, imagining that he's thinking he finally got what he wanted only because this hippie chick who showed up on the scene as the bastard child of a band member demanded it. Talk about an ego punch.

Paul speaks next. "You're an amazing musician and you have every right to be here and in on every decision we make. We shouldn't have blocked you out. It was stupid and senseless . . . something we should've known better than to do."

There's a funny tone to his voice when he says that. I look down from the ceiling in time to see everybody exchanging glances and nodding at one another. I can tell that Ty is just as out of the loop as I am about the significance of Paul's words. He's on the outside looking in, like I am.

I'm getting the impression that they have a lot of secrets I'm not privy to and probably never will be.

"How about we start this day over?" Red asks, distracting me from trying to read any more of their body language. He rubs his hands together. "Anybody here ready to play some music?"

Ty glances over at me with an unreadable expression before answering. "Are we working on new material?"

"That's the plan," Mooch says, walking over to the small booth that I had my conversation with Red in. "I'm just gonna go bang out a couple rhythms I was working on this week." He disappears into the room and shuts the door. Pretty soon we hear his drums going; the sound is muted but not completely gone. The engineers are busy with headphones on, watching lights blink on their mixers and computer screens as they make adjustments to different dials and sliders.

"What about you?" Red asks Ty. "You got any new material?"

Ty shrugs. "Maybe. I've been playing around with some stuff." He doesn't sound very confident.

"Great. Maybe you can show us."

"Sure." He turns his attention to me. "Can I have a word with you for a minute?"

I shrug. "Sure." I wish I could be excited about this private meeting, but the truth is, I'm dreading it. He's pissed, I know he is. I fought his battle for him—one he was losing for months before I got here—and won. What guy would like that?

I follow him out of the room into the reception area. There's still no one there. As soon as the door shuts, he turns to face me. "I'm sorry I was rude earlier."

I'm more than a little shocked that his first words weren't *I don't ever want to see you again.*

"Don't worry about it," I say, relief flooding through me. "I understand why you were."

He shakes his head. "No, don't forgive me that easily."

I smile, entirely charmed by the self-torture he's administering on my behalf. "Why not?"

"Because. When I'm acting like a dick, you need to hold me to it. Don't let me get away with it."

"Why not?" I can't imagine why he'd want me to extend his torture by forcing him to pay for his sins every time he makes a mistake. I'm not that much of a wench.

"Because . . ." He moves his lower jaw around and flares his nostrils, wrestling with his emotions for a few seconds before he answers. "That's what my mom did with my father all the time, and he railroaded her." Tears are threatening but he's fighting valiantly against their escape.

I nod, getting it now . . . understanding why he reacted the way he did to his own behavior. Some of the things I saw in those films are starting to make sense. I'm touched that he's looking at our interactions and measuring them against those between his parents. It tells me he sees me as more than just some woman he slept with.

I sigh and stroke his arm gently. "You don't know me very well, Ty, but I promise . . . if you spend enough time with me, you'll eventually figure out that it's not possible to railroad me. There's no need to apologize for having emotions and needing to express them."

He looks at me funny. "You were ready to forgive me without even an apology?"

"That's what people do sometimes." I reach up and stroke his cheek. He looks so sad, I just want to wipe it all away and make him smile again. "Just because you're experiencing an emotion, it doesn't make you a bad person. And if you lash out at somebody you care about in the process, well, that's life. It happens. You did apologize, and I already knew you weren't happy with yourself for doing it, so we're good."

"But I never want to be the kind of person who doesn't regret it and doesn't apologize after he does the wrong thing."

My hand drops and I shrug. "Then don't be that guy. Like I said to you last night . . . you choose. You choose how you react to the things that happen to you and the things you do. You take step one and then you decide what step two is going to be, not me."

"So, what you're saying is . . . it's all on me."

"Yeah. No matter who I am in your life and whether or not I'm still in your life two weeks from now, I can't force you to be who I want you to be; and I wouldn't want to do that anyway. You are who you are, for better or for worse."

His smile is weak, but at least it's real. "I hope it's for better."

"Me too, but that's not very realistic."

His face goes dark. "What are you saying? You don't think I can be a good person?"

I get closer and take his arm, shaking him a little bit. "Hey . . . leave your bags at the door, Ty. I'm not saying that at all. I'm saying, *you* are not perfect. You are *human*, just like me and all those old farts in the other room. You're going to have emotions, you're going to experience them, and you're going to express them . . . and those emotions aren't always going to be pretty. You have to be okay with that. I'm okay with it. I think the guys in that room are okay with it. But you can't bring your baggage everywhere you go, assuming the worst of everybody and assuming everybody hates you or is angry at you all the time."

He looks up, his eyes watery. He starts tapping his foot and then clears his throat. "This isn't easy for me. *Feelings* . . . aren't easy for me."

I pull him up against me and hold him, rubbing his back. "I know. But the good news is, you're normal. Life wasn't meant to be easy. In fact, from what I understand, it's supposed to be incredibly unfair and difficult for everyone."

He puts his arms around me and hugs me tightly, leaning his chin down to rest on my shoulder. "Who told you that garbage?"

"Two people who I'm learning to respect more and more every day." I pat him on the back a couple times and then pull away. "The band is going to give you a fair shake now. Don't blow it."

An adorable lopsided grin comes across his face. "Don't blow it? That sounds kind of ominous."

"It's not meant to be. But this is your real chance. They're going to give you a *real* shot this time. You're a hundred percent in. Don't forget to voice your opinion and say what needs to be said. You are the voice of a new generation."

"That sounds like the name of a song."

"If it isn't, it should be." I wink at him.

He leans in and kisses me on the forehead. "Thanks. Thanks for everything."

"Don't mention it." *Mission accomplished! Yeah! Who's the superhero? I'm the superhero!* There's a total fist pump coming as soon as I'm around the corner and no one can see me do it.

He jabs his thumb over his shoulder. "Are you gonna come in and listen?"

I shake my head. "No. I've been assigned a new mission. I need to find the best hairdresser in Manhattan."

"You might want to talk to Lister about that. He's got a contact list that could fill an entire room if it were on paper." He reaches up and touches a lock of my hair. "I hope you're not going to change this, though."

I look at the hair he's holding. "What?"

"At the hairdresser's . . . I like your hair the way it is. Wavy. Soft. No fake color on it."

My face goes warm with the compliment. "No, it's not for me. It's for the band."

His eyebrows go up as he releases my hair. "That's going to be interesting."

"You're not kidding." I sigh, imagining visiting Lister once more.

"What's wrong?" he asks.

"Nothing. I just don't want to have to see Lister right now, is all." He's the chief of the fun police.

He laughs. "Well, you don't have to. It was just a suggestion. If you have other contacts in the city, go for it."

"Okay, fine. Go have fun making music. I'm going to go talk to the stiff shirt."

I start to walk away, but he grabs my hand and pulls me back. At first I'm surprised and confused, but then when he leans down, his eyes falling closed, I know what he intends to do. I should tell him not to, that we're at work and there's no room for kissing when you're on the clock, but I can't. I don't even want to. I've been missing the touch of his lips on mine since the moment I left his penthouse last night.

When we connect, that Fourth of July sparkler lights up in my chest again. We're just getting into some awesome tongue action, too, when the door behind me opens all of a sudden and a slight gust of air hits me in the back.

"Oh, shit . . . I'm sorry. I didn't mean to interrupt." It's a female voice.

We quickly pull apart and I turn around to face a girl about my age with a bag over her shoulder and a pile of folders in her arms. She has a nose ring, an eyebrow ring, and a strip of purple hair down the middle of her head, like a punk rock Pepé Le Pew.

"Oh no . . . it's no problem. I was just leaving." I squeeze Ty's hand before I turn around to go.

"I'll call you," he says.

"Great." I nod at the girl on my way out as she sets herself up behind the reception desk. She waves goodbye as the door shuts behind me.

Phew. That girl walking in was like a cold shower but without the water. It's probably a good thing that it happened, because there's a couch in that reception area, and Ty was looking way too hot—and that vulnerability he shared with me made me want to tear his clothes off and make him forget how sad he was. *Damn . . . I've got it bad.*

I need to call my sisters stat and tell them what's going on. Maybe they'll be able to help me get control of my libido . . . or at least help me relocate my common sense that's missing in action.

I leave the recording studio office and head to the elevator. I guess I'm going over to Lister's office whether I like it or not, since I don't know anybody in this town other than Ray the not-so-sexy hot dog man, Mr. Blake the grouchy limo driver, Jeremy the elevator boy, and . . . wait! *James.* I can ask James the concierge for the info.

I smile, so excited that I actually have a contact in the city and I don't have to waste any more time hanging out with the most boring man on the planet, aka Greg Lister.

I'll call my sisters after I have the hair stuff figured out. I'm going to need at least a half hour of private time to catch them up on everything. I shoot off a quick text telling them to expect a call later and that everything is going really well.

CHAPTER THIRTY-FOUR

I enter the lobby of the Four Seasons, searching for James. I'm confident he'll be able to direct me to a hairdresser who can solve my problem.

My first stop is the check-in counter. The receptionist directs me to a special office where I find James sitting behind a desk shuffling papers. He looks up at me and smiles. "Hello, Ms. Fields. It's nice to see you again."

"You too, James. I'm here to see if you can help me out with something."

He stands and points at the chair across from his desk. "Please, have a seat. I'll do whatever I can."

"Cool." I sit down and arrange my fancy purse on my lap before I begin. "I have a group of men who need new haircuts. These are people who have been living in the eighties all their lives, so I need somebody who can do an updated look but not something so shocking that they can't adjust to it."

He folds his hands in front of him, resting them on the desk as he nods. "Let me think about this for a couple seconds."

I know I've come to the right place; he's not just sending me to any old salon.

He reaches into a drawer and pulls out a pad of paper and a pen. "I'm going to give you two names. The first one would be my preference, but the second one is really good too." He pauses for a moment as he's writing. "Do you have a special budget you want to stick to? Because the first one is a bit more expensive than the other one."

I shake my head. "No. There's no specific budget. Basically, whatever it takes."

He hands me the paper. "I'm pretty sure you'll be happy with either one of these. Please tell them that I sent you. Name-dropping will help you get in sooner because they're usually booked solid for weeks in advance."

I take the note and stand. "I knew I came to the right man. Thank you so much, James."

He stands and reaches his hand across the desk to shake mine. "Anytime. Did you get to see a Broadway show?"

I pause on my way out. "Nope. I don't have time for that right now." *Because I'm a busy businesswoman who works in the music industry! Yeah!* "Maybe before I leave." I feel so professional, so important. I never felt like this at the farmers' market. I refuse to think about what will happen after these two weeks are over.

"If you need tickets, let me know."

"Will do." I open the door to leave, but pause. The man I spoke to in the bar with the long hair is walking through the lobby right in front of me. He takes three more steps and stops, holding out his hand. Another man appears, moving out from behind a screen of potted plants, to greet him. He's wearing a suit. My jaw drops open when I see who it is.

I pull back into the office and close the door most of the way, leaving it open only enough for me to peek out.

"Is there something wrong?" James asks me.

"No. Nothing." What are they doing out there? How do they know each other? Did I see that guy in Lister's office? Is that why he looks familiar?

They're having an animated conversation. Neither one of them looks very happy.

What should I do? Should I go out there and confront them? Before I can make a decision, they part ways. Lister goes over to the reception desk, and the long-haired man in leather walks away, headed toward the exit. I open James' door and lean out to confirm the man is gone before I leave the office.

James is right behind me. "Are you sure you're okay?"

"Yeah, I'm good." I don't want to get him involved in my conspiracy theory, which isn't even defined in my own head yet. "I'll see you later, James." I walk away, headed for the reception desk. I can see Lister's back from here. He's speaking with the woman working at the computer. I need to get close so I can listen in.

Unfortunately, I can't get near enough to hear anything without seeming like a creepy weirdo. I chew the inside of my cheek as I try to decide what to do next. I'm just standing here staring at him, which is no plan at all.

Plan? Why am I thinking about making plans to spy on Lister? My overactive, problem-solving brain is going to take over and ruin everything. I should turn around and leave, locate these hairdressers, and talk to one of them about getting appointments for the band. Whatever Lister does on his own time is none of my business.

The moment my decision is made to walk away, Lister turns around. He stares at me in shock.

"Surprised to see me?" *Screw the hairdresser plan. Let's see him talk his way out of this one.*

"I was checking to see if you were available, actually."

I pull my phone out of my purse and look to see if he's called. The only thing on my screen is a text from my sisters asking me what's going on. "That's funny . . . I don't see any missed calls from you." I look up and wait for him to explain himself.

"I was in the neighborhood. I dropped by."

I tilt my head trying to act innocent. "Really? What were you doing in the neighborhood?"

"Client meeting. Do you have a minute to chat?"

Client meeting? Is he making up stories, or is that man really his client? The man he met looks more like a private investigator to me. But why would Lister hire somebody to follow me around? I don't know, but I'm never going to find out unless I talk to him and ask the right questions.

"Sure," I say, acting totally casual. I hope he doesn't expect me to invite him up to my room.

"How about a cup of coffee in the restaurant?"

"That's fine. But then I need to get going. I have a lot of things to do today."

Lister holds his hand out, gesturing for me to precede him. I walk over to the restaurant and let Lister take over. He quickly acquires a table for us.

"I'll have a cup of tea," I say to the man standing at the table ready to take my order.

"Espresso for me. Thanks." The waiter leaves us alone and Lister turns his attention on me.

"Have you met with the band yet?"

"Yes. We had a meeting this morning. In the studio. It went well." That's all he's going to get from me. If he wants details, he can ask his clients. I don't work for him.

"I wanted to talk to you about the legal settlement."

I wasn't expecting this. "What legal settlement?"

"The one that my clients offered to you and your sisters. The inheritance."

"Oh. What about it?"

He fiddles with the edge of his napkin. Something tells me this tiny gesture is a loss of control for him. He's nervous about something. I can't wait to hear what he has to say.

"Are you still inclined to refuse the offer?"

"I thought I was perfectly clear about it before." Is he suggesting that now, because I'm involved with the band, I'm somehow going to want their money?

"I just wanted to be certain that I understood."

"Just because I agreed to be paid for the work I'm doing now, it doesn't change anything else."

He nods, looking very satisfied. "Good. I just wanted to . . . verify." He reaches up and sticks his finger behind his tie at his neck, moving his collar around a little bit.

Sweating much? "Why?" I ask, watching him closely for more signs of strained nerves.

The waiter arrives with our drinks, ruining everything. Lister takes the moment afforded by the delivery of our beverages to collect himself. His confidence is restored; it's written all over his smug face.

Maybe Lister thinks he's off the hook for whatever it was he was worried about, but when he's done mixing in his sugar and I've poured some tea out of the pot, we're going to have a little do-over.

"Are you enjoying your stay in Manhattan?" he asks.

"Why did you want to be sure?" I ask, disregarding his attempt at redirection.

"Excuse me?"

"I asked you this before the waiter came, and I just repeated the question . . . Why did you want to be sure I was still rejecting the offer from the band?"

His finger goes up to his necktie again. "Just clarifying. It's no big deal."

Yeah, right.

He drinks his coffee in two long sips. How he does it without scalding his throat is a medical mystery.

I might be from out in the sticks, but I'm not as naïve as he thinks I am. He's nervous about something, and now that he's figured out what he needed to, he wants to get out of here before I can ask him any more questions. *Too bad, Lister. I'm on a roll.*

"Who was that guy I saw you in the lobby with?" I ask, knowing I'm turning up the heat.

Maybe I'm mistaken, but it looks like he's lost a little bit of the pink in his complexion. He uses his napkin to wipe his lips. "I didn't meet anyone in the lobby."

I fix Lister with a stare. "I saw you shaking his hand."

"Oh, that was no one. I wasn't meeting him here. It was just a chance bumping-into-someone kind of thing."

I've never heard Lister be this ineloquent before, which tells me he is completely full of baloney right now. "He reminded me of Red when I saw him the other day."

"The other day?" Lister is really paying attention now.

"Yes. He must be staying here in the hotel. I've seen him twice already before today."

Lister checks his watch. "Listen, I need to get going." He looks at my full cup of tea and the teapot that still has at least two more servings inside it.

I wave in dismissal, done playing this game with him. "Go ahead and go. I know you're a busy man." *And also totally full of shit and running away from me and my questions.*

He stands, pulling some cash out of his pocket and sliding it under the saucer of his small espresso cup.

"I'll be in touch to check in with you," he says.

I look up at him, my anger mostly contained. "Am I supposed to be reporting to you?"

He opens his mouth to answer, but nothing comes out. He presses his lips together and shakes his head before finally answering. "No. You don't report to me."

"Then why are you going to check in with me?" He is acting so weird. I wish he would just come out with whatever it is he's thinking in that sly brain of his.

"Just looking out for my clients' best interests." He checks his phone again. "I really need to go. It was a pleasure seeing you again."

"Sure," I say, but he's already gone. He probably didn't even hear me.

I watch him negotiate his way around the tables, his perfectly tailored suit fit snugly to his athletic frame. I so prefer the look of the rocker I hung out with last night to this stiff and boring butthead. I'm sure they pay him a ton of money, but he is a terrible liar. I hope he doesn't work for them in the courtroom.

I don't bother finishing my tea. I only agreed to drink it because he wanted to have a chat. Instead, I stand and walk out of the hotel, keeping my eyes peeled for that person Lister supposedly wasn't here to meet. I don't see him anywhere, so I go out to the curb and text Mr. Blake to ask him to come and get me. I only have to wait five minutes and he's there, stepping out and opening the door for me. I wish my day hadn't turned so completely gray before I got into this car, because being with Mister Stiff Neck certainly isn't going to change things.

"Hello there, Mr. Blake."

"Hello, Ms. Fields." He makes sure I'm in the car with the door shut and then gets into the driver's seat, shifting the car into drive and waiting for his moment to pull into traffic.

I hand him a piece of paper with the address for the first salon on it. "How is your family doing?"

"They are well, thank you." I see him glance down at the passenger side of the front seat before he goes back to checking his side mirror.

As the car pulls away from the curb, I pull myself forward and look around the headrest. There's a drawing on the seat next to Mr. Blake made with crayon—a few rough scribbles in red and green. There's a pattern to the patches of color . . . green on top in slightly triangular shapes, red squares under, and something jagged above the green triangles. It looks like the work of a two-year-old, but my suspicions tell me the artist is a bit older than that.

"I like your artwork," I say, sitting back and studying the side of his face, trying to read his expression.

He doesn't say anything and his face is so stern, it reminds me of one of those carved African tribal masks.

"Did Lolly draw that pretty picture?"

"She did." Life returns to his countenance as his jaw bounces out several times.

"Ah. Getting ready for Christmas early, I see."

His face twists with the emotions he's trying not to expose. "Yes."

I look out my window to my left. "My sister is doing the same thing right now, guaranteed. She gets ready really early. Always has. We start seeing red and green even before Halloween."

"It's Lolly's favorite holiday." He whispers something that sounds like *holly-day* under his breath as his hands squeeze the steering wheel over and over rhythmically.

I think about that for a few seconds. Lolly. Holly. "Is Lolly short for lollipop or holiday?"

Mr. Blake pulls up to a red light and looks at me in the mirror. "How could you possibly know that?"

I shrug. "I didn't. I just guessed."

A few minutes of silence pass before Mr. Blake speaks again. He says one word: "Gerald."

I sit there blinking for a few seconds before the meaning sinks in. Then my heart feels like it's expanding to twice its size inside my chest. "Nice to meet you, Gerald. Feel free to call me Amber."

"I prefer to keep things more formal," he says gruffly. In that moment, he reminds me a little bit of Ty . . . the beautiful man who confessed to me that he's not comfortable with feeling emotion but managed to do it with me anyway. It creates a feeling of kinship with my driver that I sure as heck never expected to experience. New York City is just chock-full of surprises, and damn, I think I actually like it. I like never knowing what crazy thing is going to happen next.

I can't help but beam with happiness. I'm breaking down barriers all over the place, kicking ass and taking names. "That's cool, Mr. Blake. I can hang with formal."

I catch his smile in the rearview mirror and notice that he doesn't bother to wipe it away.

And just like that, my gray skies turn blue.

CHAPTER THIRTY-FIVE

After chatting with the hairdresser and securing an evening appointment tomorrow for the entire band, I finally have time to talk to my sisters. I press the speed dial button and pray they'll pick up as I walk down the sidewalk. Mr. *Gerald* Blake is on his way back to the Four Seasons alone; I need some time to get my head straight.

"Hello?"

"Rose? Is that you?"

"Yes! Amber, I'm so glad you called. I was starting to get worried about you."

"Why? I'm fine."

"Because . . . you haven't called in a while, and I know you have a lot of news."

"You're right. I do." I fill her in on the details, including the fact that the band is about to start their makeover tomorrow.

"That's pretty amazing that you were able to get them appointments in one day. I thought those New York hairdressers had waiting lists."

"This one does, but when you walk in and say you need to get a bunch of celebrity haircuts, the waiting list gets a lot shorter. Normally, they close at eight o'clock at night, but tomorrow they're staying open until midnight to get them done."

"What time are you going in?"

"Our appointment is for nine. I figure it'll take about a half hour or forty-five minutes per haircut."

"It sounds like you're really getting things done over there."

"Why do you sound like you're not happy about that?" I stop at the corner of the street, waiting for the little man to turn white. Several people gather around me doing the same thing. I let my hair fall over my phone and pull my arms in closer to me. I doubt this is going to make my conversation any more private, but I have to at least try to keep the entire world from hearing my business.

"I'm happy for you. But you know I worry."

"What are you worried about? If you tell me, maybe I could put your mind at ease."

She sighs. "Nothing in particular. I just want to be sure you're okay. I feel bad that we sent you down there all by yourself."

"You have nothing to worry about. I'm happy, I promise." It's when I say this that I realize that I really am enjoying myself. I feel capable and respected. My family feels this way about the work I do at the farm, but it's not the same. The work I'm doing here makes me feel that way about *myself.* "So far everybody has been very nice to me. I think the guys in the band are trying extra hard. I'm pretty sure if I weren't related to any of them, they would've told me to go pound sand by now."

She laughs. "Are you giving them a hard time?"

"Not on purpose. But I guess I am telling them some hard truths."

"I know that Em would really like to hear what you have to say. She's not here right now, though."

"Where is she?"

"She's out in the barn, painting."

My heart leaps for my sister. "This is a good thing, right?"

"I think so. I haven't seen what she's working on, but it's been a while."

"I know. It's her way of expressing herself, and I was concerned she was going to stop altogether."

"She's been out there pretty much since you left."

A little guilt niggles at my heart. "Is it because of me? Is she upset?"

"I don't think so. I think she's a little concerned about you, like I am, but it's nothing serious."

"Will you tell her to call me when she gets in?"

"Sure. So, tell me . . . when are we going to see you?"

"In two weeks." The first few times I thought about this time period, it seemed long. Today, not so much. I fear it's going to fly by. "Today was my first day. Em told me that I have an open airline ticket waiting for me, so as soon as I'm finished here, I'll be on a plane coming home."

"Well, I'll believe that when I see it." I can hear a smile in her voice.

"What's that supposed to mean?"

"Em and I have been talking, and we think it's possible that you might want to stay there a little bit longer."

"What makes you say that?" My sisters have always been very good at reading me. *Are they right about me this time? Do I want to stay here longer than two weeks?* If they are right, that would really suck, because in order for my life to continue without conflict, I need to go back to the farm where I belong and be good with that. I can't be there, wishing I were here, and I can't be here while my entire family is wishing I were there. It sounds like a recipe for heartache to me.

"I don't know . . . ," Rose says. "Maybe a certain handsome guitar player might have something to do with it?"

My face is suddenly burning with the memories of Ty naked flashing across my mind. I drop my voice to make sure that none of my fellow pedestrians will hear me as we cross the street. "I can't talk about it now, but I do have a lot to tell you."

"Did you have sex?"

I bark out a laugh. She sounds way too excited about the idea. "Maybe."

"I knew it! Em owes me a dollar."

"I cannot believe you guys are betting on my sex life."

"Hey, you know how boring it gets out here. What else are we supposed to do? We're living vicariously through you."

"You don't have to do that. You could just come here and live it with me."

"I can't speak for Em, but I know I can't do that right now. If you decide to stay there for longer than two weeks, I might come for a visit, but for now I'm just too busy at the clinic."

I'm walking rapidly, in a hurry to get back to my hotel so that I can come up with the rest of my game plan for the band. "I'm not going to stay here past two weeks. I'm telling you; it's just a temporary job." I'm going to tell myself that as often as necessary, so that when the time comes for me to leave, I won't be tempted to ask for more. This is a two-week time-out from my real life. Rose says she's living vicariously through me, and I'm right there with her; I'm living vicariously through myself. For this short period of time, I'm no longer Amber Fields of Glenhollow Farms . . . I'm Amber Fields, personal consultant to Red Hot, currently living in Manhattan. I wish the latter description didn't fill me with quite so much excitement. It's going to suck saying goodbye to this life.

"Okay, whatever you say." Rose sighs. "I need to get going; I have a patient waiting for me."

"Why do I get the impression that you're not hearing me when I tell you that I'm coming home in two weeks?"

She's silent for a few seconds before she answers. "This might sound crazy to you, but Em and I both think that you're suited to the job you're doing right now."

"In what way?" I'm a glutton for punishment. I've asked my sister to tell me why I'm good at the thing I can't do after these two weeks are up, so I can live with even more regret after I get back to my real life.

"You're a problem solver. And once you make up your mind to do something, nothing gets in your way. That kind of person is invaluable in business. I think your talents are underutilized out here on the farm."

Her words, while meant to be complimentary, not only make me feel like I'm going to have a heart attack—because they hit so close to the thoughts I've been having myself—but they also hurt my feelings. "I thought you liked living with me and working at the farmers' market together."

"Of *course* I do. Don't be a brat. All I'm trying to say is that someone as smart as you and as talented as you are could do a lot of great things in a big city like Manhattan. You know where we come from . . . Our mothers spent the best years of their lives traveling with that band, so there must be *something* special about them. You've been given a huge opportunity to figure out what that is and maybe experience some of it for yourself. I think it would be a big mistake for you to miss out on that."

"But what about you guys?"

"What about us?"

"Don't you want the same thing for yourselves?" Maybe what I'm feeling is just a natural reaction to the situation. We've always wondered about our fathers, and now I'm being given the chance to learn all I want.

"Heck no. I have zero interest in solving anyone's problems unless they involve an injured animal. And you know as well as I do that Em would rather shave her head bald than put herself in the public eye. She has said on more than one occasion how happy she is that she doesn't have to go to the city to deal with this stuff."

"Who says I'm going to be in the public eye?" I hate that my pulse is quickening in excitement over the idea. I need to be happy living on the farm, not feeling like I'm missing out on a great life here.

"Don't even try to pretend the idea doesn't thrill you. Amber, you were meant to be a decision maker, a doer, a problem solver. It's who you are, fundamentally, as a person. Why deny it? You know it's true."

I'm almost to the hotel; I can see it up ahead. I stop so that I can finish our conversation before I get there. I'm standing in the middle of the sidewalk while people walk around me, with thoughts, feelings, and dreams swirling around inside my head. Rose has said things I never imagined someone in my family would say. All this time I thought they'd accepted and agreed with the fact that I needed to be there in order to do my part for the family business. But now to learn that at least one of my sisters thinks I could and should be doing something else with my life? That's huge. I'm almost afraid to hope it's real.

"I think you're right." My heart aches. I feel disloyal to my mothers, the women who sacrificed so much to raise my sisters and me in a safe and private place. "I'm not saying I'm going to stay here for longer than two weeks; I mean, it's not like I can just abandon my hives and my family. But this does feel like the right thing to be doing. And I really am enjoying myself . . . so far, anyway. Everybody is being really nice to me, and I feel like I'm making a difference."

"For whom? The band?"

"Yes." *And Ty*, but I'm not going to tell her that part. She'll think I'm attracted to him because he has problems that need solving, but she'd be wrong about that. I love that he's a challenge, that he wears his moods right there on his sleeve and he doesn't apologize for it, that he's a talented artist who's dedicated himself to music he's cared about since childhood, that he's unvarnished and *real*. Every other guy I've known has put on a show, pretended to be something he's not in an effort to impress me. Ty doesn't do that. You either take him at face value or not at all, and I do so like that face of his.

"And you're happy with that? Making a difference for them?" Rose asks.

"Yes. Why wouldn't I be?"

"I don't know. Maybe because when you went out there, your goal was to tell them to go screw themselves, but now you're working to help them."

I wish I could read the emotion in her words. "Are you disappointed in me?" Now I feel like crying. *Am I a traitor to my sisters and our cause?*

"Not *at all.* There's a piece of me that might've been really satisfied hearing you tell a story about flipping them off and telling them to go have a nice life. But that's the petty, mean, and small part of me that I'm not very proud of. I'm pretty sure Em feels the same way I do now; we're both glad that you found a way to put the past behind you and move forward in a positive way. It's better for everyone and your own personal karma to do that."

"I haven't put the past totally behind me. I'm still angry about what they didn't do. Or what they did. It's kind of confusing, actually. I don't have the whole story yet."

"I'm sure it is confusing. And I think, eventually, you're going to figure everything out. The important thing to know is that we support you and we trust your judgment. I know you're going to be really busy for the next two weeks, but do your best to keep us posted."

"I absolutely will. And you guys can call me or text me anytime you want. I'm just running around doing errands and stuff."

"I'm sure it's a lot more complicated than running errands, but I hear you. We'll keep in touch."

"I love you," I say, a wave of homesickness washing over me.

"I love you too. If I were standing next to you right now, I would give you the biggest hug and kiss you've ever had."

"And I'd give you one right back. Hug Em for me. I miss you guys so much."

"You don't need to miss us because we're right here. The farm is just a short plane ride away."

"They said I could use their jet."

"Wow, that's pretty generous. Those things aren't cheap to operate."

"I know. And I'd feel really guilty taking them up on the offer, but if I get too homesick, I just might."

"And we will be there to pick you up at the airport, so don't worry. Now go have fun, would you? If you don't come home with a ton of really amazing stories about your time in Manhattan, I'm going to be mad at you."

I laugh. Leave it to Rose to fix things for me. She calls me a problem solver but she is the healer of all wounds. "Okay, I have to go. I'm at the hotel now."

"Okay. Bye-bye. Have fun!"

"I will." I'm not going to let the two-week horizon get me down. Rose's words have given me a lot to think about, and for the first time in forever, I feel really, *really* excited about my future.

CHAPTER THIRTY-SIX

I'm about twenty feet from the front door of the Four Seasons when a woman who I think is going to walk right past me stops and smiles. It's a little disconcerting, but I sidestep, smile back, and continue on.

"Excuse me . . . ," she says loudly from behind me.

I pause and turn around. "Yes?"

She's definitely talking to me; she's staring right at my face as she positions herself in front of me.

"Hello. Are you, by any chance, Amber Fields?"

I stare at her, blinking in shock. I don't recognize her as an employee of the hotel, but she knows me by name, so she must be. "Yes, I am."

She reaches into her bag and pulls out a small black device. "Hi. I'm Elizabeth Mathers from OMG News. I hear you're dating the lead guitarist for Red Hot, Ty Stanz. Is this true?"

My jaw drops open. I thought the black thing in her hand was a cell phone, because it looks a little bit like mine, but now I realize it's not a phone at all; it's some sort of recorder.

"Who did you say you are again?"

"Elizabeth Mathers from OMG News." Her smile has slipped a little. "Can I get a quote from you?"

"How did you know who I am?"

"I'm a reporter; I'm pretty good at figuring things out."

My mind races. The only way she could know who I am is if she works at this hotel, Lister's office, or the airline. These are the only people I've interacted with who know my name. I think.

"What kind of quote?" She's stumped me with a simple question. I'm treading water but only barely.

"*Are* you or *aren't* you dating Ty Stanz of Red Hot?"

"That's none of your business." She's starting to annoy me, this young girl with her hair pulled back in a very tight bun and her black pantsuit and running shoes. *If I take off into the hotel, will she sprint after me?* She looks like she could and would.

"You don't think the fans of the band want to know this information?"

"I don't care whether they do or not; it's none of their business."

She puts the recording device by her mouth. "Amber is denying the existence of a relationship, but, clearly, there's something going on here."

"Hey! You can't say that!"

She gives me a tight smile. "Sure I can. It's the truth."

"No, it's not. You're misleading people."

"So, are you *denying* that you're having a relationship with him?" She shoves the recording device in my face.

"I'm not saying anything about anything." I take a step to the side and start walking quickly to the hotel. Unfortunately, she's wearing those stupid running shoes, so she easily keeps up with me. The recorder is in my face again.

"What's your connection to the band? What's your official capacity with the band?"

"Mind your own business." I push her hand away from my face.

"When pressed for answers, Amber Fields becomes violent," she says into the device.

I stop immediately and turn to face her, wondering if there's actual steam coming out of my ears; it sure feels like there could be. "You are making up nasty lies about me, and I don't appreciate it at all."

"My editor wants a quote. Make it your words instead of mine." She holds out the recorder.

I resist the urge to snatch it from her hand and wing it into traffic. "How about, instead, you go find yourself a little bit of journalistic integrity? Does that sound like a plan?"

She gives me a sly smile. "I can only do so much with people who won't cooperate."

Her words could not shock me any more than her holding a gun to me would. *How dare she threaten me!* "Since when are journalists blackmailers?"

"It's not blackmailing to get an impression about somebody I'm trying to interview."

"You know what . . . You really need a new outlook on life. I feel sorry for you." I turn around to go back into the hotel, fuming over the fact that this woman thinks it's okay to harass me about my private business. She's making life on the farm look better and better with every passing second. I think I've left her behind, but then there she is again at my shoulder. I'm walking across the lobby with long strides and she's practically running to keep up.

"How about we sit down for coffee and talk about it?"

I spin around and yell in her face. "Leave me alone!"

Several heads around the lobby swivel to face us. Suddenly, three employees in uniform appear out of nowhere.

"Are we having a problem here?" the larger one asks.

I point at Elizabeth, the so-called journalist. "Yes, we're having a problem. This woman is harassing me."

The men stare at me, looking me up and down.

I read skepticism in their expressions, which only pisses me off more. I raise my voice. "*I'm* staying here in the hotel, but this woman is *not*."

She holds up her hands, her recorder in one of them. "I'm just a journalist trying to get a story."

It must click and fit into place for them because suddenly they move to block her from me. I find myself on the outside of their circle as they usher her out the door.

I want to jump up and yell in her face that she can stay gone too, but I resist. She still has that stupid recorder and I know she's itching to use it. I turn my back on her and make my way over to the elevator.

Jeremy is standing there with his eyes wide open. "Are you okay?"

"I will be, as soon as I get upstairs and calm myself down."

We both enter the elevator and he presses the button for my floor. "Is there anything I can get for you? Wine, a shot of tequila, chamomile tea? I can bring it to your room."

I shake my head. "No. I'm going to be fine." I really need to talk to Ty. I'm afraid that stupid woman is going to print something in her newspaper, and he's going to find out about it and think I said something.

"If you change your mind, just call down to the reception desk. We'll help you out however we can."

"Thank you, Jeremy. You're really sweet." I reach out and pat him on the shoulder just as the doors are opening on my floor. I step out of the elevator and turn around to face him. "How's it going with your new girl?"

His grin is huge. "It's going really well. I have another date with her tonight."

I can't help but smile back. "Have a great time. I hope it works out for you both."

"Thank you, Ms. Fields. And don't let that lady get you down. We have the press coming in here harassing people all the time. We try to catch them at the door, but sometimes they slip through."

"I understand. It's not anyone's fault. She was very sneaky."

"Yeah. They can go too far sometimes, though."

"I'm learning pretty quickly that things don't happen here like they happen in other places." If a woman acted like that on the farm, she'd be out on her butt in two seconds. I'm really missing home right now. Why did I think I could stay here on a longer basis? One interaction with a person from the media and I fall to pieces. *Ugh.*

"Just be careful not to be . . . too trusting."

I nod. "That's good advice, especially for me."

He tilts his head. "Why especially for you?"

"Because, where I come from, it's a totally different world."

"I hope New York isn't scaring you away."

I shake my head as I consider his words. *Scared?* Since when have I ever been scared? I've handled a thousand things more frightening than a silly sneaker-wearing reporter in my life. She's got nothing on a hive of pissed-off bees or a raccoon with a porcupine quill in its nose, two situations I've dealt with on more than one occasion, thank you very much. *Please . . . Me? Scared? Not on your life.* I feel my confidence coming back in spades. I might be from the country, but that doesn't mean I'm a mouse; it means I'm a badass.

Now instead of feeling intimidated, I'm mad. How dare that woman almost ruin my dream of working here. "Nope. It's going to take a lot more than an annoying reporter to get rid of me." I want to tell him how at home I manage fifteen hives full of bees that can sometimes get a little cranky with me, but I don't want to sound like too much of a hick.

"Awesome," he says, sounding genuinely happy. "Have a great day."

"You too." I walk down the hall and pull my phone out of my bag. As I let myself into my room, I'm dialing Ty's number.

CHAPTER THIRTY-SEVEN

I leave a message on Ty's voice mail. He's probably busy in the recording studio with the band, and I don't want to bother them, so rather than call the studio to track Ty down, I leave it at that.

If I'm going to be working with the band for two weeks, I need to learn how to deal with these reporters, and I can't go running to Ty or Red every time someone tries to get an official comment from me. This person Elizabeth from whatever stupid paper she's with has figured out that I'm somehow associated with them, so I'm sure it's only a matter of time before others do too. And I doubt she's going to be satisfied with only one attempt at getting a story from me.

I stand in front of the mirror in the bathroom practicing my new plan for encounters with the paparazzi: "No comment." I change my tone to sound more confident. "No comment!" I try various inflections. "No *com*ment. *No* comment. No com*ment*!" This is the phrase I've heard other people use on television during the few occasions I've watched. It seems like it should be good enough to keep me out of hot water. What kind of story can a person possibly get with 'no comment' as their only quotable input? As long as I stick with that script and stay outwardly bland and unaffected by her taunts, she'll get nothing from me.

After settling into my hotel room, I keep myself busy doing various things—contacting Lister's office to leave a message about the hairdresser and using hotel stationery to write out my plans for the band: first, we'll deal with the hair; then we'll deal with the clothing. I don't know where I should shop for them, but I'm sure James will have some ideas for me.

Hopefully, the new material the guys are working on today will be really great, and pretty soon we'll have a whole new package to present to their fans—an updated look and not necessarily a new sound but new songs for the fans to rock out to. I sketch out ideas, slogans, and random thoughts for how we might further encourage the fans to accept the band's new image, and the time slides right on by. Before I know it, it's time for dinner.

I'm looking over the hotel room service menu when my phone rings. I recognize Ty's telephone number and pick it up with a big smile. "Hello," I say cheerily. "How are you?"

"Fine. You okay?" His tone is flat.

"I'm good. But you don't sound so great. Are you upset?"

"No. Just exhausted."

"Tough day at the office?" I'm trying to get him to laugh.

"Something like that."

The line goes quiet.

"Did you get any dinner yet?" I ask, hoping he hasn't heard about that reporter before I have a chance to tell him myself.

"No. I'm not hungry."

"Well, I hope you ate *something* today."

"Not really."

"That's not healthy." I really want to invite him over here for dinner, but I don't want to sound too forward. "I was just going to order some room service. But I could meet you downstairs for dinner if you want."

"I got your message. You said you needed to talk to me about something important?"

I suddenly feel sick to my stomach. It's one thing for him to be bummed over a disappointing recording session and another to be mad at me because I've done something wrong. "Yes. There was a reporter woman waiting for me outside the hotel when I got back today. It wasn't pleasant."

"What did she say?"

"She just asked me some questions about . . . the band. And you." There's no point in trying to talk around it. He's going to find out anyway when Elizabeth prints her story, and I can only imagine what it's going to say.

"What kind of questions?"

"She wanted to know if we're together." *There, I said it.* My face is burning.

"What did you tell her?"

"What do you mean, what did I tell her? I told her it was none of her business."

I can hear him forcing out a sigh, but he doesn't say anything after.

"Are you angry with me?"

"No, of course not. Why would I be angry with you?"

"I don't know. You sound like you are."

His voice softens. "Sorry about that. I'm just having a bad day. Don't take it personally."

"Are you sure you don't want to come over for dinner?"

He sighs. "Are you sure that's a good idea?"

I have to think about it for a few seconds. I'm not certain what he means. "Well . . . you're hungry—or you should be, since you haven't eaten all day. And I'm hungry, kind of. And there's food here, so . . ." I laugh a little, stumbling over the awkwardness of the conversation. "It sounded like a good idea at the time, but now you're making me question myself."

"Listen, you're new to this whole thing, so I'm just going to tell you straight up . . . Once these people get their teeth into something, they don't let go. You told that reporter it was none of her business what's going on between us, but she's not going to be satisfied with that answer."

"No, you're right; I don't think she is."

"So you *do* know how this goes."

"Not exactly. But whenever I wouldn't answer her question the way she wanted me to, she would say stuff into her recorder that wasn't true. She started making things up."

"Great. One of those."

"Yeah, she wasn't very nice. She seemed okay at first, but then she started playing that rude game, and I realized she wasn't."

"Not all of them are like that."

I hate talking about this woman who single-handedly did a great job of screwing up my whatever-it-is with Ty—not a relationship exactly, but the potential for one.

Time to change the subject. "Are you sure you don't want to come over for dinner?"

"No . . . yeah . . . I do. I do want to come over. Just give me an hour to get ready." He sounds completely defeated.

"Take all the time you need. I'll be up here in my room." I'm going to leave it up to him to decide whether he goes to the front desk and asks me to come down or if he comes up to my room for food here. I would definitely not be opposed to another roll in the hay with him. I've been thinking about him all afternoon, and I'm pretty sure, after talking to him now and hearing his defeated tone, that he would enjoy a little playtime too. He had a tough day, and my interaction with the reporter certainly didn't help. Maybe I'll be able to cheer him up.

"Great," he says. "I'll see you soon."

"Okay. Bye."

"Wait . . . Amber?"

"Yes?"

"Thanks."

"You're welcome," I say a little mystified.

"For everything you did with the band today. It was really cool of you to do that."

"Of course. I want to do anything I can to help all of you."

"I hear there's an appointment at the hair salon for tomorrow night."

"Yes. Is the band excited?"

"I'm not sure *excited* is the word I would use to describe it." He chuckles.

"Do you think it's a mistake?" I'm starting to doubt the wisdom of my choices.

"No, it needs to happen. But these are old guys, and it's hard to teach an old dog new tricks sometimes."

"Okay. Well, I'm going to do my best."

"I know you will. I'll see you soon."

"Okay. Bye." I wait to see if the conversation is truly over this time. When I finally hear the line go dead, I hit the red button on my phone.

I have an hour to shower, put some of that yummy-smelling lotion all over me, and figure out which outfit I'm going to wear. I don't know if I'll be leaving this room tonight, but I'm going to dress like I will. Hopefully, Ty will take one look at me and decide it's better to stay in. I don't want to chance seeing that Elizabeth person again, and I'm honest enough to admit that I'm really looking forward to being naked with him again. I just hope he feels the same way about me.

CHAPTER THIRTY-EIGHT

A simple knock at my door nearly gives me a heart attack. *It's him.* Ty is here.

I walk over and look through the peephole. He's in the hallway, dressed all in black. His hair is crazy and his makeup dark. I'm afraid it matches his mood.

I open the door to let him in. "Hi." I'm suddenly shy.

"Hi." He looks me up and down, giving me no indication of what he's thinking or feeling. "Can I come in?"

I move out of the way. "Sure. I'm glad you came."

"Me too."

The moment I shut the door, he pulls me into a hug. His arms wrap around me and hold me tight. Whatever misgivings I might have had before he got there melt away.

I'm surprised by how enthusiastically he's embracing me, but I'm not complaining. I hold him tightly, just breathing and enjoying the sensation of his body against mine. He's warm, solid, and all man. I had no idea what I was missing out on not having a boyfriend. Not that he's my boyfriend or anything, but this is two nights in a row we've been together, and I'm loving every minute of it. Maybe his moodiness should be putting me off, but I'm finding it intoxicating. I never know what I'm going to get with him, and I love the challenge. It's like looking at a birthday present and wondering what's going to be inside the box under all the wrapping paper. So far, it's always been something good.

"I really needed this," he says into my shirt at my shoulder.

"Me too." It seems monumental to be admitting this to one another. We've only known each other for a couple days. I've gone my whole life without his hugs, and I've been just fine, so why does it feel like I can't survive without them now?

"What's for dinner?" he asks, finally pulling away. He moves through the room over to the windows.

The abrupt change from intimate hug to businesslike request for a meal throws me for a loop. I stand there stunned for a few seconds before I can answer. "Whatever you can find on the menu, I guess. Or we could order something from somewhere else if you want and have it delivered."

He's staring out the window with his hands shoved deep into his front pockets, his shoulders rounded forward. "No. I'm sure the restaurant here is fine."

I take the menu from the desk and walk over to him, reading out a few of the options.

"The steak sounds good," he says absently. "I'll have that. Medium rare."

I look over the menu, trying to pick something for myself. I feel his hand on my shoulder and look up.

"I don't expect you to call it in for me. I can do it."

I shrug. "It's no big deal. I'll do it."

His hand falls from my shoulder. "Sometimes I forget that not everybody is at my beck and call."

"What do you mean?"

He goes back to staring out the window. "I gave you my order like you're some kind of waitress. I didn't mean to do that. It's just that . . ." He looks down at the floor and sighs. "The only people in my life these days are people who have been hired to take care of me or people who play music with me. It's new to me. I'm not doing well with it."

I think I understand where this is coming from. "When was the last time you saw your brother or your parents?"

He shakes his head slowly. "I haven't seen my brother in more than a year. The last time I saw my parents was right before I came here, six months ago."

"Where are they now?"

"My parents are outside of Philadelphia. My brother . . . Who knows?"

"Is he okay?" I ask delicately. I'm so worried about his answer and what it might dredge up for him, but to not ask would be cruel and insensitive.

"I assume so. I haven't heard otherwise."

I rest the menu on a nearby table. "Do you mind if I ask you what the circumstances were of your brother going missing?"

"No, I don't mind." Ty actually sounds a little relieved. "He's not missing. Not exactly." He walks down the length of the room, still looking out into the night. He stops at the corner where two windows meet. "He just couldn't take it anymore. He left. For a while he was living with a friend of his, but then he moved out and didn't leave a forwarding address."

"Have you tried to find him?"

"No. But I'm thinking about doing that now."

"Why now?"

He doesn't answer for the longest time. Then he turns around and looks at the leather-bound folder on the table. "You want me to call in our order?"

I pick up the menu and walk over to the telephone. "No, I'll do it." He obviously doesn't want to talk about his brother right now and I'm not going to push him. I hope he does open up to me, though, because I think this is important . . . maybe even critical.

When the ordering is done, I hang up the phone and turn to face Ty. He's not looking out the windows anymore. He's staring at me.

"What?" I look down at myself. "Is there something wrong?"

"Why would there be something wrong?"

"You're staring . . . It's pretty intense." I try to laugh through it, but the look on his face stops me.

He walks slowly over to me, his gaze smoldering. I'm no mind reader, but I don't need to be in order to know what he's thinking; I've already been stripped naked in his head and now he's reaching out to touch me.

His fingers come up and trace from the hollow in my throat down to the middle of my chest. He slowly releases the top button of my shirt.

"I thought of you all day today," he says in a hoarse whisper.

"Me too," I whisper back. My pulse is racing and I'm already wet between my legs.

My second button is now undone. His finger glides across my skin to my left breast, where he slips it under the edge of my bra. It both tickles and makes me hot. I shiver. He stops to undo the rest of the buttons of my shirt. It falls off my left shoulder, but I do nothing to stop it. Cool air brushes across my skin, bringing up goose bumps.

"You are so sexy. So natural. So real." He seems mesmerized.

"Thank you. I'm glad you feel that way." I can't believe my luck; I think I've found the one musician in the entire world who doesn't want a woman with bleached-blond hair and boobs up to her neck.

"I do. I really do." He pauses, his expression going almost pained. "I want to be inside you so bad right now."

His directness sends a shock through me, but not the unpleasant kind. I'm warm all over, trembling in anticipation of what he's suggesting.

"What's stopping you?" I ask.

He looks up at me as if to verify whether I'm joking, but when he sees that I'm not, he rushes in.

Suddenly, our arms are around each other and we're stumbling toward the bedroom. My shirt falls to the floor and my bra quickly follows.

He yanks his T-shirt off and flings it across the room. We fall to the bed in a heap, him on top of me. He has a raging hard-on and I can't get my pants off fast enough.

"You smell nice," he says, trailing kisses across my chest.

I was just going to say the same thing to him. He smells like a man, so different from me and the scents I'm used to at home. It's alien and foreign and entirely sexy.

He moans, pressing into me, reaching around to squeeze my rear end. I moan too, unable to stop myself. The sensations are too much. I'm losing control already and we're just getting started.

He pulls my panties down with little finesse. I'm only able to get one leg out before he's released his rock-hard cock from behind his zipper. I hear the ripping of material and feel a jerk around my waist, and then suddenly he's there pressing inside me.

"Condom!" I squeak, in a panic.

"Fuck. Sorry." He pulls away and scrambles around, trying to get into the back pocket of his pants that are still halfway down his legs. He finds a package and rips it open, quickly taking care of business. He rolls over partially on top of me and looks down into my eyes. "I'm sorry about that. That was stupid."

"Don't worry about it. You fixed it."

He reaches up and strokes the hair away from my face. "You are so beautiful. I don't want to fuck this up."

I reach up and take his hand away from my face and place it on my breast. "You are not going to fuck anything up, unless you stop what we started before we finish."

He smiles for the first time since walking into my room. "Yes, ma'am." Then he's there again, so physically present—heavy and solid—pushing against me and then into me.

I close my eyes with the pleasure his body brings me. This is so much better than I imagined it would be. He goes in and out, smooth like silk yet hard as a rock. *How did I get so lucky?* I've found a guy who challenges me and keeps me guessing while also making me feel like a million bucks in bed.

This time it's different with him. There's a sense of urgency and desperation. I think he's using my body to exorcise the demons from his life. I don't mind; I want to help him find peace, even though I love his intensity. And it's not like I'm not getting something out of the deal too. It feels amazing to have our bodies communicating on this level, almost like we're enjoying a spiritual experience. I feel closer to my creator, closer to understanding why my body was built the way it was. Ty and I were meant to be together like this. I can feel it in the deepest part of myself.

"I'm sorry, babe," he says between gasps. "I can't hold back for very much longer."

That crazy feeling is coming over me again, the one I can't control, whose origin is the place where Ty and I are most intimately connected—the spot he's rubbing and stroking, heating up with every inch of his rock-hard body. I'm so close, nearly there too. "It's okay," I say, sounding like I'm pleading. "I'm ready for you."

My words work like magic for both of us. He loses control at the exact moment that I do. He's yelling and then so am I. The two of us cling together as we rock out a rhythm that rubs me in all the right places. Our bodies strain toward each other and then suddenly there's an explosion of light in my mind.

I close my eyes and fall into the abyss that follows when the fireworks fade out. Tears gather in my eyes as emotions overwhelm me. This was meant to be. I'm so glad Ty is in my life, and now I'm worried about what will happen when I leave New York in two weeks.

As Ty is collapsing on top of me, a knock at the door causes me to stiffen. *Someone is here.* He rolls off to the side, giving me a quick kiss on the mouth. "I think our dinner has arrived."

Oh, yeah. Dinner. I had forgotten all about it.

I go to roll off the bed and get to my feet, but he grabs me around the waist and pulls me back, burying his face in my neck.

I giggle uncontrollably. "What are you doing?"

"Kissing you goodbye."

"I'm just going to the door." I push him away and he pretends I'm stronger than I am, flying backward to land against the pillows.

"Rejected," he says, grabbing his chest near his heart and pretending to cry.

"Please." I snort. "If what I just did is rejection, I can't wait to see what acceptance is."

He winks, his fake crying disappearing in a flash. "Me neither."

I grab the fluffy white bathrobe and wrap it around me, grinning the entire time. I love this playful side of Ty. "Stay there," I say, adjusting the belt around my waist. "I'll take care of this."

"Yes, ma'am," he says, saluting.

I go to the door and let the hotel employee inside. He rolls in a fancy cart loaded down with food, napkins, condiments, silverware, water, beer, and my tab. I sign it, giving him a generous tip before seeing him out the door.

I roll the cart into the bedroom and grin at the handsome man who has settled himself under my covers. "Dinner is served."

He smiles lazily back at me, his makeup smeared and his hair standing out everywhere. "Come over here and let me feed you."

I let the robe drop to the floor and give Ty a few seconds to feast his eyes. Grabbing a strawberry off one of the plates, I bring it to bed with me, giggling when I hand it to him and join him under the covers.

"What are you laughing at?" he asks me, grinning like a fool.

"Nothing. I'm just happy."

He takes a bite of the strawberry.

"Hey!" I say in mock outrage. "That was supposed to be for me. You were going to feed me, remember?"

He leans over and presses his lips to mine, transferring the bite of strawberry into my mouth.

"Mmm. Yummy." I giggle again. This is so ridiculous, but I don't care.

I slowly chew the fruit as we continue to kiss. It's a little gross, but I have to admit, strawberry kisses are pretty damn awesome. I don't know where the rest of that fruit ends up, but suddenly his hands are on my breasts again. Our food is going to get cold, but my body is heating up, and that's all I care about right now.

I climb on top of Ty, straddling his naked body. "This time, I'm in charge."

He puts his hands on my hips and looks up at me, a sexy grin lighting up his dark eyes. "Yes, ma'am, if you say so." He leans over to grab his pants off the floor and locate another condom.

Soon enough, he's ready for me and I'm ready for him. As I slowly lower myself over his erection, I grin with pleasure and satisfaction. *Oh, yeah*. This is going to be a long, beautiful night.

CHAPTER THIRTY-NINE

Ty and I are lying in bed together the next morning, still half-asleep, when he rolls over and begins stroking my shoulder. He's spooning me from behind and I wiggle, trying to get closer to him.

"I need to talk to you about something," he says, his morning voice rough from sleep.

His tone tells me sex is temporarily out of the question. "What's up?" I hope he's not regretting all the fun we had last night. We went four rounds, and I'm probably not going to walk right for a week, but I'm happy about *everything* we did, and I wouldn't change any of it for the world.

"Yesterday . . . during practice. Things didn't go so well."

I twist my head sideways, trying to see his face. "What happened?" I slide around to my back so I can see him more clearly. His hair is tousled and his eyeliner smeared. I lift myself up enough to give him a kiss and rub his cheek before falling back down onto the pillows. "Tell me. Maybe I can help."

He shakes his head. "I don't think you can. We're having some trouble coming up with new material. It has nothing to do with you, though, so don't feel bad. That's not why I told you. I was just . . . bothered by it. And I didn't want you to think it was you that was making me act like an asshole yesterday."

I nod in commiseration. "I can imagine how tough that must've been for everybody, especially after the conflict that started out the day."

"Conflict, yeah. Which you resolved, by the way, so that's cool. Nobody's blaming anybody for anything. I think we're all under a lot of stress."

"I can imagine. Did you guys talk about what you're going to do?"

"No. But I was thinking about something . . . Maybe it's crazy, though."

When it doesn't sound like he's going to finish, I reach up and shake his shoulder. "What? Tell me."

"I don't know. I was thinking maybe I'll try to get in contact with my brother."

I frown, trying to understand. "Do you think you're having trouble writing new music because you're sad about him?"

"Nah. I was thinking that maybe he could come and try to write some music for us."

"Would the band be open to something like that?"

He lifts his shoulder. "I don't know. But I figured it was worth a shot."

"Why don't you talk to them first? It might be better to get the green light from Red before you offer anything to your brother or get his hopes up."

He nods. "You're right. But I need to contact him, anyway. It's been too long."

I reach up and smooth his hair down. "I'm glad you're doing that. I could tell from the movies you showed me that you two were close. I don't know what I'd do without my sisters. They're my whole life."

He stares at the sheets over my chest. "My brother and I have a lot of garbage to work through, about stuff with our parents and shit that was said and done over the years. Neither of us handled it well in the end. We didn't part on great terms, but still . . . we're close . . . or we were, growing up. I think enough time has passed that we could find a way to work through it."

"Sibling relationships are the best ones you can have. You need to work things out, regardless."

"I don't think our relationship is like the one you have with your sisters."

"Probably not. But don't let that stop you. If nothing else, you both have a lot of common ground."

"Maybe too much."

"Don't say that. Don't be so negative." I tap him lightly on the cheek so he'll look at me. "Remember, you are the architect of your life—that control does not belong to your past or your parents. *You* decide what your next step is going to be." It strikes me as I say this to him that maybe I should consider taking my own advice. It's not that anyone has tried to control my life, but I have let my family's expectations—or the expectations I think they have—guide me in making my decisions . . . maybe too much.

He leans in and gives me a long, sultry kiss. "You're right," he says, finally pulling away. "Thanks for reminding me." He gives me a more chaste kiss and then throws the covers off, quickly climbing out of bed. "I've gotta get going."

"Do you have time for breakfast?"

"Nope. I need to get back to the studio."

"I'm going to come over too, but I need to eat first and get ready."

He pulls his pants on. "I'll meet you over there?"

I lean back on the pillows, pulling the sheets up over me. "Yep. I should be there by nine." A glance at the alarm clock on the bedside table tells me I have two hours to get ready and get my buns over there. *No problem.* I'll even have time to talk to my sisters.

"Cool." He leans over to give me another kiss, gently stroking my arm before standing up and hunting down his shirt. He pulls it on over his head and then runs his fingers through his hair, making it worse.

I giggle.

"What's so funny?" He looks at me with a lopsided grin. He couldn't be more adorable if he tried.

"That hair." I pull the covers up to my face to hide my smile.

"What's wrong with my hair?"

I draw the sheet down to my chin so he can hear me better. "It looks like you stuck your finger in a socket."

He fake-glares at me and then stomps off to the bathroom. "Holy shit . . . what in the hell happened to my head? Look what you did to me, woman!"

I can't stop laughing as the happiness bubbles up inside me. The water starts running and then there's some splashing around. A few minutes later he comes out with his hair slicked back and most of the makeup removed from his face. He points to his head. "Better?"

I shake my head no, pulling the sheets up to my face again. My stomach hurts from holding in the laughter.

"What? I combed it. That's what you wanted, right?"

"I thought I did . . ." I can't finish because I'm laughing too hard. He looks like Pee-wee Herman.

"You are so going to get it . . ." He enters the room with long strides and jumps onto the bed, making me squeal with surprise and delight.

Then he's on me, pushing against me, his heavy body and faded cologne washing over me, making me go all warm inside. Here go those fireworks again . . .

"You're lucky I have to get to work," he growls, leaning in and biting my neck.

I scream and slap at him. "Ack! Go away!" I'm laughing as he tickles me back.

And then suddenly he's gone. He's back on his feet, walking out of the room.

"You're leaving me?" The words are out before I can stop them.

He pauses in the doorway, his hand on the frame. He looks back at me with all the humor gone from his expression. "Only if you want me to."

I shake my head, all my good humor gone too. "I don't."

His grin slowly comes back. "Can I go to work, though?"

I nod, my heart swelling to twice its size in my chest. *Huh* . . . I never knew that happiness can sometimes feel like cardiomyopathy. I'm going to have to tell Rose that I actually remembered one of the medical descriptions she's talked about over dinner.

Ty winks and disappears. I hear him putting on his shoes and banging around in the other room and then the sound of the door opening and closing behind him. When I'm certain he's gone, I tiptoe into the other room and grab my phone off the table. I quickly dial my sisters as I climb back into bed.

Em answers on the second ring, her voice very sleepy. "Oh my *god*, it's been forever since I've talked to you."

"I know. I just had to call. Sorry it's so early. I'm *so* excited, though, I couldn't help myself."

"Why? What happened?"

The words burst out of me like there's an explosion going off behind them. "I think I'm falling in love!" Saying what's been in my heart since last night feels amazing . . . like I just injected myself with pure helium. I've given voice to the light I feel warming my heart.

"Oh my god . . . Are you serious? Are we talking about the lead guitarist?"

"Yes. His name is Ty." I can still picture his beautiful face and the angst in his eyes.

"I remember. Tyler Stanz from Philadelphia."

"Somebody's been doing her research."

"My sister is spending a lot of time with this man. I need to learn something about him, since she never calls me anymore."

"Hey, no fair. No guilt trips allowed. I called the other day and you weren't around."

"No, you're right. I was busy. I'm just kidding."

"I hear you've been painting."

"It's possible I've been painting, but let's not talk about that right now. Let's talk about the L-word you just said."

I take a deep breath and let it out. "Okay, so I may have been a little overexcited. I don't *love* the guy. But I really, really like him a lot."

"Did you have sex with him?"

"Yes. Many times. And it just keeps gets better and better. It's the best I've ever had by a mile."

"I'm happy for you. I really am."

I sense something in her tone that notches my excitement level down a bit. "Why do I not believe you?"

"I may be just a tiny bit worried at how fast you're moving with this guy. I'm not judging . . . you know I like having sex as much as the next girl. And our mothers raised us not to be uptight about that kind of thing . . . But it's only been *three* days."

"I know. Believe me, my common sense has been lecturing me all day and night for those three days. But I can't change how I feel. And I can't change how he makes me feel whenever he's around."

Em's tone goes philosophical. "Do you think it's in our DNA?"

"What do you mean?"

"This attraction we have for musical people. I mean, our mothers basically put their lives on hold for two whole years following the band around. Do you think you're going to do that too?"

I shake my head even though she can't see me. "No. No way. I don't want that kind of life. I'm coming back to the farm in two weeks." I nod over and over, hoping it will help me to convince myself. The problem is, when I picture myself going back and living my old routine again, it makes me want to cry.

"Even though you *really*, *really* like this guy?" Em asks.

"Yes. My life is not in New York." Saying it makes my heart feel heavy. It literally hurts.

"Okay. Whatever you say. So . . . what else is going on, besides all that red-hot sex you're having?"

"Well, I had a really good first day. And today is the day I bring them to get their haircuts."

"We're saying goodbye to the mullets?"

"Yes. Forever and always. The mullets shall be banished to hell where they belong."

"Good for you. What else is on the menu?"

"Wardrobe changes."

"Out with the old and in with the new?"

"Kind of. I'm using Jon Bon Jovi as my model."

There are a few seconds of silence before she responds. "I can see that. That could work."

"Yeah, I thought so."

"So, you're officially an employee of the band. What does the manager think about that?"

"He is apparently on a long vacation while they're in the studio, so I don't even know if he's aware of it."

"I hope he doesn't get upset and think you're stepping on his toes."

"I'll be long gone before that can happen." Again, the idea of leaving makes me way too sad. But I'm not going to deal with that right now. Nothing has changed, even though I'm loving this time I've been spending with Ty. *Two weeks. That's it.* After that I am gone. I force down the urge to hyperventilate.

"I wish you could talk to Rose, but she's not here."

"Isn't it a little early for her to be at the clinic?"

Em sounds mad now. "Somebody dumped a box of puppies at our door, so she had to go over earlier than she'd planned."

I hiss in disgust. "What kind of asshole does something like that?" I don't know why I bother to get enraged over it; it's not the first time it's happened and it won't be the last. And Rose always says she'd rather they do that than worse things.

Em answers, "I guess somebody who doesn't want the puppies but is also nice enough not to drown them in a lake."

"You have a point. Anybody who gives their puppies to Rose knows that she's going to take good care of them and find them loving homes."

"Yep. Listen, I'd better go. Are there any messages you want me to pass on to anyone?"

"Just tell the moms that I said hi and that I'm doing fine and they shouldn't worry. And give Rose an extra-big hug for me. Tell her I wish I were there to help her with the puppies." Imagining myself being gone for good in the context of Rose's clinic makes me feel guilty. I help her a lot there, and if I don't go back soon, she'll struggle to do everything with fewer hands.

"I will," Em says. "Be safe, okay? Take care of yourself. I'm sad that I'm not there to watch you do your thing. I'll bet you're amazing at it."

My heart feels like it has a cramp in it. I miss my sister so much. "I will. I promise. Wish you were here too . . . Feel free to come anytime."

"No, thanks. I'm happy to leave all the hard work to you." She giggles. "Love you! Bye!"

"Bye." The call disconnects.

I slowly pull the sheets back and sit on the edge of the bed, contemplating the day ahead. I'm going to put my worries to the side and focus on the band. They're paying me to do this job, and I want to get it right.

First things first: I need a shower. Then I'm going to grab some breakfast downstairs and head over to the studio. And if Ty needs me to, I'll do my best to help him locate his brother. Maybe getting some younger blood into the music-writing part of the band's business is exactly what the doctor ordered. I cross my fingers and send a prayer up into the sky that Red won't be offended by the idea.

CHAPTER FORTY

I enjoy watching the band jamming together more than I thought I would. Time just flies by. Before I know it, we're ordering dinner in and sitting down to enjoy pizza and beer together.

"I thought that went pretty well," I say to the group, biting into my slice of pepperoni. It's delicious—cheesy and hot.

"It's a little rough, but we'll get there," says Paul.

"We might get one song out of it," Red says, not sounding as positive.

Ty clears his throat. "What would you guys think about bringing in a songwriter?"

Cash, Paul, and Mooch glance at one another before turning their attention to Red. Everyone waits silently for his response.

"Who did you have in mind?" He stops eating his pizza and stares at Ty. I would hate to have him look at me like that; he doesn't seem exactly thrilled about the idea.

"Maybe my brother. If I can find him."

"Where is he?" asks Mooch.

"I don't know. He moved out of my parents' place a few years back, and I lost track of him. I think he's still in Philadelphia."

"If he's in the music business, it won't be difficult to find him," says Paul. "Have you done a search on the Net yet?"

"No." Ty keeps eating his pizza like it isn't a big deal to be talking about finding his missing brother.

I know for a fact that Ty could have done a search for Sam on his telephone, because I've seen him on there hunting down other things before. It's very telling that he hasn't bothered to do it yet. *What is he afraid of?*

"What's his first name?" Mooch asks, pulling his cell out of his back pocket.

"Sam." Ty puts his plate with a half-eaten slice of pizza on it down on the table, rubbing his hands on his legs. He's nervous. I'd love to go hug him to make him feel better, but I'm pretty sure he'd want to kill me for doing that in front of the guys. And since I want to have sex with him later tonight, it's probably better that he not want to kill me.

We all stare at Mooch as he presses buttons on his phone. "Looks like he's in LA. I don't see him performing anywhere, though."

"No, he doesn't perform. That's not his thing."

After seeing Ty onstage, I find this hard to believe. Ty is a natural; it's in his blood. And I know that Sam grew up playing right alongside him. I wonder why he doesn't perform onstage. Maybe he's shy like my sister Em.

"I don't mind you giving him a call," Red says. "And if he wants to come over here and jam with us a little bit, he's welcome. But I'm not making any promises." He looks at the other members of the band, and they all stare at one another with the strangest expressions on their faces. Nobody actually says anything, though.

I put my pizza down. "What's going on?" I look from one face to the other, wondering who's going to answer my question.

Mooch shoves a giant bite of pizza into his mouth, shrugging. I think he's trying to come off as innocent, but he couldn't look guiltier if he tried.

"Nothing's going on. We're all cool," Red says, smiling, thinking I won't notice that he's faking it.

Cash puts his plate down on the table and gets up, walking back into the booth. He shuts the door behind him, and very soon thereafter we hear the sounds of a guitar coming through the door. This tells me more than Mooch's innocent act ever could.

"There's definitely something going on here, and the fact that you're hiding it is not cool." I glare at Red, since he's the ringmaster here. "What is it that you're not telling me? If you don't want to share it with me, that's fine. But you need to bring Ty in on it. You agreed."

Red slowly chews his pizza, the expression on his face mutinous. He wants to deny me, but then he looks over at Paul, who lifts his eyebrow at his bandmate, silently challenging him.

Red throws his plate of pizza onto the coffee table and looks away, his expression twisting into something angry. He punches his leg with his fist. "God *dammit*."

I glance at Ty, but he's just as confused as I am.

"There's some stuff going on," Paul says.

"Yeah," I say sarcastically. "I got that." I scold him as best I can with my eyes.

I turn my attention to Red. "Tell me what's going on. I signed your NDA. I'm not going to tell anybody anything."

I've finally got Red's attention. He looks up at me sharply. "Why would you say that?"

I shrug. "I just figured that it must be a big secret or you wouldn't be getting so upset about it. And there's already some woman from a newspaper bothering me, so I wanted you to know that I'm not going to do anything to screw things up for you. Your secrets are safe with me."

"She's not from a newspaper," Ty says. "She's from OMG. An online rag."

"Fucking vultures," Red says, hissing out a sigh of annoyance.

"Don't worry about her. I can handle her," I say. "But what's going on? Tell us and maybe we can help."

"The only one who can help us is Lister," Paul says. He stands and walks over to the booth, looking through the window at Cash and tapping on the glass to get his attention. The music stops and he comes out.

"Amber wants to know about Darrell," Paul says.

"Are we really going to do this?" Red asks. He sounds tired all of a sudden.

"I think it's better if she knows everything," Paul says.

"Forewarned is forearmed," Mooch adds.

Forearmed? "I'm not sure I like the sound of that." I fold my arms over my chest. It feels like the temperature in the room has dropped several degrees.

"There's nothing you need to worry about," Red says to me with his hands pressed together. "We're taking care of everything."

"Forgive me if that doesn't make me feel any better." I'm slowly losing my temper. They're hiding something from me, and everyone but Red thinks I should know what it is. I don't like being patronized, and that's what this feels like.

"Just tell her, Red. Get it over with." Now Cash sounds annoyed.

Red leans back on the couch, resting his hands on his thighs. "Darrell was with the band back in the beginning. We were friends in high school."

A lightbulb goes on in my head. "Ohhh, I remember. He was with you for your first album."

"Yes. But then we had differences of opinion about some things, and decided to part ways."

"More specifically, we got into a big argument with him about your mothers," Mooch says.

I'm not sure I'm hearing him correctly so I sit there and replay what he said in my mind. *Yep. I definitely heard that right.* "My mothers?"

"Yes," Cash confirms. "It was about your mothers and them being with us on tour."

"What was the argument about specifically?" I am completely and totally fascinated now. All-in. I had no idea this had anything to do with me and my life. I feel like I'm on the cusp of getting some answers to questions I've had for a long time.

Red takes over the explanation. "Your mothers had been traveling with us for going on two years at this point. Everything was cool. Then they started acting a little cagey, and we couldn't figure out what was going on."

"Cagey?"

"They just didn't seem to be into the partying as much," Cash says. "At the time, it felt like they weren't into the scene anymore. Looking back, of course, we realize it was something entirely different. But things were going really great for two years and then . . . suddenly . . . they weren't going great anymore."

Now I get it. "Because they got pregnant." My heart goes cold. This is the story titled: *The Beginning of the End of My Mothers' Lives as They Knew Them*. The part where my mothers' hearts got broken, and my sisters and I got left behind. I'm not sure I'm ready to hear it, but Red is already talking again.

"Yes, but at the time we had no idea that that's what was going on." Red rubs his hands together, massaging his knuckles. "We were in the dark about what was happening behind the scenes, but we were also really busy. We were writing a lot of music, we were touring nonstop, and we had constant attention on us, coming from all directions."

"From our label, from fans, from inside the band." Mooch is shaking his head. "It was pretty awful, actually. We didn't know what hit us. We were still new to the attention."

"So what does Darrell have to do with any of this?" I ask.

"He was giving us a hard time about all the women hanging around. He thought they were a bad influence," Cash says.

"He thought my mothers were a bad influence?" I could use a lot of words to describe the women who raised me, but *bad influence* would never fit.

"He thought they were a distraction from the music," Mooch clarifies. "But we told him at the time—and we still believe—that they were great for us. They helped us de-stress. With them around to lighten the mood, we never had to take ourselves or anything we were doing too seriously." Mooch looks over at Red. "They were like our haven from all the craziness."

Red is nodding his agreement. "They were. And then we lost them." I hear the pain in his words, and I feel it inside my chest, too.

"I don't understand how it all happened. Explain it to me." My heart is beating rapidly. *Will they answer me? Will they explain what happened all those years ago? Do I really want to hear this story?* I fear it will shatter some beliefs I've held as truths for way too long.

Ty walks over and drapes his arm across my shoulders, silently giving me his support.

"Are you asking how it worked out that your mothers left and you never saw us?" Red is staring right at me. He is offering me exactly what I thought I wanted. *Do I still want that? Am I ready to hear something I may not like?*

"Yes. I'm asking."

Red looks at his bandmates. "Are we sure we want to go here?"

Paul nods.

"The truth shall set you free," Cash says. He has tears in his eyes.

"Like a Band-Aid, man," Mooch says. "Rip that sucker off."

Red faces me again. "Fine. You want to know the story? I'll tell it to you."

CHAPTER FORTY-ONE

Like I said, everything was going great and then it wasn't," Red explains. "The four of us—Mooch, Cash, Keith, and I—were trying to hold things together. But Darrell was fighting us on it. He kept telling us we needed to cut the dead wood and focus on the music."

"He was jealous," Cash says. "He wasn't getting the attention from the girls that some of us were, and it made him angry."

"It wasn't just that," Mooch says. "He had a point. We *were* partying a little too hard. After the success of the first two albums, we started taking it easy. Too easy. We were more focused on having fun than working."

Cash nods his agreement. "True."

"What about my mothers leaving? How did that happen?" I can't believe how nervous I am; I'm actually trembling as I wait for his answer.

"We went to Albuquerque for a show. It was the first one that your mothers didn't go to with us. I remember Barbara telling us that her mother was sick and they all needed to go spend some time with her. I assumed they were going to Vegas, but I didn't double-check. Things were always cool with us; we trusted each other."

"It was a very unique relationship," Cash says. "We were really close, but there was total freedom. We didn't harsh their vibe and vice versa. It worked perfectly."

"Exactly," Red says. "But when we got back to New York, they weren't there. We waited a couple weeks, expecting them to come back or call, but they never did."

This relationship sounds a little too free and easy to me. "Didn't you worry about what happened to them?"

"Of course we did. But then we got word that they were fine and that they were dropping out and didn't want to be contacted anymore." He looks down at his hands, his shoulders slumping.

"Who sent you that word? My moms?"

"Yeah. Through our manager, Ted. At least, that's what he told us at the time."

I'm having a hard time processing what he's telling me. "But I thought you really cared about them."

"We did." Red raises his head and his voice. "We loved them. I still do." He glances over at his friends. "I can't speak for anybody else, but they're still right here." He thumps his chest with his fist a couple times, right over his heart. "But they wanted out. We couldn't force them to come back, and none of us were ready to end our careers."

"So, when you found out they were expecting babies, you just walked away?" I try not to sound bitter, but it's impossible.

Red jumps to his feet. "No!" he yells. "We didn't know!"

Paul goes over and grabs Red by the arm, making him sit back down on the couch. "Easy, man. Relax. Remember, you said you weren't going to get angry about this."

Red jerks his arm out of Paul's grip. "What do you care? You weren't involved. You don't know them at all."

Paul's voice is calm and smooth, soothing in effect. "I may not've been there, but I know how important Amber's moms were to you, and I know how much it hurt you when they left. Just chill, man. You're going to scare her away." He glances at me.

Red looks at me too and nods, letting out a long sigh. "You're right." He pats Paul on the back. "Thanks, man."

"Don't mention it." Paul relaxes into the couch.

Red drops his face into his hands, too overwhelmed with emotion to continue.

Mooch takes over the storytelling from there. "When we got back from Albuquerque, Ted told us that your mothers were gone and weren't coming back."

"The same band manager you have now?" I ask, just to be sure.

"Yes. And they told him—or so we understood—that they didn't want anyone to bother them. They didn't want to be in the limelight anymore, and they didn't want the press finding out where they lived. They just wanted to move on with their lives."

"And after all the time they spent with you, the times you shared, you believed that?"

Cash responds. "The last month they were with us, they really weren't into it. Of course we know now it's because they were all pregnant and probably sick and worried about what was going to happen with their lives. I mean, living the way we were . . . It was no place for pregnant women or babies. I said it enough times in front of your mothers . . . Red said it too, and Darrell . . . he practically shouted it on a daily basis. He fired one of the roadies when he found out the guy's wife was pregnant, and we didn't do a damn thing to interfere." He looks over at his bandmate. Red is nodding sadly. "It was kind of our mantra—no kids, no ties, no hassles. It's how we channeled the music, or so we thought."

I heard that same thing from my mothers when they told Rose, Em, and me why they left the band . . . that it was no place for kids and families, so I can't take offense at it. I know they would agree with what Cash is saying.

"But what about natural curiosity?" I press. "Didn't you wonder?"

"Of course we did," Red says, lifting his face out of his hands. "It practically killed us not knowing what they were doing or where they went."

"So why didn't you look for them?"

He shrugs. "Guilt. Pride. Drugs. You name it, I suffered from it."

"We all did," Cash adds.

"Things fell apart pretty quickly after that," Mooch says. "We got in a huge fight with Darrell. He was happy that your mothers were gone; it's what he wanted all along. But it was too much for us. Even though he wrote good music with us, we couldn't even stand to look at his face after everything went down."

"That's where I came in," Paul says. "There was no way they could work with Darrell anymore. He and Keith got into a huge fistfight. Keith broke two fingers, putting a crack in Darrell's orbital bone. It made it impossible for him to play for several weeks."

"So, my mothers disappeared, Darrell got kicked out of the band, and you came in to take over his spot."

Paul nods. "Nobody was even sure the band was going to be able to continue. But then Keith's fingers got better, and the guys were so devastated by everything that happened, they poured themselves back into the music and touring."

"We made a lot of money," Red says. "But I'd give it all back if I could do that part of my life over again . . ." He can't finish.

Tears rush to my eyes. I'm too choked up to speak.

Ty clears his throat. "Wow. You guys just blew my mind. I've been following your music since I was a kid, but I didn't know anything about this."

"You knew that Darrell left," Paul says.

"Yeah, but the official word on that was artistic differences."

Cash shakes his head. "Nah. We could play together, we just couldn't stand to be in the same room with a guy who was happy about the women leaving, who was so insistent that they were bad influences."

I try to wrap my brain around what these men have said and how it relates to where we started this conversation. Something about my mothers leaving has to do with a person they're thinking of hiring to write music. Then it hits me . . .

"Is Darrell the one you're thinking about bringing back?" I look at each of them, wondering if I'm right.

Mooch shrugs, looking guilty.

"That man will never step foot in any studio that I'm a part of," Red says with passion, his tears forgotten in favor of fury.

"Maybe we won't need him," Paul points to Ty, "if you can find his brother. Maybe it'll work out. Or we could find someone else. Or just keep working on what we have now."

Red nods. "I'd give Lister's dog a try before I let Darrell have anything to do with my musical life."

I can't let that one pass. "His dog?"

Red shakes his head, back to looking exhausted again. "It's a little rug rat. Barks at everything that moves."

"I've seen it, actually. When Lister first came to our house." I had temporarily forgotten their lawyer's heart isn't completely made of stone.

It makes me think of Lister showing up at my house. "So how did you find out about us, then? After twenty-five years, who spilled the beans?"

"Darrell," Cash says. "He told Lister and Lister told us."

"Why would he do that?" I look at Ty, wondering if he gets it, but he seems as mystified as I am.

Cash shrugs. "He was trying to use it as leverage to get back in with the band."

"What on earth was he thinking?" I cannot imagine any scenario where Darrell admitting he helped our mothers disappear would help him get back into the band's good graces.

"Who the hell knows?" Red says. "And who the hell cares? All he did was seal his fate, as far as I'm concerned." He glares at his bandmates, as if daring them to disagree. None of them appears to feel any differently from the way he does, though.

The room goes silent. I look at these men sitting in front of me, seeing them with new eyes. Twenty-five years ago they had the world at their feet, and then it all blew up in their faces. Women they loved, who it sounds like they would've done anything for, disappeared from their lives without saying goodbye, and a couple of selfish assholes—Darrell and Ted—made a decision to keep them apart at any cost. And our mothers, who were young and scared, listened to these men and believed what they said. They let them influence the direction they took with their lives . . . a direction that led our moms away from allowing my sisters and me to know our fathers.

Maybe I should be angry at those two men . . . maybe I should want to seek revenge and destroy them. But I don't. And maybe I should be angry with my mothers for being so easily influenced and maybe even selfish. But I'm not. I stand here in front of the band, feeling their pain but knowing there's a way past it. I can't change the past, but I can influence the future.

"I understand that your hearts were broken twenty-five years ago. I know my mothers had a hand in that. There were other people involved too, though. Your friend Ted probably hasn't given you the whole truth about his role in it." I haven't heard from anyone yet that they know he's the one who gave my mothers the money to leave and set up a new life. "But I'm not sure it matters in the long run."

Realization is washing over me in waves. I expected to feel anger and regret at learning the story of my mothers' relationships and my beginnings, but I don't. I feel grateful and hopeful. "The fact is, my sisters and I were better off being raised where we were. Like you said, the road is no place for kids or families. It would've been a kind of suicide for you to stop touring when you were doing so well, and I can't say that I would've been happier having a famous dad drop by every once in a while to say hello between tours, especially when it would have also meant reporters constantly hounding us and ruining the peace and quiet that our home promises to us and all its visitors."

I have their complete attention, and even Paul is getting choked up. "Our mothers were sure you wouldn't want them around anymore if you found out they were pregnant. You had said in no uncertain terms that pregnant women and children were not welcome on tour. They heard you repeat that thought many times during the two years they were with you."

"We know," Red says. "And I can't tell you how angry I am that I was so selfish and short-sighted."

"It doesn't matter now," I say, fully believing that. "The past is in the past. It's time to move on."

"I wish they had just told us," Cash says. "We could have avoided so much pain."

"They didn't want to pressure you into changing your minds about that, because in their hearts they knew you and Ted and Darrell were right: they didn't belong on tour with you anymore. It was time to move on. And they knew if they told you, they risked starting huge fights and destroying the band. The band was everything to you and very important to them, too."

"Ted has a lot to answer for when he gets back," Mooch says.

"We could all be angry at Ted and pissed off at the circumstances that caused him to do what he did, but I think that would be a waste of our time and emotion. Yes, Ted sent our moms away under maybe somewhat false pretenses, but he also made sure they had the means to live and raise my sisters and me in a beautiful place. We've had a wonderful life because of him, and I can't be angry at him for that."

I look around to see if they agree, and I think they do. They don't look nearly as upset as they did a minute ago. "No one is innocent in this situation, and playing that blame game is only going to dredge up more hurt feelings that'll take forever to heal. I would really appreciate it if we could just move forward from here—clean slate, no more misunderstandings or bitterness to bog us down. No more pointing fingers and getting angry at something someone did or said twenty-five years ago."

"I think that would be really great," Mooch says through his tears. He gets up and comes over with his arms out.

I happily enter his embrace and give him a big hug. "Thanks, Mooch."

He pulls away a little, tears going down his cheeks. "Do you think . . . maybe . . . you could ever call me Dad?"

Shocked at his proposal and the emotion behind it, I burst into tears, unable to answer. I never in my life thought I'd have the chance to call any man Dad. When I turned eighteen, I officially turned the page, telling myself having one wasn't in the cards for me, and yet here is this man that millions of people adore, asking me if I'll be his daughter. He doesn't even know if I really am biologically his, but he doesn't seem to care. It's beyond overwhelming.

Red stands and so does Cash, both of them coming over to join in our hug.

CHAPTER FORTY-TWO

I think it's a good thing that we have hair appointments tonight. The conversation got so heavy, there was no way out of it without a lot more tears, except for the fact that José Fernando Luis Velasquez was waiting for us at his salon.

I wish more than anything I could call my sisters and tell them what's going on, but I have no private time except for five minutes to use the bathroom before we're on our way over. I'm sharing a ride with Ty.

"So, that was kind of crazy, huh?" he asks. We're holding hands in the backseat.

"You could say that again." I still can't believe what I heard in the studio.

He glances at the driver and lowers his voice. "Do you want to talk about it?"

I lean into him so I can give him a quick kiss on the cheek. "Maybe later. Maybe tomorrow." It's too raw for me right now. I need to let things settle. Not to mention the fact that when I have this conversation with Ty, it won't be in front of a stranger who's driving the car we're in.

He squeezes my hand. "We've got time. All the time you need."

I could cry over that sweet comment, except I don't have any tears left in me. Thank goodness the salon isn't far. The limousine holding the other band members stops at the curb ahead of us and we park behind it. All of us get out at the same time.

A few strangers walking by on the sidewalk stop to stare. There's no way six people and their two drivers all exiting limos at the same time isn't going to attract attention. A few of them recognize the band members, so Red and the others pause to sign autographs.

I enter the salon ahead of everyone and introduce myself to the master. "Mr. Velasquez . . . Thank you so much for fitting us in on such short notice."

He's looking over my shoulder with a big grin on his face as he pets my hand. "Oh, darling, I need to thank *you*," he says with a Hispanic accent. "Do you have any idea how long I've been wanting to get my hands on their hair?"

This man is exactly what I needed. I smile. "Twenty years?"

"At *least* that long." He gives me an enthusiastic hug. "Who are we starting with?"

"I think you should start with the boss," I say in a near whisper. "As soon as Red's on board, you'll have no problem with the rest of them."

He nods sagely at me, narrowing his eyes. "Girl, I like how you operate."

"I'm sneaky."

He leans in. "I love sneaky."

He raises his hand above his head and waves it like a windmill at the wrist. "Let's go, friends. Snap, snap! Hop to it! We have hair to make fabulous!"

Out of the back room come several people to do his bidding, young men and women of all shapes and sizes.

I stare, not sure whether to be impressed or upset. "I thought *you* were cutting their hair."

"These are my protégés. They are here to assist me."

I nod, suitably impressed. "Okay. I'm just going to get out of your way."

He points to a chair that looks like a throne at the edge of the room. "That is for you, Queen Bee. You go sit your little buns down over there and I'll have somebody bring you something to drink. What would you prefer?"

"Green tea?"

He looks me up and down. "I knew it. I can read you like a book. Hippie chick from day one."

I hold up my hand for a high five. "You know it."

He grasps my hand in his and squeezes it. Then he kisses my knuckles. "We are going to be good friends. I know this."

This is the happiest I've been since I came to New York, save all the moments I've spent with Ty. I wish I could live in this salon instead of the Four Seasons.

The door opens and the band comes in, leaving a crowd of people behind them.

I walk over to the throne and sit down in it as José yells, "Shades!"

His troupe of assistants rushes over to the windows and lowers the blinds so that we have complete privacy. The fans are probably still out there, but even their cameras aren't going to get a shot of anything going on in here now. I'm so relieved; I no longer feel like a fish in an aquarium.

A couple minutes later, someone shows up with a nice mug of hot green tea for me. All the men in the band are brought into another area of the salon to have their hair shampooed and de-rat-nested.

José is barking out orders left and right. He introduces himself to each of the band members, sharing a little quip about a song of theirs or a story about one of their concerts he attended.

I can't believe how lucky I am. You'd never know it by looking at him in his hot-orange pants, high-top sneakers, and yellow spandex top, but José is a true Red Hot fan. No wonder I got an appointment in one day.

I sip my tea, reflecting on my day. I guess I would call it a success—seriously crazy, but good. I think about all I learned and how sad it is that the lives of people I care about were influenced by a lack of communication that would have been so simple to fix.

I'm seized by the desperate need to reconnect with my roots. I have to talk to my sisters right now, and I don't care that I'm in the middle of a hair salon. The band members are getting shampoo head massages, and I can hear them moaning with pleasure from here. I don't think they're going to be ready to get their haircuts anytime soon.

Rose picks up the phone immediately. "Oh, I'm so glad you called. I missed you last time."

"I know. How've you been? I miss you so much."

"I'm exhausted. I have a whole litter of puppies and no mommy to feed them, so I guess I'm the mommy now."

"How many are there?"

"Seven border collies. They are *so* adorable."

"And I'll bet they're eating every two hours through the night, right?" This is not the first batch of orphan puppies my sister has nursed. The guilt hits me again that I'm not there to help her.

"I've got them up to three hours. We're doing pretty well. So what's going on with you?"

"I have a lot of news, actually. But I don't have a lot of time, so I'm going to speed through it."

"Go for it. I'm all ears."

"Is Em there? She's going to want to hear this too."

"Yeah, she just walked up. I'm putting you on speakerphone."

"Hi, sweetie," Em says. "How are you doing?"

"Great. I was saying to Rose that I have some incredible news and I don't have a lot of time, so I'm going to go in fast-forward."

"Oooh, news. I love news. I'm listening."

I give them the play by play, reliving the conversation I had in the studio. When I'm done there's complete silence on the other end of the line.

"Hello? Did you guys hear me? Oh crap . . . If my phone died . . ."

"No, we heard you." It's Rose, and she sounds terrible.

"What's wrong?"

"Nothing's wrong," she says, sniffling. "It's just a lot to absorb."

I nod, my heart breaking for my sisters who are having to hear this for the first time. I should have been more sensitive. "I know. I've had more time to adjust to the idea. It's crazy, right?"

"The moms are going to be sad," Em whispers. "They always felt like the band would have agreed with them that leaving was a good idea."

I've been so busy thinking about myself and my sisters, I haven't taken too much time to consider how our mothers would take the news, other than to think that they'll be happy to know the guys still love them.

"Maybe we shouldn't say anything," I suggest. "At least not right now."

"But when?" Rose asks. "You can't keep it from them forever. They should know that the band never forgot them, and that those men would have wanted them to stay if they'd been given the choice."

"No, you're right. It wouldn't be fair to not tell them something we know," Em adds.

"Agreed. I don't want to hide things. But can we wait until I get back? I really would like to be there for them when they find out."

"We can wait until then," Rose says. She pauses. "Em's nodding at me, so she agrees."

I really wish I could be there to wrap my arms around my sisters. I know they're both crying. At least they have each other.

I look over at the band and see that their hair is being rinsed and some of them are sitting up with towels on their heads. "I need to go. I'll call you back later or tomorrow."

"Thanks for calling. We know you're really busy, but we appreciate you keeping us in the loop."

"Rose, you need to go to sleep. I can hear how tired you are in your voice."

"Yeah, I will." She yawns.

"I'll put her to bed right now," Em promises. "Just take care of yourself. You're dealing with a lot of stuff there, and it can't be easy doing it all alone in the middle of a strange city."

"I will." Funnily enough, Em's concern feels out of place. I don't feel burdened or worn-out; on the contrary, I feel energized. Electric. I could go another twelve hours.

"How's Ty doing? Is he cool with everything?" Em asks.

"He's being really wonderful. Very understanding."

"I'm glad he's there for you," she says.

"Me too." Rose sniffs. "I'm looking forward to meeting him."

"I don't know if that's ever going to happen, but I would love for you to do that. I think you guys would really like him."

José heads in my direction, so I make a kissing noise into the phone. "Gotta go, love you, bye." I hang up the phone and slide it into my purse.

He stops in front of me but faces the men, placing his hands on cocked hips. "So, what are we talking here? Total makeover or something a little less drastic?"

"I'm thinking Jon Bon Jovi, renewal-type look."

"Jon Bon Jovi, nineties renewal? Or Jon Bon Jovi, two thousands, serious-actor look?"

"Let's start with the nineties; hair no longer than the shoulder but nowhere near the ear. Can you do this?"

He gives me a sassy look. "Sweetie, I can do *anything*."

I grin. "I heard that about you."

He points at my head. "And what about you? What can I do for you?"

I shrug. "Nothing. I think I'm good."

He picks up a lock of my hair and looks at the ends, nodding and squinting as he makes me turn my chin left and then right. "I have something in mind for you. You should let me do it."

Ty walks over in time to hear him say that. "Don't change too much about her. I think she looks great how she is."

José shakes his head. "Oh no, nothing drastic. You're right. She's a natural beauty. Earth mother all the way. But I'd like to get rid of some of the split ends and put a little shape to her style."

When I see the four men with the towels wrapped around their shoulders, looking like wet dogs, I don't have the heart to resist. *If they can do it, so can I.* "Why not?"

"That's the spirit!" José yells as he raises his hand and snaps his fingers. "Team! I need a shampoo here, stat!"

"Him too!" I say, pointing at Ty.

He holds his hands up. "I'm good."

"Get under that damn faucet," Red growls from beneath his towel. "All for one and one for all."

Ty's shoulders sag. "Please don't buzz all my hair off."

José grabs him by the arm and steers him toward the shampoo area. When Ty sits down next to me and they're wrapping a towel around his neck, he gives me a dark, sexy look. "You're going to pay for this."

"You can thank me later," I say, winking at him. The protégé in charge of my hair tips my chair back and puts my head under the warm water, and I quickly fall into a blissful sleep as the shampoo suds are slowly massaged into my scalp.

CHAPTER FORTY-THREE

José has worked his magic. We are walking out of the salon as new people. Gone are the mullets and in their place are sophisticated rocker looks, their hair layered but long enough to touch their shoulders. For the first time ever, I actually find them handsome, and I'm pretty sure they think so too; they're walking taller and prouder than when they came in.

Ty looks pretty much the same. They took some of the length off the top and shortened the back and sides, but they've gelled it up into his trademark spikes, making it hard for me to keep my hands to myself.

Red looks at his phone, frowning and putting it to his ear as we approach the front door of the salon.

"What's the matter?" Paul asks. I hardly recognize him. He's way better-looking with his hair shorter. It's as if fifteen years have been taken off.

"My driver says there's a crowd outside."

"Just go straight for the car," Ty says to me, putting his arm around my lower back.

I nod. José is standing at the front door with his hand on the lock. "Are we ready, people?" We all gather in a tight group at the door, Red in front.

"Let's do it," Ty says.

They head out the door, but I hold back.

"I need to pay you," I say to José. Camera flashes are going off and people start yelling. I ignore them, trying to listen to José.

"Come back tomorrow, sweet girl. We'll take care of it then."

"Okay." I'm not sure that this is how business is usually done, but Ty is pulling on my hand, dragging me out the door.

"I'll talk to you tomorrow, José. Thank you so much for my hair." I reach up and touch it. It feels lighter even though he really didn't take much length off.

"It was my pleasure. Come back soon."

I'm pulled into a crowd of people that's a lot bigger than I expected it to be. It's not just regular fans hanging out, but television crews and reporters too. There are flashes going off everywhere. Red hasn't made it to his car. He's standing in the middle of the whole thing, under a bright light shining on his face.

"Whose idea was it for you to change your look so drastically?" a woman asks, sticking her microphone in Red's face.

"Let's just say it's somebody the band trusts." He looks behind him, but thankfully can't see me over the taller heads in front of me.

"What do you think your fans are going to say?"

"I hope they're going to say we look good." He smiles and everyone laughs.

"Aren't you worried that abandoning the look that's worked for you for so many years is a mistake?"

His good humor disappears in a flash. "No comment." He puts his head down and pushes past her. The rest of the band follows quickly on his heels.

My plan is to do the same, but somebody grabs me and pulls me back. I find the bright lights in my face now and the microphone just under my nose.

"Are you the person responsible for all the changes we're seeing?"

My eyes go wide. Ty is on the fringe of the group, trying to get to me, but he's being blocked by people wanting his autograph. He tries to ignore them, but they're very persistent, shoving paper and pen in his face.

I panic. "Maybe?"

I can't believe how badly I just failed at that. I imagine watching myself on television later and being humiliated at what a wiener I've become. The wall of people is several feet thick so I'm not going anywhere right now. The reporter is throwing another question at me before I can come up with a plan of how to get out of this mess.

"How are you associated with the band? Are you this long-lost daughter that we've heard about? Are the rumors true?"

"What?" Now I'm pissed. *What the hell is going on?*

"Rumor has it there's a love child on the loose in New York City. It's you, isn't it?"

I glare at her. "No comment."

"What do you hope to accomplish coming out as a daughter of Red Wylde now after twenty-five years?"

"No *comment*," I say louder.

"Are you looking for money? Are you going to demand a paternity test?"

"Which part of no comment do you not understand?!" I shout.

Her microphone is still in my face. She almost hits me with it, shouting her question at me. "Do you know their music? Are you even a fan?"

I grab the top of the microphone and shove it down toward the ground, ripping the spongy black part off. I toss it out into the crowd and glare at her. "I told you no comment, and I meant it."

"Just give me something I can use," she says, shouldering people aside so she can get even closer than she already was.

Suddenly, Ty is there and he's wrapping his arm around my shoulders and pulling me away. His forearm slides up to my neck, but I don't care that I'm almost in a headlock at this point. I just want to get away from these people.

The woman falls in behind us, yelling questions at the back of my head. Ty easily ignores her, but it's grating on my nerves. I pause, intending to give her a piece of my mind, but Ty pulls me toward him. "Don't do it. You'll regret it."

He's right. I know he is. I keep going and we finally make it to the car. The door is open and the driver is there, protecting my right to enter the vehicle with only Ty at my side. I swear, some of these fans and reporters are so nutty they'd climb in with us if they thought they could get away with it.

My heart is beating like it's trying to escape my chest. I can't believe how awful and scary that was. Once we're closed up in the car, I look at Ty, knowing my eyeballs are practically falling out of my head. "How do you put up with that?"

He looks incredibly sad. "I think it's easier for me than it is for you."

"They're so intrusive . . . so *rude*."

"They make money by selling news, whether it's true or not, doesn't matter. In fact the more awful it is, the better."

I shake my head. "I need to learn how to deal with these people, because I'm obviously in way over my head."

He reaches over and takes my hand, holding it on his thigh. "You did really well, actually. You kept saying no comment, which is exactly what you should be doing."

"Are you sure?" I look at him, trying to figure out if he's just being nice. "I really wanted to give her a piece of my mind."

"She was baiting you so that you would. You don't want to give her what she's looking for. It's not going to be good for you no matter what you say. When you're ready to talk, you can schedule a real interview with a quality network and prearranged questions. It'll be fine."

"You're right." I know he's right. I just really wish I could be one of those people who has the perfect answer ready at the right moment and enough confidence to pull it all off. Maybe I'll be there someday, but I'm definitely not there now.

"You did good." He kisses the back of my hand. "For somebody who has no experience with it, you did exactly what you should have. I'm proud of you."

"Thanks." It's just a few simple words, but he manages to turn the evening around for me.

"Your hair looks great," he says, grinning at me as he reaches up to touch it.

I smile at him. "Now you're just shining me on."

"No, I swear." He holds up his hand in a pledge. "You look seriously hot."

I giggle. "Stop." I look out the window, watching the buildings and other cars go by. This day has been the craziest of my entire life, hands down.

"Can I come up to the room with you?"

I look at him and bite my lip. *Is he thinking what I'm thinking?*

He winks.

I know then that we're of the same mind, and pretty soon we're going to be naked together. I cannot wait. I nod and he smiles back at me.

I pass the rest of the car trip in silence, letting my thoughts run their own course. Now that I have some distance between myself and those reporters, things are becoming clearer.

If I'm going to make this my life . . . for two weeks or whatever . . . I need to remember who I am, where I come from, and what I'm all about. I can't let people intimidate me or scare me. I think Rose was right about me; I think I was meant for this life. And Ty said I handled myself exactly right when I was being pressured by those reporters. I practiced saying *No comment* in the mirror and then when I needed it to come out right, it did. All I need is practice and a can-do attitude, and I'll make it.

And if I can make it through these two weeks, who knows what I could do next? The possibilities are endless, and I can honestly say that this is the first time in years that I've felt this way about my future. It fills me with excitement to even contemplate that.

My mothers made a huge decision about their lives twenty-some odd years ago that affected no fewer than ten people forever. They made a critical decision about how they were going to move forward into their future without talking to all the people involved. I need to learn from their mistakes and not repeat them.

I decided years ago that I had to stay on the farm and make my future there, but I never actually asked my family what they thought about my decision. I just assumed they'd agree. But after talking to Rose and Em, and after experiencing this New York City life, I'm starting to think that was a mistake. I'm doing the same thing my moms did all those years ago, which is beyond foolish. If I'm going to base my entire future on someone else's needs, I at least have to be absolutely sure I know what their needs are first, right? My family and I should probably have a conversation about it, but I'm not going to get ahead of myself. First I have to kick butt during this two-week period. Then . . . we'll see.

CHAPTER FORTY-FOUR

When I wake up the next morning, Ty is sitting on the edge of the bed looking at his telephone and frowning. I angle up onto my elbows. "What's wrong?"

He shakes his head. "You don't want to know."

I sit up more fully, pulling his arm over so I can look at his phone with him. He's reading a news headline, and my picture is right on top of the article.

"What the hell?" *At least my hair looks good.*

He pulls his phone away. "Never mind. It doesn't matter."

I hold my hand out. "Give it to me. I need to read it."

He passes me the phone and stands. "I'm going to jump in the shower." He hesitates, standing over me. "Promise you're not going to get upset about anything you read there. It's just people trying to sell their newspapers or get clicks on their websites."

"No promises," I mumble.

I read the article, which is full of conjecture and out-and-out lies. Apparently, I'm some sort of gold digger who has crawled out of the woodwork to claim my rightful throne as the heir to the Red Wylde fortune. They've dug up all kinds of stuff on me including where I live and the fact that I have two sisters who are the same age.

I cannot believe I dragged my family into this garbage. Who told these reporters all this stuff? I can't imagine anyone in the band or my family saying anything. I put Ty's phone down and grab mine from my bag that's on the floor next to the bed. There are two missed calls from my sisters waiting for me.

I press the green button and chew on my thumbnail while I wait for someone to answer. My call goes into voice mail. I press the red button and then dial the house number. After three rings, somebody picks up.

"Hello?"

"Barbara?"

"Who the hell is this?" She's pissed.

"Mom, it's me; it's Amber."

"Prove it."

I'm not sure I heard her correctly. "Excuse me?"

"I said prove it. I'm sick and tired of you reporters calling here and making up stories, pretending to be my daughter."

No wonder she's so angry. *How dare they!* "I'm the beekeeper and the wheeler-dealer at the farmers' market."

She lets out a long sigh. "Thank God."

"Mom, what is going on over there?"

"Well," she lets out a bitter laugh, "the shit has hit the fan, as they say."

"Why? How?"

"Apparently, somebody let the cat out of the bag. I think half of New York City is camped out in our backyard right now."

My heart sinks. "Please tell me you're joking."

"I wish I were. The good news is, we have completely sold out of all of our honey, jams, and jellies. And at this point, I'm going to start pulling things out of the barn and selling them as antiques."

"Mom, don't." I feel sick to my stomach.

"Hey, don't be upset. Now you know why we chose to leave when we did. We had a feeling this was going to happen eventually. It's just happening a lot sooner and more quickly than we thought it would."

I picture all those strangers ruining our grass and leaving their trash behind as they conjure up gossip about my family. "Kick them out! Tell them they can't stay."

"That's not who we are, you know that. Our home has always been available to anybody who wants to be here."

"But they're vultures! They're not *people* who want to stay there and get in touch with themselves or nature."

"Maybe they are and maybe they aren't. Who am I to judge?"

"They're going to *use* you, Mom. They're going to take advantage of you."

"Listen, sweetie . . ." She sighs. "I know what I'm doing. I spent a couple years living the life, okay? I know how to handle reporters."

I'm grouchy now, knowing she probably does know what she's doing, whereas I am a complete nincompoop when it comes to public life. "Well, that only makes one of us."

"Hey, I hear you didn't do too bad, actually." She sounds proud.

"Oh yeah? Then how did they find out all the stuff about the family? I must've done something wrong."

"No, that's got nothing to do with you. Somebody's feeding them information, and I know it's not my girl."

The first person who jumps to mind is Lister. If he were standing in front of me right now, I'd set his pants on fire. "I am going to *kill* him."

"Who are you going to kill?"

"Never mind. Do me a favor: tell Rose and Em that I'll call them later. I have to go take care of something."

"Don't do anything rash," she warns.

"You do know who you're talking to, right?"

Her voice softens. "My little gladiator. Just don't take anything too personally, okay? No matter what you see or hear or read, know that it really has nothing to do with *you*. It's just people's egos getting in the way of their common sense."

"I know. The only people who really know me are you, Carol, Sally, and my sisters. Everybody else can go eat worms."

Ty walks out of the bathroom just in time to hear me say that.

"I gotta go. I love you."

"Love you too. Bye-bye." She hangs up.

"What's going on?" he asks, his expression impossible to read. He's holding a wet towel around his neck on either side; another one is draped around his hips.

"I have to go see Lister." I jump out of bed and start pulling on my clothes, finding them in heaps around the room.

"Don't you want to take a shower first?"

"No, I don't have time. I need to go kick some ass and take some names."

"Can I come watch?"

At first I'm going to say no, that this is between me and Lister, but then I decide I'd rather have Ty standing by my side than be alone. I can trust him. "Be my guest."

Ty rubs his head with the towel from his neck. "I'll be ready in five minutes." He disappears into the bathroom as I rake a brush through my hair. I know I look like a crazy fool with yesterday's clothes on and old makeup, but I don't care. The look matches my mood. That Lister better look out, because I'm not going to put up with any of his lawyer crap. Things are about to get *real*.

CHAPTER FORTY-FIVE

The people sitting at the reception desk in Lister's office try to stop Ty and me from going past, but I'm not having any of their nonsense. I buzz right past and walk as quickly as I can down the hallway that I'm pretty sure leads to Lister's office.

I pass the copy room on my right. "Hi, Linny!" I yell as I rush by. She sticks her head out, but I'm gone before she has time to respond.

I see the conference room next. I signed papers in there. Knowing Lister, I probably signed a contract donating one of my kidneys without even realizing it.

"Take your next left," Ty says. I turn around to thank him and realize that Linny is right behind him.

I stop for a moment. "Sweetie, you're not going to want to see this. I'm really angry at your uncle."

"Good. So am I."

"Why don't you go make a photocopy of your butt? I'll be there in a minute to do one with you."

She grins. "I already did."

I walk over and give her a quick hug. "You are so adorable. Please go wait in the copy room. I don't want you to see me so upset."

"Do you know each other?" Ty asks, mystified.

"We're old friends," Linny says. She sticks her tongue out at him and then turns around to leave, her ponytail swinging back and forth.

He's taken aback, first staring at her for a few seconds and then at me. "I guess she told me."

"Don't try to make me laugh right now. I'm righteously pissed, and I want to stay that way."

He holds his hands up in surrender. "Yes, ma'am."

I turn around and keep going. I eventually end up at Lister's office and, miracle upon miracle, find him at his desk. A woman I saw once before here is leaning over with a very see-through blouse, showing him something in a folder.

He looks up. "Amber. Ty. I wasn't aware we had an appointment."

"We don't have an appointment." I stop in front of his desk, glaring at him.

He looks up at the woman. "Veronica, could you give us a minute, please?"

She nods, taking the folder from his desk and walking out the door, barely glancing at Ty or me.

Ty shuts the door behind her, and I fold my arms across my chest.

"Why don't you have a seat?" Lister points at the chairs in front of his desk.

"No, thanks; I'll stand."

"You look upset."

I tilt my head. "Do I? That's funny. Why would I be upset right now?"

He looks at Ty. "Is this about the news coverage?"

Ty shrugs. "Don't ask me. You're talking to her."

I wave at him. "Yeah . . . Hello? Mr. Misogynist? I can speak for myself, you know."

He frowns at me. "I don't know what this has to do with me."

"What this has to do with you is *you're* the one feeding the press information about me."

He frowns and drops the pen that was in his hand, placing his hands on the arms of his chair. "I did no such thing."

"Really? Because they sure know an awful lot about me, and it wasn't me who gave them anything."

He glances at Ty before refocusing on me. "I did notice they had a lot of detail."

"Did you? Was that *before* or *after* you sent them all of my personal information?"

He stands up. "I did no such thing. I would never do that."

"Well, then, who did?" I unfold my arms. "Somebody in your office?"

"No. Anyone who works here protects our clients' confidentiality. And anyone who didn't would be fired instantly."

"Fine, then. Call them in here. Anyone who touched my file is a suspect."

He grabs his telephone handset and starts pressing some buttons. "I don't think that's going to be necessary." He puts the phone to his ear and waits for it to connect. I hear a male voice on the other end of the line answer. "It's Lister. I need to ask you a question."

He hesitates before he continues. "Have you talked to the press about Amber and her family?"

I wish I had been watching the numbers he pressed on the telephone. I need to know who he's talking to so I can call him or her and bitch them out myself.

He frowns. "I don't know what you hoped to accomplish by doing that, but it was a mistake." He pauses while the voice on the other end of the line is going.

"How do I know?" he asks. "I know because Amber is standing in my office right now and she's very upset. And I'm angry too. You had no right to do that. I told you nothing good would come of it."

He hisses and shakes his head as he listens to the man on the other end.

"Whatever. Like I told you before, I cannot represent you. I don't want you contacting my office ever again. We're done." He hangs up the phone with a bang.

I open my mouth to speak, but suddenly Ty is at my side and he's furious. "Who in the hell was that?"

I put my hand on his shoulder. "Let me handle this."

Ty turns his glare on me and then returns it to Lister. But I feel his muscles relax slightly under my hand. "Fine. But then I've got some things to say to him."

I turn my attention to Lister. "Who was that on the telephone?"

He presses his lips together and says nothing.

"He's not your client, so don't tell me you have some sort of confidentiality between you two."

He still doesn't respond.

A flash of memory moves across my mind. "Is it that guy from the hotel? The guy with the long hair and the leather?"

He flinches.

"Who the hell is she talking about, Lister?" Ty asks.

Lister's gaze drops to his desk and he picks up his pen, poking the top of his desk blotter with it. He lets out a long sigh.

"You'd better start talking, buddy, or you're about to lose some really valuable clients," Ty says.

Lister looks up at him with a challenge in his eye.

Ty laughs at him. "Don't think I won't tell the band everything I'm listening to right now as soon as I leave this office. And trust me . . . if Red finds out that you screwed Amber, you're done. There will be no forgiveness. He'll probably sue you for malpractice, too. You'll burn, Lister. You will *burn*, and I'll be standing right there next to him with lighter fluid and matches in hand."

"I didn't do anything to Amber," he finally says, defeat written all over his face. "It was Darrell."

"Darrell?" I can't believe I'm hearing that name again. *What the hell?*

Lister throws his pen on his desk. "You might as well have a seat."

I think about remaining on my feet, but then decide against it. Lister appears as though he's ready to confess, and I want to keep him talking. I sit down and give Ty a look that asks him to do the same. He follows my lead silently. Once we're seated, Lister begins.

"I was approached by Darrell a couple months ago. Everyone in the band knows—except you, Ty—that he tries every once in a while to work his way back in."

"You're right. I didn't know." Ty's jaw is twitching.

I reach over and touch his arm. "That was in the past." I'm referring to him being left out of decisions by the band. We're beyond that now, and I'm not going to let him be hurt by it anymore.

He nods curtly at me and we both turn our attention back to Lister.

"Like always, I told him the band isn't interested, but this time he had more information with him. He knew about Amber's mothers and he somehow found out about the girls, too. I don't know how—he tracked them down, somehow—he wouldn't tell me how. But he was planning to use it as his way in. Blackmail the band if necessary."

"How?" I ask, totally in the dark. "How could he do that?"

"Do you mean how could he do it technically, or morally?"

"Both." I try to picture the man I saw in the lobby. He seemed a little cold, but downright mean? I don't know. Maybe.

"He assumed that if he told the press that twenty-five years ago the band got three women pregnant and then dumped them out in the backwoods in Maine, it would seriously damage their image. We're in the middle of contract negotiations with a new label, and it wasn't going to look good for them if this news came out right after the signatures were on the papers. It would have looked like they were hiding their dirty laundry with full knowledge of the damage it could have done to their brand. They could have been sued by the label for fraud, and the damage to their reputations would have been pretty bad."

"Is that why they offered me money?" I feel sick all of a sudden. They came across as so genuine. *Did I completely misjudge them?*

He shakes his head. "No. They wanted to meet you. The money was my idea. Kind of."

"Kind of?"

"They wanted to give you money as a way of making up for not being there. I had different reasons for offering it."

"What? I thought you didn't want us to have any money. I thought you didn't like us." Thirty million bucks is an awful lot of dough to hand over to people you dislike.

"As I've told you on several occasions, how I feel about you is irrelevant. There aren't many people in the world who find out their fathers are multimillionaires and don't ask for some of it. I figured we'd offer you something that's more than generous and end it right there. You'd agree to complete confidentiality and you'd agree never to seek more."

I stare at him with something akin to hate in my eyes. "We're not those kind of people."

"So you say. But it doesn't matter. When I refused to play the middleman in his scheme and the band refused to bend, Darrell leaked the information to the press anyway. So now your secret is out, and I'm sorry about that. I never intended for that to happen. I thought Darrell was smarter than that."

"Does Red know about your involvement?" Ty asks.

"He knows most of it. He knows that I've been fending Darrell off for years. He doesn't know that Darrell tried to strong-arm me, and I specifically didn't share that information with him because I cannot trust him to be reasonable about it. Red would go after Darrell with violence, and all that'd do is land him in jail."

"I guess we can agree on one thing," Ty says, not sounding very happy about it. "Not telling Red—that part was smart."

"So, what do we do now?" I ask. I'm at a total loss.

Lister pulls his chair forward and picks up his pen again, spinning it between his fingers. "You have several options. You can keep doing what you're doing, work as a consultant for the band, and then go back home. After a while, the press'll leave you alone. If there's no story there, they'll find other people to talk about."

"What's my other option?"

"You go home now. End it, and walk away. The story will go away a lot faster if you choose to do that."

"I don't think you should just walk away," Ty says, reaching out and taking my hand.

"Why? Because you'll miss me?" I'm so sad now, bitter words are flying out. I'm trying not to cry in front of Lister, though; I don't want to give him the satisfaction.

"Yes, I'll miss you. But that's not all. The band really needs you. Look at what you've accomplished already, in just *two* days. You got our relationship back on track, we've got them agreeing to bring in Sam for a trial, you've changed their look for the better. And there's still so much to do. We *need* you."

I want to believe him. I really do. The hope his words give me makes me feel like I could fly over all these skyscrapers with just my arms as wings.

Lister drops his pen on the desk, drawing our attention back to him.

"You don't agree with that?" Ty asks.

"It's not up to me. It's up to the band. Have you talked to Red about this yet?"

Ty shakes his head. "I haven't, but I know how he feels. He wants her to stay."

"Maybe he won't when he realizes it could hurt their reputation."

I really hate Lister for saying that, but mostly because I know it's true. Red and the rest of them do have to think about it. A person's reputation is a very valuable thing. My mothers realized that when they left, and I will make the same decision twenty-five years later, if necessary. I won't destroy the careers of a whole group of men, careers that for some of them span almost three decades, just so that I can find professional fulfillment.

"Bullshit. Red doesn't give a shit about any of that. He wants Amber and her sisters in his life, no matter what it takes." Ty looks at me, pleading with his eyes. "You know I'm telling the truth, babe. He said that to you himself. Mooch asked you to call him Dad, for chrissake. You can't back out now."

When I start crying, Lister stands up. He walks over to his bookshelf and comes back with a box of tissues, setting it down in front of me. He hikes his hip up onto the edge of his desk and rests his hands on his leg as he looks at me.

"Amber, you need to do what's best for you. I can't tell you what that's going to be, but whatever it is, you should decide soon and let everybody know. There's a lot of money riding on your decision, and a lot of other things that need to be put in place depending on which direction you decide to go."

Ty looks up at him, furious. "She can take all the time she needs. Nobody is going to rush her into anything."

I wave the tissue at both of them, my heart breaking into a thousand pieces. Staying is what I want to do more than anything in the world, but I realize now how selfish that is. The band was fine until I showed up. They were packing stadiums with fans, touring the world, and making money hand over fist. The press wasn't making up horrible rumors about them that could jeopardize their future contracts with new labels. I can't just think about myself here; I have to do what's right for the band, or I won't even be worthy of working for them.

"I don't need any more time. I've decided. I'm going home."

CHAPTER FORTY-SIX

I leave Ty in Lister's office, telling him I need to go to the bathroom, but instead I just go. With my heart breaking, I exit the building and jump into his car, telling the driver to take me to the Four Seasons. I rush up to my room, throw my new clothes into the shopping bags they came in, and go back downstairs. I ignore the phone calls coming to my cell as I get into the car with Mr. Blake driving.

"I'd like to go to JFK, please."

He glances at me in the mirror but does as I ask. I cry all the way there. I make it to the ticket counter to claim my seat on the next and only flight out, which leaves in forty-five minutes. The universe has spoken; I was meant to leave now.

I make it through security, but I'm forced to abandon all my delicious-smelling lotions. It makes me cry all over again.

I don't remember much of the flight; it passes in a blur and I'm too numb to think about what happened. The only thing that goes through my mind over and over again is that I'm a failure. I don't have what it takes to be in business in the city. The farm is where I belong. I wish it made me feel anything but completely depressed.

It doesn't take long to get from Manhattan to central Maine. I take a taxi back to the house, paying for it with some of the cash I have left in my wallet. It reminds me that I never paid José for the haircuts.

I send a text to Lister before I arrive home. *Please pay José the hairdresser for all of the haircuts for the band. I promised I would pay today. Ty will give you the address.*

I send another text to Lister two minutes later. *I forgot to tip the concierge, James, and the guy who is always in the elevator, Jeremy. They've taken really good care of me. Could you please leave them a tip? I'll pay you back.*

I shut my phone off and sleep until I arrive at the farm.

The car drives me right up to the porch, helping me avoid the crowds of people who are camped out at the end of the driveway. I'm glad to find that my mothers have put their foot down and at least insisted on *some* privacy.

I walk in the front door but find the house empty. I drop my things on the floor and go into the dining room, sitting down in one of the chairs and resting my head on my folded arms.

I don't even realize I'm sleeping until a hand on my back jolts me out of a hazy dream.

"Amber? Honey, are you okay?"

I sit up in a daze. Sally is standing over me.

"Sally? What are you doing here?" I look around and realize where I am. For a moment, I'd forgotten that I came home.

"I live here, sweetie," she laughs as she strokes my hair. "You look really sad. What happened?"

The door bursts open, and Em enters with Rose at her heels. They both have big grins on their faces until they see me. Their smiles are quickly replaced with looks of surprise and then worry.

"What happened? Why are you home?" Em asks.

"Oh my goodness, something happened," Rose says, rushing over. They gather around me, touching me, stroking my hair, leaning over and kissing me.

I can't stop the tears. "I decided I needed to come home. I'm done with New York City. It's not the place for me."

Em takes the seat on one side of me and Rose takes the other. Sally disappears out the front door.

"What happened?" Rose asks. "Just tell us." She reaches up to play with my hair. Em does the same thing on my other side. This is what we always do; when one of us is sad, we play with her hair and talk to her until she can work out the problem. It's very relaxing and helps us form a connection while we unload our sorrows. I don't think it's going to work this time, though.

"Do you remember a guy named Darrell who was with the band in the beginning?" I ask.

Em stands up all of a sudden and runs over to our record collection. She pulls out the album that has his picture on the front. She puts it down on the table.

Now I see the resemblance. *I knew I'd seen him before.* "Yes, that's him."

"He's not with the band anymore, though, right?" Rose asks.

"No, but he wants to be. But the band doesn't want anything to do with him, so they've been shutting him out. So he decided to try to blackmail them through their lawyer, and when that didn't work, he went to the reporters and told them everything."

"Everything? Like what?" Em asks.

"Well, lies, actually. He's telling them that the band knew about us all along and abandoned us, but that's not true." I look at my sisters, so sad that we have to go through this. "They didn't know. The band manager kept the information from them. They were trying to respect our mothers' choice to be done with the rock 'n' roll lifestyle. They had no idea they were walking away from women who loved them and children they had fathered. It's so unfair."

Both of my sisters cry with me. The door opens and all three of our mothers come in. They take one look at us and come over. We all stand together in a circle, hugging one another.

There are many, many tears, and then one of us snorts accidentally. It starts somebody laughing, and that laughter becomes contagious. Then we're a mess of tears *and* laughter. Eventually, we move into the living room and collapse onto the sofa together. We don't fit; it's not big enough for six women, but we squish ourselves in anyway.

"What on earth are we going to do with ourselves?" Barbara asks when we finally calm down and can breathe again.

"I don't know about you guys, but I hear there's going to be a concert in New York City next week, and I'd love to go to it," says Sally.

Everybody looks at her. "What are you talking about, Sally?" Carol asks.

She grins, pulling something out of her apron pocket. It's a piece of paper all folded up. She reads aloud from it. "Red Hot. Hell's Kitchen. Tickets on sale at the door. Welcome back tour. Intimate venue. Show starts at nine." She folds the paper and slides it back into her apron.

I shake my head. "No way. I'm not going back there."

Barbara pats my hand. "It's okay, sweetie. You don't have to go back if you don't want to."

We sit on the couch like that for ten minutes, until our mothers start complaining about their legs falling asleep. It's only three in the afternoon, but I'm exhausted. As soon as I'm untangled from everyone else, I go up to my room and fall into a deep sleep with Rose on one side of me, Em on the other, and a pile of border collie puppies in every crack and crevice between us.

I dream of Darrell yelling that I've ruined everything, and then I dream of a band I love—playing music I know by heart—but every time I try to get their attention, they turn their backs on me.

CHAPTER FORTY-SEVEN

My phone shows eighteen missed calls, all from the same number. When I'm alone and the last puppy has been deposited in the laundry basket that is his temporary home, I press the green button on my phone.

"I was starting to think you were never going to return my calls," Ty says. "Are you okay? Where are you? I went to the hotel, but they said you checked out."

"I'm sorry. I'm home at the farm. I needed to get away, and I've been sleeping. I was exhausted."

"I get it." He sounds as sad as I feel. "Trust me. I want to fall into a coma myself after that meeting at Lister's place."

"Is everybody angry at me?" I cringe, waiting for his answer.

"No. Why would anybody be angry at *you*?"

"I don't know. If I hadn't come to New York, none of this would've happened."

"If that dick *Darrell* hadn't stuck his nose into everybody's business, none of this would've ever happened. You are not the problem, Amber. *He* is."

The phone goes silent. I can't think of anything else to say.

"Please come back," he whispers. I hear the pain in his voice, and I really want to make it go away, but I can't. This is a problem I cannot solve, and it's killing me.

"I can't," I say, crying silently.

"Is it because of me?"

"No. You're the only reason I'd want to come back."

"I thought you were enjoying working with the band."

It almost hurts to admit this. "I was, actually. It just . . . stopped being fun, I guess." I can't tell him the truth, that I loved every minute of it. That would be selfish.

"It's just a momentary setback. Lister is going to be lucky if he keeps his job after this."

I sigh. I'd love to hang on to the hope he's offering, but it's all just an illusion. "I think you guys live a life that is full of temporary setbacks."

"What do you mean?"

"You always have somebody who wants to get into your business, who wants a piece of you. There's always somebody who doesn't care about your privacy, or wants to learn dirty secrets about you so they can spread them around the world."

"That's the price we pay for fame."

"I know. But I think that price is too high for me. I don't want to be famous. I just want to be me." I thought I wanted to be a businesswoman in the city too, but when it comes at the cost of destroying my family, the price is too high.

He's quiet for a long time. When he finally speaks, his voice is hoarse. "You're leaving me."

I feel like I've been stabbed in the heart with a sharp piece of glass. "I'm not leaving you. I care about you very much, but I've only known you for a few days. You'll get over it." He deserves to be with someone who loves that life of being hounded, of having news articles written about her, who doesn't take it personally when her family is attacked. I'm too sensitive to be that person for him. When someone attacks my family, I want to attack back. I'll end up in jail or worse.

"I won't get over you. I'm telling you, I won't."

The piece of glass that lodged in my heart isn't going anywhere. I'm afraid it's going to be a permanent part of my body now. "Ty, I have to go. This is too painful for me right now."

"Can I call you later?"

I should tell him no; it's not fair to lead him on. But I don't have the strength to do that. I keep picturing his eyes, and how dark they can be sometimes. And I remember those home movies, and how badly that little boy wanted to play guitar, even when people were making him miserable. "Sure. Call me later."

I hang up the phone and go back to sleep, all alone in the bed this time. I can't wake up and face reality. Not yet.

CHAPTER FORTY-EIGHT

I have no idea what time it is when I wake up again. My cell phone is dead. The light outside my window is dim, suggesting it's either early in the morning or nighttime. I haven't heard our rooster crowing, so I'm betting it's the latter.

I wander into the bathroom to pee and take a moment to brush my teeth. My hair looks like crap, but nobody in this house is going to care. As I reach the top of the staircase, I hear voices down on the main floor—deep voices. I slowly go down the steps, holding on to the railing. The lower I get, the more familiar those voices become.

When I reach the bottom I stop and my jaw falls open. My living room is full of people, and they're all looking at me.

"Amber." Mister Bigger-Than-Life himself, Red Wylde, is standing in the middle of our living room. My mothers are beaming, and I don't think I've ever seen them look so happy. Cash is sitting in the recliner with a beer resting on his belly. Mooch is on the floor, feeding a puppy with a bottle. Paul is on the couch between Rose and Em. And Ty is standing off to the side, isolated from the rest, but now the center of my attention.

"What are you doing here?" I ask him.

He shrugs. "We took the jet."

Red takes two steps toward me. "Amber, we need you to come back."

I hang on to the railing with two hands, shaking my head. "You don't need me."

Red goes to take another step, but Ty stops him, holding up a hand. When I'm ready to race up the stairs, overwhelmed by the idea that all these people flew to Maine to talk to me, I stop for the man before me; Ty reaches the bottom stair and takes my hand.

"I know you're exhausted, and this is probably the last thing you want to see right now, but we felt really bad about what happened to you and wanted to apologize."

"In person," Mooch says loudly. The puppy he's supposed to be feeding starts squealing. "Sorry, sorry, little guy. Geez, you're hungry."

I try to smile at Mooch's silliness, but my cheeks tremble with the effort. I bite my lip to keep from crying.

"We really do want you to come back. You were in the middle of doing great things for us, and it's already making a difference. Look." Ty unlocks his phone and presses a few buttons, holding it up for me. The big headline is impossible to miss. *Red Hot is back and hotter than ever.* It's a perfect photograph of the band as they're standing outside the hair salon. They do look great, I have to admit. I take his phone so I can get a closer look. I can't help but smile. I'm proud of myself. I did good.

"You did that," Red says. "And we know you have other plans for us. Come back and make them happen."

I give Ty his phone. "This is all very flattering, but I have things I need to do here." My heart is hammering in my chest. I want to hope so badly, but my brain won't let me. My brain is rational, realistic. It's telling me this is too big a risk to take.

"We can cover for you," Carol says loudly.

"Not that we don't love you to pieces," Sally says, "but your presence here is not needed. Not for the farm to function, I mean." She reaches up to tug her braid. "I mean, don't stay here just for us." She looks at Barbara. "Help . . . I'm screwing this up."

My mom walks over and stands next to Ty. "Baby, you need to be happy. You're not happy here on the farm. You know it and we know it. Go be who you are in the city."

"But . . . what about the farm?" I ask. "My bees?"

"Smitty can take care of the bees," she says, stroking my hand. "He knows this farm like the back of his hand, and he's already asked if we need help."

Good old Smitty . . . the boy next door who we've known since early childhood. It's kind of crazy that I never thought about him taking over for me. Of course he's perfectly capable, there's no question about that.

"Come back," Ty says. "You can stay at my place. It's a lot more private than that hotel. Nobody will be able to bother you there."

Hope keeps beating away at me, demanding to be let into my heart. "They'll just be waiting for me outside the studio, or the hair salon, or wherever else I go."

"You get better at avoiding them with more practice. And we'll work with specialists who can help you come up with ways to deal with them, answers to give them that will satisfy them so they won't harass you."

"People like that exist?"

"You bet," says Paul. "I had to have several sessions with them."

"We all did," Cash says.

"Even me," Ty says. "It's not easy, but you can find ways to make it bearable. The rewards are so great. I know you were enjoying your time in the city. Let me show it to you. Let me show you the fun parts of living in New York." He pulls me down to the ground floor and hugs me, whispering in my ear. "Just give us a real chance. That's all I ask."

Barbara puts her hand on Ty's shoulder and looks up at him, silently asking him for a moment. He nods and steps aside.

My mother stands before me, placing her hands on my cheeks. She kisses me on the forehead. "Baby girl, it's time for you to leave the nest. We love having you here, and you are an amazingly fun, lovely, intelligent person we love to be with. But the farm is not the place for you right now. You can come back whenever you want, but you need to spread your wings and fly a little bit."

I start to cry. "What if I don't want to?"

She nods in understanding. "You want to. You just need to be honest with yourself. We've seen it for a long time, but we also knew you weren't quite ready to go. You're ready now. We release you from any obligations you feel you have toward the farm or your family. Go with our blessings."

I take a deep, shuddering breath. "There's a lot of really rude people in that city."

"Yes, there are. But there're also a lot of really great people there who care about you very much." She looks briefly over her shoulder before coming back to me. Her voice drops to a whisper. "Don't make the same mistake that I made, okay? Take a chance on life. Don't let those mean people scare you away from your future."

I think about it for a while, and then I nod. She's right. I know she is. Hope explodes in my chest, now joined by the rational part of my brain. This makes sense. I might be out here, living in the sticks, wearing cotton and hemp, but that doesn't mean I need to be intimidated by people who live in the city, wear three-inch heels, carry microphones around, and make up lies. I'm not going to let these people scare me. I need to learn to follow my own advice. And if my moms say I'm not needed for the functioning of this farm, then I'm not going to argue with them.

"I think I can handle it for two weeks."

Red comes over and stops just next to my mother. "We were kind of hoping we could convince you to stay for longer than two weeks."

Now I'm scared all over again. "What exactly are you saying?"

"Can we call that two weeks a trial period? And if you're still happy at the end of it, maybe you could consider staying for longer?"

"Like a permanent job?"

He nods. "We can get you an apartment, a driver—anything you need."

I frown at him. "I'm still not taking that money." I haven't quite worked out in my mind yet what ten million dollars is supposed to represent, so I can't consider taking it. Not yet, anyway. Most important, I don't want it to come between me and the men standing in this room. Those potential relationships are worth a lot more to me than that.

He grins. "We'll talk about that later. What do you say about the job?"

I look over at the group of people standing in my living room . . . my moms, my sisters, this guy I'm falling in love with, my *father*, whoever he is . . . They're all here for *me*. It's pretty damn overwhelming, to be honest. I've never felt more loved in my entire life. I don't want to let any of these people down, and I don't want to let myself down either.

My mom is right. My future isn't out here in the middle of a hippie commune in Maine. It's in New York City.

So what am I waiting for?

CHAPTER FORTY-NINE

"Are you happy?" Ty asks me.

I flatten the last moving box from the kitchen and throw it on the pile next to the front door. I've been in New York for three months now, and this is my biggest move yet: I've settled into a high-rise apartment in Midtown on the top floor, with my new roommate—the love of my life, Ty Stanz—who also happens to be the lead guitarist of Red Hot.

Yeah . . . so, I'm officially a groupie, but it's no big deal, because I'm also a high-powered businesswoman working my way up the corporate ladder in the music industry. I earn my keep, running a well-oiled PR and branding machine that no one can find fault with anymore, not even me. Miracle of miracles, I have a knack for the business, and every one of my instincts has paid off. An industry executive just called me yesterday, trying to lure me away so I could come work for his people. Of course I said no, since I kind of love the band I'm with now.

"I'm very happy," I say, accepting the glass of wine Ty hands me.

"Let's make a toast." He holds up his beer bottle and tips it toward my glass.

I smile, biting my lip as I wait to hear what he's going to say.

"Here's to our future together. Full of love, laughter, and *privacy.*" He wiggles his eyebrows at me.

I look around at this new, big, mostly empty apartment that we just moved into together. Nobody but family knows that we live here, and it has a private entrance to a parking garage with all kinds of security measures, including three doormen—two of whom I poached from the Four Seasons Hotel. I'll be able to come and go as I please without anybody bothering me.

"Cheers to that," I say, taking a sip of my wine.

"Are you happy with the progress you've made?" he asks, taking a sip of his beer.

"Very. Did you see the reviews?"

"I sure did. Did you see what they said about that sexy lead guitarist?" he asks, smirking.

"Yes, I sure did. 'Hotness personified' I think is how they described him."

His face turns a little red and he shakes his head. "If they only knew."

I move closer, pulling him against me. "I'm glad they don't know, because if they did, you would *never* get any privacy from the rest of the world."

He puts his beer down on the counter and holds me closer. "Is that so?"

I nod as he leans down to kiss me. We're really going at it too, until somebody behind us clears her throat.

I turn around. "Can I help you, Mother?"

Barbara holds up a bowl. "Where am I supposed to put this?"

Sally and Carol come into the room behind her. "You need to come in here and supervise this move," Sally says. "Carol's putting things in the weirdest places."

"I'm putting them in the places they *should* be," she says, tugging on one of Sally's braids.

I pull away from Ty's embrace. "I need to go."

"Go. Handle. Organize. Supervise. It's what you're good at."

I walk away smiling, corralling my mothers and leading them back into the living room. They're here for a few days helping me move in to our new place while I get the band ready to head off to Japan for two weeks. I'm almost tempted to go with them, but I have too much to do here. Ty's brother, Sam, is going to be here soon, and I'll be busy integrating him into New York City life until the band gets back.

I stand in the living room looking at the chaos my mothers have created unpacking boxes when I don't yet have enough furniture to store things in. I blink a few times and then turn around and leave the room.

I go straight into the kitchen and grab Ty by the hand.

He smiles. "Where're we going?"

"To the bedroom."

"Mmm, I like the sound of that."

I yell over my shoulder. "We'll be out when Ty has to leave for Japan." I drag him into the bedroom and lock the door behind us.

He slowly pulls his shirt over his head. "I like it when you take charge."

"Good, because I'm about to show you who's boss right now." I slowly unbutton my blouse as I step toward him, a devious smile playing on my lips.

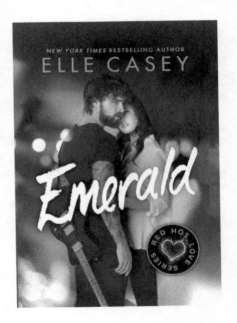

ABOUT THE AUTHOR

Elle Casey, a former attorney and teacher, is a prolific *New York Times* and *USA Today* bestselling American author who lives in southwest France with her husband, the youngest of her three children, and a bunch of cats, dogs, and horses. She writes in several genres, including romance, suspense, urban fantasy, paranormal, science fiction, dystopian, and action/adventure.